Accolades for America's greatest hero Mack Bolan

"Very, very action-oriented.... Highly successful, today's hottest books for men."
—*The New York Times*

"Anyone who stands against the civilized forces of truth and justice will sooner or later have to face the piercing blue eyes and cold Beretta steel of Mack Bolan, the lean, mean nightstalker, civilization's avenging angel."
—*San Francisco Examiner*

"Mack Bolan is a star. The Executioner is a beacon of hope for people with a sense of American justice."
—*Las Vegas Review Journal*

"In the beginning there was the Executioner—a publishing phenomenon. Mack Bolan remains a spiritual godfather to those who have followed."
—*San Jose Mercury News*

EVERLASTING WAR

There's nothing in this Everlasting
War that should influence anyone to
follow in my footsteps. Mine is a
very grim existence. I have
submerged my life into these
missions, sacrificing everything I
hold dear. I, too, have dreams, but
I've forgone them all to hurl myself
in a holy war.

—Mack Bolan

"Mack Bolan stabs right through the
heart of the frustration and
hopelessness the average person
feels about crime running rampant
in the streets."

—*Dallas Times Herald*

DON PENDLETON's

MACK BOLAN.

ASSAULT

A GOLD EAGLE BOOK FROM

WORLDWIDE.

TORONTO · NEW YORK · LONDON · PARIS
AMSTERDAM · STOCKHOLM · HAMBURG
ATHENS · MILAN · TOKYO · SYDNEY

First edition May 1990

ISBN 0-373-61419-5

Special thanks and acknowledgment to
Mike Newton for his contribution to this work.

It's perfectly obvious that somebody's responsible and somebody's innocent. Otherwise, justice makes no sense at all.
—Ugo Betti

The triumph of justice is the only peace.
—Robert Ingersoll

It's time for justice to start making sense again. I have identified the guilty, and they have passed judgment on themselves. All that's left, from this point on, is the restoration of the peace.
—Mack Bolan

PROLOGUE

The fortress-villa stood twenty miles north of Beirut on the highway connecting Lebanon's capital with its northern neighbors, Al-Batrun and Tripoli. The owner, when in residence, commanded views of both the highway and the eastern Mediterranean. On clear days—which were most days in that region of the world—he could stand on the balcony outside his bedroom window and observe the long, low silhouette of Cyprus, one hundred-odd miles to the west.

The villa had been raised by a long-forgotten architect, before the pall of endless violence had descended over Lebanon. Its "extras," from the sentries on patrol with automatic weapons to the various security devices tucked away from casual inspection, had been added in the past five years. Above all else the present owner had a passion for self-preservation.

To various observers and "authorities," the civil warfare that had shattered Lebanese society and slaughtered thousands since the latter 1970s was an unmitigated tragedy, perhaps a curse from God. The villa's present owner took a different view, regarding each historical event and each new day as one more opportunity provided for the benefit of those with strength and foresight. If the violence couldn't be eliminated, it could still be channeled, used against selected enemies, the private risks translated into profit. Peace was highly overrated as a backdrop to prosperity. The money lay in war and in the sundry lower passions man was heir to.

Sometimes in the evening he could see Beirut in flames. The once-great city was a charnel house these days, but he had little sympathy for those who lingered on, ignoring danger to themselves, their families. He understood religious warfare at a cold, objective level, but he lacked the zealot's passion, leaving that for others who believed with heart and soul. His passion was survival, in the lavish style to which he had become accustomed. If profit lay in war and human suffering, he was prepared to claim his share without compunction.

Glancing at his heavy Rolex watch, he saw that it was nearly time for him to greet the others. None of them were ever late, and while he might not have preferred their company in normal circumstances, this was business, and the villa's owner had a reputation as a gracious host. His chef had spent the past two days preparing menus that would satisfy his guests without offending Shiite sensibilities, and half a dozen prostitutes were quartered on the premises, prepared to serve with style if any of his less religious visitors were so inclined.

He crossed the broad veranda with an easy stride that spoke of confidence and self-assurance, closed the sliding plate glass doors behind him to preserve the air-conditioning—another late addition—and moved on through various luxuriously furnished rooms to reach the villa's entryway. Before he stepped outside again, he donned a pair of mirrored aviator's glasses to diffuse the glare of sun on polished marble.

The villa was of Greek design, with sturdy columns harking back to the Acropolis, their bulk providing fair concealment for the television cameras that monitored his driveway and the open lawn on either side. Inside the house a single claustrophobic room had been reserved for monitors, a dozen screens manned constantly against the possibility of an assault from land or water. Four men were employed to watch the monitors, trading off in six-hour shifts to avoid fatigue, and only one of them had ever fallen asleep on the job. He was still on the payroll, and the memory of ear lobes severed with a cutthroat razor was enough to keep him constantly alert to any hint of danger from the outside world.

In the event of an attack by land or sea, a mobile team of gunners could be instantly deployed to meet the threat. Trained attack dogs provided a substantial first line of defense, with automatic rifles, hand grenades and submachine guns in reserve. Atop the villa's roof, concealed inside a stucco dome of relatively recent vintage, twin-mount .50-caliber machine guns had been mounted on a small rotating turret. An assault by air would be met with concentrated antiaircraft fire, while sentries on the ground adjusted their response to meet the threat.

Security. In the unstable modern world, it came with wealth and wisdom, unattainable without experience and a supply of ready cash. If one elected to become a predator, survive outside the herd, eternal vigilance must be the price. With a secure base of operation, anything was possible.

The Palestinian, surprisingly, was first to arrive—usually it was the Shiites. He traveled with six bodyguards, their vehicle bristling with weapons, paranoid eyes concealed behind cheap sunglasses. The obligatory checkered *keffiyeh* and the khaki uniforms of his entourage clashed with the Palestinian's tailored business suit, invoking memories of an American politician, playing dress-up to impress the gullible natives in a backward congressional district.

"Good health to you, brother."

"Good health to you. Have the others not arrived?"

The host smiled patiently, observing the traditional amenities. A servant led the Palestinian inside, his squad of riflemen remaining with the vehicle, their weapons tucked inside. The villa's owner paid them no attention, trusting their discretion to a point, secure in the knowledge they were covered by his own crack troops in the event that anything went wrong.

A second vehicle rolled up the drive and parked some distance from the Palestinian's car. The single occupant climbed out and left his keys in the ignition, brushing past the clutch of Arab gunmen with determined strides. The trip from Cyprus had consumed his morning, and the new arrival would be anxious to conclude his business, clearing the decks for rest and relaxation.

The servant reappeared and led the man from Cyprus into air-conditioned comfort. It was almost noon, and from his shaded vantage point, the villa's owner scanned the stretch of highway visible beyond the wall he had erected to protect his property from prowlers. He saw a shiny speck approaching from the north, assuming detail as it closed the gap and took on the familiar outline of a limousine. The vehicle was slightly larger than his own, coal-black in contrast to the beige that he preferred, and it was making decent time in spite of heavy armor plating that would add an extra ton or more.

The three Iranians arrived together, somber in their funereal robes and turbans, mouths etched in perpetual frowns above trailing beards. The Shiite temperament allowed no compromise with earthly pleasure, and the government's chosen spokesmen knew their role by heart. They might be forced by circumstances to deal with infidels, but they wouldn't enjoy it, even if it made them rich beyond their wildest fantasies.

He greeted them with courtesy and ushered them inside. The Cypriot and Palestinian had taken seats across from each other at the conference table, leaving four seats vacant, and the villa's owner moved to take his usual position at the table's head. The three Iranians sat close together, drawing spiritual strength from one another in the presence of uneasy allies.

"Gentlemen," their host began, "I'm delighted we could meet once more before commencement of our joint operation. It pleases me to tell you that I have established contacts in New York. They have assured uninterrupted distribution of our product, with a guarantee of full indemnity in the event of loss through confiscation or diversion."

On his left the Cypriot allowed himself another fleeting smile. "Full payment?"

"In advance. Our contacts will assume the risk with customs and the drug enforcement bureaucrats. Potential danger to our syndicate is thereby minimized, confined to transatlantic shipment and the territory we already control."

"The price?"

"Reduced by ten percent to offset risks incurred by the Americans. It's a bargain, I assure you."

"As you say."

The eldest of the three Iranians leaned slightly forward, elbows resting on the table, pale hands clenched in front of him. "The price is insignificant," he said, the flankers nodding like a pair of puppets. "We are more concerned about the prosecution of our holy war against the Great Satan."

"Understood." Their host had little patience for the Shiites' posturing, but they were partners of a sort, and any rift between them now might doom the enterprise to failure. "There was some initial reticence among our contacts in New York—these men are patriots, after their fashion—but an extra two-percent reduction in the wholesale price convinced them to accommodate our special needs. Your agents may expect cooperation...to a point."

"They will require assistance with their documents and weapons."

"All has been agreed, upon my promise of discretion. If your men are taken into custody, however—"

"They will not be taken. Each of them has been selected for his personal commitment to jihad."

"Of course. And we are in agreement that their 'special' operations will not jeopardize the pipeline?"

Stiffly the Iranian replied, "We are agreed that export of the poison to America will further undermine our enemies and strike a revolutionary blow against their parasitic government. With that in mind, we shall maintain security where possible."

It was a feeble promise, but the best he could expect, all things considered. The Iranians were zealots, rich with oil and largely out of touch with human feelings. They would do their part, but he would have to watch them closely, making certain that their precious holy war didn't obstruct the cartel's higher purpose.

"Very well," he said at last, his tone approximating satisfaction. "If we are agreed upon our purpose...?"

"We're agreed." The Cypriot presumed to speak for those around him, but this time he got no arguments. The three Iranians remained impassive, while the Palestinian smiled knowingly.

"Reports?"

The owner of the fortress-villa listened while they spoke in turn about their separate phases of the operation. All appeared to be in order, ready to proceed on schedule. After eighteen months of planning they were on the move, or nearly so.

For the Iranians, it meant a new expansion of jihad, their holy war against the West. The Palestinian would balance profit motives with an opportunity to strike another blow at Israel and her friends abroad. As for the Cypriot, his motives were, perhaps, the most uncomplicated and sincere of all. Self-interest ruled his every waking thought, and he would spare no effort to advance his own position in the world.

The villa's master understood them well enough, and understanding gave him all the edge that he would ever need.

CHAPTER ONE

From all appearances, the terrorists were looking for a place to start. Mack Bolan picked them up outside the Metropolitan Museum of Art and trailed them south along Fifth Avenue, maintaining distance while they dawdled at Temple Emanuel and the Fifth Avenue Synagogue, shifting east to check out the CBS building and Radio City Music Hall. They carried nothing in the way of packages or parcels, and he had no fear that they were leaving bombs behind. The men were window-shopping, memorizing entrances and exits, angles of attack, surveying one-way streets where they might lose pursuers if they drove against prevailing traffic.

The Iranians had nearly slipped away from Bolan, as they had eluded immigration officers and customs men, the FBI and Secret Service, state police and local homicide detectives. They would certainly have shaken him if Stony Man hadn't been able to rely upon a source in Teheran to leak a portion of the duo's planned itinerary. They had entered the United States from Canada on phony passports that identified them both as Indians from Delhi, touring North America on holiday. Mack Bolan didn't know their names—the source in Teheran hadn't been privy to such information—but he knew they weren't what they appeared to be.

The pickup had been a relatively simple matter. Bolan could have left it to the FBI, let them have some friendly headlines for a change, but the head shed at Stony Man had been concerned about potential repercussions. If the play went bad for any reason, spilling over into blood, it would be easier to cover Bolan's tracks than for the Bureau to explain itself before congressional inquisitors.

And there was bound to be some blood, the Executioner decided, following his targets south on Seventh Avenue toward Greenwich Village. An arrest would mean a show trail, offering the terrorists a public forum while their sponsors set about the task of infiltrating other hit teams into the United States. They might be in the U.S. already, but the warrior had no time to waste on empty speculation when an enemy of flesh and blood was right before his eyes.

The details of their mission posed a mystery for Bolan, but their covert presence in America confirmed his suspicions that Iran's new, accommodating attitude toward the United States had been a sham. The late ayatollah's program for Islamic revolution in the Shiite mold remained unchanged. The bogus Indians might have specific targets singled out for execution, but it seemed more likely they were fishing, sizing up the possibilities before they made their move. New York was like an endless smorgasbord for zealots, offering innumerable targets drawn from every creed and color of the human rainbow.

In Greenwich Village Bolan trailed them south on Bleecker Street and watched them disappear inside a small café. He found a parking space a half block farther on and doubled back on foot, arriving as the two Iranians prepared to place their order with a bouncy waitress. The warrior took a counter seat and scanned the plastic menu briefly, ordering a sandwich and a cup of coffee while he kept a sharp eye on the dark men at their table by the window.

The Iranians were nearly finished with their meal when a short Italian entered, sizing up the scattered patrons at a glance. Without a trace of hesitation, he approached the terrorists and sat down at their table, smiling vacantly, his eyes belying any muscular contortion of his lips.

The conversation took perhaps three minutes, start to finish, and the terrorists apparently were satisfied by what they heard. One of them tried to pay the check, but he was waved off by the new arrival. Bolan watched as the Italian palmed a roll of currency and peeled off two crisp bills, folding them once in half before he dropped them on the table. Sweating out the fractions of a second, knowing he could lose them if their escort had a car outside, he let the trio reach the sidewalk. When the door had closed behind them, Bolan dropped a ten-spot by his plate and followed casually, acknowledging a thank-you from his waitress with a lifted hand.

He hesitated in the doorway, zipping up his jacket as he watched the three men crossing Bleecker Street on foot. Bolan struck off on a parallel course, keeping to his own side of the street, merging with the normal flow of pedestrian traffic. They covered three blocks before the Italian led Bolan's targets into a narrow side street, eastbound, and the warrior took his chances crossing in the middle of the block.

Their destination was a cheap hotel of 1930s vintage. Bolan watched them duck inside and followed cautiously, lingering outside the glass revolving doors and giving them a chance to reach the elevator. It was one of the old-fashioned kind, its destination indicated by an arrow set above the sliding door. As the Executioner's quarry disappeared, he entered, crossed the lobby swiftly, drawing no reaction from the solitary clerk behind the registration desk. Distracted by the charms of *Hustler*'s centerfold, the clerk let Bolan pass without a second glance.

He lingered at the elevator, waiting as the arrow quivered, rose and stopped on number five. There might be time, if he was quick enough.

He gave the clerk another hasty glance and took the service stairs.

SADDAM KASSIM BELIEVED it was an honor to be chosen as a martyr for jihad. To die in the United States, battling against the Great Satan, was the highest aspiration of a Shiite warrior. And if by the grace of God he should manage to survive, so much the better.

Kassim had been allowed to leave Teheran with only vague instructions, free to strike against the targets of his choice, selected in agreement with his comrade, Abdel Bazargan. New York had been selected as their field of operation as it was the largest, richest city in America, its teeming streets jam-packed with Jewish banks and infidels of every stripe. You couldn't fire a shot or detonate a hand grenade in New York City without killing several of the enemy. It was a zealot's happy hunting ground.

Kassim and Bazargan had spent their second morning in the city scouting out prospective targets, killing time until the hour of the one and only task that was specifically ordained by their superiors. They'd been told to purchase lunch in a specific restaurant on Bleecker Street, at noon, and to accompany the man who met them there. The stranger would convey them to his master, and Kassim had been instructed what to say upon their meeting. He didn't approve of catering to infidels, but this one knew the city inside out, and he had access to the weapons they would need to carry out their mission. In return for his cooperation, he would be allowed to prosper from the fallout of jihad.

Despite his Shiite fundamentalist beliefs, Kassim wasn't put off by dealing drugs. He saw the poison as another weapon, no different than an automatic rifle or grenade— except that drugs could undermine the whole American society, instead of merely picking off a politician or a group of soldiers here and there.

In retrospect Kassim was startled by the ease with which they had been able to invade America. There had been routine questions at the customs terminal in Buffalo, but no one seriously questioned any of the counterfeit ID they'd been issued in Teheran. He had been nervous on the flight from Pakistan to London, cautious on the transatlantic journey to Toronto, shaking off his final apprehension as they entered the United States without a hitch. The prophet was correct about the holy power of jihad. Kassim thought nothing could delay them now.

Their escort smelled of olive oil and garlic, the aromas conjuring an image of Kassim's home village near the western border with Iraq. Five years of fratricidal warfare destroyed the village and surrounding farms, wiped out his family and friends, but still Kassim survived. His mother, had she lived, wouldn't have recognized him on the street. He was a new man, forged in white-hot flame and dedicated to the cause of vengeance. He knew well enough whose money had supplied Iraqi soldiers with their weapons and the lethal gas they used against civilian populations in the hinterlands. America, as always, was the author of atrocity.

And it was time to pay her people back.

On the street outside the restaurant, Kassim imagined they were being followed, glancing surreptitiously across his shoulder, but the streets were crowded and he caught no glimpse of a familiar face. It had to be paranoia, he decided, the result of plotting covert action in a country where the enemy was all around him, everywhere he turned.

If Abdel Bazargan felt any apprehension on the walk up Bleecker Street, he kept it to himself. Kassim had watched his partner closely through their journey from the east, and he had finally decided Bazargan was either fearless or a fool. The simple faith of God was enough to keep him satisfied, whereas Kassim required some vestige of a strategy incorporating safety measures, backup systems for escape.

The hotel lobby was a musty cave that smelled of age and long neglect. Their escort led them past the registration desk, the clerk oblivious to their arrival. Waiting for the elevator to arrive, Kassim experienced a sudden tingling of the scalp, the short hairs rising on his nape. He swung around to face the lobby's only entrance from the street, too slow to catch the figment of his own imagination. He was being foolish, acting like a child afraid of shadows, and he steeled himself against anxiety as listless bells announced the elevator's slow return.

Their escort punched the fifth-floor button, and the sliding door wheezed shut. Had there been just a hint of movement on the street, a dark shape stepping into the revolving door before his view was blocked?

Kassim ignored the worm of doubt that wriggled in his belly, concentrating on the context of his scripted conversation with the infidel. An hour, give or take, and he could go about his business, carrying the torch among his enemies. Before his work was finished, they would tremble at his name.

WHEN ANTHONY SILVESTRI checked his watch again, he discovered that the Iranians were late. They seemed to exist in a state of culture lag that left them trailing well behind the pack. Before you made a lunch date with a Persian, you were wise to fix yourself a sandwich for the road and count on sitting down to lunch at dinnertime.

If anyone had asked, Silvestri could have told them why a state the size of Israel had been kicking ass in the Middle East for over forty years. The Jews were punctual—compulsive, even—and they seldom made mistakes. The Arabs spent their free time stabbing one another in the back and pumping up the artificial price of oil until the bubble burst and they were left without a pot to piss in. Snakes and sand dunes, sheikhs all parking brand-new limousines outside their tents—and the peasants didn't get a dime. Silvestri knew he could have broken OPEC in a week if he was president. Cut off the food handouts and you'd see how fast the sons of bitches fell in line.

Unfortunately he was being forced by circumstance to deal with people he despised. It wouldn't be the first time, but it rankled all the same. The Golden Crescent of the Middle East was turning out some heavy stuff these days in terms of heroin and hash, supplying ample quantity to balance deficits of quality compared to more expensive China White from Southeast Asia. At the moment, the Iranians were selling cheap, and if the Ayatollah's successors wanted help with certain special projects in return, it served the Family's interests to cooperate.

Silvestri wasn't thrilled about the prospect of a bargain with the Shiites, and he worried that the shock waves of a terrorist attack on U.S. soil might harm the Family, but the word had come direct from Don Grisanti. They were dealing with Iran; case closed, next case. If anybody didn't like it, he could argue with the boss one-on-one and name his beneficiary.

Silvestri had no secret death wish. When the boss of New York's second-largest Family told him it was time to deal with Iranians, Anthony was ready to oblige. If Don Grisanti ordered him to jump, he asked: On who?

The good news was that pushing Golden Crescent heroin and hash could make him filthy rich. Silvestri wasn't poor by any means, but there was no such thing as too much money. He remembered playing store in kindergarten, stealing from the till and squirreling plastic coins away until he found out they were worthless. From the time that he was old enough to count his pennies, he'd wanted more.

The Iranians could be helpful with their bargain-basement smack. Silvestri didn't care why Teheran was underselling everybody else in town. If they were doing penance by forsaking profits, it was fine with him, and if the new Shiite leader had some wild idea about destroying the United States with smack, well, let him try. Silvestri was an expert on the subject, and he knew his fellow countrymen were indestructible. They had an infinite capacity for chemicals in every form, from sleeping pills and steroids to the goodies that you wouldn't find in any local drugstore. Americans were snorting, toking, mainlining fools, and they spent more money on recreational drugs in one year than most Third World nations earned in a decade. The Islamic revolution would be ancient history before Americans burned out on doing drugs, and in the meantime, Anthony Silvestri was prepared to do his bit for the promotion of supply-side economics.

Footsteps in the hallway slowed outside his door. The hotel was a dump, but dumps had their advantages—like creaky floors to let you know when you had company. Silvestri slipped the single button on his jacket open, reaching for the automatic that he wore beneath his arm. He knew it would be Shelly, bringing the Iranians for their little rendezvous, but there was still one chance in ten or fifteen thousand that a wild card might attempt to take him by surprise. The world was full of losers looking for that one big score, and when they interfered with business, there was nothing you could do but whack them out.

He listened for the knock—two quick ones followed by another after six or seven seconds, then two more—and let himself relax. Ten minutes late, but that was pretty good for Iranians. Straightening his tie and buttoning his jacket, Anthony Silvestri checked the peephole just to put his mind at ease. The fish-eye lens made Shelly look like Jackie Gleason, risen from the grave.

He slipped the double latch and threw the door wide open, putting on the plastic smile he always used when he was dealing with inferiors. "Good afternoon," he beamed at the new arrivals. "You're right on time."

IT WAS A GAMBLE from the start, and halfway up the stairs, Mack Bolan knew that he was bound to lose. The elevator was a clunker, granted, but it had a fair head start, and there was no way the Iranians would hang around the corridor outside their destination. By the time he got to the fifth floor, the Executioner was mulling over ways to single out their room without disturbing every tenant on the floor and putting the Iranians to flight.

The worst scenario would be a total miss, if they had punched up number five, then ridden to a different floor in an effort to confuse pursuers. Bolan shrugged the notion off. If they were conscious of the tail, they'd have bolted and scrubbed the meeting. From the look of their companion in the restaurant, he'd be used to breaking legs, not cracking codes and running rings around surveillance. No, the meet would be on the fifth floor, but where?

When Bolan cracked the access door and pressed one eye against the narrow opening, a wedge of empty hallway was all he saw. He shifted his position, opening the door another inch or two and praying that the hinges wouldn't squeal in protest. Scoping out the left-hand side, he spied a slouching figure halfway down the hall, on guard outside a door, and recognized the contact from the restaurant on Bleecker Street.

He pegged the range at close to sixty feet, the dingy light a handicap to accuracy. Still, he had no choice. A rush would leave him open to defensive fire, and even if the sentry missed, his enemies inside the room would be forewarned of danger. They might bolt or arm themselves and stand their ground, but Bolan would have sacrificed surprise in either case.

A distance shot was risky, too. The Executioner might miss, or only wound his target, leaving time enough for shouted warnings. If his aim was true, the sound of a collapsing body might alert the others, prompting them to flee or fight.

Another gamble. And again he had no choice.

He palmed the sleek Beretta 93-R, balancing the weapon to accommodate the extra weight of its suppressor. Flicking off the safety, Bolan thumbed the hammer back and raised his free arm, crooked to grant support across the elbow as he aimed.

One shot, to make or break the game, and it would have to be a killer. Bolan fixed his sights upon the target's head, the dark face offered up in silhouette.

One shot . . .

He stroked the trigger, riding out the automatic's recoil, retinas recalling vivid images of muzzle-flash.

Downrange the sentry lurched and staggered, slumping back against the wall where abstract patterns had been etched in something that resembled crimson ink. The dead man's legs began to fold a heartbeat later, and he ended in a crouch, buttocks resting on his heels before he toppled over, sprawling on his side.

No time to waste. Emerging from the stairwell, Bolan double-timed in the direction of the fallen sentry and the door that he had guarded with his life.

His ears picked up no sounds of voices from behind that door, but he could almost feel the concentration of his enemies concealed from view. As Bolan braced himself to crash the gathering, a shadow fell across the built-in peephole's tiny lens, approximately level with his chin. The Executioner was moving forward, one leg raised to smash a heel against the lock, when instinct made him change direction, veering to the left and going down.

Behind him bullets ripped the flimsy wooden panels, slicing through the empty space that he had occupied earlier and drilling the opposite wall.

CHAPTER TWO

"Supply's no problem, then?" Silvestri asked.

"No problem whatsoever," replied the Iranian on his left.

Deliberately they had avoided introductions. The Iranians were worried that their holy mission in America might come to grief unless they kept their names a secret, and Silvestri, for his part, didn't want them naming him if they were captured and interrogated. Don Grisanti had a lot of blue-suits on his payroll, and they closed their eyes to gambling, drugs, a murder now and then. But it would be a different story if the Iranians started tossing bombs in school yards, sniping politicians on the street. There would be hell to pay, and when the dust began to settle, Anthony Silvestri meant to have his own hands clean.

"Okay," he said. "The price is fair enough. If you can guarantee supply..."

"No problem whatsoever," said the man on his right.

Silvestri forced a smile. "You realize that we'll be taking all the risks of importation. I'd be interested to know exactly how your people plan to make delivery."

The dark men traded shifty glances. Neither one had cracked a smile since their arrival. He'd seen hit men have a better time in jail than these two seemed to have while they were laying down a multimillion-dollar deal.

"When all has been agreed, you will receive the name and address of a trusted friend in Nicosia. He will handle all the details of delivery in bulk. From Cyprus, transportation of the merchandise is, as you say, your problem."

"Right. I understand you need some special items while you're in the city?"

"Uzi submachine guns," said the dark man on his left, "with ammunition. Hand grenades, fragmentation type. Perhaps one dozen. And automatic pistols, chambered for the Uzi's parabellum round. With extra magazines."

Silvestri had expected worse, and he refused to think about the hell two men could raise in Macy's or Grand Central Station with that kind of hardware.

"That's easy," he said. "Where and when?"

"At six o'clock. Our room—"

"No good," he interrupted, frowning. "Nothing personal, but you two boys are new in town. For all I know, the Feds may have you spotted. It's a gamble meeting here, but my employer owns the place, okay? I can't send anybody up to your hotel with Uzis and grenades."

Another glance between them, and they seemed to grasp the logic of his argument. "Perhaps the restaurant," one said, "on Bleacher Street."

"That's Bleecker, and it's not a bad idea. Go in at six and order dinner like it's no big thing. I'll give you half an hour, and—"

The sound was difficult to place. It came from just outside the door, Silvestri knew that much, but what the hell would make a noise like that? At first it sounded like a clump of soggy paper towels thrown against the wall, and then there was a heavy shuffling and sliding, like Shelly might have tripped and fallen on his ass.

The Iranians stiffened in their seats, exchanging pointed looks before they focused on Silvestri. He was on his feet before they had a chance to start with any questions, moving toward the door and hauling out his automatic on the way.

"Hey, Shell?"

No answer came from beyond the door, although he knew damn well that Shelly should have heard him. Smelling trouble, he stepped closer to the door, the automatic cocked as he leaned forward, listening.

Silvestri glanced across his shoulder and discovered that the Iranians both had fisted snubby .38 revolvers. It crossed his mind to wonder what they needed pistols for, and he decided that it didn't matter either way. If they were being raided—by the Feds, for instance—he was up shit creek and no mistake.

Silvestri turned away from the Iranians and pressed one eye against the peephole. He was hoping desperately for Shelly's Jackie Gleason imitation, but instead he saw a tall, dark stranger with a jazzy automatic in his fist. The guy was standing back and taking stock, as if he were about to kick the door, and that meant they were being raided.

Or worse.

Silvestri didn't waste his energy on calculating the possibilities for rip-offs, double crosses and the like. Relying on his instinct now, he took a short step back and snapped off three quick rounds directly through the door, chest-high. He was retreating toward the startled Iranians when a rapid, 3-round burst ripped through the door, immediately followed by another.

Silvestri figured Shelly must have bought it right away. That meant the sons of bitches didn't plan on leaving any witnesses, and he'd have to kill them all or find another exit in a hurry. Wasting precious heartbeats on a rundown of his possible assailants, anyone who might have tried to queer the old man's action with Iran, he saw the other men breaking for the window and the fire escape beyond.

The mafioso scowled. They might be late for meetings, but the bastards didn't mess around when it was time to hit the bricks and save their asses. Bringing up the rear, Silvestri felt a fleeting urge to waste them both, and then the world fell in behind him.

Someone gave the door a flying kick, and by the time Silvestri turned to face the opposition, it was too damned late to save himself. He recognized the big guy, startled to discover that there was no one crowding in behind him, but he only had a fraction of a second as their guns went off together.

Anthony Silvestri saw his single bullet strike the wall, and then three rounds punched through his rib cage, knocking him off balance. Sprawling on the floor, he felt a seeping wetness through his clothes, but nothing else. That was strange.

Silvestri thought that dying was supposed to hurt.

THE CARPET SMELLED of urine, urging Bolan to his feet once he'd sidestepped the initial rounds of hostile fire. He triggered two quick bursts in answer, anything to keep their heads down as he gained his balance, closing in to strike the locking mechanism with a well-placed kick.

The door flew open, splinters trailing from the jamb, and Bolan entered in a combat crouch. He had a brief impression of a body scrambling through the window, shoe soles rattling on the fire escape, and then his full attention was commanded by the rearguard sentry.

Bolan knew the face, but there was no time for a conscious recognition as he saw the automatic pistol rising in his adversary's hand. They fired simultaneously, the Executioner sideways to present a smaller target, but it didn't matter in the last analysis. His enemy had jerked the trigger, panic taking over in the crunch, and Bolan heard the bullet strike the wall. His own Beretta stuttered, scoring three for three, and then his man was down, a stunned expression on his face, the light of life already winking out behind his eyes.

Silvestri. First name, Anthony, an underboss in charge of moving drugs for Don Patrice Grisanti. Flashing through his mind, the information raised a question mark that Bolan had no time to cope with at the moment. He'd come for the Iranians, and they were slipping away.

He rushed to the window, stepping across Silvestri's corpse. A glance had been enough to show him that the room was empty, and if one of his intended targets had escaped by crawling through the window, it was safe to bet the other had been out before him. Precious seconds had already slipped away. He might not have another chance to make the tag.

He hesitated on the sill, then risked a glance outside. Ten feet below him, crouching on the fire escape, Abdel Bazargan was leveling a snub-nosed .38 at Bolan's face. The Executioner recoiled as splinters blasted from the window frame and stung his cheek. A second round drilled glass above his head and set in motion a jagged, tinkling waterfall.

Bolan poked his hand around the corner, squeezing off a burst that had no realistic hope of striking flesh. One bullet struck the fire escape and whined away, the others lost in empty space.

Another glance, and this time there was only frenzied motion on the metal stairs. He followed, scrambling across the windowsill and craning far across the rail. One of the terrorists had reached the pavement, sprinting north, and Bolan was about to try a shot when number two cranked off another round from somewhere just below his feet.

The rusty grating saved his life, but the warrior felt the bite of shattered fragments on his ankles. The fire escape was lurching as his adversary made a break, and Bolan followed, skipping two or three steps at a time to reach the landing just below him. Someone must have heard the shots by now, and even in the apathetic heart of New York City, neighbors could be dialing 911. Patrol cars might be swinging off their normal beats and turning toward the scene of the disturbance even now, surrounding Bolan and his prey.

He gained a flight when the Iranian got careless, slipping on the rusty stairs and nearly going down. The effort cost him time, and Bolan's target compensated by reversing his direction, thrusting out the snubby .38 and triggering a round that passed within an inch of Bolan's ear.

Precision work wasn't an option in the circumstances. Bolan fired a 3-round burst from twenty feet and saw one slug rip through the gunman's thigh, another tunneling his shoulder as the third broke wide. His target staggered, reeling with the impact, and he stroked the trigger one more time with greater accuracy, stitching three neat holes along the Iranian hitman's spinal column.

The 93-R's slide locked open on an empty chamber, pale smoke curling from the breech. The warrior pulled the magazine and snapped a fresh one home, released the slide to chamber up a live round as he shouldered past the sagging corpse, continuing pursuit.

His quarry was within a few short strides of disappearing, merging with the flow of afternoon pedestrians, and Bolan knew he had no time to waste. He holstered the Beretta, vaulted easily across the rail, and saw the pavement rushing up to meet him from a range of twenty feet.

ACCORDING TO TOUR GUIDES, there are no such things as
alleys in Manhattan. There are only streets, among which
some—like Orwell's thinking animals—are clearly more
equal than others.

The "street" that waited for Saddam Kassim below the
hotel fire escape was narrow, lined with trash receptacles
and heaped with refuse that had never made it into cans or
Dumpsters. Homeless alcoholics might be found there,
sleeping after dark, but it was vacant at the moment. He
had ample room to run.

Gunshots echoed on the fire escape behind him. He
recognized the crack of Abdel's .38 revolver, answered by
the whisper of a silenced automatic. From the sounds of
ricochets on metal, he deduced that Bazargan was still
alive, a guess confirmed in seconds as the .38 went off
again. This time, when the silenced weapon answered, he
imagined that he heard the bullets striking home, a dying
gasp from Abdel as his spirit separated from the flesh.

Still running, he was conscious of a heavy impact on the
pavement. Abdel falling? Someone leaping from the fire
escape in close pursuit? He wasted no time glancing backward, knowing that the enemy wouldn't be far behind. If
he could reach the street in time, he had a chance.

Emerging from the alleyway, Kassim took time to tuck
his .38 inside the waistband of his slacks. He turned left,
an easterly direction, shoulders hunched to minimize his
height and change the general outline of his silhouette. He
didn't run, but moved with swift, determined strides,
bypassing several dawdlers, putting them behind him and
his pursuers. If he was forced to break away or stand and
fight, his adversaries might think twice about the danger
to their fellow men before they opened fire.

Kassim, for his part, wouldn't hesitate.

The terrorist had covered half a block before his ears picked up an angry murmur in the crowd behind him. Glancing back, he saw a tall man jostling past pedestrians, ignoring glares and bleats of protest from the sluggards. Kassim didn't recognize the man, but he knew the face of danger well enough. He palmed the .38 revolver, thumbed the hammer back and whirled to greet the stranger with a bullet, quickly aimed from forty feet away.

A youngish black man saved the runner's life, selecting just that moment for a change of course that brought him into Kassim's line of fire. The bullet drilled a clean hole in his nylon jacket, the surprise of impact mirrored on his face as he began to fall. Approaching from the rear, Kassim's opponent made the catch and knelt to ease his burden to the sidewalk, both hands momentarily occupied.

Kassim took off and left him to it, racing through the crowd, his .38 in hand. The weapon was a magic scepter, parting the impenetrable ranks in front of him as he ran. A woman screamed, and someone cursed him as he passed, but no one tried to stop him.

Spinning in midstride, he saw the stranger gaining, long legs eating up the sidewalk in his wake. Another running spin and he squeezed off a second shot, aware that it would take a miracle for the slug to find his target. He was dizzy now and veered off course, across the curb, colliding with a vendor who was selling pretzels on the street.

"You stupid—"

Slashing with the .38, Kassim cut off his words and drove them down his throat, along with broken teeth. At that he nearly stumbled on the falling body, almost lost his balance, gasping out a prayer for strength. He kept his footing somehow, weaving through the traffic which, at this point, had been slowed to a crawl. He ducked behind a sports car, slipped between two taxis and across the concrete island toward the eastbound lanes.

The blue-and-white patrol car seemed to come from nowhere, looming up to block his path with all its chrome and mounted lights. Two faces, black and white, regarded him with shocked expressions through the windshield. In a city where the police had seen it all, Kassim's abrupt appearance, gun in hand, apparently still came as a surprise.

Before they could recover or react, he got a running start and leaped up on their hood, the polished metal slippery beneath his feet. One of them had a microphone in hand, but he hadn't begun to speak, and the Iranian wasn't about to let him start. Kassim fired two shots through the windshield at point-blank range, one at each stunned face, before he sprang away and lurched in the direction of the nearest sidewalk.

Screams were all around him now, but he could lose them if he was fast enough. The tall man on his heels would be another matter, but his luck was bound to change. He'd survived a confrontation with American police, and he would kill the tall American as soon as possible.

But he must plan the move precisely, making no mistakes.

He only had two bullets left.

BOLAN CURSED BITTERLY and plunged after his quarry, scuffing the hood of a shiny Mercedes as he took the path of least resistance. Passing the patrol car, he saw two bluesuits slumped inside, their bloody faces slack and unresponsive. The warrior passed them by, aware that there was nothing he could do to help them now, and reached the

sidewalk after narrowly avoiding a collision with a
Cadillac.

His prey was eastbound once again, and Bolan wondered if he had some destination in mind, or if panic was
directing him. In either case the Executioner was bound to
follow, and he took off in the gunner's wake, shouldering
the idle gawkers aside with deliberate roughness, contact
stoking up his need to win the race.

A hard right on MacDougal Street, and Bolan thought
he might be gaining when the shooter changed his tack and
ducked inside a small boutique. Ignoring the potential for
an ambush, the warrior followed, palming the Beretta as
he entered in a combat crouch. A tiny blonde with eyes the
size of saucers pointed toward the rear of the establishment, and Bolan edged in that direction, past the dressing
cubicles.

The back door stood ajar, presenting Bolan with a view
of yet another alley. Clutching the Beretta in a firm, two-
handed grip, he kicked the door wide open, waiting for a
bullet that would spring the trap, proceeding in a rush
when none was fired.

His prey was halfway down the alley, running as if his
life depended on it. Bolan thought of shouting at him, but
he knew that it would be a waste of breath. He couldn't
even fire a warning shot, because the silencer would ren-
der it a futile gesture. He could drop the runner, with a
little luck, but there would be no guarantee of merely
wounding him at such a range.

And so he ran.

The Iranian's in-and-out at the boutique had added to
his lead, and he was taking full advantage of it now. Instead of glancing left or right as he exploded from the
alley, the man dashed straight across the intersecting street.

Or rather, tried to.

Bolan heard the screech of tires on asphalt, watched the taxi clip his target like a blade of grass before a mower, dragging him beneath its wheels. The chase was over, and he holstered the Beretta, slowing to a walk as he prepared to join the crowd of rubberneckers flocking to the accident.

He would remain until the ambulance arrived. No hurry there, judging by the appearance of the runner's crumpled form, the blood slick spreading out from underneath the cab. And while he waited, he would try to solve a riddle lacking any decent clues.

CHAPTER THREE

When Bolan made it back to Bleecker Street, there was a parking ticket on the windshield of his rented car. He stuffed the paper in a pocket, slid behind the wheel and waited for a slot to open up in traffic, engine idling at the curb. In motion, the warrior let his instincts do the driving, rolling north through Greenwich Village into Chelsea, as his military mind sought different angles on a new and unexpected problem.

Bolan had been asked to take the two Iranians before they had a chance to find themselves a target. He had done the job, or seen it done, but now there was a wild card in the game, and simply taking down the gunners didn't put his mind at ease.

Silvestri was the problem, and his death at Bolan's hands did nothing to resolve the issue. Why were two Iranian assassins meeting in a cheap hotel off Bleecker Street with an underboss of the Grisanti family? And why Silvestri, who was known to handle drugs exclusively? By all accounts, the gunmen had been hard-core terrorists, not dealers. Logically—if there was any logic to be found—they should have met with someone else in the Grisanti hierarchy. Joe Tattaglia, perhaps, in charge of weapons for the family. Or Mickey Andriola, *consigliere* to the clan.

Silvestri's involvement made no sense at all, and while irrational behavior might have been expected from the members of a Shiite hit team, New York's mafiosi were a different breed of cat. They looked at every option, sized up all the angles prior to making any move, and when they made connections, it was always with a concrete goal in mind.

The puzzle had too many missing pieces. He'd have to look for answers elsewhere, and while Don Grisanti doubtless could have filled him in, the Executioner suspected he might have a problem wangling the necessary invitation to a sit-down. If he dropped in to see the don, unexpectedly, he'd run the risk of touching off a major brushfire war, and this time Bolan hadn't come prepared for full-scale military operations in Manhattan.

He'd have to find another way, and that meant calling Hal Brognola.

Cruising north along Ninth Street, he found a shopping mall near Chelsea Park and left his car a short walk from the outdoor pay phones. One was in use, two others out of order thanks to vandals, but his luck improved on number four. He fed a handful of assorted coins into the slot and punched out Hal Brognola's office number, with the prefix for the District of Columbia.

It was a private line, and Brognola picked up before the phone could ring a second time.

"Hello?"

"I've got a number for you," Bolan told him.

"I'm listening."

He read the pay phone's number off and waited as it was repeated in the gruff, familiar voice.

"Affirmative."

"Three minutes."

Bolan cradled the receiver, waiting, and the call came through with seconds left to spare. Brognola would be scrambling and recording all at once, the tapes erased before the day was out, unless they seemed to have some evidentiary value.

"How's the weather?" the big Fed inquired when Bolan answered.

"Heating up."

"It has a tendency to do that. Have you had a chance to meet our friends?"

"Just now. They didn't have a lot to say."

"I guess they're tired from all that traveling."

"You'd be surprised. When I dropped in, they were already entertaining company."

A note of caution crept into Brognola's voice. "That's interesting. Anyone I know?"

"A local Family man by the name of Silvestri."

"He's the one who deals in pharmaceuticals?"

"He used to. Last I heard he was retired."

"That makes it sticky. I'd prefer to have this conversation in the flesh. What kind of schedule are you working on? Do you have any time to spare?"

"Could be. I've got some questions of my own."

"Let's hope I have the answers."

"Are we talking Stony Man?"

"Where else?"

"I'll drive," the soldier said on impulse. "Look for me tomorrow, close to lunchtime."

"Fair enough. That gives me time to check some odds and ends."

"It's gotten odd enough already."

"Yeah. We'll have to see if we can fix that. See you."

Driving back to his hotel in midtown, Bolan tried to read between the lines of Hal Brognola's conversation. Was the man from Justice holding out, or had he truly been surprised by the news about Silvestri? The warrior flipped a mental coin and factored in his knowledge of the big Fed's personality, deciding Brognola's expression of surprise was genuine.

And in its own way, that made matters worse.

A relatively simple game of tag was turning complicated, and he didn't like the sudden twist. It made him nervous when the savages began to work in concert, laying ego baggage and petty jealousies aside. A common interest was implied, and Bolan didn't even want to think about the cause that would unite a team of Shiite terrorists with New York's Mob.

He didn't want to think about it, but he had no choice.

His enemies had served the problem up before him on a platter, and he couldn't turn away. Tomorrow at Stony Man Farm there might be answers to the questions that were nagging at his mind.

If not, the Executioner would have to seek them somewhere else.

"SILVESTRI?" Leo Turrin's frown seemed carved in granite. "*Anthony* Silvestri?"

"As I live and breathe," Brognola said. "*He* doesn't, though, anymore."

"It couldn't happen to a nicer guy."

"Agreed, but that's beside the point. Our question of the moment is, what was the Brooklyn smack king doing with a pair of triggers from Teheran?"

"Converting?"

"That's a scream. I'll laugh next time I get a chance."

Brognola's sour tone wiped Turrin's smile away. "All right then, if Silvestri was involved, I'd say the boys were talking drugs. We know the Families are shopping in the Golden Crescent nowadays. The China White's too pricey for a lower class of clientele."

"Agreed, but when did participants of the Islamic Revolution start dealing? These guys won't touch pork, for

God's sake. You think they're moving smack and hash now?''

Leo shrugged and spread his hands. "Right now," he said, "I don't think anything. Silvestri was the mover for Grisanti's Family. That's solid. If he's started branching out to other lines, I haven't heard about it."

"No," Brognola agreed. "Me, neither."

"Well?"

"I've got a date with Striker at the Farm, lunchtime tomorrow. Can you make it?"

"Absolutely."

"Fine. Reach out for Jack Grimaldi, will you? Make it top priority."

"Will do." The frown was still in place. "What's going on?"

"It's just a hunch," Brognola said.

"That bad?"

"The worst. I've got some calls to make, loose ends to wrap up before I lay it out. If nothing proves me wrong, I'll fill you in tomorrow, along with Striker."

"Right."

There was a worried look on Turrin's face as he departed, and Brognola saw no profit in a futile bid to lift his spirits. It was just a hunch, but he had learned to trust his instincts in a quarter century of service to the government. Brognola's intuition was responsible for solving countless cases where "police technology" had failed. The human factor, after all, was still what made the world go 'round, for good or ill.

And that included Bolan.

The guy had taken on Brognola's New York operation as a favor, using time he doubtless could have spent on other projects, tracking other enemies. It was supposed to be a simple touch-and-go, two killers neutralized by force, a message telegraphed to their employers in the Middle East. Instead, with the involvement of a New York mafioso who was known to deal exclusively in drugs, the game was complicated, turning in upon itself to form a riddle...and perhaps a snare.

Brognola had a hunch, all right, and he wasn't about to leak the details in advance. With any luck, a call or two would prove his fears unfounded, and he could dismiss the notion as a bit of job-related paranoia.

He reached across the desk and lifted the receiver for his private line. No point in going through his secretary this time. A mistake would cost him nothing more than time. A solid hunch, by contrast, just might cost the life of Hal Brognola's closest friend.

If he was right and everything proved out, the secret would be his. And he would keep it to himself until tomorrow when he shared it with the Executioner.

GRIMALDI SWUNG the chopper east, along the nonexistent line that was the border, with Nogales at his back. The desert was invisible below him, lost in darkness, with a smudge of light that would be Bisbee, Arizona, showing up around eleven o'clock, some forty miles ahead. Without his running lights, he was compelled to trust the instruments explicitly and pray the mufflers on the whirlybird's jet engines were performing as designed. Inside the cockpit there was no way he could tell.

It hadn't been Grimaldi's first time flying dark, but he'd never cared for the experience. Bush pilots running drugs from Mexico would do the same, and every moment he was braced to meet a blacked out Piper Cub, propeller growling like a buzzsaw as it churned his windscreen into dust. So sorry, Jack...but, anyway, you stopped the shipment.

Great. Except he wasn't after drugs tonight. His target was a so-called human being, or a group of same, who had been working nights along the Arizona border for the past six months, surprising wetbacks in the darkness and relieving them of any cash or personal belongings they were dumb enough to bring along when they went looking for a new life in *El Norte*. Having pocketed the goodies, Mr. X and company wiped out the risk of witnesses by mowing down their victims, execution-style.

As targets go, the wets were relatively "safe." They weren't citizens, most spoke no English, and the new arrivals had no special status under terms of federal amnesty. The border rats who preyed upon them knew that local cops—most cops—in Texas and in Arizona had more pressing problems than the fate of half a dozen wetbacks every now and then. It was a shame they had to die on U.S. soil, of course, but what the hell, it wasn't like the border rats were murdering Americans.

The Border Patrol expressed greater concern, unsettled by the prospect of armed predators operating at will in the wasteland, realizing perhaps that the raiders must inevitably run afoul of a patrol. The explosion had come two weeks earlier near Lukeville, when a pair of officers had stumbled onto something and gone down before a hail of automatic fire. The Feds were angry now, and with the possibility of international connections in the case, a subtle word had been relayed to Stony Man Farm. Grimaldi and the chopper had been detailed to assist in scouring the border for a man, or men, who made the rules up as they went along.

It would have been a hopeless task with searchlights, swooping in like something from an alien invasion, warning their potential prey before he came within five miles of making contact. In the place of running lights and floods,

Grimaldi used an infrared device designed for stalking human prey in Vietnam's impenetrable jungles. Recently it had been used on the domestic front to turn up missing children, stranded hikers and remains of victims buried by a psycho killer in a Sacramento suburb. An adjustment to the unit kept Grimaldi from receiving false alarms on every rabbit, stray dog or coyote that he passed, but if a human being or an engine-driven vehicle turned up along his flight path, he would know about it. Once a contact had been made, he'd communicate with units on the ground and close the net.

It was a piece of cake. Except they'd been running sectors for the past eight days without results. In all that time, they'd surprised perhaps two hundred wetbacks, plus a naked teenage couple, sweating up the seats of daddy's station wagon. In the process, Jack was conscious of the fact they might have been observed by their intended prey.

The border rats had no apparent schedule, and their territory ranged from Yuma, Arizona to Del Rio, Texas. The odds of spotting them on any given night were minuscule, ridiculous to contemplate. Forget about your basic needle in a haystack. This was more like searching for a drop of water in the ocean. Hopeless unless—

The scanner came to life, directing Jack's attention to a group of bodies and at least one vehicle ahead. Most likely it would be another gang of wetbacks coming over from the south, perhaps a party warming up. In either case, he had to play the game.

Grimaldi keyed the floods and saw two off-road vehicles, one black, one camouflage, with five or six armed men around them. Ten or fifteen feet away, about half a dozen Mexicans were standing with their hands raised, staring into leveled guns.

The floodlights startled all concerned, and Jack was barking orders as he brought the air speed down and swung the chopper back around to face the gunmen. Hovering, he lighted the scene from thirty yards away and fifty feet above the desert floor. His earphones told him troops were closing on the ground, and all he had to do was keep the gunmen more or less in sight. No sweat.

The punks had other notions, though. They scrambled for the vehicles, ignoring a demand for surrender that Grimaldi broadcast over the helicopter's loudspeaker. Two of them opened fire on the chopper, and Jack took her out of range, as engines roared to life beneath him. He was satisfied, at least, to see the wets had disappeared, their shadows melting into darkness on the fringes of the lighted stage.

The vehicles were moving now in opposite directions. Choosing one at random, Jack advised the ground pursuit team of the runaway's direction and received an anxious "roger" in return. If someone let the runners slip away, it wouldn't be Grimaldi's fault.

He stuck behind his chosen target, noting that the off-road number was an open Jeep. Three men were hanging on as ruts and potholes shook the vehicle, and they were conscious of pursuit. First one and then the other passenger glanced back in the direction of Grimaldi's chopper, shouting something to the driver, and with every bulletin the wheelman urged his vehicle to greater speed.

There was a limit, even so, and they could no more lose a helicopter in the open than they could produce a set of wings and fly. The chopper had greater speed, and it wasn't delayed by the necessity of bucking surface obstacles. Grimaldi ran no risk of blowouts, broken axles or fractured oil pans.

The raiders recognized their problem and decided that the quickest way to shake the tail would be to shoot him down. Both passengers were packing automatic rifles, and they started pegging rounds at thirty yards. Amused, he took the chopper up and out of range, continuing pursuit from higher altitudes.

The driver of the Jeep was running dark, as if extinguishing his headlights would defeat surveillance from the sky. In his position, anything was worth a try, but there were risks involved. He never saw the gully just ahead, carved out of sand and stone by flash flood waters, and the Jeep was airborne by the time the driver realized he had a problem.

Impact, halfway down the far wall of the gully, solved his problem, permanently. Skewered on the steering column, dead before his vehicle made contact with the desert floor, the driver probably had time for one last scream before it all went black. In any case, he never felt the rush of crackling flames that instantly consumed the vehicle and his companions, burning bright enough to bring the search teams home without Grimaldi's help.

He thought about returning to the contact point and looking for the other punks, but he decided not to bother. They were in the box by now, and if they chose to shoot it out, he didn't care to watch. Enough, for one night, was enough.

Grimaldi had the microphone in hand and was preparing to report, when static whispered in his earphones, followed instantly by the dispatcher's voice.

"Command to Airborne One."

"I copy."

"Airborne One, we need you back at base, ASAP. You're wanted on the land line. That's a Blue Ridge Top Priority."

Grimaldi felt his pulse rate quicken as he recognized the code from Stony Man. He didn't hear the Blue Ridge Top Priority that often—maybe once or twice a year—and it would mean that Brognola was in a flap.

"Affirmative, Command. Good timing. We're just finished here. I'll disengage and see you on the ground in fifteen, tops."

"We copy fifteen minutes, Airborne One. Command out."

Talking to the ground, he gave the hunters clear directions to the weenie roast and told them he was breaking off. They asked no questions, and Grimaldi offered nothing in the way of explanations. Hell, he had no answers, even if he felt inclined to flap his jaw.

The summons was a mystery, like always. Everything would be explained on his arrival, and until that time, he would be left to play a game of solitaire with his imagination.

Grimaldi didn't notice that he was smiling as he turned the chopper back toward the command post, opening the throttle on her jets. Perhaps, he thought, enough was *not* enough.

Not yet.

IN HIS HOTEL ROOM, Bolan spent the night packing. He had traveled light, one suitcase and a carryall that never would have passed security in any airport, but the weapons were expendable. He could have ditched them in the case of an emergency, but he had opted for the longer, slower drive from selfish motives.

Bolan wanted time to think.

He could have traveled on a military or commercial flight to Richmond, but the riddle of Silvestri and the two Iranians was preying on his mind, and forty minutes in the air wouldn't allow him time to scrutinize the different angles, looking for a way inside the puzzle box. He might not solve it on his own, but he could try. And anyway, the act of driving tended to relax him. After the recent hit, it would help him wind down and clear his mental decks for action.

Television news was covering the Greenwich Village shootout as a case of underworld diplomacy gone sour. No one in the media or law enforcement was surprised to find Silvestri dead. It happened all the time to dealers, and if every human death diminished mankind as a whole, some cases generated less alarm than others. Frowning TV anchorpersons might not say so, but for New York's finest and their federal counterparts, "good riddance" was the password of the day.

Silvestri's bodyguard had been a four-time loser, with convictions on the books for rape, grand theft, extortion and impersonating a policeman. In his younger days, Vincenzo ("Shelly") Manganiello earned his keep by posing as a vice detective, shaking down male prostitutes and their embarrassed johns for payoffs to avoid "arrest." The scam was strictly business, Manganiello leaning strongly toward the ladies after hours. Sadly, for his victims, he preferred to pick his "girlfriends" out of parking lots and shopping malls, persuading them to serve him at gunpoint. Like Silvestri, he wouldn't be missed.

The two Iranians hadn't yet been identified as such. The media suspected that their passports might be bogus, but the Teheran connection hadn't been deduced so far. "Smart money" pegged the pair as Pakistanis, interrupted while negotiating a narcotics deal with Brooklyn's king of smack. As for the gunman who had dropped Silvestri and the two Iranians, homicide investigators had no clues. No useful fingerprints had been recovered, and eyewitnesses were hopelessly confused.

A shower helped the Executioner unwind, and he had turned the television off by nine o'clock. His bags were packed, the car secured downstairs, his clothing laid out for the morning's journey. Naked, Bolan killed the lights and slipped between cool sheets, settling in as he waited for his body heat to warm the bed. Beneath his pillow, one hand curled around the grip of his Beretta. He closed his eyes.

Tomorrow would bring the answers to his riddle, one way or another. He'd either scope the problem out himself or pick up a solution from Brognola at the Farm. If neither of them had a solid answer of his own, they would discover one together. In the meantime, there was nothing to be gained by stalling sleep.

He shifted once or twice, adjusting to the mattress, blanking out the images of violence that had marked his afternoon. Accustomed by experience to sleeping when and where he could, the soldier focused on a spinning void and let it swallow him alive. Within the space of ninety seconds, he was breathing deeply, face and form relaxed in sleep.

But, for the Executioner, escape would bring no respite from his everlasting war. The images of death and violence would return to him, as always, in his dreams.

CHAPTER FOUR

The Bear was tired of waiting. Action was his strong suit, even from the confines of his chair, and killing time before arrivals always set his nerves on edge. Distractedly he punched up a display of Hal's itinerary and confirmed the ETA from Wonderland.

Another fifteen minutes.

He'd been working through the night to nail down answers for the questions Hal had asked him yesterday by phone, and while another man might have displayed the symptoms of fatigue, it didn't show on Aaron Kurtzman. Rather, he was brimming with excitement, anxious to report his findings and observe Brognola's personal reaction to the news. He could expect an "attaboy" on this job, if the man from Justice wasn't too disgruntled by the information Kurtzman had amassed.

In fact, he had been lucky with his queries, striking a responsive chord in places where he had expected only silence—or at best a grudging nod of confirmation. Hal had been on target with his supposition, but he hadn't grasped the full dimensions of the problem they were facing. If the truth were told, Brognola's guess had barely scratched the surface.

That was bad, and Kurtzman was relieved that these days no one killed the messenger who brought bad news. Brognola would be angry, perhaps depressed, but he'd hardly be surprised. If Aaron knew the guy at all, his first reaction would be digging in to find a viable solution.

And the viable solution, Kurtzman knew, was driving south that morning from New York. If anyone could take the ball and run for daylight on a play like this, Mack Bolan was the man.

Brognola had to know that, too, and it wouldn't improve his humor. He didn't enjoy dispatching friends—or strangers, when it came to that—on missions that could easily result in sudden death. For this one, scratch out "easily" and write in "probably," providing an assessment of the grim reality that Aaron's monitors and printers had disgorged since 4:00 a.m.

Eight minutes now, and Kurtzman hoped the plane would be on time. He wheeled his chair back from the double keyboard, flexing forearms roped with muscle. Somewhere in the house there was a motorized contraption he could use, but Aaron let it gather dust. He had already lost his legs, the price of failure to detect a traitor in the ranks, and he wasn't about to let his arms go by default. If nothing else, maneuvering his chair around the house and grounds provided him with daily exercise.

These days he seldom thought about the night when he was shot. The human body has a talent for dismissing pain once it is safely past, and while the mind recalls an incident as painful in the abstract, it can seldom specify the suffering involved. Was there an ache? Or stabbing pain? How had it *really* felt?

In fact, the spinal wound that left him chairbound hardly hurt at all. The shock of impact had immediately rendered him unconscious, and there had been numbness afterward, supplied in equal parts by local anesthetics and the severance of all the major nerves below his waist. He wouldn't walk again, the doctors were unanimous on that score, but he could adjust and lead a fairly normal life within the limits of his handicap.

And so he had.

But in the old, preambush days, he'd been prone to pacing under stress. If he was sweating out a rendezvous or waiting on a bulletin from distant sources, he would stalk the floor with long, determined strides. More recently, in lieu of wheeling back and forth like something from an animated shooting gallery, he fumed inside and worried the computers, firing queries off around the country and around the world, on any topic he could think of. On occasion he received surprising answers.

When it was almost time, he caught the elevator from the war room and wheeled himself across the first-floor computer room, through its coded access door and the spacious entryway beyond, onto the long covered porch of the farmhouse. Facing north across a field of fallow ground, he had a clear view of the landing strip, three hundred yards away.

He wouldn't go to meet the plane, as it would mean a transfer to a vehicle and back again when he returned. The effort would be wasted on a ten-minute round trip, and there would be no time to brief Hal in the car, regardless.

He could hear the sound of engines approaching from the east. It circled once, the military pilot getting clearance from the house before he lined his aircraft up and brought her in. A car rolled out to meet Brognola and his lone companion, doubling back in the direction of the farmhouse as the pilot shut his engines down and waited for the fueling truck.

Emerging from the car, Brognola looked the same as ever, with the possible addition of some brand-new worry lines around his eyes. Behind him, Leo Turrin flashed the Bear a grin composed in equal parts of friendship and determination. Neither man was overjoyed about the purpose of their visit, and the station chief of Stony Man

Farm regretted that their day could only go from bad to worse.

When they had decently disposed of the amenities, Brognola followed Kurtzman to the war room, leaving Turrin on his own to scout out sandwiches and coffee in the mess.

"How goes it?" asked the man from Wonderland.

"It goes," the Bear replied.

"You have the information I requested?"

"That's affirmative. I was afraid we'd come up empty—lean, at best—but it appears we tapped the mother lode."

Brognola read the answer on his comrade's face and forced himself to ask the question anyway.

"Is it as bad as I expected?"

"Nope. It's worse."

"WE'VE GOT Grimaldi on the scope," Aaron Kurtzman announced. "Anybody want to do the honors?"

Leo Turrin snuffed his cigarette and pushed his chair back. "Sure. Why not?"

In fact, he'd grown tired of waiting even prior to their arrival at the Farm. Brognola had been playing sphinx again, refusing to discuss his suppositions on the case at hand, and Turrin knew that the big Fed would only talk when he was good and ready—which in this case meant when everyone was present and accounted for. Grimaldi's touchdown put them one step closer to the show-and-tell, and Leo thought the guy deserved a welcome for his trouble at the very least.

Grimaldi's aircraft was a light, twin-engine Cessna. Leo sat beside a young, athletic-looking "farmhand" as they motored out to meet the pilot, and he knew enough to skip the conversation. Staffers at the complex were close-mouthed, even grim, around outsiders, and it didn't matter if they saw you once a week for months on end. Unless you were assigned to Stony Man Farm full-time, or answered to the names of Bolan or Brognola, you were merely passing through, a "stranger" to be treated with the proper blend of courtesy and caution.

Grimaldi let the ground crew handle fuel and any necessary servicing, a tribute to his faith in those around him. He was smiling as he crossed the tarmac, wringing Leo's hand and nodding absently in the direction of their silent driver.

"What's the shake-up, Leo?"

"Damned if I know. Hal's been suffering from an attack of lockjaw since last night. He wants to lay it out all at once for everybody."

Grimaldi's face lighted up. "So, Striker's coming in?"

"We're looking for him noonish."

"And I take it he'll be needing wings."

"I wish I knew."

They rode back to the house in silence. Kurtzman met them in the entryway and shook Grimaldi's hand. "You made good time."

"That's motivation for you. Where's the boss?"

"He's running down some loose ends in the war room. We'll be going down to join him after Striker shows. You hungry?"

"I could eat."

They followed Kurtzman to the dining room, and Turrin sat across from Jack, content with coffee while the pilot wolfed down two thick sandwiches and chased them with a frosty mug of beer.

"Not bad," Grimaldi told the Bear when he was finished. "You should open up a chain. The price is right."

"Tell that to John Q. Public, will you?"

"I'd be glad to. Where's he living nowadays?"

Their banter was designed to ease the tension, but it failed to work on Leo. He'd been absorbing the Brognola vibes since Striker bought the mission to Manhattan, and the late addition of Silvestri as a wild card seemed to be the final straw. Hal was preoccupied with doom and gloom just now, a situation that evoked bad memories for Leo, images of other cases where the odds had seemed impossible.

It would be better, he decided, when they knew the worst. However bad a situation got, it never held a candle to the terrors of imagination run amok. When problems were defined and quantified, their limitations measured, you were that much closer to attaining a solution.

Right.

And that was easily said, considering the fact that Turrin wouldn't be compelled to solve the problem either way. It would be Striker on the firing line, perhaps alone, when everything began to fall apart and all their boardroom theories turned to shit. It would be Striker carrying the ball on their behalf and taking all the lumps along the way.

Like always.

Leo wondered why he did it, and the answer came across at once, as plain as day.

Because he could. The possibility and the necessity were one, combined in Bolan's sense of duty. He could no more pass a dangerous situation by than he could voluntarily stop breathing. One recourse would be as fatal as the other to a man of Bolan's temperament and dedication.

Striker was a solid-gold original, and no mistake.

It would be tragic if they had to throw the guy away.

BROGNOLA FINISHED reading through the file a second time and closed it gently, almost reverently, before he sat back in his chair and removed the cellophane from a fat cigar.

"You've read all this?" he asked Kurtzman rhetorically. "Okay, what to do you think?"

"It's not my choice."

"I know that, dammit. All I'm asking for is input here."

Brognola thought that Kurtzman looked incongruous, his massive torso rising from the wheelchair. When he shrugged, it seemed that he was on the verge of rising to his feet, as if the past few years had been some kind of ghoulish put-on.

"I suppose, if it was me, I'd say we have to go ahead."

"You mean, *he* has to go ahead."

"That's what I mean."

"Goddammit."

"Think about the options, Hal."

"I have."

The "options" were delay, procrastination, inactivity. There would be other contacts, other meetings, and they might not have a handle on the players next time. If they didn't follow the trail while it was fresh, they ran a risk of losing out entirely.

"What's the time?" Brognola asked. He'd already checked his watch, but hoped it might be fast, allowing him a bit more time in which to think.

"I show eleven forty-five," Kurtzman said.

"Damn."

"He's got a choice, remember? If he doesn't think that he can pull it off—"

"He'll try it anyway. You know that, same as I do."

"So? His choice."

The Bear was playing devil's advocate, and Brognola was in no mood for philosophical discussions.

"Where's the choice?" he asked. "The guy hasn't walked away from trouble since he learned to tie his shoes. He'll take the job, regardless . . . if it's offered."

"If?"

"We could delay response." The words were bitter in his mouth. "Put Able Team or Phoenix on the case when they wrap up their present missions. That way, anyhow, we'd shave the odds."

"You think so? Putting three men—maybe eight men— on the ground instead of one? Why don't we drop a coin and send in the Marines?"

"That's not a bad idea." Brognola scowled. "If it was thirty years ago, or even twenty, there's a chance the President would do exactly that. Gunboat diplomacy, and no apologies for taking care of business. Now we've got to turn the other cheek and keep one eye on world opinion every time some piss-ant, third-rate power takes a shot. Some days I wonder if we're even holding ground."

"And other days?"

"Hell, then I *know* we're losing."

Kurtzman wheeled himself around and headed for the war room's elevator. "I'll go up and dust the welcome mat. You want me to direct the gang downstairs when everybody's in?"

"No, thanks. I'm right behind you."

"Okay."

Brognola listened to the elevator doors and spread one hand across the flat manila file in front of him. It wasn't thick, but it was loaded all the same, and it could blow up in his face if it was handled carelessly. Retaliation was a two-way street, and the United States had been engaged in skirmishing with Teheran for about a dozen years. Neither side had scored a clear-cut victory as yet, and that was bad enough, considering the obvious discrepancies in population, size and military strength. Brognola didn't want to be the man responsible for one more grand snafu. And yet if he did nothing...

The big Fed stuck the unlighted cigar into a corner of his mouth and pushed his chair back, shambling toward the elevator. As an option, inactivity didn't exist. It was surrender, plain and simple. If you let the savages walk over you, they kept on going. There would be no sudden change of heart, no magic revelation to the error of their ways. Negotiation merely bought time for the enemy.

A pair of Kurtzman's staffers concentrated on their printouts as Brognola exited the elevator and crossed the computer room. It wouldn't be long now, he thought, familiar faces staring back at his from their positions at the conference table, while he dealt the cards of life and death.

Disgusted with a world that always seemed to stack the deck against him, Hal Brognola wondered how much longer he could play the game.

THE DRIVE HAD BEEN a gift from Bolan to himself. He needed time to think, and driving from New York to Stony Man Farm, due west of Wonderland, had given him the perfect opportunity to sort his various impressions of the Greenwich Village strike.

He caught the Holland Tunnel from Manhattan to New Jersey, following the Pulaski Skyway through Newark and southward, picking up U.S. Highway 1 at Elizabeth. Bolan stopped for breakfast at Trenton, purchasing coffee and pastry from a roadside shop, parking his car in a turnout that offered a view of the Delaware River. The trees were alive with birds, and he wound up feeding them the best part of his breakfast, grateful for the company and the distraction they provided.

Any way he looked at the Iranian connection, it spelled trouble. Granted, there was nothing new about Grisanti's Family shopping in the Golden Crescent, but as far as Bolan knew, the deals had all been cut on Middle Eastern turf, without suppliers visiting America, and there had been no solid evidence of terrorist connections. Now, if instinct served him, it appeared the picture might be changing for the worse.

From Trenton Bolan motored south on Interstate 95, skirting Philadelphia, Wilmington, Baltimore, finally plunging into the snarled heart of Washington, D.C. Emerging from Wonderland, he caught westbound Interstate 66 through Arlington and into Gainsville. There he veered southeasterly on U.S. Highway 211, holding his course well into the Blue Ridge Mountains, picking up Skyline Drive east of Sperryville.

The final approach to Stony Man Farm inevitably filled Bolan with a sense of awe. He knew the region's history, including four long years of bloody civil war, but Bolan marveled chiefly at the landscape. Virgin forest lined the road on either side, protected from human trespass as part of the Shenandoah National Park. Five miles south of the U.S. 211 intersection, the rugged profile of Stony Man Mountain loomed to an altitude of four thousand feet, following Skyline Drive with an inscrutable gaze. Pioneers gave the man-mountain its name, and Civil War combatants bled before the silent watcher, dying for the high ground. Lately Bolan liked to think that Stony Man would voice approval, if he could, of the establishment that shared his name.

Stony Man Farm sprawled over some 160 acres, much of it in trees, and where the property hadn't been fenced, it was protected by an interlocking screen of sensors and security devices. Barring failure of the installation's several generators all at once, it was impossible for human beings to approach the Farm unseen. Since its establishment, the base had suffered one attack and thirty-seven false alarms, the latter incidents involving hikers gone astray. The innocent were guided back to Skyline Drive and pointed toward the nearest town, occasionally offered rides to speed them on their way. They never reached the airstrip or the buildings that comprised the installation's heart.

Television cameras monitored the gate at Stony Man, and Bolan rolled his window down as he approached the entrance, leaning out to give the monitors a full-face view. The gate could only be unlocked by staffers at the house; there was no way to spring the locks by hand or override commands with a remote control, since buried cables made the linkup with the base command post. High explosives or a heavily armored vehicle would do the job, of course, but either method would alert the Farm's defenders, and a hot reception would be guaranteed for the intruders.

Bolan waited briefly while his photograph was analyzed by the computer, confirmation sought and rapidly secured on the registration of his vehicle. He would be covered, even so, until he reached the house and passed a personal inspection, ruling out the possibility of hostile forces slipping in a "face" to breach the Farm's defenses.

Rolling in through trees that had been thinned in places to provide the guards with fields of fire, he concentrated on the topic of his meeting with Brognola. The big Fed had played it cagey on the telephone, and Bolan wondered whether that was due to strategy or simple lack of concrete information. Either way they had a problem on their hands, and they would have to find a viable solution soon.

He parked beside the house and left his keys inside the car. A member of the staff would stow the vehicle and bring his bags inside when he or she had time. Four men were waiting for him on the porch, and Bolan asked himself how many men could count on friends as true as these.

Brognola was the first to shake his hand, and Bolan worked his way along the line from there, with words and smiles for Leo Terrin, Jack Grimaldi and the Bear. These men were special, and each had risked his life for Bolan in the past. The war had taken Kurtzman's legs, but he'd never once complained or tried to wangle easy duty for himself. Across the board these members of the team were family, pledged to carry on the everlasting war while strength remained.

He spent a good half hour in the mess with Jack and Leo, eating charbroiled burgers while they spoke in generalities about the recent New York set. Grimaldi filled them in on Arizona, where a dirty job had been wrapped up with three men dead and four in jail, awaiting trial on counts of Murder One. It felt like old times in the trenches, but they knew the gathering wasn't intended as a sort of class reunion. There was brutal work ahead, and while it was a safe bet Leo would be staying home, Grimaldi's presence smacked of foreign shores, a mission that demanded wings.

When Bolan finished with his lunch, they caught the elevator to the war room, riding down in silence, each man busy with his private thoughts. The Executioner examined his sensations, searching for a trace of apprehension, but he had to settle for a burning curiosity. Whatever was decided in their conference, whether he accepted or declined the mission, he was bent on knowing why a pair of terrorists had traveled halfway around the world to huddle with the second-largest group of mafiosi in New York. He owed himself that much at least.

Brognola and the Bear were waiting for them in the war room, huddled at the far end of the conference table, speaking softly as they entered. Kurtzman heard them coming, and he flashed a smile that came off looking strained. When they had settled into empty chairs, Brognola spent a moment scanning faces, saving Bolan's for the last.

"I think we've broken the Silvestri riddle," he declared. "We know the guy was moving smack for Don Grisanti in New York and parts of Jersey. We've confirmed his contacts were a pair of hard-core Shiite terrorists, although we still don't have their names. It didn't click until we played a hunch last night and Aaron scored the touchdown with his magic modem."

"Piece of cake," the Bear put in without enthusiasm.

"That, it wasn't," Bragnola replied. "We got damned lucky with the information, but you may not think so, once you've heard the punch line."

Bolan held Brognola's gaze, unblinking. Several seconds passed before Grimaldi got impatient. "Do we have to guess, or what?" he asked the room at large.

"We're looking at the absolute worst-case scenario," Brognola said. "A transatlantic terrorist connection with the old-line Syndicate. New York, for starters. If it spreads, the sky's the limit."

Bolan raised an eyebrow. "And the roots?" he asked.

Brognola tried to catch the frown in time, but failed. "They're planted in the Bekaa Valley."

CHAPTER FIVE

The name produced a sudden rush of adrenaline, but Bolan concealed the effects, easing back in his chair and waiting for the others to respond. Kurtzman had already known the punch line, and Leo took it silently, a stern frown carving dark parentheses around his mouth. Grimaldi was the only member of the team who voiced his agitation.

"What?" The pilot seemed astonished, or perhaps angry. "The Bekaa Valley? Jeez, you must be kidding, right?"

Brognola's hands were folded on the conference table, giving him the aspect of a man at prayer. "I wish I were."

Grimaldi wouldn't let it go. "The Bekaa is a frigging nightmare, folks, in case you haven't heard. Why not try something easier, like climbing Everest with a blindfold on and both hands tied behind your back?"

"Nobody said it would be easy, Jack."

"Well, that's a consolation. But did anybody mention that it just might be impossible?"

"Let's hear the story."

Bolan's voice cut through Grimaldi's agitation, stifling the pilot's protest. Strangely Brognola didn't appear relieved. Instead he dropped his eyes to focus on the slim manila file in front of him. It took a moment for the Fed to put his thoughts in order, then his eyes came up again and locked on Bolan's as he spoke to the assembled warriors.

"We've confirmed through Aaron's contacts that the two Iranians you iced were hard-core Shiite terrorists. There's no mistake on that score. The Silvestri angle threw us off because we hated to believe the worst . . . but, what the hell, it's all there is."

"A new alliance?"

"Maybe not so new. We should have seen it coming, I suppose. A large minority of native Lebanese are Shiite Muslims, so Iran's got a captive audience right there. They've got their own militia, and they've been waging civil war against other factions, off and on for thirty years. Ike sent Marines in 1958 to help a Christian president hang on, but congress didn't like the smell of things and he was forced to bring them home again. They muddled through a while without us, but the war's been going strong since the late seventies, with no end in sight."

"Whatever happened to peace on earth?" Grimaldi asked.

"Let me know if you find some," Brognola grumbled. "I'll order a six-pack."

"My treat."

The big Fed resumed his interrupted narrative. "If holy war's not bad enough, the Lebanese have had to deal with multiple invasions in the past ten years, with everyone from Israel to the Syrians and PLO grabbing a slice of the pie. Whole towns have been wiped off the map, and Beirut looks like a travel brochure for Nagasaki on D-plus-one. The government, if you can call it that, is facing double-digit unemployment—well over thirty percent at last count—and the country's economic credibility is shot to hell. We're talking anarchy, with momentary spasms of repression thrown in for variety. It's perfect, when you think about it."

"For Iran," Bolan said.

"Hell, yes."

"Let's hear some more about the Bekaa, shall we?"
Jack Grimaldi's voice was terse.

"My pleasure. Basics first?"

Brognola glanced at Kurtzman, and the Bear made
magic with a keyboard mounted on the table just in front
of him. The lights were dimmed but not extinguished,
while a screen against the wall descended from the ceiling
on Brognola's left. Another keystroke put a detailed map
of Lebanon on-screen.

"Geographically the Bekaa Valley occupies the north-
eastern corner of Lebanon, north of Baalbek and east of
Al-Hirmil. The climate is idyllic—lush gardens, balmy
breezes, the works. Before the latest round of civil war, the
region was primarily a getaway for wealthy Lebanese. They
liked the weather and the scenery, the isolation. It was like
Palm Springs for Arabs."

"But?"

"Precisely. Everything that made the Bekaa Valley
popular with tourists also made it ripe for cultivation. In
this case, the growers started with hashish and worked their
way up to opium poppies. The top hoods from Beirut and
Damascus discovered the Bekaa around 1975, and they
didn't take long to dig in. The valley is perfect for growing, refining and shipping narcotics. Most of the local
peasants are Shiite Muslims, and they were recruited for
grunt work, one way or another."

Bolan knew what that meant. First would come the offer of employment in the fields or a refinery. The salary
would be a pittance, but for those who hadn't worked in
years, a crust of bread was better than an empty plate. If
there was serious resistance, an example might be chosen
by the growers, sacrificed in public as an object lesson to
the rest. It might take two or three such lessons, but the

people would inevitably fall in line. And with each passing year, abiding hatred of the rich and powerful would grow in every peasant's heart until he hungered for revenge.

"Come 1982," Brognola continued, "when Israel made her push across the border, blitzing Tyre and Sidon on the way to occupy Beirut, our dearly departed pal Khomeini saw a chance to make some hay in Lebanon. He packed off several hundred of his revolutionary guards to Baalbek, and they settled in an old, dilapidated downtown building called 'Hosseinieh.'"

On cue the map of Lebanon was whisked away, supplanted by a color snapshot of a squat, four-story blockhouse. Graffiti, scrawled in Arabic and Farsi, covered the outside walls as high as a tall man could reach. Red crescent banners were draped from the second-floor balconies, and a forest of shiny new antennae sprouted from the roof. Otherwise the building might have been another derelict awaiting demolition.

"The ayatollah's missionaries started searching high and low for dispossessed and disaffected Shiites, signing up as many as they could to join Khomeini's revolution. It didn't take much coaxing, and the holdouts had their price. We've logged reports of Shiite women in the Bekaa region being paid to wear the chador in public, covering their faces to give the general impression of a strong, united Shiite front. It's bull, but the truth is bad enough."

"And the recruits?" Grimaldi prompted.

"Losers going nowhere, for the most part," the big Fed responded. "Suddenly they had a holy cause to fight for. Khomeini told them they were invincible soldiers of God, stoking up the anti-Semitism while he played on their inbred hatred of Westerners and the wealthy in general. The actual training took place, still does, at a former Le-

banese army outpost—the Sheik Abdullah barracks—
overlooking Baalbek.''

As Brognola spoke, the screen was changing to display
an aerial reconnaissance photograph of a desert military
installation. Bolan could pick out the barracks and mess
hall, the slit trench latrines, tiny figures in khaki and *kef-
fiyehs* swarming over an obstacle course, others lying
prone on the firing range.

"The training covers four months on the average. I'm
told that ideology takes precedence over logistics, but recruits get the full course on firearms and explosives, sabotage, hijacking and kidnapping. There's even a special
graduate course for suicide troops. Yesterday's nobodies
come out as professional terrorists, fanatically committed
to their faith, sworn to die for the Islamic revolution.''

"I thought they were invincible,'' Grimaldi cracked.

"A contradiction. So what else is new? The Iranian
government keeps things rolling with a local welfare program, using petro-bucks to provide basic social services for
Shiite villagers. Even so, health care is minimal, and there's
no running water to speak of, no sanitary services of any
kind. Outbreaks of typhoid and dysentery are routine in
the Bekaa Valley, and bubonic plague's making a
comeback.''

Leo Turrin cleared his throat and said, "It must cost a
bundle for this Shiite summer camp.''

"Surprisingly the outlay has been minimal. Since 1984
or so the terrorists and missionaries have been self-
supporting, pushing hash and heroin along with revolution. Mostly they've been dealing with the Corsicans,
around Marseilles, and buyers from the old-line Mafia in
Sicily. Of course, we know a lot of stuff gets back to the
United States, but the DEA and Interpol have always concentrated on the middlemen. We bust a French supplier,

and our Bekaa buddies sell to the Italians for a while. We turn the heat up on the pizza connection, and Iran's finest look for outlets in Morocco, Greece—you name it."

"And we're back to Anthony Silvestri," Bolan said.

"You guessed it. It's the first time we've connected any Iranians with a sale on U.S. soil. No middleman this time. It's a development we're anxious to discourage, if you get my drift."

"Why would they run the risk of a direct approach?" Grimaldi asked. "It sounds like things were cooking fine before they made the change. Now they've got two dead players and a serious potential for embarrassment. What's in it for Iran?"

"We can't be sure at this point. Don Patrice Grisanti has been interviewed, concerning the demise of his lamented nephew—and of course he's ignorant of Tony's business dealings."

"Naturally."

"I don't like guesswork," Brognola continued, "but I'm working on a hunch, if anybody's interested."

"Let's hear it," Bolan said.

"Okay. Suppose Iran's mouthpiece in the Bekaa Valley wants to mix a little revolution with their business enterprise. They've tried to infiltrate the States before, and we suspect they've scored a minor hit or two. It worked for the SAVAK, why not the revolutionary guard? Whatever, they've been hungry for a major score outside the Middle East. By dealing one-on-one with Don Grisanti's people, even offering a discount if they have to, there's a chance that they could bring the war right to our doorstep."

"You're talking an exchange of bargain-basement drugs for a strategic helping hand?"

"Why not?"

"Would Don Grisanti play?"

"He might," Brognola said, "if he was insulated well enough. And then again, it may have been Silvestri's baby. I'm conversant with the literature on 'patriotic' mobsters, but we all know how that goes. In '48, the customs boys were looking at a Jewish faction of the Cleveland outfit. Seems the kosher crowd were shipping guns to Israel at the same time they were selling fighter planes and bombers to the Arabs. It's a wacky world, my friends."

"It couldn't help the Families to show up holding hands with terrorists," Grimaldi said.

"Silvestri didn't plan on making headlines," Brognola replied. "It should have been a routine sit-down. Would have been, except for Striker. And I'm not suggesting that Grisanti plans to send his buttons out to blow up synagogues. If I'm on track with this, I picture something in the way of a logistics trade-off—weapons and explosives, documents and hideouts, anything the shooters need to make their day. It lets them travel light, and contacts with the Syndicate would smooth the way, before and after any play they had in mind."

"You can't keep shit like that a secret," Leo said.

"The Iranian leadership wouldn't care. They brag about retaliation and intimidation of their enemies. You'd think that crap would've ended with Khomeini's death. If they have to sacrifice some mercenary allies in the process, what've they lost? Exposure of a Syndicate connection just might be the propaganda coup they're looking for. It emphasizes 'decadent American corruption,' and it leaves the G-men chasing gangsters while the Iranians burrow in and start the whole routine from scratch, with their connections in Marseilles, Sardinia or Casablanca."

"Hal," Grimaldi said, "if that's the action, who's to say they haven't got another team inside already?"

"It's a possibility we're checking out," Brognola answered, "but I'm still inclined to think the sit-down with Silvestri was a ground breaker. Iran's not going to flood the country with shooters before they find out if the big boys will play. My guess is they're biding their time and waiting to see what comes next. They'll be looking for contacts. I'd like to provide one."

Four pairs of eyes turned toward Bolan, each with its own message of anxiety, concern, anticipation. The Executioner met each in turn, keeping his own face impassive.

"I'm listening," he said.

The aerial photo dissolved into a street scene, snapped outside an anonymous sidewalk café. The Bear's electric pointer found a table in the center foreground, lighting first on one man then another, as Brognola made his introductions.

"On the left," Brognola said, "we have Ahmad Halaby. He's a PLO defector who regards the new, improved Arafat as the worst kind of Jew-loving traitor. Halaby's people make the Black September crowd look like a troop of Boy Scouts. No job's too small or too dirty for a dedicated 'liberation warrior.' He's also got a practical side— his men take on contracts for profit. We've linked them to quasi-political murders in Libya, Italy, France and West Germany. The DEA suspects Halaby of supplying muscle for an international drug pipeline run by his friend in the picture."

"A lovable guy," Grimaldi said.

"A prince. On the right, meet Bashir Moheden. There are maybe half a dozen warlords in the Bekaa Valley, and you're looking at the top dog. Moheden was among the first to set up cash crops in the Bekaa, and he also led the shift from hash to opium. He's got connections with the ranking syndicates in Turkey, Sicily, Morocco and the south of France. There was a spot of trouble with the Corsicans a few years back, but that's all taken care of now. His family are all Druze Muslims, but Moheden is the first generation to worship the holy profit margin.''

The scene changed again, presenting a grainy news photo of four bearded men in black turbans and caftans. Kurtzman's electric pointer circled the second dour face from the left.

''Mir Reza Bakhtiar,'' Brognola said. ''The Islamic Revolution's spiritual leader in the Bekaa Valley. Since the spring of 1984, he's been in charge of supervising missionary work and training programs for the revolutionary guard in Lebanon. He's also been continuously in touch with Moheden and our old friend Ahmad Halaby, coordinating traffic in narcotics. Bakhtiar sells Shiite crops to Moheden's wholesaler, and rumor has it that Moheden toes the party line in public, just to keep things copacetic.''

''Rumors from where?'' Bolan asked.

''The Bekaa population isn't all one happy Shiite family,'' Brognola told him. ''In addition to the Druze contingent, you've got Christian rebels in the area, plus troops from Syria patrolling in the name of peace. Throw in some bandits looking out for number one, and you begin to get the picture. We've got sources in the region that we share with the CIA.''

''Who moves the cargo?''

''There you're looking at another threesome.''

Aaron touched his keyboard, and the screen was filled with faces, clipped from separate photographs and mounted side by side, like suspects in a lineup.

''On your left,'' Brognola said, ''is one Hussein Razmara, pulling duty on behalf of Bakhtiar in Nicosia. On the record, he's a Shiite holy man, concerned with saving souls. Scratch the surface and you're looking at another ayatollah wanna-be, committed to exporting revolution even when it's packaged by the kilo. The cherub in the middle is a Lebanese supplier, Rashid Sarkis, also working out of Nicosia. He's Moheden's man, some kind of childhood friend or something. Sarkis is a Shiite convert, but our analysts regard it as a marriage of convenience, firming up the link with his suppliers in the Bekaa. Last time Sarkis prayed, it was for God to strike a jury blind and make them set him free on smuggling charges.''

"Did it work?" Grimaldi asked.

"With help—and cash donations—from his earthly friends.''

"I love religion.''

"On your right, the local broker, one Spyros Makarios, a native Cypriot. His father joined the EOKA push against the British back in 1955. A military court condemned him two years later for the bombing of an outpost at Kirinia. The widow couldn't hold her tribe together. Spyros grew up on the streets and taught himself the necessary skills. He's basically a smuggler—three convictions, two with prison time—but he's suspected in a string of homicides that date back over ten or fifteen years. He's hard on competition, as they say.''

"He deals with foreign buyers?" Bolan asked.

"He used to, pre-Silvestri. Now I have a hunch he's playing wait-and-see. Their new approach has blown up in their faces. I picture all concerned as being worried, miffed and plain old everyday pissed off. They may shift back to basics while they lick their wounds and try to find out what went wrong. If so, Makarios will be the man to see for product booking out of Nicosia.''

"Who's your contact on the street?"

"A native by the name of Nikos Kiprianou. He's a youngster, but he's done successful work for people in the Company and DEA. I'm told that he can fix an introduction to Makarios."

"Direct approach?"

"Seems best to me. They have to know Silvestri's dead, but they can read it different ways. He may have been a ringer overstepping his authority, or outside forces may have tried to jump his claim. Whatever, if I read the players right, they should be hungry for a new connection, even if it comes off looking like a consolation prize."

The soldier smiled, despite himself. "No need for flattery."

"If you decide to take it on, I'd say that you could almost flip a coin. Go in as one of Don Grisanti's people, or approach them as a scout from someone new."

"It's risky if you use Grisanti," Leo said. "Makarios may have some kind of hot line to the Family. You could get burned before you have a chance to do your thing."

"Agreed." Brognola's face was stern. "Of course, if Spyros is in touch with Mr. G., he might report the contact with another customer. Grisanti might put two and two together on Silvestri and induce Makarios to whack you as a favor."

"It's a gamble," Bolan said, his choice already made before he spoke. "Let's play it as a new approach. I'll go in independent of the Family."

"Fine." The worry lines were forming on Brognola's forehead. "I'll arrange a meet with Kiprianou, let him make the introduction. After that you'll have to play it pretty much by ear."

"That sounds familiar."

"Right. Don't underestimate these characters, okay? You've got fanatics on your hands, along with pros who would eliminate their mothers to preserve the paying status quo. Among them they can field a fair-sized army, and they know the territory.''

He recognized a friend's concern and pointedly ignored Brognola's pessimistic tone. ''You mentioned opposition in the valley?''

''That's affirmative. The Company has opened channels with a group of Christian rebels in the Bekaa, covering their bets against the day they may be authorized to move against the Shiites. I don't have the details, but we'll pin them down before you fly. Which brings me back to Jack.''

Grimaldi raised an open palm to silence the big Fed. ''I'm way ahead of you,'' he said. ''No self-respecting narco dealer would go east without his faithful sidekick.''

''Sorry, nothing so direct,'' Brognola told him. ''Still, if things work out in Nicosia, I anticipate the need for an insertion into Lebanon. Can do?''

Jack's face had settled for a look that Bolan read as two parts insult, one part irritation. ''I suppose I might squeak by,'' he groused. ''Are the Israelis in on this?''

''They will be when the time comes. Listen, bringing in a private plane on Cyprus would make you stand out like a neon sign.''

''Yeah, okay. I read you. Anyway, don't say I didn't try.''

''I've never pegged you for a shortage of initiative.''

''I'll need some earnest money,'' Bolan said.

''It's in the works. We're borrowing a bit from the DEA and matching what they give us from the Farm's slush fund.''

Bolan smiled. The slush fund had been built up over time through strategic withdrawals from Mafia war chests, the money invested by Kurtzman for maximum yield.

Stony Man wasn't by any means a self-supporting operation yet, but the return from those investments banked a cool two hundred thousand dollars every quarter, just like clockwork. It amused the Executioner to think of using gangland money to oppose the Mob. Poetic justice.

"We're set, then?"

"More or less," Brognola said. "I'll schedule detailed geographic briefings, let you read our dossiers on all the principals—the usual. Let's call it two, three days, to iron out all the details."

"Fine."

He was amazed to note the total lack of apprehension. Later, maybe, after he was airborne. In the meantime Bolan had an opportunity to stand down from a state of constant readiness and spend some time with friends. Whatever happened after that would take care of itself.

There would be time enough for worry when he reached the killing ground.

CHAPTER SIX

Bashir Moheden sat on a lounge chair on the wide veranda of his fortress-villa, sipping wine and waiting for the others to arrive. It was unusual, to say the least, this second meeting in a ten-day period. The cartel normally convened no more than once a quarter during normal operation, but the news from New York City wasn't normal.

They had failed somehow and suffered losses in the bargain. It was not disaster yet, but there was danger in the air, a scent Moheden had been quick to learn in childhood, running with the street gangs in Beirut. Someone, somewhere, had tampered with their operation, throwing it off track, and that meant danger for them all unless they found the problem and corrected it at once.

He didn't mind the loss of life so much—they were Iranians, in any case—but it was troubling that their emissaries had been killed so easily. Three dead, according to reports, and not an enemy among them. He expected better from a pair of men who had been schooled in taking human life. They should at least have left their mark on the opposition as they died.

It would be touchy, briefing his Iranian associates about the problem. They were steeped in paranoia at the best of times, and while the loss of two commandos would mean little to their precious revolution overall, they would at once suspect Moheden or the other cartel members of some treachery. The personal suspicion might not be expressed in words, but he would see it in their eyes; it would be audible when they began to speak with slow, deliberate words.

He would refuse to take the bait, of course, but what about Halaby? Could the Palestinian restrain himself if accusations were implied? He was notoriously quick to anger, and his rage, unchecked, could lead to violence that would tear their little group apart.

Moheden made a mental note to brief his guards before the others came. If bloodshed seemed inevitable, he would throw his weight to the Iranians who managed his supply of drugs. Halaby was a friend, of sorts—albeit an unstable one—but he could be replaced. There was a young lieutenant in the Palestinian's command who might be useful if a change of leadership was indicated by events.

It never crossed Moheden's mind to strike at the Iranians. Aside from being his suppliers, they were backed by thousands of fanatics who would gladly dedicate their lives—and deaths—to seeking vengeance on their enemies. No matter that their thinly veiled suspicions might be groundless. If it came to choices, he would opt to save his business and preserve the status quo as much as possible.

In time Moheden thought he might be able to eliminate his Teheran associates by indirection, planting rumors of disloyalty with the revolutionary guard or speaking to the new president, but it would have to be a last resort. A hasty move, instead of solving problems, might reduce his life to chaos. It might even get him killed.

Moheden was familiar with the face of death. It had a hungry look, as if the appetite for fresh red meat was never satisfied. In younger days he had occasionally smelled the Reaper's breath—a cold draft from the charnel house—when danger came too close for comfort, but he always managed to survive. It was a specialty he had developed over time.

Together, if they kept their heads, they could determine what had happened in New York, and they could put it right. If the Iranians insisted on a scapegoat, he would find them one and supervise the sacrifice himself. It would be strictly business, after all.

Moheden drained his goblet, setting it aside, and shed the final vestiges of apprehension as he rose. He had an hour left, and there were final preparations to be made, precautions to be taken. Everything must be in readiness before his guests arrived, with no mistakes among the servants or the guards about their several cues.

Ideally they would meet and talk, agree upon a strategy for future operations and disperse in peace. If things went badly, though, Moheden was determined to survive.

As always.

Mir Reza Bakhtiar was terrified of flying. He concealed his fear behind excuses, daring anyone to challenge him and risk his anger, but the fact remained that he had only twice set foot inside an airplane. On the first occasion, fleeing from his homeland to escape the Shah's police, he had been ill throughout the flight, humiliated by the weakness that betrayed him in the face of strangers. Twelve years later, when the hand of God smote his enemy and he returned to help Khomeini lead the Shiite revolution, Bakhtiar had fortified himself with tranquilizers prior to boarding. On arrival in Teheran, he kissed the ground and swore that he would never fly again.

So far that promise had been scrupulously kept. When he was sent to tame the Bekaa Valley for Khomeini, Bakhtiar had traveled overland through Turkey and along the coast of Syria. Iraqi gunmen made two separate at-

tempts upon his life, but he'd grown accustomed to the
danger of assassination. Anything was better than the
panic he experienced while airborne.

For the meetings with Moheden, he inevitably drove to
Tripoli and waited for Hussein Razmara to arrive by boat
or plane from Cyprus. They would always visit the Lebanese together, showing him a strong, united front,
though Bakhtiar had reason to suspect Razmara's personal commitment to the revolution. Lately, when he
spoke about their operations with Moheden, there was an
avaricious air about Razmara, prompting Bakhtiar to
think he might have been seduced by gold. It was a shame,
if true, but he was still a useful pawn. Elimination wasn't
indicated yet.

This trip the car was smaller than his usual, the latter
sidelined by an engine failure, and he welcomed the announcement of arrival at their destination. Though Moheden was an infidel, he set a proper table for his guests,
and Bakhtiar felt more or less at ease within the villa's
walls. His guard wasn't relaxed, precisely, but he understood the man's greed and knew the Lebanese wasn't prepared to risk his life, his fortune, on a bit of cheap intrigue.

Outside the Bekaa Valley, Bakhtiar didn't employ a
troop of bodyguards. His driver was a member of the
revolutionary guard and was always armed, but Bakhtiar—aside from staying clear of airplanes—made no fe-
tish of his personal security. He trusted in God for
protection, balancing the odds with half a dozen riflemen
when he was forced to travel in the Bekaa. Only there, with
enemies on every side, did he suspect that God might need
a helping hand.

They passed through wrought iron gates and rolled
along the curving drive. Moheden waited on the marble
steps, his smile solicitous, a servant at his elbow. Was he

worried? There was something in his eyes, around his mouth, but Bakhtiar refrained from asking any questions as he left the car and greetings were exchanged. His host would provide them with the details of the problem in his own good time, when they were all assembled.

Bakhtiar and his companion trailed Moheden's servant over parquet floors to the familiar conference room. He spent several moments at the picture window, studying the garden just outside. The Lebanese would have no time for flowers, but he paid a gardener to keep the grounds immaculate. It was a symptom of his personal compulsion to succeed, divorce himself completely from the poverty of childhood.

The Iranian took care to seat himself directly opposite their host, where he could view the others comfortably, never being forced to crane his neck or otherwise reveal a trace of special interest. It was better if they had to guess what he was thinking, search for hidden meaning in his words.

He knew the proper way of dealing with an infidel. You kept him guessing, doled out promises when necessary, conscious of the fact that God recognized no obligation to an unbeliever. If the faith demanded treachery, so be it. God and the Prophet owned his first allegiance, followed closely by the holy revolution. Nothing else held true significance.

He waited for the others, knowing that, if necessary, he could manage to destroy them all.

THE ARMORED LIMOUSINE was crowded, and Ahmad Halaby was relieved to stretch his legs on their arrival at Bashir Moheden's villa. Leaving his commandos to their own devices, trusting them to be alert at need, the new arrival shook hands with his host and followed him into the conference room. The others were in place before him, but Halaby took the time to pour himself a glass of iced tea before he took the only empty chair.

A glance around the table showed him five stern faces, and he wondered what was going on. The summons from Moheden had been urgent, with the passing mention of a problem in New York, but there had been no explanation. Privacy, in Lebanon, didn't extend to telephones or radio transmissions, and Moheden had been wise to spare the details. But his very secrecy allowed Halaby's own imagination to run riot.

Had their emissaries been arrested? Were the Western powers girding their loins for yet another fruitless war on drugs? Would they be forced to change procedures and discover brand-new outlets?

Moheden leaned forward in his chair, both elbows on the table, to address them in a confidential tone. "I thank you all," he said, "for rearranging busy schedules to accommodate our small emergency. I trust you were not greatly inconvenienced, but the matter is, as I suggested earlier, of some importance."

Pausing for effect, the Lebanese examined each of his guests in turn before continuing.

"It grieves me to inform you that our representatives in the United States, Saddam Kassim and Abdel Bazargan, have both been killed. I have no details yet, but it appears their contact—Anthony Silvestri, of the New York Mafia—was also murdered. The investigation is continuing."

Halaby bit his tongue and glanced at the Iranians, impressed that neither of them registered a visible emotion. Such men would couch their fury in quotations from the Prophet and avenge themselves at leisure. He admired their style, but had no patience for such games himself.

"I have anticipated certain questions from the floor," Moheden said, "and I will try to put your minds at ease, if possible. My contacts in New York are keeping track of the police investigation from a distance, and I hope to be informed within a day or two if any suspects are identified. So far the relevant authorities haven't identified our people. I believe they never will. Silvestri's murder is regarded as a consequence of friction in the local underworld, related to the traffic in narcotics. There appears to be no intimation of an overseas connection."

"So much for the notions of American policemen." Under stress Mir Reza Bakhtiar retained a tone of measured courtesy. "What are the facts?"

Moheden didn't flinch from Bakhtiar's examination. "I can tell you that our people made connections with Silvestri as arranged. A hostile force of unknown strength surprised them, murdering Silvestri and a bodyguard, along with Abdel Bazargan. Kassim escaped the trap and was pursued. More shots were fired, and several bystanders were injured. Two policemen are reported dead. Kassim was killed while running from the scene. Apparently a traffic accident."

"Apparently?"

"A taxi driver was involved. I have no reason to believe he was involved, except by sheer coincidence."

Halaby saw an opening. "How badly are we damaged in regard to traffic with America?"

Moheden seemed relieved to hear from someone other than the stern Iranian. "In theory," he replied, "our losses have been minimal. No cargo was involved, and our connections on the European continent haven't been jeopardized. The plans for a direct approach should be delayed, in my opinion, while we reassess our friends and enemies. In any case, Silvestri's syndicate will need some time to nominate a suitable replacement and evaluate security procedures. It's possible that they suspect us of duplicity.''

"And if they do?" Halaby thought he knew the answer in advance, but he was interested in hearing it confirmed before the others. He wasn't prepared to waste his time on stagnant schemes.

"We forge ahead," Moheden told him, hesitating long enough to add, "with the consensus of you all. Silvestri's syndicate isn't the only outlet in America, or even in New York. If we proceed with caution, I'm confident that we can find associates who meet our several needs."

Halaby sat back, satisfied. As he had hoped, Moheden wasn't frightened by the sight of blood.

"My countrymen have given up their lives," Bakhtiar said, his voice and manner solemn. "I'm interested in seeing them avenged."

"As are we all." Moheden glanced around the table, waiting for a voice of opposition to be raised. "It may be wise, however, to forgo that vengeance in the interests of our common goal."

"*My* goal is furtherance of the Islamic revolution," Bakhtiar replied. "Our list of martyrs has grown long enough already. When an enemy confronts the revolutionary guard, our uniform response is total war."

"With all respect, may I remind you of our common purpose? None of us assembled here has any love for the United States. Our motives vary, granted, but we have agreed upon a common course of action. Risks and setbacks were anticipated from the first. It does no good for us to fall apart the first time we encounter obstacles."

Halaby watched the two Iranians, deciding which way he should jump if things began to fall apart. The meeting wouldn't come to blows—Moheden had too many guards outside for that—but bitterness engendered by a major quarrel could rebound in violence later. He'd seen it happen in the councils of the Palestinian resistance, when the traitor Arafat began to whisper of accommodation with the hated Zionists. Sometimes Halaby still regretted his defection from the PLO. It would have been more manly in the long run if he had assassinated Arafat and seized the operation for himself, but he had been successful in his way. He wouldn't let an argument across the conference table ruin everything when he had worked so hard to come this far.

Makarios, the Cypriot, had risen from his chair, the move evoking memories of proper school boys asking for permission to relieve themselves. Moheden and Bakhtiar fell silent, swiveling around to face Makarios.

"May I suggest," the Cypriot began, "that we postpone discussion of revenge until the common enemy has been identified? Meanwhile it would be advantageous to secure new contacts in America, perhaps employing them to isolate our opposition while our plan proceeds."

Halaby smiled. The young man had a good head on his shoulders, even if his face was too effeminate and soft. A beard might help, if he could cultivate a darker growth than the existing peach fuzz on his cheeks and upper lip.

Moheden favored his associate from Cyprus with a smile. "Makarios is right, of course," he said. "Our fellowship was organized for mutual advantage. We must not allow a private grievance to defeat our purpose, thereby wounding everyone at once."

Across the table Bakhtiar appeared to reconsider, but Halaby didn't trust his smile. "We shall defer our vengeance," the Iranian declared, "but we do not forget. In time, when circumstances have revealed our enemies, the proper action must be taken."

"As you say," Moheden answered. "Every man among us will be proud to lend a hand when that day comes. In death, Kassim and Bazargan have warned us of potential danger, and they will not be forgotten."

They observed a moment's silence in respect for men Halaby hadn't known or even seen in life. When everyone was satisfied—except, perhaps, for the inscrutable Iranians—the Lebanese raised his voice again.

"With the permission of the group, I will initiate new contacts in America as soon as possible. If suspects are identified in the assassination of Silvestri and our representatives, you will be notified at once. There is a possibility, in that event, that the employers of Silvestri may proceed to mete out justice on their own, before we have an opportunity to strike. Such men are volatile, and violence in America isn't unusual."

Halaby nodded solemnly with the others, as if Beirut and Lebanon in general hadn't become an open killing pit in modern times. It would have been amusing, all this talk of dignity and honor, if Halaby hadn't grown accustomed to it from his youth. The Palestinians were no less prone to speeches, declarations of their love for God and their homeland. In the end, it all came down to justifying actions that were calculated to enrage the world at large.

For his part, it would be enough to turn a profit on the drugs and strike a telling blow against America. He didn't share the Shiite's personal obsession with jihad, but nine American administrations had identified themselves with Israel, lavishing their gifts of arms and money on the Zionists who had usurped Halaby's native soil. While the United States continued its support for Israel, there could be no hope for liberation of his people. Only when the war became too costly would Americans be moved to reconsider their established policies. There was a striking justice in allowing the Americans, through sale of drugs, to help raise money for defeat of the oppressive Zionist regime they had so long supported.

And if Ahmad Halaby should, perchance, become a wealthy man while waging war against his mortal enemies, so much the better.

BASHIR MOHEDEN SAW Halaby settled with the woman of his choice before retreating to his den. This time, instead of wine, he poured himself a double whiskey. It was sustenance and celebration all at once, relieving nerves stretched taut by confrontation with Mir Reza Bakhtiar, and celebrating his success at heading off a split in the cartel.

It had been close, and the Iranians might still decide to take some action on their own, but he'd managed to extract for the record a promise of cooperation. If they later changed their minds and went in search of private vengeance, Moheden couldn't be held responsible.

Establishing new contacts in Manhattan might be difficult, but he would have to try without delay. His leadership of the cartel had been approved primarily because of his extensive foreign ties. The Bekaa Valley militants had managed to support themselves through his connections up to now, but phasing out his European contacts was a ticklish matter. The elimination of the middleman increased Moheden's profits, even with the discount Bakhtiar demanded, but it also might make enemies.

He wondered, briefly, if his long-time partners—Corsicans, perhaps, or the Sicilian Mafia—had taken steps to queer the meeting with Silvestri in New York. They all had ways of gaining "secret" information, and the cartel's more direct approach to dealing with America might threaten some of those with whom Moheden had done business in the past. Retaliation was a possibility, displeasure couched in graphic terms that anyone could understand.

The Lebanese hoped that he was being paranoid. He didn't want to fight a war with the Sicilians or the Corsicans. It would be costly all around, and while Halaby would undoubtedly support him for a price, the damage done to ancient friendships would be totally irreparable. In the event that former allies were identified as modern enemies, Moheden thought it might be wise to let Silvestri's people seek revenge. While outlaws in the New World and the Old were battling among themselves, he would be free to look for other buyers, other ways to make a profit on the sidelines of the killing ground.

The best scenario for all concerned would be the one put forward by the American police. Silvestri and his "Family" had enemies throughout America...perhaps throughout the world. The Mafia was known for its perennial resort to treachery, with blood relatives stabbing one another in the back on any lame excuse. For all its vaunted interest in diplomacy, the stateside Syndicate was torn by petty rivalries that made the European underworld seem stable by comparison.

Moheden would proceed with caution, testing each new step before he was committed to a move, retreating if he spied a danger signal. There was nothing he could do until tomorrow, though, and in the meantime...

Moving through the house, he passed the bedroom where Halaby and the whore were going through their paces. He walked along the corridor, past several other doors, until he reached the last one on his left.

Inside, the tall Israeli prostitute was standing by the windows, facing Beirut. With darkness, if the fighting was intense this day, she might be able to observe the glow of distant fires.

The woman turned to face him as he entered, offering the barest hint of a submissive smile. Moheden told himself that she was his, in heart and soul, as well as in the flesh. He wanted to believe the drugs and money made no difference.

"I want you," he informed her simply. In his conversation with the woman, "need" was never mentioned or implied.

She shrugged the caftan off her shoulders, stood before him, naked to his gaze.

Moheden offered her his hand.

CHAPTER SEVEN

Mack Bolan was familiar with divided lands. He'd seen the different ways in which partition could make enemies of neighbors, even relatives. This afternoon, as flight attendants started picking up their plastic cups and checking seat belts, scuttling around the first-class cabin of the Boeing 727 circling Nicosia's airport, Bolan wondered whether it would be the same in Cyprus.

He had brushed up on geography at the Farm, refreshing dormant memories from high school. Bolan knew that Cyprus was the Mediterranean's third-largest island, after Sicily and Sardinia, with a population approaching three-quarters of a million people. Eighty percent of those were ethnic Greeks, another eighteen percent ethnic Turks, with various Arab and Eastern European minorities making up the difference. Despite a full generation of independence, Cypriots had a tendency to think of themselves as "Greeks" or "Turks," and the ancient antagonism would probably keep right on simmering into the twenty-first century.

Political control of Cyprus had been changing hands since Phoenician times, winding up with Britain in charge after World War I. Over the next four decades, Greek Cypriots dreamed of *enosis*, a reunion with their ancestral homeland, and when diplomacy fell flat, they launched a no-holds-barred guerrilla war against the British in the latter 1950s. Members of the EOKA "liberation army" had been learning from the Viet Minh in Indochina and the

IRA in Belfast, plotting acts of terrorism and assassination to accommodate their local needs. In August 1960, Cyprus won her independence, guaranteed by Britain, Greece and Turkey and the pipe dream of *enosis* was abandoned in the cold, hard light of day.

The Cypriots had recognized their ethnic differences and tried to make allowances for same. Their brand-new constitution specified that the vice president, three of ten cabinet ministers, and thirty percent of the national legislature must be ethnic Turks, but old rivalries died hard. In Ankara, hungry politicians cast covetous eyes upon Cyprus, carefully logging reports of real or imagined discrimination against the island's Turkish minority. In June 1974, Turkish forces assaulted the island by sea and air, capturing forty percent of its northern territory before they ran out of steam. Over the next six months, 45,000 ethnic Turks moved north, into the "Turkish Cypriot Federated State," while an estimated 200,000 Greek Cypriots fled south, abandoning their homes to the invader. Fifteen years of U N votes, debates and consultations had done nothing to relieve the situation. Cyprus was—and likely would remain—a land divided, torn apart by ethnic and religious animosity.

The situation would affect Mack Bolan's mission only inasmuch as he was called upon to read his opposition, crawl inside their heads and puzzle out their strategy before it took him by surprise. The target group was obviously international, including as it did a Cypriot of Greek descent, a Lebanese and an Iranian. Behind them stood another Lebanese, a Palestinian commando leader, and a spokesman for the government in Teheran. It was the kind of merger that made Bolan nervous, organized criminals crawling into bed with political zealots, producing a bastard offspring that was neither purely mercenary nor entirely dedicated to a cause. That kind of schizoid union made the players unpredictable, and Bolan knew that he'd have to watch himself each step along the way.

He started watching in the airport terminal, remembering that he wasn't supposed to meet his contact there. Too obvious, they had agreed, and as a "casual tourist," he'd only draw attention to himself if he was greeted by a native on arrival. Still, the absence of a scheduled contact didn't mean security was guaranteed. There might be other watchers at the airport, checking new arrivals as a matter of routine, or looking out for someone in particular.

It might not hurt if he was marked—the Executioner didn't intend to pass unnoticed in the city, after all—but he couldn't afford to have his cover blown this early in the game. He had an image to protect, and he had flown first-class to bolster the impression of a wealthy rogue, prepared to mix some shady business with his pleasure. If a lookout took the time to snag a copy of his ticket, they would learn that he was traveling as "Mike Belasko," paying with a credit card that matched the name, and all his correspondence had been picked up from a mail drop in Manhattan. He wouldn't be found in any telephone or street directories for New York City—or the Eastern Seaboard if they chose to look that far. Discreet inquiries in the halls of Justice might turn up a rumor that "Belasko" was a dealer with a heavy rep but no convictions.

Waiting at the carousel to claim his luggage, Bolan wished he could have found some way to pack a pistol, anything, before he left New York. Security precautions had been tightened drastically across North America and Western Europe in recent months, authorities recalling the destruction of Pan Am Flight 103 by a terrorist bomb over Lockerbie, Scotland, and check-through luggage was now routinely X-rayed on all American carriers flying out of

JFK. Inspectors were trying new gadgets, designed to replace bomb-sniffing dogs by revealing plastique with a dull yellow tinge on the viewer, regardless of its innocuous shape. Guns in the cargo compartment were no threat, per se—and they could be shipped legally by air, if you were into reams of paperwork—but Bolan had preferred to skip the hassle.

The alternative, a military flight to carry all his hardware transatlantic, would have branded Bolan from the moment that he stepped on board. It would have been more economical to simply take out an ad in the local papers, publishing his name and mission for the world to see. In either case, the ultimate result would be the same.

His bags arrived, and Bolan showed his claim stubs as he left the terminal, flagging a taxi outside. The driver understood enough English to find his hotel, deliberately selected by Aaron Kurtzman as the most expensive in Nicosia. A glance at the aging facade told Bolan that "luxury" on Cyprus clearly had a different definition than it did in the United States.

He was expected, and a porter lugged his baggage to the elevator, riding up with Bolan to the seventh floor. His room was clean and spacious, decorated in an early-1960's style, as if the march of time had frozen in its tracks a short time after independence had been achieved. He tipped the porter, tried out the shower and was relieved to find the water neither brown nor tepid. Locking the door and wedging a straight-backed chair under the knob to frustrate intruders, Bolan peeled off his clothes and tossed them on the bedspread, moving on to wash the miles and his fatigue away.

His local contact would be checking in sometime that evening, but the Executioner had several hours before he'd be called upon to meet the enemy. From that point he'd have to trust his instincts, play the cards as they were dealt and call the opposition's hand whenever possible. He knew the players, more or less, and recognized the natural advantage of their own home turf. It was a problem he had coped with in the past.

This time, however, he'd have to be especially careful. With the different personalities involved, reactions to his overture were unpredictable, potentially explosive. In effect he'd be juggling vials of nitro, and it might not make a difference if he kept them in the air or not. One slip could take his head off, either way.

Like always.

FOR NIKOS KIPRIANOU, cloak-and-dagger work had started as a hobby, somehow winding up a full-time job. At first it was a lark—the hush-hush errands; runs for "cultural attachés" at the U.S. Embassy, with tax-free folding money paid upon completion of a job; a shadow mission now and then, with Nikos trailing this known Communist or that suspected criminal around the streets of Nicosia, logging destinations, sometimes snapping pictures of their contacts on the sly. On various occasions there had been clandestine meetings in a restaurant, a park or a museum, where Nikos handed off a slip of paper or received an envelope.

By that time Kiprianou knew that he was working for the CIA. He didn't mind—if anything, the knowledge added spice to his activities, a hint of danger—but the risk had seemed illusory. All that had changed, when his control inside the embassy began to farm him out on drug enforcement business, dealing with a different class of agents and another breed of human targets. In the drug trade, spies and government informants were routinely murdered, dumped in alleyways or simply made to disappear, and lately Nikos had begun to wonder if his choice had been a foolish one.

Tonight would be the worst. It was the first time he'd been required to carry weapons, and it made no difference that the pistol, ammunition and accessories were meant for someone else. If he was stopped by the police, his briefcase searched, it would mean prison time. Conversely if his actions were discovered by the other side, he might be killed.

It was a problem, but he'd decided to proceed, at least until the point of contact. Afterward, if things went badly, he could still plead ignorance and disavow all knowledge of the stranger's government connections. And if things went well, he just might be a hero.

Nikos squared his shoulders, entering the hotel lobby with determined strides, as if he were expected there. In fact he was, but the American wouldn't have briefed the concierge about their meeting. It was possible that Nikos might be intercepted, questioned by the house detective. The American would be disturbed, compelled to fabricate a story that might prove embarrassing. It would be best for Nikos to avoid a confrontation with the staff if possible.

He took advantage of a family checking in, the clerk distracted, porters wrestling with their baggage. Kiprianou had the number of his contact's room, and he relaxed a little when the elevator door slid shut behind him. Moments later he was stepping out on number seven, the briefcase dragging on his arm as if it weighed a ton.

The first time, Nikos thought he might have knocked too softly. He was poised to try again when footsteps sounded on the other side and someone threw the bolts back and opened the door. He'd prepared himself for anything, and yet his first sight of the tall American was startling. The eyes bored through him, seemed to peer inside his soul, and Nikos Kiprianou wondered what it must be like to face this man in battle.

"Yes?" The voice was smooth and deep, without the rasp affected by so many thugs.

"Mr. Belasko? I'm Nikos Kiprianou. I believe you're expecting me?"

No password had been specified, and Nikos was relieved, as it might easily have slipped his mind. The man who called himself Belasko checked the corridor, then stepped aside to let him in. The door snicked shut behind him, and the double locks engaged.

"You have the items I requested?"

"Here."

The case changed hands, and Nikos watched Belasko place it on the bed, extracting a Beretta Model 92, its muzzle threaded for a silencer that he would also find inside the briefcase. There were extra magazines of fifteen rounds apiece, together with a shoulder holster and a cleaning kit. While Nikos waited on the sidelines, the American broke down the pistol, checked its internal mechanism and reassembled the gun in seconds flat. He worked the slide to place a live round in the firing chamber, eased the hammer down and set the safety switch before he dropped it on the bed.

"Sit down."

The young man did as he was told.

"What are your orders?"

Nikos made a stab at looking nonchalant. "This evening I'll take you on a tour of Nicosia. We'll dine together at a restaurant where it is probable that we will see Makarios. If not, there is a tavern he frequents. We'll find him, one way or another."

"When we do?"

"You'll examine him, but from a distance. Strangers don't meet Makarios without a proper introduction."

"That's where you come in."

"Correct. However, it would be a foolish thing to take him by surprise. The first approach is critical. I have a friend who has a friend. These things are delicate, you understand? Tonight—tomorrow morning at the latest—I'll be in touch with those who schedule meetings for Makarios. If he is interested, and I believe he will be, you should plan on meeting him tomorrow, or the next day."

"Fine. I leave it in your hands."

The man was reasonable and Nikos was relieved. He'd expected something in the nature of a blustering commando type who had to have things now or not at all. Belasko obviously had enough experience to understand that nothing beneficial ever happened instantly.

Nikos made a show of glancing at his watch. "We have two hours at the least. Are you ready for a tour of Nicosia?"

"Ready as I'll ever be," the tall American replied.

Bolan slipped on the shoulder holster and clipped the anchor loop around his belt. The weapon hung beneath his left arm, with a pouch for extra magazines below his right. A roomy jacket kept the hardware out of sight, though practiced eyes might spot a telltale bulge.

"Have you got wheels?" Bolan asked.

"A car? Of course."

"Let's go."

THE WHIRLWIND TOUR took an hour and a half, with Nikos pointing out assorted mosques, museums and ancient ruins, plus the several enterprises owned by Spyros Makarios and his colleague, Rashid Sarkis. Roughly one-sixth of the Cypriot population resided in Nicosia, and Bolan had a feeling he'd seen them all before his tour guide parked outside a stylish restaurant downtown. The doorman obviously doubled as a bouncer, but he smiled at Nikos like a long-lost friend and ushered them inside. The maître d' conveyed them to a corner table where they had a view of both the entrance and the smallish dance floor. Just across the polished hardwood rectangle, a set of drums and other instruments awaited the arrival of a band.

Their waiter brought the wine list and a pair of menus, lingering while Nikos rattled off a string of questions in his native Greek. From what the Executioner could tell, the answers seemed to be affirmative.

"Makarios has made a reservation for this evening," Nikos said in English when they were alone. "This is his favorite restaurant in all of Nicosia. Possibly because he owns it."

"How long has he been in bed with Sarkis?"

"Bed? Ah, you mean business. Four, five years—perhaps a little longer. Sarkis brings the merchandise from Lebanon and sells it to Makarios in bulk. Makarios has friends in France and Italy, Morocco, even London. Lately some say he has friends in the United States."

"Let's hope he's got room for another."

Nikos frowned. "If you have money, then Makarios will be your friend. At least until he has your money. Then…" The young man spread his hands and cocked one eyebrow, his expression speaking for itself.

Brognola had expressed his confidence in Nikos Kiprianou, based on classified reports from contacts in the Company and DEA. On impulse Bolan made the choice to trust him with at least an inkling of the game plan.

"I don't need undying friendship," he explained. "I'm looking for the next step up the ladder, following their product to the source."

"Is this not dangerous?"

The warrior smiled. "Could be."

"These men are ruthless," Nikos told him. "They will stop at nothing."

"So, I'd say it's time that someone got around to stopping them."

A shadow crossed the young man's face. He had a message to deliver, but the words were sticking in his throat, dammed up by pride.

"Mr. Belasko, I'm happy to assist you," he began at last. "But you must understand that I have always been a messenger and nothing more. Sometimes I follow someone here and there, reporting on their movements, but I take no action. Do you understand?"

The speech was costing him, in terms of self-esteem, but Bolan let him forge ahead.

"Perhaps you have been...how should I say... misinformed. I'm not armed. If there is danger, I will not desert you, but—"

The steward brought their wine and appetizers, silencing the young man's protest for a moment. Bolan seized the opportunity to let him off the hook.

"I'm not anticipating any trouble," Bolan said, delivering a version of the truth. "If I can get Makarios to pass me up the line, I'm out of here. No pain, no strain."

He didn't dwell upon Plan B, which would involve a squeeze play on Makarios and Sarkis. If they bought his cover, Bolan would be satisfied to take the next step on his journey, homing on the dragon's lair. When he was finished with his work in Lebanon, there'd be time enough to stop in Nicosia overnight and tidy up loose ends.

The young man sipped his wine and poked the appetizer with a fork. His face was solemn, almost brooding.

"You must understand," he said at last, "that I'm not a coward."

"Never crossed my mind," the Executioner replied. "You sign on for a job, it just makes sense to know the terms. I wouldn't hire a deep-sea diver for a guide if I was set on mountain climbing."

Nikos was about to answer when a small commotion near the entrance stole his train of thought. "Makarios!" he hissed.

In life, the dealer had a softer visage than his mug shots indicated. Years of living well and eating better had provided padding on his five-foot-two-inch frame, and he was working on another chin to match the two he had. The hairline was receding, but he grew it longer in the back and combed it forward, in a style preferred by balding men around the world. Designed to make him look more youthful, the coiffure failed miserably, giving him the aspect of a burned-out, aging rock star. The impression was accentuated by his open shirt and hairy chest, with several golden pendants dangling from his neck.

A stunning redhead clung to Makarios as he moved across the room, escorted to his private table by the maître d'. The dealer didn't seem imposing in the flesh. He might have been a used car salesman or accountant posing as a playboy on his annual vacation, spending money it had taken twelve long months to save. If there was danger here, deceptive first impressions might have said, it lay in being bored to tears by conversation with a dull, insipid man.

The Executioner reviewed his knowledge of Makarios provided by the files at Stony Man, and weighed the facts against the image. He was looking at a killer credited with half a dozen single-handed executions, listed as the moving force behind a score of others. Multiply deliberate homicides by several hundred—even thousands—to accommodate the lives Makarios had stolen by exporting heroin to Europe and America. How many children had he killed? How many families had he destroyed without a backward glance?

The waiter brought their food and lingered long enough for both of them to voice approval of the fare. Across the room, an easy pistol shot away, Makarios was busy with the redhead, chuckling to himself, his dark hands moving underneath the table as she whispered something in his ear. A slender man approached the dealer's table, standing at a simulation of parade rest while he waited for permission to be seated.

Nikos Kiprianou leaned across his steaming plate of seafood, nodding toward the new arrival. "Constantine Pappas," he said. "My friend. I will be speaking to him later. He'll fix the meeting with Makarios."

"We hope."

"Have confidence. There is no problem."

Bolan forced a smile he didn't feel. "I hope you're right."

"Of course."

The young man's confidence was catching, but he took the optimism with a grain of salt. A hundred different things could still go wrong, he knew, and any one of them could be a killer. For the moment it would be enough if Nikos could deliver on his promise of an introduction. Failing that, the Executioner would have to try another angle of attack.

A more direct approach, perhaps, with fire and thunder standing in for invitations and the small talk of polite society. If necessary, he was ready, but he hoped it would not come to that just yet. It would be so much easier for all concerned if he could get the necessary information short of launching all-out war.

But he would have it either way, regardless of the cost. And if the killing started here, so be it.

Staring at his enemy across an empty dance floor, waiting for the band, Mack Bolan knew the cleansing fire was overdue.

CHAPTER EIGHT

The call from Nikos came at half-past seven, catching Bolan as he stepped out of the shower, and it verified a luncheon meeting with Makarios at one o'clock. The car would be downstairs at half-past twelve precisely.

Bolan dressed and armed himself, his mind a cool, deliberate blank as he ordered breakfast from room service. There was no point in rehearsing hypothetical dialogue, and he'd long since given up on practicing expressions in the mirror. He was either ready for the meeting or he wasn't, and it wouldn't make a bit of difference either way.

When he had finished breakfast, Bolan broke down the Beretta and scrutinized its action, killing time. He emptied out the several magazines, reloading them himself to guarantee a proper feed. Last up, although he wouldn't take it with him to the sit-down, Bolan tried the silencer for size and weighed the automatic in his palm, becoming comfortable with its balance.

The Beretta in his hand wasn't designed to handle 3-round bursts, but it was fast and accurate enough without them, having recently edged out the venerable Colt .45 as America's official military side arm. Bolan preferred the Beretta, with its graceful contours and superior firepower. Fifteen rounds, versus the Colt's seven or eight, could make all the difference in the world, and Bolan thought the 9 mm parabellum compared favorably to the big .45's in stopping power. Granted, he'd be using factory loads this time out, but placement of rounds was at least half the battle, and Bolan was confident that the Beretta would serve him well.

He caught himself borrowing trouble and frowned. The meeting with Makarios was meant to be exactly that: a meeting, not a battle in the streets. If Nikos Kiprianou knew his business, there should be no problem. As he holstered the Beretta, Bolan knew that he'd have to play it that way, trusting Nikos, hoping for the best until he spotted evidence of things unraveling around him. Gambling with his life was a familiar game for Bolan, and he knew the rules by heart.

With four hours remaining before he kept his date with Kiprianou, he stowed the silencer and spare Beretta magazines inside his luggage, locked the bag and left it in the closet. He wasn't especially concerned about a search, and if the articles were found—by someone other than police—they would be useful in providing confirmation for his cover.

Bolan locked the door behind him, rode the elevator down and left the building. The narrow streets were teeming with pedestrians and traffic, drivers changing lanes and leaning on their horns in classic European style. The shops were opening, and Bolan dawdled past their windows, scrutinizing jewelry, clothing, tacky souvenirs and baked goods. Noting landmarks as he traveled, the warrior started putting flesh upon the bones provided by his hasty tour with Nikos yesterday. Accustomed to the tourist trade, the natives passing by appeared to take no notice of the tall American.

It crossed his mind to see if he was being followed, but a glance behind yielded no surprises. No one suddenly bent down to tie his shoe, no one veered across the street through traffic. It was possible, of course, that he had missed the tail—God knows the crowd was thick enough to cover a professional surveillance team—but Bolan let himself relax a bit, suspecting that Makarios wouldn't have had him followed. Trailing Bolan through the streets of Nicosia would have been a futile exercise, all things considered, and he thought the dealer would be looking for another angle of attack.

Makarios was said to have connections stateside, and a well-placed phone call would provide him with the basic information laid for Bolan's cover. If he wanted further data on the life and crimes of "Mike Belasko," he'd have to wait until they met, and supply his own assessment of the stranger from America.

Near ten o'clock he stopped for Turkish coffee at a sidewalk restaurant and spent the best part of an hour watching tourists jostle natives on the sidewalk. There was something in the attitude of foreigners on holiday that made them pushy and rude, as if their manners had been left at home. Bolan marveled at the fact that wars didn't erupt in tourist areas. It was a testament to human stamina and greed that such behavior could be borne in silence, even with a smile.

He chose a different route on his return to the hotel, completing a circuit of downtown Nicosia. Greek and Turkish cultures had been clashing here for generations, but he saw no signs of animosity around him as he strolled the winding avenues, intent on savoring the morning while it lasted.

A man in constant motion, forced to travel widely in pursuit of enemies, the Executioner regretted that he seldom had the time to linger and appreciate exotic cities, scouting out their secrets for himself. He saw the world as soldiers saw it during wartime, broken down in terms of battlefields and theaters of operations, base camps and objectives. Did the troops who liberated France from

Nazism cherish memories of Paris in the spring? Would veterans of Vietnam recall Saigon as anything other than a maze of bars and strip joints, whorehouses and opium dens? And in the long run, did it really matter?

Bolan found his tour guide waiting for him when he made it back to the hotel. Nikos was perched on the hood of his car, watching the hotel entrance, when Bolan stepped up beside him and placed a firm hand on his shoulder. The young man jumped, then did a rapid double take and smiled.

"All ready?" Bolan asked.

"When you are."

"Great. Let's do it."

As a CHILD, before the British soldiers shot his father in Kirinia, Spyros Makarios believed in magic. It had been a natural mistake, a symptom of his youth, but violent death and the attendant curse of poverty had stripped him of illusions almost overnight. At nine years old, he learned to steal from market stalls to feed his family, and when the older, stronger boys had robbed him once or twice, he learned to fight. There was no magic after all, unless he made some for himself.

Makarios had prospered as a smuggler, moving drugs and other contraband, because he was a ruthless man and a perceptive judge of character. The ruthless aspect of his nature served him when competitors encroached upon his territory and he had to drive them out. Perception helped Makarios to choose his friends and allies in a world where treachery was an accepted part of doing business.

Thus far he had managed to survive without a major setback, serving time for minor violations of the smuggling laws, emerging as a wiser, more determined businessman. He cultivated contacts in the outside world, but he was cautious in selecting those to whom he gave his trust. Such men, the worthy ones, were few and far between.

Was it coincidence, perhaps, that the American should make his overture precisely at this time, when he was under orders from Moheden to recruit new customers in the United States? Makarios didn't believe in fate, and accidents of timing sparked a natural suspicion in his mind. Pappas had carried word from one of his associates, a Nikos Kiprianou, that the spokesman for a new and powerful American concern was spending time in Nicosia, searching for a dealer to supply his needs.

Like magic.

It was only common courtesy to meet the stranger, take his measure, and Makarios had opted for a luncheon gathering at one of several restaurants he owned in town. Security was guaranteed in a controlled environment, and healthy bribes ensured that they wouldn't be interrupted by police. With any luck, the meeting might pay off for all concerned.

Pappas appeared and whispered something to the maître d', two strangers trailing in their wake as they approached Makarios. The younger man had a familiar face, perhaps observed in passing on the street, or in a nightclub. His American companion was tall and dark with somber eyes, a killer's eyes. Makarios decided he would be a man to reckon with, perhaps a steadfast friend, most certainly a lethal enemy.

The dealer rose as they approached, a gesture of respect. Pappas performed the introductions, leading Nikos Kiprianou toward the bar while the American, who called himself Michael Belasko, sat across from Spyros in the private booth. A waiter hovered over them as they perused the menus.

"I can recommend the lobster."

"Fine. I'll have a beer to start, and white wine with the meal."

Makarios approved and made it lobster, twice. He ordered ouzo for himself, in place of beer.

"Have you enjoyed your trip?" he asked.

"So far so good."

"What brings you into Nicosia?"

"I've been hired to represent a group of businessmen in the United States," Bolan said. "They're kicking off an import operation, and they need reliable suppliers. Men of substance who can spare them the necessity of dealing with the East."

The drinks arrived, and Makarios sipped his ouzo, waiting for the waiter to withdraw.

"You mention imports. Is there any special product they desire?"

"Right now they're concentrating in the field of pharmaceuticals. I understand that you're the man to see."

"You flatter me."

"I do my homework," the American replied. "For instance, I'm aware that you were doing business with a gentleman named Anthony Silvestri. He can't use your product anymore. I can."

"Silvestri, I believe, has had an accident?"

"Things happen. Some guys try to move more weight than they can handle, if you get my drift."

"And your associates are men of proven strength?"

"Together, they've got all the muscle they can use."

"There are inquiries to be made."

"That goes both ways. If we do business, I'm instructed to review the source and meet the man in charge."

Makarios felt angry color rising in his cheeks. He flashed a smile to cover his immediate reaction. "That is much to ask on short acquaintance."

"Not so much, considering my people have allotted thirty million dollars in their budget for the first two years of operation. When they lay out cash like that, they like to know who's pocketing the change."

Makarios was busy multiplying and dividing in his head. "Of course," he said, "I can relay your message to my own suppliers. Sadly I'm not in a position to predict their answer."

"How much time?"

"A day or two. No more."

Bolan appeared to think it over, finally nodded. "Fair enough. I'm out of here on Wednesday, either way."

"Perhaps this evening you will be my guest for dinner? This is only one of various establishments I own in Nicosia. Others, I believe you will agree, provide more stimulating entertainment."

"Sounds okay to me. No harm in mixing business with a little pleasure."

"As you say."

Their food arrived on steaming platters, and Makarios dismissed the waiter with a nod. He filled their wineglasses to the brim, raising his own in a toast.

"To friendship."

Makarios made small talk as they started on the lobster, but his thoughts were elsewhere, flitting back and forth between a three-million-dollar payoff—his prescribed percentage of the figure mentioned by his guest—and the problems that could still arise to rob him of his fortune. He would pass the offer on without delay, of course, but there were still inquiries to be made. Makarios wasn't prepared to risk his life and liberty on dealings with a total stranger, and his partners would demand a briefing on Belasko's background, his associates in the United States, before they voted on the deal.

Had this man, or a member of his group, eliminated Anthony Silvestri and the two Iranians? If so, the Shiite delegation might reject his bid on principal, demanding vengeance. It would be Moheden's task to calm them down in that event, persuading them that business must take precedence over personality.

Makarios had trouble reading the American, as if his heart and mind were veiled to outside scrutiny, but on occasion he had found the same with others in his trade. He hoped the background check would tell him more, but there was little time to spare. With thirty million dollars in his pocket, the American would have no trouble finding other friends to welcome him with open arms.

Makarios didn't intend for that to happen. One way or another he would have to deal with Mike Belasko quickly. In the world he occupied, a loser got no consolation prize, and there was always someone waiting in the wings to take his place. The first mistake was normally your last, and even if you managed to survive it, you were never quite the same.

A born survivor, Spyros smiled across the table at the tall American and started making plans.

"WERE YOU SUCCESSFUL?" Nikos asked.

"I've got a dinner date," the Executioner replied. "No verdict, yet."

"Still, that's something. If Makarios mistrusted you, he'd have found some pressing reason why the two of you couldn't do business."

"Maybe."

Bolan scanned the crowded sidewalks as they motored back to his hotel. His mind replayed the conversation with Makarios from start to finish, searching for a turn of phrase or an expression that would tell him whether he had sold himself. The dealer's words came back to him: "There are inquiries to be made."

Okay. The cover story prepped by Stony Man would hold up under normal scrutiny. Makarios wouldn't have time to put "Belasko's" whole life story through the wringer, and he doubted that the dealer had sufficient stateside contacts for a truly thorough scan in any case. Silvestri's death had closed the door on any informational exchange with the Grisanti Family, and if the dealer's people had a line to Justice, it would only help his case.

Beyond those preparations, there was nothing he could do but watch and wait. Could Spyros rake the necessary information in by dinnertime? It seemed improbable, but Bolan would be on his guard against an ambush, just in case.

"When shall I pick you up?" the young man asked.

With genuine relief, the Executioner replied, "Not this time, Nikos. It's supposed to be some kind of one-on-one experience. I'll rent a car through the hotel."

The new arrangement wasn't sitting well with Nikos. "I was instructed to assist you with your mission."

"And you have," the Executioner assured him. "Take the evening off and call me in the morning."

Nikos drove for half a mile in silence, finally working up the nerve to ask a question. "You're leaving me behind because you think I'm a coward?"

Bolan frowned. It hadn't crossed his mind since their discussion of the night before in his hotel room, but the question brought it back.

"Not even close," he said. "Makarios is handing out the invitations, and he obviously doesn't want an extra pair of ears. If you're looking for a job tonight, check out Hussein Razmara and his buddy Sarkis. I have all the basic background information, but I need an inside reading I can trust. The personal perspective from a native. Can you handle it?"

The young man thought about it long enough to make himself believe the job wasn't mere busywork. "Of course," he said at last, a measure of his old vivacity returning. "Anything you wish to know."

"Primarily how well they work together. Are they friendly or antagonistic? If there's any weakness there, I'd like to know about it going in."

"No problem."

"Watch your step, all right? I've got no use for dead men."

Nikos cracked a smile. "I know just how to do it."

Bolan hoped that it wasn't bravado talking, but he had to give the guy a chance. If he instructed Nikos to remain at home, the young man might be driven to attempt some action on his own, provoking unforeseen retaliation from the enemy.

He cursed the driver's macho personality and made a mental note to keep him occupied as much as possible with harmless errands for the next two days. The last thing Bolan needed in his present situation was a kid, still wet behind the ears, hell-bent on demonstrating that he was a man.

The Executioner's experience had taught him that the "men" who tried to prove themselves the hardest often failed. In combat that meant risking other lives as well, and taking others with you when a grandstand play fell through. For Bolan's part, he couldn't spare the time to baby-sit a wounded ego.

Nikos and his pride would have to take care of themselves.

The Executioner was gearing up for war.

THE MIDTOWN TRAFFIC slowed him down, but Nikos Kiprianou still had time. Belasko's meeting with Makarios was scheduled for the normal dinner hour, starting off at eight o'clock with cocktails, and the young man thought he should be able to produce some interesting information in the meantime. He would telephone Belasko in his room before the meeting, and he would impress the tall American with his initiative.

At first it worried Nikos, his reaction to the thought of being left behind. Why should he care what happened with Makarios? He could be safe at home while the American took all the risks. But something deep inside—a pang of shame, perhaps—had forced him to complain. In all his missions for the drug enforcement people and the "cultural attachés," he had never failed. There was no reason for Belasko to dismiss him now.

It was his own fault, Kiprianou thought, for showing weakness when they met. He had been frightened at the prospect of a shooting war against Makarios, and he had let it show. Small wonder that the agent tried to shake him off when there was danger in the wind, but he wouldn't be thrust aside as if he were a child.

Belasko had been playing with him when he offered the alternative assignment, digging up more information on Hussein Razmara and the Lebanese supplier, Sarkis. Still, it was a job that Nikos knew he could perform, and he might yet surprise Belasko with his range of contacts.

There were ways to find out anything in Nicosia, if you tried, and Kiprianou thought he knew them all.

His first stop was a coffeehouse that catered to the Shiites. They didn't touch alcohol, and they were close-mouthed even with their own, but there was always gossip, even in the tightest circles. Nikos had a friend who had a friend, and by the time he left the coffeehouse at four-fifteen that afternoon, he also had a name.

The latest information led him to a smoky tavern where the conversation ran to whispers and the clientele regarded him with frank suspicion. It was slower going there, and cash changed hands before he heard another name, together with an address in a section of the city that police avoided after nightfall. Still, if there was information to be had, it was his duty to pursue the lead.

Traffic thinned as Nikos neared the target neighborhood. Most local residents couldn't afford to buy or operate a car, and Nikos thought it might be wise to double back and find a parking place outside the district. He could walk from there, attracting less attention to himself, but what if he was called upon to make his exit in a hurry? Pounding through the maze of streets with enemies behind him, darkness falling like a shroud, held no appeal for Nikos Kiprianou. He'd run the risk of theft or vandalism, making sure to lock the vehicle before he left it on the street.

His destination had been charitably dubbed a "nightclub." On arrival Nikos recognized it as a sex club, with a bar on one side of the smoky room, a small stage on the other. Naked "dancers" occupied the stage in shifts, performing with a startling array of foreign objects while the scratchy background music rasped and sputtered from an ancient record player. Nikos ordered wine and then paid double, as he fed the bartender a name.

Kiprianou's contact was so short that Nikos first mistook him for a midget. Swarthy, scarred about the face and neck, he gave off menacing vibrations that belied his size. The careless stitching of an ancient wound had forced one eye to squint forever.

It was difficult to talk around the music, and the short man led him through a beaded curtain, up a flight of stairs, the sounds of drunken men in heat receding as they climbed. A narrow corridor led off the landing, several painted doors on either side, and Nikos guessed they'd be bedrooms where the "dancers" and selected customers would make a little extra money for the house. The young man understood such things, though he had never paid for sex.

His contact chose the nearest door and led the way inside a tiny office. If the room was small to start with, its dimensions positively shriveled with the addition of the two behemoths stationed by the desk, a pair of animated bookends, scowling down at Nikos Kiprianou. He felt giddy as the door swung shut behind him and the bolt was thrown.

"You have been asking many questions," Scarface said, relaxing in a swivel chair that had been fitted out with extra cushions. "It is time for you to give some answers of your own."

CHAPTER NINE

From where he sat, it seemed to Rashid Sarkis that his world was shrinking daily, dwindling to the extent that he'd wake one morning with the Japanese for neighbors and Americans camped out in his front yard. Within a decade he had risen from the ranks of petty crime around Beirut to deal with foreign buyers, moving major quantities of contraband. Each day he dealt with customers in Rome and Paris, Bonn and Barcelona. Twice he'd been called upon to speak with the United States, but the Americans were treacherous, and he preferred to deal with them through intermediaries.

Now the damned Americans had come to him, and he was being forced into a corner, pressed for a decision that would either save his life or throw away a thirty-million-dollar deal. The utmost caution was required. He couldn't risk an inappropriate decision based on lack of information. Neither could he stall too long, when Spyros was prepared to close the deal.

They had discovered nothing yet about the man who called himself Belasko. Sarkis had no interest in the name, per se. He was aware that men in certain lines of business were required to change their names as often—and sometimes, regrettably, more often—than they changed their underwear. Belasko might be known by many different names at home, and it wouldn't support a case against his suitability for the transaction he proposed. If anything, a shady reputation only served to make him seem legitimate in present circumstances.

Likewise Sarkis wasn't troubled by the possibility that Anthony Silvestri had been murdered by Belasko or his agents. Some of the dealer's best friends were assassins. He recognized the role of violence in their industry and made allowances, reserving judgment when potential customers waged war against each other on their native soil. A small delay, perhaps, but he could always strike a bargain with the winner. Bakhtiar and his associates would be more difficult to pacify, but thirty million dollars was a powerful inducement to forgiveness.

All things being equal, Sarkis worried most about the young man, Nikos Kiprianou. He'd set the meeting up between Belasko and Makarios, remaining in the background as they gingerly began negotiations. It was normal practice in the world of shady deals, employing intermediaries to unite two men of substance and prestige. If only Nikos had been satisfied with his achievement and the normal finder's fee.

But he'd started asking questions, prying into matters that were better left alone. Worse yet, instead of seeking information on Makarios—an indiscretion which, at least, would bear some plausible connection to his work for the American—he had begun to sniff around the fringes of the Sarkis empire, peering into corners that had never seen the light of day.

Inevitably, swiftly, word was carried back to Sarkis. As a spider monitors each tremor of its web, so did the Lebanese absorb each bit of information pertinent to his continued safety and prosperity. He was accustomed to inquiries from police and offered the appropriate response, in cash or vague, misleading answers, but he bristled when the questions came from strange civilians.

Questions on the street meant competition at best, or le-thal enemies at worst. In either case, experience had taught him to respond with swift, decisive action.

Sarkis had begun by asking questions of his own. Within an hour's time he learned enough to know that Nikos Kiprianou didn't represent a local syndicate, nor was he rich enough to tackle Sarkis on his own. He was an errand boy, of sorts, and that told Sarkis that his questions had been posed by someone else, outside the young man's normal sphere of operation.

It remained to be determined whether the American, Belasko, was responsible for Kiprianou's sudden curios-ity, or whether Nikos had some other sponsor waiting in the wings. Interrogation was a tiresome, messy business, but there seemed to be no option. Sarkis needed answers, and his time was running short. He had to get a fix on Ni-kos soon, before Belasko kept his next appointment with Makarios.

And that meant he'd have to supervise the job himself, as he had in the old days.

Sarkis raised his hands and held them before his face, blunt fingers spread for individual inspection. They were clean hands—physically, if not in theory—and his nails were manicured with loving care. It had been years since he'd been called upon to personally violate another hu-man being, but he couldn't trust the present task to his subordinates. They would assist him, naturally, but the work required a master's touch.

Some things, like making love, were never quite forgot-ten once you learned the trick.

THE PAIN RETURNED with consciousness, by slow degrees, and Nikos Kiprianou realized that he was still alive. It came as something of a shock, all things considered, but the throbbing in his skull, the aching ribs and groin, assured him that the beating hadn't been a simple nightmare. Somehow, after they had gone to work, the scarfaced midget and his pet gorillas had decided not to kill him. They had spared his life, and with that certain knowledge came a flash of cold, mind-numbing terror.

Nikos spent a precious moment taking stock of his surroundings. He was lying on his back, spread-eagle on a rigid surface, with his wrists and ankles bound securely. It wasn't the floor, because it shuddered slightly when he moved.

A table, then.

The cool air on his body told him he was naked, and the nagging rasp of friction burns confirmed that he hadn't been stripped with tender, loving care. His garments must be little more than rags by now, but Nikos didn't care. He'd be glad to walk home naked through the teeming streets if they would only spare his life.

But who were "they," and where had they transported him?

The ceiling had been different in the sex club's office, where the questioning began and ended with a vicious beating. This was certainly a different room, more spacious, and the new acoustic ceiling tiles suggested that he might be in a different building altogether. So, they had abducted him as well as beating him unconscious, but the information failed to help him in his search for a solution to his plight.

The early questions had been crude, simplistic. Scarface wanted Nikos to explain his interest in the Sarkis operation. Had another prompted his inquiries? And, if so, what was the stranger's name? The young man had surprised himself by holding out, but on reflection, he couldn't attribute that to any special strength of character. The hulking animals who beat him had enjoyed their work so much that they refused to stop upon command, and blessed darkness had descended in a tidal wave of jolting, crushing fists.

He thought they would be more deliberate and thorough when they started up again. They wouldn't let him slip away so easily next time. His very posture, splayed out on the table, indicated that his captors were adopting a more calculated, reasoning approach.

His skin was crawling, and he feared that he might soil himself, but Nikos Kiprianou spent a moment breathing deeply, trying to control his runaway emotions. Fear was paramount, but there was also anger, outrage, and a trace of morbid curiosity. If Scarface had relinquished him to other hands, who would his new interrogator be? Would more intelligent assailants be amenable to reason? Could he spin a web of cunning lies that held up long enough to win his freedom?

Behind him—or above him in his present posture—Nikos heard a door click open, whisper shut. The sound of footsteps told him that the floor was vinyl, possibly linoleum. No carpeting to stain with flecks of blood or human waste.

A human silhouette moved into Kiprianou's field of vision. Nikos didn't recognize the man at first, but he made the obvious connection in another moment. Despite familiar features, Sarkis nearly fooled him with the denim overalls.

"My friend," the Lebanese addressed him simply, "you appear to be in difficulty."

"A misunderstanding," Nikos answered, fighting to enunciate with lips that felt like sausages.

"No doubt." The dealer sounded rational. "My people misconstrued your questions as a gesture of hostility. Myself, I have no doubt that you were merely curious, attempting to collect some simple information."

"Yes." The pain prevented him from smiling, but he felt a sudden rush of hope. How easy this was turning out to be!

"I must confess a certain curiosity, myself. When strangers question my employees, seeking information on my business operations and my movements, I become suspicious. Surely you must understand."

"Of course." What could he say to pacify the enemy and save himself? "I only..."

"Yes?"

He tried again. "You are a wealthy man, while I have next to nothing. I was anxious to improve myself by emulating your example. How could such as I pose any threat to you? You must believe me."

"Must I?" Sarkis studied Nikos Kiprianou with a flat, disinterested gaze. "In your place I believe I would say anything, do anything, to save myself and fend off further pain. Of course, the most successful remedy is truth. I recommend it."

Nikos clenched his sphincter muscles as a rising surge of panic threatened to betray him. "I have spoken truthfully," he answered, instantly disheartened by the hopeless tenor of his voice.

"You will, of course, forgive my skepticism," Sarkis said. "I fear that you haven't convinced me, Nikos. I must cause you further suffering, unless you can persuade me that you speak the truth."

"I beg of you—"

"You must not."

Sarkis reached behind him and retrieved a long, flat tray of stainless steel. He placed it on the table next to Nikos, just beyond his line of sight, and spent a moment studying its contents. Nikos felt his scrotum twitch and shrivel as the dealer started holding up his instruments in turn for mutual inspection.

First there was a six-inch corkscrew, followed by a pair of butcher's shears, designed for clipping bone and gristle. There were knives in several sizes, and a brand-new hacksaw. The soldering iron, by contrast, was discolored from frequent use.

"Once more," the dealer said. "Who sent you to inquire about my business?"

Nikos Kiprianou closed his eyes and gave no answer.

He would need his breath when he began to scream.

BASHIR MOHEDEN TOLERATED telephones around the house because his business was dependent on communication, but he never answered them himself. Their ringing grated on his nerves, and practical experience had taught him that the shrilling rarely heralded good news. He let the servants field all calls, reporting the identity of callers, while Moheden picked and chose among them, spending time with some, rejecting others.

This time there was something in the jangling of the telephone that set his teeth on edge. He was relaxing in the shade of his veranda, half-asleep, but he could hear the strident chimes through walls and windows closed against the midday heat. He braced himself for the inevitable summons, wondering what sort of crisis he would have to cope with this time.

Soft soles whispered across the flagstones as the house-man brought a cordless telephone, in case Moheden deigned to take the call.

"Who is it?"

"Master Sarkis."

Frowning, he received the instrument and waited for the houseman to retreat before he lifted the receiver.

"Sarkis?"

"Here."

"Have you secured the line?"

"Of course."

"Proceed."

"There is a problem."

"Go on."

"A stranger from America. He calls himself Belasko, first name Michael. He's been in touch with Spyros to initiate discussion of a major purchase."

"Ah."

"Makarios believes his backers may have killed Silvestri."

"Is that a problem?"

"Not to me. I'm concerned about the youth."

"Explain yourself."

"A local small-time hoodlum. He approached Makarios for this Belasko and arranged their meeting. Spyros and Belasko are supposed to meet again tonight. Perhaps an hour from now."

"I'm listening."

"The young man was intercepted asking questions all about Razmara and myself. He stands up fairly well to questioning, but I have learned that he runs errands sometimes for the U.S. Embassy. My people think he may be tied to drug enforcement, possibly the CIA."

"And the American? What was his name?"

"Belasko. I have nothing to connect him with the government, except for his association with the youth."

"A possible coincidence?"

"Perhaps."

"What was his offer to Makarios?"

"They were supposed to work the details out tonight. I understand that over two years' time he planned on spending thirty million."

"Dollars?"

"So he told Makarios."

It was approximately twice the figure quoted to Silvestri in New York. Moheden felt his pulse accelerate, swiftly reminding himself that the man was a probable Judas.

"Opinions?"

"None." He could feel Sarkis scowling down the long-distance line. "I haven't spoken with the man. Makarios smells money and believes that he may be sincere. As for the young man..."

"Ah, yes."

"If I could only get the truth from him—"

"You have an hour. Will he crack?"

"It's possible. Who knows?"

"Be ready. If you break him and he gives up the American, they must be made to disappear. If you convince yourself of this Belasko's bona fides, Spyros may proceed... but cautiously."

"There is another matter," Sarkis said.

"Indeed?"

"Belasko says his syndicate—whoever they may be—demand an interview with the suppliers prior to closing any deal."

"Demand?"

"It stands as a condition of the deal."

Moheden hesitated briefly, then made up his mind with customary swiftness. "Satisfy yourself that this Belasko's business is legitimate," he ordered. "If the man is still alive tomorrow, call me back. Call back, in any case, and let me know what happened. Not tonight. I need to think this through and make some calls myself."

"And if he lives tomorrow?" Sarkis pressed.

"A meeting may be possible. The sum of thirty million dollars is deserving of some minimal respect."

"The youth?"

"Find out what else he knows, if anything. When you are finished with him, make him disappear."

"It shall be done."

"Rashid?"

"Yes?"

"Be careful."

"Yes."

Moheden set the cordless phone on the flagstones beside his lounge chair. In his mind he pictured the interrogation room where Sarkis would be questioning the young man. It was unfortunate, but such techniques were sometimes necessary. Fortunately Sarkis had a background in the work, and he would learn the captive's secrets one way or another, if the youth survived that long. Exuberance occasionally ruined an interrogation, ending with the subject dead or comatose before the crucial answers were elicited. Moheden thought that Sarkis could be trusted with the job, as long as he kept track of factors such as shock and loss of blood.

The Lebanese concentrated on the problem of Belasko and his thirty million dollars. Did the cash exist? Was his involvement with the young man a careless error in selection of a guide, or could there be a more sinister interpretation?

For the moment he'd leave the problem to his representative in Nicosia. Thus, whatever happened could be blamed on Sarkis, or—if things went well—Moheden could preempt the credit for himself. He instantly dismissed the thought of warning Bakhtiar, and saw no need of troubling Ahmad Halaby with the sketchy news.

This time tomorrow they would all be safe from harm, or on their way to being thirty-million-dollars richer. Either way, Bashir Moheden stood to be the hero of the hour, praised for his decisive and insightful handling of a touchy situation.

Smiling in the sunset, he decided there was no way he could lose.

SPYROS MAKARIOS COULDN'T stand still. He'd been pacing rings around his office, snapping at employees for the past two hours, and his mood grew worse each time he checked his wristwatch. Forty minutes left until his scheduled meeting with Belasko, and he had no final word from Sarkis yet, no way of knowing if he was supposed to greet the tall American with smiles or kill him in his tracks.

The way Makarios felt now, one option seemed no better than the other.

He'd been encouraged by their luncheon meeting, though a lifetime of suspicion had prevailed. A call to Sarkis had initiated certain inquiries, but dredging information from the vastness of America took time, and they might not retrieve the details of Belasko's background for a period of days, if ever. Spyros was prepared to move ahead with caution, lured by the prospect of his own commission on a thirty-million-dollar sale, but that had been before his second call from Sarkis.

Who was this Nikos Kiprianou, that he tried to play with men who had devoted lifetimes to their craft? Did he suspect his clumsy questions would elude them? Did he take Makarios and Sarkis for a pair of fools?

It was insulting, but Makarios wasn't concerned about his pride just now. An insult called for punishment in kind, depending on its circumstances and severity. A roughing-up, perhaps—or worse, if honor was at stake. If only insults were involved, they could have settled it like men.

Nikos, however, had been guilty of a greater indiscretion. Spyros shuddered at the thought of Pappas sitting at the bar with Nikos Kiprianou, smiling, sipping ouzo as they talked. How long had they been friendly? What had Constantine let slip, in this or that unguarded moment? How much of their small talk had been sold to the Americans in hopes of building up a case for trial?

The youth was an informant, that much was apparent, and as such his fate was sealed. The problem of Belasko lingered unresolved, and soon—in less than half an hour now—Makarios would have to sit across a table from the tall American, all smiles, as if his stomach wasn't twisted into knots. Belasko would expect an answer, and Makarios wasn't convinced that he could speak, much less talk business in his normal, measured tones.

He had suggested a postponement, but Sarkis flatly rejected the notion. Delays would only put Belasko off—alerting him if he was guilty, sparking anger and suspicion otherwise—and they couldn't afford the risk in either case. The meeting must proceed on schedule, Spyros buying time while Sarkis plumbed for answers in the ruin of Nikos Kiprianou.

So little time! Makarios stopped pacing long enough to pour himself a glass of ouzo, draining it in one long swallow. In the past he had occasionally turned to liquor as a sedative, but this time Spyros thought that he could drain the bottle where he stood and still find no relief. He tried deep-breathing exercises, thrust his hands inside his pockets to control their trembling. Nothing seemed to work.

At last, in desperation, he sat down behind his desk and forced himself to focus on the wall directly opposite. The paneling was cedar, and it gave a fresh outdoors aroma to the office. He concentrated on the smell, eyes closing, picturing himself in the woods outside Kirinia when he was just a child, before the British soldiers threw his father into jail and later shot him as a rebel.

They had been simple days, before responsibility and hunger taught him that the world wasn't so simple after all. The intervening years had taught him to survive in any circumstances, cope with any danger that arose. It was ridiculous for him to pace the floor and tremble at the thought of meeting with a strange American. He owned the restaurant where they would meet, and paid the salary of every person whom Belasko would encounter after passing through the doors. A signal from Makarios would summon up a dozen men to deal with the American.

His eyes snapped open as the telephone began to ring. He snared the receiver and was gratified to find his hand rock-steady, firm.

"Hello?"

He recognized the voice without an introduction, nodding to himself as he received his orders, halting the reflexive motion when he realized the caller couldn't see him.

"Yes," he said at length. "I understand."

And so the choice was made. Makarios was pleased that it hadn't been his decision. All he had to do was carry out his orders, letting Sarkis take the heat for any errors of judgment. Life and death were truly simple matters, once the problem of decision making was resolved.

He checked his watch again. Ten minutes. Spyros rose and crossed the room to pour himself another brimming glass of ouzo, drank it down and felt the liquid fire begin to spread. It wouldn't hurt if he was slightly drunk this evening. It might even help him see his duty through.

He wondered if Belasko would be drinking.

Anything at all to blunt the pain.

CHAPTER TEN

The concierge at Bolan's hotel arranged for the rental car, and a dark blue compact was waiting outside when the warrior emerged from the lobby at seven o'clock. He wore a lightweight suit, the jacket a concession to his side arm, and a smallish airline flight bag swung from one of Bolan's hands. Inside, the silencer, spare magazines, and other backup gear were wrapped inside the jet-black nightsuit, just in case.

He slid behind the steering wheel and stowed the flight bag underneath the driver's seat, where it would be invisible to passersby while he was parked. The Executioner had made a point of memorizing landmarks on their trip to meet Makarios that afternoon, but he was having dinner with the dealer at a different restaurant, and so had bought a street map from the gift shop in the hotel's lobby. Bolan found the small red X that signified his lodgings, then spent five more minutes tracking down the street his host had named. The map was short on detail, and discovery of alternate escape routes would be best accomplished at the scene.

Bolan had allowed himself an hour, and he wasted half of that in midtown traffic, nearly being sideswiped twice by drivers who appeared to be auditioning for demolition derbies. Watching out for further hazards, the warrior noted that the lion's share of vehicles around him had been marked by dents and scrapes, the wounds deliberately untended, like a haughty swordsman's duelling scar. He wished the rental luck and forged ahead, arriving at his destination twenty minutes early.

He used the extra time to scout the neighborhood, alert for telltale signs of ambush, charting alternate approaches and retreats. The options were distinctly limited, but he felt better after driving twice around the block, examining a narrow alley set behind the nightclub. Bolan followed local custom, parking on the street with two wheels on the skimpy sidewalk, making sure to lock the vehicle. The strains of sultry Eastern rhythms ventured out to greet him as he drifted toward the entrance of the club.

Keeping faith with the establishment's motif, the hulking doorman had been dressed in imitation of a harem guard, complete with turban and an open satin vest, exposing well-developed muscles. Bolan wondered if the ornate dagger tucked inside his sash was merely there for show.

He was expected, and the doorman shook his head when Bolan palmed a roll of bills and tried to pay the cover charge. Inside, he spent a moment waiting for his pupils to accommodate the dark and smoky atmosphere. The music, louder now, accompanied a pair of dancers who were stripping down to bare essentials on a long, low stage. Though both, presumably, were going through the same routine, one shed her veils and filmy harem garments with a certain style, the other grinding through her act mechanically, disinterested in her surroundings. From the rapt attention of the all-male audience, it didn't seem to matter either way.

He scanned the room and saw Makarios approaching through the haze, all smiles. They shook hands like a pair of long-lost friends, and Bolan trailed his host in the direction of an elevated booth to one side of the stage. A sultry waitress took their order—wine for Bolan, ouzo for

Makarios—and Bolan watched her hips as she retreated toward the bar.

"You like?"

"What's not to like?"

"Perhaps, if we do business, I'll give her to you."

Bolan smiled. "I don't believe she'd fit inside my luggage."

When the drinks arrived, Makarios threw back a brimming glass of ouzo, quickly filling it again. He leaned in closer, to be heard above the music.

"How you like my club?"

"It's different."

"For the Turks," Makarios explained. "They like to feel at home, as if they all had harems back in Ankara, instead of ugly wives and ten or fifteen children. See, they like the blondes and redheads best. Where did they ever see a blonde at home? Such children."

Bolan watched his host put down another shot of liquor, wondering if Spyros always drank that way at night, or if he had a special need for artificial courage. Either way he knew enough to keep his guard up, using the distraction on the stage as an excuse to scan the room for lurking enemies.

A signal from Makarios had brought the waitress back with menus.

"First we eat, then talk some business. Yes?"

He slipped the single button on his jacket open, granting quicker access to the gun beneath his arm.

"That's why I'm here."

CONSTANTINE PAPPAS released the safety on his Turkish Kirikkale pistol and returned the automatic to its pancake holster. Extra magazines weighed heavy in the pockets of his suit coat, and a second gun—an ancient .38 revolver with the finish worn away—was tucked inside his belt, against his spine.

The other members of the firing squad were also armed with pistols, and a small Beretta submachine gun had been hidden behind the bar in case their hasty plan fell through. Pappas wasn't impressed with the American, for all his size and fierce demeanor, but Makarios insisted on a backup plan. Insurance, he had called it.

Death insurance.

Constantine hadn't been briefed about the stranger's crimes, and he wasn't concerned with motivation. An employer judged his workmen on the basis of results. This seemed an easy job, and yet...

The tall American was armed—Pappas knew that much—and Makarios had vetoed a suggestion that their target should be forced to check his weapon at the door. It would have been "unfriendly," Spyros said, arousing dark suspicions, possibly initiating violence if the man refused. The plan required their target, this Belasko, to be seated in the special booth when Spyros left the table to relieve his bladder. Constantine and others would approach the table then and open fire, before Belasko recognized his peril.

Spyros was convinced that it would work. He had derived the notion from a gangster movie filmed in the United States and dubbed in Greek. The movie followed Lucky Luciano's Prohibition-era war against a rival mafioso known as Joe the Boss, resolved when they sat down for dinner in a stylish restaurant and Luciano went to use the toilet. It was foolproof on the screen. Pappas saw no reason why it should not work tonight.

Despite his nervousness, Makarios had thought of everything. The booth's location would prevent stray rounds from wounding any of their customers, providing Constantine and his associates were swift and sure enough with their initial shots. Police wouldn't arrive in time to halt removal of the corpse, assuming they were called at all, and drunken Turks made most reluctant witnesses.

In three years' time, Pappas had killed five men on orders from Makarios; the tall American would be his sixth. His normal duties ran toward supervising shipments of narcotics and collecting debts from wayward gamblers. On occasion he discouraged competition with a beating or a well-placed firebomb, leaning on the independents who were rash enough to trespass on the territory ruled by Spyros and his partners.

When he killed, Pappas had always favored privacy—a darkened alley or an empty parking lot, perhaps the target's home—and this would be his first attempt at murder with a paying audience. The shooters would wear stocking masks, erasing any threat from witnesses, but it was still a change of pace. Pappas had swallowed several pills to help himself unwind, and he could feel them kicking in as he stood waiting in an alcove set behind the stage.

From where he stood, the other gunners were visible. Two waited in the kitchen, peering through a porthole in the door, and one was loitering outside the men's room. When Makarios was clear they would converge, with masks in place and weapons drawn, and do their job before Belasko—or the other customers—had time to realize that anything was happening. A well-aimed round of shots and they would haul Belasko's body out the back to where a stolen car stood waiting in the alley. They would strip his corpse and dump it on the highway south of town for the police to puzzle over at their leisure.

It was simple.

Just like in the movies.

"THE SUM YOU MENTIONED, I believe, was thirty million dollars?"

"Over two years' time," the Executioner replied. "If that works out, there might be larger orders down the road."

Makarios had cleaned his plate, and he was looking somewhat groggy, the result of too much food and ouzo. Still, there was a glint in his eyes. Raw greed, perhaps . . . or was it something else?

"Your sponsors must be wealthy men," he said, speech slurring just a fraction from the drink.

"They plan to make a profit on the deal."

"Of course. We aren't Communists." He chuckled more than necessary at his own small joke, the laughter interrupted as a strained expression surfaced on his face. "I drink too fast," he said. "My bladder tells me so. You will excuse me for a moment?"

"Sure."

He watched the dealer waddle off in the direction of the rest room, turning his attention to the girls onstage. An Arab and another blonde, but Bolan couldn't peg her nationality. Perhaps Italian, from the north, where blondes weren't uncommon. The drunken audience showed no interest in her ethnic background, concentrating on the flesh she was revealing to their gaze, a little at a time.

He checked his wristwatch, squinting in the gloom. It was already half-past nine, and so far they had only talked around the deal, Makarios avoiding any mention of his earlier request to meet the men behind the traffic. Balkan temperament was part of it, a need to take things slowly that was rivaled only in the Latin nations, but he wondered if the dealer might be stalling with a more deliberate goal in mind.

Perhaps . . .

A lanky gunman was attempting to adjust his stocking mask as he emerged from hiding near the stage. He held the automatic pistol low against his leg, to screen it from the dancers and the audience as long as possible. On Bolan's left, another figure drifted into view from the direction of the rest room, where Makarios had disappeared. Two more were just emerging from the kitchen, jostling a waiter in their eagerness to get it done.

Four guns. Would there be others waiting on the sidelines to attempt a save if things went sour for the home team?

Bolan had no time to mull the question over as he palmed the new Beretta, hunching lower in his seat. His free hand rose beneath the table, seized it by the lip for leverage, and kept on rising, plates and bottles spilling to the floor as he thrust it over on its side. He dropped behind it, seeing weapons on the rise, and triggered two quick shots before he hit the floor.

One of the dancers screamed. Downrange the toilet gunner lurched and staggered, groping for the wall to keep himself from falling. It was hopeless, and the guy was dead before he hit the floor.

His comrades opened up in unison, their wild rounds knocking chunks of plaster from the walls and drilling knotholes in the table. Bolan wriggled back into a corner of the booth and twisted so that he could see a portion of the room. A shoulder, clad in leather, and a denim leg— the gunner from the kitchen shifted, trying for a better shot, and Bolan took one of his own.

He winged his adversary, nothing serious, but it was still enough to drive the shooter back. The other kitchen gunner followed, seeking cover, and a group of rowdy Turks dispersed before them, scattering to safety.

There were screams from both the dancers now, accompanied by shouts and curses from the patrons as they ducked beneath their tables, half a dozen of them breaking for the door. Would any of them hail police? No matter. Spyros more than likely had the fix in locally, and Bolan would be on his own.

The lanky backstage gunner had approached within a range of twenty feet, an automatic pistol counting cadence. Six shots...seven...eight. A momentary silence spurred the Executioner to action, and he burst from cover, catching his assailant as the gunner tried to draw another weapon he wore tucked behind his back.

It was the rough equivalent of point-blank range for the Beretta. Bolan drilled a mangler through the gunman's stocking mask and watched the impact punch him backward, flattening a table as he fell.

The two surviving gunners opened fire in unison, and Bolan vaulted from the booth. He hit with a flying shoulder roll and came up firing, scrambling across the floor and under cover of another capsized table as his adversaries found the range.

Four up, two down—and he'd have to do a damn sight better in a hurry if he meant to catch Makarios. The dealer might have slipped away already, and he surely wouldn't hang around if he perceived his troops were losing. If he lost Makarios—

The warrior shifted cautiously, again, and he was in the open, worming toward a new location under cover of the semidarkness. Customers had scattered from the area around his booth, but he could feel them watching from the shadows, huddled under furniture to duck the next barrage of slugs.

He found another table lying on its side and burrowed in. The gunmen were impatient, anxious to complete their "simple" job, and he was banking on their eagerness to breed mistakes. They had to move, and it was either rush or run.

Whichever way it played, the Executioner was waiting.

But he didn't have the time to wait all night.

MAKARIOS HADN'T BEEN shamming when he told Bolan that he had to use the toilet. He was standing at a urinal, his free hand braced against the wall, when rapid pistol fire erupted in the outer room. Two shots, at first, and then a crackling string like fireworks. He was zipping up his trousers when he realized that it was taking much too long. Belasko should be dead by now, and still the gunfire echoed through his club.

Alarmed, Makarios allowed himself a quick peek from the men's room, but his view was blocked by corners and a screen of hanging beads. Emerging from the rest room, he killed the alcove lights to give himself some cover, and it helped a little. Now he saw a pair of legs protruding from around the corner, feet splayed out in death.

Belasko had been lucky, and continued gunfire told Makarios his luck was holding. Sober now, the dealer knelt and drew the stubby Walther automatic from its ankle holster. Flicking off the safety as he rose, Makarios edged closer to the beaded curtain, glancing downward for an instant at the fallen gunman's prostrate body. Blood had pooled beneath him and escaped in shiny rivulets across the floor.

He tracked in the direction of the empty booth, his stomach lurching as he recognized the corpse of Constantine Pappas. Two other members of his firing squad were still alive, occasionally popping up from cover, firing toward a table in the middle of the room, but Makarios couldn't see Belasko, with the shapes of furniture and huddled patrons in his way.

Behind the bar his backup gunner had begun to pace, the submachine gun in his hands, but he had no clear target either. Makarios sized the situation up and knew that he'd lost control. They still might kill Belasko if he tried to reach the door, but a prolonged exchange of fire was bound to draw police. Makarios couldn't afford to wait around and answer probing questions. It would take time to prepare himself, rehearse his answers, and for that he needed breathing room.

His car was parked out front, and that meant crossing in between Belasko and the other guns unless he worked his way around in back. Retreating, Makarios tucked the Walther automatic in his belt and raced toward the exit. If their plans hadn't been shattered, Constantine and his companions would have carried Mike Belasko's body out this way, a simple flourish of the mop sufficient to eradicate all traces of his passing.

Suddenly, behind him, pistol fire erupted in a storm. Two weapons hammered before another made it three, and then the submachine gun opened up. Makarios heard bullets ripping into plaster, gouging woodwork, as his gunners gave it everything they had.

Too late to stem the rising tide of panic that propelled him forward, Makarios hit the alley running, turning right and pounding past the car Pappas had stolen for tonight. He left it there, uncertain whether there were keys or where to find them, sliding on the gravel as he ducked around another corner, headed for the street.

No more than twenty yards and he'd be safe. Makarios's car was locked, and he fumbled with the keys, alert to fleeting time. He flicked a glance in the direction of the entrance, saw the doorman taking to his heels, a spectacle in turban, satin vest and flimsy harem trousers.

He slid in behind the wheel, jabbed at the ignition, missed it, tried again. He got it on the second lunge and mouthed a silent prayer of thanks for swift response beneath the hood. Belasko couldn't stop him now.

But where to run?

If the police were summoned, they would quickly trace him to his home. With corpses in the club, they were obliged at least to pull him in for questioning. He needed time to think, but where?

He had it!

Sarkis had demanded that he kill Belasko, and the order had presumably been handed down from Bashir Moheden. Makarios could hide with Sarkis and let the Lebanese attempt to salvage something from the chaos of his master plan.

Relaxing now that he had found a destination, Makarios concentrated on his driving, easing up on the accelerator. He couldn't afford a confrontation with police, on any charge, before he spoke with Sarkis and resolved their difficulty.

Soon.

In a few more moments all his troubles would be over.

IT WAS RUSH OR RUN, and when he heard his adversaries scrambling to their feet, Mack Bolan knew instinctively they had decided on the rush. For all they knew, he might be wounded, even dying, and they had to take the chance. Their skirmish had already lasted long enough to draw police, and their only ready exit lay within a hostile line of fire.

They rose together, squeezing off in rapid fire with two guns each, and Bolan had to give them points for accuracy. Dead on target from a range of fifteen yards, they doubtless would have nailed him if he hadn't scurried clear in time.

He let them close the gap a little, easing up from cover with the Beretta braced in both hands, tracking on the nearest figure first. A double punch ripped through the guy's chest and sent him spinning like a dervish, jostling against his partner as he fell.

The second man, still bleeding from the graze above his elbow, caught himself before he fell and spun to face the enemy. He got off two more shots before he died, but both of them were wild, and then a single slug made contact like a hammer blow between his eyes. The shooter's head snapped back, and Bolan watched him melt away, a snowman disappearing in a sudden heat wave.

He was expecting backup gunners, but the burst of sub-machine-gun fire surprised him even so. He caught a glimpse of muzzle-flashes as he hit the floor, and then a storm of bullets started eating up the furniture around him, wild rounds scattering some patrons who had gone to ground nearby.

Their flight distracted Bolan's adversary for an instant, tricking him with decoys, and he chopped down two runners before he realized his fatal error. By the time he swung the weapon back on target, Bolan had him cold at thirty feet, the first round drilling through his sweaty forehead, lifting off a section of his scalp. Another clipped his dying vocal cords before he had a chance to scream, and number three was simply icing on the cake, a heart shot, as he fell away behind the bar.

There was no time to waste. It took a moment for the Executioner to reach the men's room, scan its empty stalls and double back to try the exit. He found the door ajar and pushed on through. The solitary car out back was going nowhere.

Bolan played a hunch and doubled back, past milling patrons who appeared to realize the worst was over. Half expecting opposition from the doorman, the warrior hit the sidewalk in a gallop, nostrils flaring at the scent of burning rubber in the air. Downrange, a pair of fleeing taillights winked across the nearest intersection.

Bolan got the door unlocked and threw himself behind his rented compact's steering wheel. Makarios was working on a decent lead, but there was time, if he could let the dealer think that he had made it free and clear. If common sense prevailed and panic was suppressed, he had a chance.

The engine came to life, and Bolan gave the little car its head, running dark through the short quarter-mile without oncoming traffic. Makarios was slowing by the time he crossed a major intersection, and Bolan turned on his headlights, an innocent motorist pulling away from the curb.

In fact, he had a fair idea of where Makarios was going. If he called it right, the dealer would be doing him a favor, simplifying matters for what lay ahead. The soldier still had ugly work to do, and it would go down easier if he could find his targets—some of them, at any rate—mobbed up together in a handy shooting gallery.

The "soft" approach had failed spectacularly, and he wondered who had blown his cover. Moments later Bolan's mind coughed up a possible solution, but the answer raised more problems than it solved. If he was not mistaken, then his killing mission might take on the aspect of a rescue.

Soft was definitely out.

The Executioner was going hard.

CHAPTER ELEVEN

"And so, you *left* him?" Sarkis made no attempt to disguise the venom in his tone. He pinned Makarios with an accusing stare. "You have no way of knowing whether he is still alive?"

His unexpected, uninvited visitor turned open palms in the direction of the ceiling. "The police! I couldn't wait, Rashid. He must be dead by now, but I need time."

"For what? To find your balls?" He was delighted by the way Makarios recoiled before his anger. "You were dining in your own establishment, alone, when all the shooting started. You have never seen the tall American before. The other men wore masks, you say? How could they possibly be recognized?"

"But the police know Constantine. He works for me. That's not a secret."

"So?" Rashid felt confident, as always, when he solved the problems of a less intelligent associate. "Are you responsible for everything that your employees do in leisure time? How could you possibly suspect that Pappas was involved in criminal activity?"

"You think they will believe me?"

"It isn't important whether they believe you, Spyros. The police must prove you guilty of a crime before you go to prison, eh? Who testifies against you in this case? Not Constantine. His men?"

"They wouldn't dare."

The Lebanese took time to pour himself a glass of wine.

"That leaves Belasko."

"But a dead man—"

"Trust his death when you have seen his body, Spyros. As it is, you *think* he might be dead. Where is your car?"

Makarios looked honestly bewildered for a moment, then cocked a thumb in the direction of the street. "Outside."

Sarkis made an effort to suppress his mounting anger and disgust. The whining bastard had arranged an ambush for Belasko, then ran out before he saw it through. If that wasn't enough for one night, he had run directly to Sarkis, at his home. No warning call. No hasty rendezvous on neutral ground. If anyone suspected Spyros, if he'd been followed...

Sarkis stiffened, dark eyes boring through Makarios.

"You took precautions?" he demanded. "Coming here tonight, you weren't followed?"

"Who would follow me, Rashid?"

The dealer's mind was racing, searching for the reassurance of an answer. "Are we certain that Belasko was alone in Nicosia?"

Makarios frowned. "There was Nikos Kiprianou..."

"Forget him." Sarkis smiled. The young man wasn't a problem any longer. He was simply rubbish, waiting to be carted out and thrown away. Perhaps a memory. "Can you be certain there was no one else?"

Makarios looked worried now. "I made inquiries of the concierge at his hotel. Belasko was alone when he arrived. He had no visitors other than Kiprianou."

"Were any other hotels scrutinized? Was this Belasko followed when he left his room? Did he make contacts on the street?"

The Cypriot was staring at his shoes. "I ordered no surveillance," he replied. "There wasn't time. The usual inquiries—"

"Brought the usual results. Our problem," Sarkis said, "is that Belasko might turn out to be a most unusual man."

"But he's dead! I don't see—"

"One moment!"

Sarkis raised an open hand to silence his companion. A small red light was flashing on his desk. It appeared to be a silent pager for his intercom, but any message heralded by that light had to be bad news. The beacon was, in fact, connected to a series of strategic "panic buttons" planted all around the house, positioned where his sentries would have easy access in emergencies. Another red light would be flashing in his bedroom, with a muted buzzer chiming in to wake him from the soundest sleep. The system had been tested after installation three years earlier, and Sarkis hadn't seen the flashing light since then.

"What is it?" Spyros asked.

"Perhaps a visitor."

"Police?"

"Unlikely."

The police were never unexpected, and his men had been well trained to use the panic button only in a case of dire necessity. A full-scale raid might qualify, but Sarkis knew he'd have been forewarned by friends in uniform, whose loyalty he'd purchased over time. Eliminating the police, that only left—

The burst of automatic fire was muffled, barely audible inside his study, but it was enough to put Makarios in motion, short legs driving him across the room and back again. His face had lost its color. Sarkis wondered if he might be on the verge of cardiac arrest, a blessing in disguise.

He pulled a desk drawer open, slipped his hand inside and palmed the Browning automatic, drawing reassurance from its weight. He flicked off the safety and drew the slide back, just enough to verify a live round underneath the firing pin.

"Who is it?" Makarios whispered hoarsely.

"We'll have to go and see," the dealer replied. His pistol waggled toward the only exit from his study. "After you."

MAKARIOS HAD LED the Executioner on a winding, quarter-hour drive, but Bolan had maintained surveillance, hanging back just far enough to seem innocuous, occasionally turning off his headlights if he found a street devoid of other traffic. Once, he thought the runner might have spotted him, the way Makarios had taken three quick rights, to double back upon his course. In fact, the guy had simply missed his landmark, circling the block to get it right. He took no other measures to avoid pursuit, and Bolan trailed him back to Sarkis, switching off his lights and pulling in a full block from the dealer's home.

The street was dark and empty. Bolan took a chance and stood beside the rental car to change his clothes, the night breeze warm against his naked flesh before he pulled the blacksuit on. He snugged the shoulder rigging back in place and mounted the Beretta's silencer. Spare magazines were evenly distributed among his several hidden pockets, and he finished off the job by smearing camouflage war paint on his face and hands.

He knew there would be guards and they'd probably be armed with more than pistols. Bolan could have used a submachine gun—some grenades, perhaps—but it was no good wishing. He'd left an SMG at the strip joint, but he would have wasted precious time retrieving it and scouring the bar for backup magazines. He might have lost Makarios and any chance he had of wrapping up the pipeline's western terminus in Nicosia.

Granted, he'd known where Sarkis lived from the beginning. Brognola had briefed him on the dealer's current residence—along with that of the Iranian, Hussein Razmara—but he hadn't been convinced Makarios would run directly to his crony. If the Cypriot had tried to make a break—the airport, for example—Bolan would have been compelled to take him down in public, prior to searching out his other targets.

It was better this way. If, by chance, he found Razmara in the house with Sarkis and Makarios, his mission would be simplified. If not, he had the address and his street map. He could still be finished with the job by dawn.

But first he had to make his way through any sentries Sarkis might employ. Not *past* them, for the risk of leaving one alive would be too great. They played the game and took their chances. They would have to die.

Unless, of course, they killed him first.

He crossed the street and moved in, under cover of the night. The neighborhood lay north of downtown Nicosia, and it had been occupied for generations by the city's affluent elite. The homes were large, by Balkan standards, built with breathing room between them, walls dividing neighbors and accentuating the distinction of the neighborhood from Nicosia's standard residential press. If the abodes were something less than mansions, if they offered less than total privacy, at least their tenants had escaped the teeming warrens of the lower classes.

Sarkis had a prime location, with his house set back away from traffic and screened by olive trees. The wrought iron gates were closed across a gravel driveway leading to his door. The grounds were relatively small—two acres, more or less—but that spelled status for a city dweller. And, the Executioner was quick to note, it also gave the home team ample opportunity to lay a trap.

If Bolan had an edge, it had to be surprise. Makarios couldn't be certain he was still alive. At worst the pusher would suspect a foul-up, but he'd be hoping for the best. He might be reassured by Sarkis, or the Lebanese might kick his ass for running under fire. Whichever way it went, they wouldn't have the time to mount a new offensive now.

He found the dealer's telephone connection, scrambled halfway up the pole, and used his vantage point to scan the grounds. No foot patrols were visible, and Bolan took his chances, squeezing off two silenced rounds to clip the cable. That accomplished, he reversed directions, scaled the six-foot wall and hesitated long enough to whistle for the nonexistent dogs before he dropped inside.

He found the first guard urinating on some ornamental shrubs, and solved his bladder problem with a single round behind one ear. A second man, closer to the house, was lighting up a cigarette when Bolan helped him kick the habit with a slug dispatched from skin-touch range. The smoker had an Uzi slung across his shoulder, with a pair of extra magazines tucked through his belt, and Bolan claimed them as the spoils of war.

The odds were looking better all the time.

He circled wide around the large three-story house, approaching from the rear. Lights burned behind a number of the windows, but he met no more sentries on the last leg of his trek. The blinds were drawn upstairs, and no one moved behind the downstairs windows as he left the cover of the trees, advancing in a rush across the strip of manicured lawn. Tall, sliding doors gave access to the house from a veranda, and he tried them, startled to discover that they weren't locked.

Chalk up another fumble for the opposition.

Bolan slipped inside and closed the sliding door behind him, leading with his Uzi, feeling slightly foolish as he got the drop on half a dozen empty chairs. It was a smallish, casual dining room, illuminated dimly by a pair of fixtures mounted on the wall. The overheads were dark, the table bare. Connecting doors to Bolan's right and dead ahead were closed.

He crossed the dining room and tried the right-hand door for starters, finding that it opened on the kitchen. Stainless steel and polished copper gleamed from racks above a good-sized range, reflecting tiny images of Bolan as he scanned the empty room. A double-door refrigerator hummed to life as Bolan made his exit, moving on.

Beyond the second door he had his choice of left or right, along a corridor with paintings on the walls and thick shag carpet underfoot. The lights and stairs were to his left, and Bolan ventured off in that direction, following the Uzi, eyes and ears alert to any warning signals of impending danger.

Like the gunner on the stairs.

The guy was halfway down, descending silently, when Bolan crossed his field of vision. The discovery was simultaneous, or nearly so, and the Executioner saw his adversary reaching for a pistol as he swung the captured Uzi up and into target acquisition. There would be no time to switch in favor of his side arm, with its silencer, and he was dead unless he stopped the gunner's play.

So be it.

Bolan stroked the trigger of his submachine gun, ripping off a short, precision burst that stitched his enemy across the chest and put him down without a whimper.

Somewhere overhead, a startled voice was shouting questions, rallying the troops, and Bolan knew he had no time to spare. All hope of a surprise forgotten, literally shot to hell, he started up the stairs.

"THIS WAY."

Makarios glanced back at Sarkis, saw him pointing to the left, and veered in that direction, covering the empty hallway with his Walther automatic. They were safe, or should be, on the topmost floor, but he didn't believe in taking chances where his safety was concerned.

Below them on the second level of the house, a burst of automatic fire revealed that Sarkis's men had found the enemy. Makarios felt dizzy from the rush of questions swirling in his mind. How many raiders were there? Were they cronies of Belasko's? Had they somehow followed him without his knowledge?

If not, then it could only mean that Sarkis was the target. The thought was reassuring, until Makarios remembered his position. He'd doubtless be mistaken for a member of the Sarkis household, either guest or staff, and from the sound of things downstairs, the raiders meant to leave no witnesses behind. By running to Rashid, he'd unwittingly become a target in the shooting gallery.

The stairs were twenty feet in front of them, guarded by a solitary gunman who stood on the landing. Gunfire echoed in the stairwell, and as Makarios watched, a stray round clipped the banister, diverted from its course, and struck the ceiling overhead. A stream of dust and plaster filtered down, then petered out and stopped.

"Your place is here," Sarkis informed him, nodding toward the landing and its solitary guard. It took a moment for Makarios to realize that he was being left behind.

"Where are you going?"

"I have calls to make. Razmara must be warned."

"But, I—"

"Stay here!" the Lebanese commanded in a tone that caused Makarios to wince. "You needn't be afraid this time. My soldiers will protect you."

Sarkis turned and stalked away before Makarios could formulate an answer. Fury brought the color to his cheeks, and when he turned around, the solitary gunner shifted his eyes away from an examination of the man his master had humiliated.

Balancing the Walther in a sweaty palm, he moved to stand against the railing, listening to sounds of combat from the second floor. As if on cue, the gunfire faltered and died. Could it be over? Did the sudden lull spell victory or death? How long before a frightened neighbor called police?

Not long.

He jumped, surprised, as shooting suddenly erupted on the floor below. The gunman at his side regarded Makarios with a look of thinly veiled contempt, then turned his full attention in the direction of the stairwell. Stepping closer to the rail, the young man raised his submachine gun, braced the stock against his shoulder, covering the stairs.

Below, a gunman—one of those employed by Sarkis—hit the stairs full tilt, his face contorted by exertion. Halfway up, he turned to fire a parting shot and lost his balance, nearly falling as he lurched against the banister. Before he could recover, half a dozen rounds of automatic gunfire ripped through him and punched him backward in a lifeless sprawl.

The young man at his elbow cursed, but held his ground. Makarios had seen enough, and he ignored a second curse that was directed at his back as he retreated. Surely there was somewhere he could hide, with all these empty rooms. And where had Sarkis gone? He must have reached Razmara by this time. How long could warnings take?

He tried the first door, found it locked and veered across the hall. This time the knob turned easily beneath his hand, and Makarios stuck his head inside the bedroom, frightened at the thought of running into Sarkis. Theoretically an equal of the Lebanese, Makarios knew Sarkis could be unpredictable and violent in a crisis situation. If he witnessed Spyros in the act of disobeying his command . . .

The room was empty.

Hesitating on the threshold, Makarios turned in time to see the young man on the landing die. He didn't hear the fatal shots, but witnessed their result: a spray of crimson from a head wound, and the gunner twisting, falling, holding down the trigger of his weapon as he melted to the floor.

Makarios was torn between reaction and retreat. If he was quick enough, he might be able to surprise the enemy while they were vulnerable on the staircase. On the other hand, he still had time to find himself a sanctuary— underneath the bed, a closet, anything—before the raiders reached his floor.

He split the difference, crouching in the doorway with his gun arm braced against the wall, his sights trained on the landing. He had seven rounds and one spare magazine before he was defenseless. Could he stop them all? Could he stop one?

The dealer offered up a prayer to long-forgotten gods and settled down to wait.

THE UZI'S LAST SIX ROUNDS had gone to kill a gunner on the stairs, and Bolan knew he had no time to cast about for other magazines. They would be waiting for him on the floor above—Makarios and Sarkis at the very least—and any stalling now would only let them plan a better ambush.

Bolan dropped the empty submachine gun and drew his Beretta as he started for the stairs. Without a stun grenade or two, there was no easy way to do it. He'd have to take the staircase any way he could, and that meant dropping anyone who tried to stop him.

How many hostile guns? It was the question you could never really answer, going in without a recon, but he had no options left. It was the stairs or nothing, and he hadn't come this far to turn back empty-handed.

Bolan visualized his move and then made it, pounding up the stairs and past the fallen gunner's body, twisting as he ran to bring the landing under fire. He'd been ready for a firing squad, prepared to kill as many as he could before they cut him down, and he was startled to behold a single lookout, staring down the barrel of a compact submachine gun.

The warrior triggered two quick rounds before his adversary had a chance to fire. The shooter's head snapped back, and impact drove him off the rail, his weapon spraying walls and ceiling as he fell. More cautious now, expecting the appearance of a backup gunner, Bolan tried to cover both the landing and the stairs behind him as he climbed.

He took the last three steps in a determined lunge and threw himself across the landing, rolling into touchdown as a pistol opened up with rapid, close-range fire. The sniper had a precious edge, but he was firing carelessly, like something from a grade B Hollywood production, and his haste gave Bolan time to aim a well-placed double punch.

He recognized Makarios in profile as the dealer fell. No other weapons joined the party, and he scuttled over to the doorway where Makarios lay on his back, his arms flung out, red blotches soaking through his shirt. The guy was fading fast, but he was conscious. Bolan slipped a hand beneath his head and lifted him so he could breathe a little easier.

"Where's Sarkis?"

Was the dealer trying to respond, or merely grimacing in pain? It hardly mattered, for the light went out behind his eyes as Bolan watched and he became a deadweight in the soldier's hands.

That made it door-to-door, and Bolan started with the closest one at hand. The lock surrendered to a flying kick, and Bolan crossed the threshold in a crouch, retreating just as swiftly from the empty storage room. He checked another pair of bedrooms, getting nowhere fast, ears straining for the wail of sirens that would force him to evacuate.

The fourth door opened outward like a closet. It was locked, and Bolan cracked the mechanism with a silenced round before he whipped it open, stepping back to cover the enclosure from an angle.

Stairs.

He felt a burning in his gut, the knowledge that his major quarry might have already slipped away.

Descending into darkness, Bolan kept his automatic leveled, ready for a surprise at any moment. It was possible he might have missed his prey, that Sarkis could be hiding somewhere on the floor above, but he'd learned to trust his instincts under fire. His gut was telling him that the dealer would attempt to slip away while Makarios and the home guard took the heat.

What kind of lead would Sarkis have? If he'd bailed out at Bolan's first encounter with the troops downstairs, he'd be free and clear by now. The soldier's only hope lay in confusion, indecision and delay. Makarios would certainly have been a factor slowing Sarkis down.

How much?

The stairs ran out, and Bolan faced another door. Ground floor or basement? He tried the knob and found the door unlocked. He took a long, slow breath, expelled it softly, counting down the doomsday numbers in his mind. Leaning forward in a crouch, he pushed off.

The first shot gouged a tunnel in the doorjamb, several inches to the right of Bolan's face. He felt the sting of flying splinters, ducked and rolled before a second-round correction drilled the space where he'd been standing. As the floor came up to meet him, the warrior had a brief impression of the room: acoustic tiles on walls and ceilings, a fluorescent fixture overhead, a makeshift operating table in the middle of the floor, the darting figure just behind it, angling for another shot.

The gunfire echoed loud in Bolan's ears, confined within the soundproof chamber. Bolan squeezed off silenced rounds in answer, striking sparks as one slug struck the stainless steel operating table, veering off to drill the wall. He kept himself in motion, scrambling around the table as his adversary circled clockwise, like some lethal parody of a lecher chasing his secretary around her desk.

It had to end, and swiftly. On an impulse, Bolan changed direction, veering counterclockwise, taking Sarkis by surprise. For something like a heartbeat, they were face-to-face, their weapons leveled, fingers tightening on triggers.

Bolan got there first, with three rounds fired so rapidly they lifted Sarkis off his feet, the dealer's single shot exploding harmlessly in space. He fell against the wall and slithered down into a seated posture, leaving bloody skid marks in his wake. His eyes were open, locked upon a private view of hell.

The operating table captured Bolan's full attention now. Its occupant was bagged for transport, lumpy and misshapen in a giant burlap sack that was discolored with his seeping blood. Before he pulled the drawstring, Bolan knew what he would find inside the sack, and yet he had no choice.

The battered face of Nikos Kiprianou was relaxed in death, released from the ungodly pain that had consumed his final hours. Bolan pulled the burlap back to scrutinize the other damage, feeling instantaneous regret that he couldn't raise Sarkis from the dead and kill the bastard one more time, with feeling.

How much had the dealer learned from Nikos? When it came to that, how much had Nikos really known? He was Bolan's contact in the embassy, of course, and that would certainly have been enough to seal his fate—and Bolan's—with the syndicate. Had Sarkis telephoned the news to his associates outside of Cyprus? Was Hussein Razmara on the run?

The young man on the table had absorbed prodigious punishment before he died. Assuming Sarkis hadn't carried out the mutilation for his personal enjoyment, that would indicate that Nikos was resistant to interrogation, holding out as long as possible before he broke. How long? It had been nearly seven hours since they parted, Nikos dropping Bolan off at his hotel. Allowing time for several contacts, with the ultimate betrayal, there had still been ample opportunity for Sarkis to alert his partners.

Time.

It was the final enemy, impervious to any weapon in the soldier's arsenal. When time ran out, the game was over. Simple. No debate and no discussion.

Bolan tugged the burlap back in place and left the two dead men together. The police would sort it out or not, depending on their own involvement with the smuggling operation. The warrior had no interest in their progress, rounding up the small fry. He was bent on larger game, and one of his intended targets still remained at large in Nicosia.

He had nothing to lose, except his life.

CHAPTER TWELVE

Hussein Razmara's home lay east of Nicosia in a landscape marked by rolling hills. The Shiite spokesman cherished solitude, avoiding the conspicuous display of wealth that Sarkis and Makarios had cultivated while alive. From everything that Bolan knew about Razmara, he was dedicated to the revolution in his heart and mind. If anything, he may have been more zealous than the ayotollahs in his observation of the strictest Muslim doctrines. His fanaticism made him doubly dangerous, an enemy to reckon with.

The Executioner had taken time to arm himself before he left the Sarkis household, picking up another submachine gun and a quantity of extra magazines from fallen sentries. He was still in his blacksuit, with his jacket covering the shoulder rig, the SMG and ammo clips laid out beside him. As he left town, he made a point of scrupulously following the traffic laws, aware that any routine stop would quickly escalate into disaster.

The police would be at Sarkis's now, and if the Lebanese hadn't found time to warn Razmara of his danger—if the dealer recognized the danger—the authorities might know enough to make a call themselves. A few of them at least were certain to be on the pad with Sarkis and Makarios. The sudden termination of their off-the-record contract might forestall a tip to the Iranian, but Bolan wouldn't count on any favors.

All he needed was a chance, one shot, before he took his act across the water into Lebanon. Loose ends on Cyprus would compound the danger in the second phase of his assignment, and he knew that if Razmara was allowed to live, he would establish new connections by the time the week was out. It wasn't Bolan's mission to disrupt the pipeline; rather, he'd been commissioned to destroy it at the source. It would defeat his purpose if the Nicosia outlet should remain in operation while he made his run against the Bekaa hardmen.

Bolan saw the lights before he came within a mile of the Razmara compound. Pulling off the road, he stashed the rental in a grove of trees and locked it, trusting isolation to protect his wheels from thieves and vandals. Carrying the submachine gun and the extra magazines, he took a shortcut overland and saved himself a quarter mile. In minutes Bolan stood atop a hill behind Razmara's house, examining the layout of the grounds.

The lights, he saw, were concentrated at the single entry gate, four hundred yards away, and in a ring around the house. Where Sarkis had preferred an opulent three-story home, Razmara occupied a simple ranch-style, flanked by smaller quarters for his staff. The Shiite's home away from Teheran was drab, flat-roofed, with no exterior adornment. On the roof, a solitary rifleman kept watch—or dozed, it was impossible to say—from a position at the northeast corner of the house. No other guards were visible from Bolan's vantage point, and he spent several moments waiting, on the chance that roving foot patrols might show themselves.

It looked too easy.

Even if Razmara had no inkling of the fate that had befallen Sarkis and Makarios, he was a man with countless enemies, whose life had been in danger, one way or another, since the era of the Shah. A veteran of the survival game, Razmara wouldn't leave his home unguarded ... but he might attempt to cultivate an innocent facade, thus luring assassins into killing range.

The soldier waited several moments more, then scaled the wall behind Razmara's house at a position where the rooftop sentry's view was theoretically obscured by standing trees. There might be sensors on the grounds, or other personal security devices Bolan couldn't pick out in advance, but he'd have to take his chances.

Using darkness as his cover, Bolan climbed the nearest tree until he reached a level even with the sentry on Razmara's roof. The man still faced away from Bolan, sitting with his shoulders hunched, a rifle braced between his knees. Again he didn't move while Bolan watched, and it seemed probable that he was dozing at his post. A bullet would have made his sleep eternal, but the range was better than one hundred feet, too far to trust the strange Beretta and its silencer for guaranteed precision work.

He slithered down again, lost contact with the rooftop gunner as he hit the ground, and spent another moment verifying the apparent absence of patrols. An entry to the house meant passing underneath the floodlights, but the lights would only be a problem if Razmara's men were watching. So far Bolan saw no evidence that they were on the job. He should be safe enough, unless a battery of gunmen lay in wait behind the darkened windows at the rear.

Again, no options.

Bolan used the shadows where he could and took his time, alert for anything from mines to sensors. On the far perimeter of lighted ground, he hesitated for another moment, secured his liberated SMG and made his move.

The killing shot might come from anywhere, at any moment. If the combat scuttlebutt was true, if he was lucky, Bolan wouldn't hear it coming. One clean shot, perhaps a burst like sudden thunder, and he'd be dead before he hit the ground.

His eyes were more or less adjusted to the floodlights by the time he reached the house and crouched against its western wall. No battle cries or clamoring alarms broke the silence. If anyone had marked his rush, they'd be waiting for the target to move closer, where a killing shot was guaranteed.

Close by, no more than twenty feet to Bolan's right, a covered carport offered sanctuary from the glaring lights. He worked his way along the wall and let his pent-up breath escape when he was safely under cover.

Safe? He forced a smile. It was a relative position in the hellgrounds.

The carport sheltered a Mercedes, a Jeep and a pair of all-terrain vehicles that Bolan assumed would be used for patrol of the grounds in the daylight. Two of the walls were bare; the third and nearest supported a workbench, littered with mechanic's tools. Bolan slipped around the ATVs and tried a door connecting with the house, but it was locked. He doubled back to search, found the tools he needed and began to strip the lock.

He worked as quietly as possible, aware that noise would make no difference if the enemy was waiting for him on the other side. It took a moment to defeat the lock, then Bolan had it, laying down his tools and palming the Beretta as he eased across the threshold.

WHEN HE HAD the opportunity, Hussein Razmara liked to get a full eight hours' sleep. Since he believed in rising with the sun, beginning every day with a praise to God and the Prophet, he would often be in bed by nine or ten o'clock. A man whose passions were directed toward fulfillment of the revolutionary dream, he kept no woman to distract him in the night.

All humans dream, but the Iranian knew he was special. It was rare that he couldn't recall at least one vision from the night before, and he recorded them in diaries bound with leather, noting their significance, interpreting the symbols as befitted a man of piety and wisdom. On the very rare occasions when he dreamed of sex, Razmara knew that he was being tested, and he willed the images away. More often he dreamed epic battles, with the infidel in flight before the righteous sword of God, wielded by himself.

This night he dreamed the subjugation of America. Razmara led a fighting column through the streets of New York City, rolling over spotty opposition in the capital of U.S. Zionism, pleased to note that most of the Americans he met were docile, hollow-eyed and passive. They were roused to action only when their drugs didn't arrive on time, and then they turned upon one another in a suicidal frenzy. It was priceless, watching a society of infidels collapse before his very eyes.

Razmara jerked awake, with automatic fire ringing in his ears. His elbow banged against the nightstand as he groped to find the lamp, and caution stayed his hand. Instead of turning on the light, he reached inside the nightstand's single drawer and found the automatic pistol that he kept there for emergencies.

The sounds of firing close at hand could only mean his enemies had tracked him to his home. But who? How many? Thirteen months before the late Ayatolleh Khomeini rose to power, half a dozen gunmen from SAVAK— the Shah's gestapo—had attempted to assassinate Razmara in Beirut. Two lost their lives in an exchange of gunfire with his guards, who also died, and he had killed the other four himself, sustaining only superficial wounds. He knew the face of death, and he wasn't afraid.

It would be difficult to dress in haste without a light, and he refused to give himself away by turning on the lamp. Razmara left his muslin nightshirt on as he prepared to meet the enemy. His slippers lay beside the bed, and he stepped into them, benefiting from routine.

His pistol was a Chinese copy of the Russian Tokarev, a sturdy weapon that Razmara favored for its weight and stopping power. He could drop a man at thirty paces with a single shot, and any armed encounters in the house were bound to be fought at closer range.

Razmara hesitated at the bedroom door, a sudden thought delaying him. Should he call Sarkis and Makarios and warn them of the danger? There was nothing they could do to help him now. If gunmen were inside the house, the issue would be settled swiftly, one way or another. Still, there was a possibility that the attack might be related to their common business, and the others might be facing danger, too.

It was inconsequential. Time was of the essence, and if Sarkis or Makarios was under fire, neither would pause to take his call. If they were safe, a few more moments of delay would make no difference. Either way, Razmara had to save himself before he could be any help to others.

Carefully he cracked the bedroom door and scanned a wedge of dimly lighted corridor outside. The sounds of gunfire had drawn closer, but the echoes were deceptive, muffled and distorted by the carpeting and walls. He slipped outside and closed the door behind him, looking like a derelict with unkempt hair and beard, the nightshirt hanging to his knees, pale legs below. He cocked the automatic pistol, held it ready as he moved with shuffling steps along the corridor.

Razmara's enemies had tried to kill him more than once, and he was still alive, still fighting for the holy cause. Assassins faced him at their peril, used to dealing with the infidels who hid themselves and trembled in the face of danger. Razmara feared no man alive, including those whom he regarded with devout respect.

He hesitated at a turning in the corridor. Around the corner, from the general direction of the dining room and parlor, gunfire hammered out a terse, staccato cadence. Angry voices cursed in Farsi, rasping out commands, but he couldn't surmise the progress of the battle from a distance. He'd have to see it for himself.

Prepared for anything, Hussein Razmara edged around the corner, following the sounds of combat.

AFTER GAINING ENTRY to the house, Mack Bolan found himself inside a utility room. There was no lock on the connecting door, and he followed his Beretta through a spacious pantry, checking out the kitchen as he passed. Razmara's home might not be opulent compared to that of Sarkis, but his kitchen would supply a fair-sized troop of riflemen at need. Moving forward, the Executioner could only hope those troops weren't in residence.

He checked the dining room, and had the parlor in his sights before he met the opposition. Breezing through an open doorway, speaking softly to avoid disturbing sleepers in the house, two gunmen froze at sight of the man in black, wasting precious seconds as they tried to cope with the disruption of their day-to-day routine. They both had Czech-made Skorpions, slung for comfort rather than convenience, and the guy on Bolan's left was quicker off the mark at swinging his around.

A muffled cough from the Beretta, and the sentry staggered, spouting crimson from a blowhole in his chest. The partner bought himself a scrap of time by dodging sideways, triggering a wild, reflexive burst before he had a chance to aim. The nearest bullets came within a yard of Bolan, wreaking havoc with a china hutch behind him, and the Beretta answered with a deadly one-two punch from twenty feet.

The gunner lurched and lost his balance, giving up the machine pistol as he tried to catch himself, too late. A high-backed chair went with him when he fell, and Bolan plugged a mercy round behind one ear.

The shooter's dying burst hadn't been wasted. Bolan heard the household come alive, doors slamming open, startled voices shouting questions. He was entering the parlor when a group of sleepy-looking soldiers challenged him. Their automatic weapons seemed incongruous with baggy cotton underwear.

Bolan holstered the Beretta, shifting to his captured submachine gun as the hostiles opened fire. The racket numbed his ears, but he was covered for the moment, with the sofa's heavy frame and padding soaking up incoming rounds.

To Bolan's left there was a fireplace, separated from the couch by several yards of open floor. An easy chair stood on his right, upholstered in material that matched the sofa, with another couch beyond. The room was furnished to accommodate at least a score of visitors, and Bolan glimpsed the possibility of his survival in Razmara's hospitality.

The move would take precision timing, and he had to shave the odds a bit if he was going to succeed. He waited for a lull, the opposition either pausing to reload or send a scout ahead, and when he burst from cover, Bolan gave it everything he had.

They were prepared to flank him with a pincers move, and Bolan caught them in the open, lunging from his place behind the couch, the submachine gun rattling away at almost point-blank range. The nearest gunner took a burst across the chest and went down in a sprawl, his comrades frozen for a heartbeat in the face of armed resistance. Bolan drilled another where he stood, then he ducked behind the easy chair and out of sight, the three survivors scrambling for cover and returning fire in ragged bursts.

He let them cut the chair to pieces, scuttling behind the couch and along its length while they were wasting precious rounds. The body of the first man down was now within his reach, blood soaking through the simple undershirt that was his final combat uniform. Before he left his room, the guy had thrown his daily combat rig across one shoulder, with its pouch for extra magazines, and Bolan offered a silent prayer of thanks to the universe as he saw two grenades clipped on the harness.

Reaching out with both hands, Bolan grabbed the dead man's feet and pulled him closer, unhooking the grenades. One of the opposition saw his move and shouted to the others, streams of automatic fire converging on the sofa.

Too late.

He pulled the safety pins on both grenades, pitched one and then the other, huddling for cover behind the couch as the lethal eggs hatched. Shrapnel exploded against the walls and ceiling, loosing gritty streams of plaster from above. A strangled scream wound down to nothing on the far side of the room, and Bolan rose from cover, cautiously, to check the damage.

Reeling through the haze of smoke and dust, a tattered scarecrow wobbled into the warrior's line of fire. One naked arm was hanging by a flap of skin, the other raised to press a hand against the gunner's bloody face. As Bolan watched, the dying man collided with a piece of furniture and toppled over on his face.

The Executioner heard reinforcements coming, and he moved to intercept them, staking out the parlor entrance as he fed his liberated SMG another magazine. How many guns this time? And would the sounds of battle summon others from the barracks out back? He felt time slipping through his fingers, concentrating on Razmara and the next phase of his mission in the Middle East.

He counted seven men, all jammed together in the hallway, drawing closer. It was close enough to get him started, and Bolan let them have a burst in greeting, dropping two before they had a chance to recognize the danger. He kept firing as the others went to ground, a couple of them answering with rounds that chipped the wall and doorframe overhead.

Not good enough. He had to flush them out and kill them in the open, before Razmara slipped away. The soldier fired off half a magazine to pin them down, then scuttled backward to the parlor's fireplace, searching briefly and recovering a can of lighter fluid from the mantelpiece. Returning to his post, he snagged a scrap of undershirt from one of his assailants, dousing it with fluid, knotting it around the can to make a wick.

His disposable lighter worked the first time, and he lighted the scrap of cloth, flames licking at his hands as he wound up to pitch. It was an easy toss, despite the wise-ass gunner who got off a burst as Bolan showed himself. The makeshift firebomb dropped behind his adversaries, bounced along the carpet, and erupted as the fumes caught fire inside.

One gunner took the worst of it and staggered to his feet, arms beating at the flames around him, and the others bolted, firing wildly as they broke from cover, two men peeling off in each direction. Bolan met them with a string of short, precision bursts that swept them off their feet and scattered them around the entryway. He used the remnants of his magazine to halt the human torch's breathless screams.

One clip remained, and he snapped it into the receiver of his submachine gun as he rose, a silent specter on the field of death. Behind the barrier of smoke and flame, he caught a hint of movement, drawing closer, and he braced himself to meet a new attack. How many more would he be forced to kill before he had a clear shot at Hussein Razmara?

Bolan didn't recognize his target at a glance. The Shiite mouthpiece hadn't dressed for company—had scarcely dressed at all, in fact—but the warrior saw that he had found himself a gun. The knee-length nightshirt didn't slow Razmara as he approached the flames. Unflinching, he passed through them, stepping wide around the bodies of his fallen bodyguards, intent on closing with his enemy.

The Executioner stood fast and waited, fingering the trigger of his submachine gun. At a range of forty feet, Razmara swept his pistol up and fired a hasty round that whispered close to Bolan's ear. He kept on firing as the submachine gun stuttered in response, a line of crimson blotches sketching abstract patterns on his nightshirt. Dying on his feet, he triggered two more rounds before he toppled backward in his tracks.

Retreating through the smoky parlor, Bolan checked his track for late arrivals at the party, meeting no more opposition by the time he reached the carport. Using caution as he left the shadows, the Executioner braced himself to face the rooftop gunner, but the guy was gone, his station empty. Bolan wrote him off, assuming that the rifleman had made his way inside and died there, fighting for his master.

His work was finished on the island, and the time had come for him to face the greater enemy. If Nicosia had been hairy, Lebanon was shaping up to be a killer, and the Executioner had lost his cover in the bargain.

Hadn't he?

A notion came to Bolan as he left the lights behind and found his solace in the darkness. It would take some thought, and it was far from foolproof, but it might be worth a try.

Sleep first, and then he'd apply himself to the solution of his problem, working out the bugs. And in the morning it was time to call Grimaldi.

For the next leg of his journey, Bolan would be needing wings.

CHAPTER THIRTEEN

Twelve hours after Bolan's raid on Cyprus, Bashir Moheden stood waiting for his houseguests to arrive. The meeting had a single topic on its brief agenda.

The news from Nicosia had begun to filter in at daylight. First a member of the metropolitan police had dialed his private number to inform him that Sarkis and Makarios were dead, as well as a dozen of their men. Detectives had no motive and no clue to the identities of their assailants.

Immediately Moheden had tried to call Hussein Razmara, but the line was out of order. Trembling, he'd placed a most uncustomary call to the police, connecting with his toady after several minutes of listening to empty air. The Lebanese voiced his suspicions, made suggestions, and a pair of uniforms had been dispatched to check Razmara's compound in the hills outside of town. An hour later, Moheden received another call and learned what he had dreaded.

The other calls had been a matter of necessity. Moheden would have liked to meet with his associates at once, but Bakhtiar was holed up in the Bekaa Valley. Time would be required for him to make the journey overland. The Lebanese understood that Bakhtiar would have to bring an escort this time. Twenty men, perhaps?

In fact, the extra time was beneficial, granting him an opportunity to sort the puzzle pieces in his mind and try to find an answer for himself. Who wished to hurt him, and

why? There were competitors, of course. For all of his
success, Moheden hadn't managed to monopolize the sale
of drugs in Lebanon or Cyprus. Ticking off the names of
his important rivals, he could think of no one with the
cunning, strength and nerve to kill all three of his associates in Nicosia. One or two, perhaps. But three? Until that
morning, Bashir Moheden would have believed such an
event to be impossible.

Dismissing local enemies, his mind leaped back to the
American connection and the stranger Sarkis had reported only yesterday. What was his name? Belmondo?
No, Belasko! First name, Michael. Hasty calls to the
United States had turned up nothing in the way of useful
information, but Makarios suspected that the stranger—or
his sponsors stateside—might have been responsible for the
Silvestri murder. Another case of gangland competition,
with the loser going out of business for eternity.

The sum of thirty million dollars had been mentioned,
and Moheden wondered now if it had been some kind of
lure to trap Makarios, then Sarkis and finally Razmara.
How? As best the Lebanese knew, his men in Nicosia
hadn't briefed Razmara on their contact with Belasko.
Moheden hadn't forbidden them to do so, but Makarios
and Sarkis shared his views on Shiite temperament, and
they'd certainly have tried to close the deal before inviting
the Iranian to ruin everything with talk of vengeance for
the murders in New York.

Where was Belasko now?

It had been nearly ten o'clock before Moheden got his
final call from the police in Nicosia. There had been three
shootouts, altogether—first, a spot of trouble at a sex club
owned and operated by Makarios left six men dead, with
several others nursing minor wounds; a second battle, at
the Sarkis home had killed Makarios and Sarkis, plus a

number of the men employed by Sarkis as his body-guards. The Lebanese had been discovered in a secret, soundproofed room, beside the mutilated body of a young man who was obviously tortured prior to death. The latter victim was a Cypriot whose name was meaningless to Moheden.

Finally the unknown raiders had attacked Hussein Razmara's compound east of Nicosia, slaughtering at least a dozen of the Shiite's men and killing off Razmara in the bargain. All the dead had been identified, including Cypriots, Iranians and Lebanese. There had been no Americans, no strangers, in the lot.

And what had happened to Belasko?

Two scenarios ran parallel across Moheden's mind, a double feature playing simultaneously. In the first, Belasko was a potential customer, perhaps responsible for killing Anthony Silvestri, eager now to strike a bargain of his own. The other cast him as a villain—what Americans would call a "ringer"—sent to wreak deliberate havoc on the pipeline and destroy Moheden's empire if he could.

But why? Dispatched by whom?

Again, the operation was beyond his local competition, even if they had been able to dismiss their petty differences and work together for a change. The locals had no contacts in America, and Moheden had made no enemies in the United States.

Or had he?

The Silvestri case came back to haunt him. By the simple act of choosing one distributor, had he created opposition on a lethal scale? Would it have been more prudent to approach the Mafia's Commission, as a body, and allow the capos to select participants themselves? Had his attempt to cinch a deal ensured Silvestri's death and brought this havoc down upon himself?

The Lebanese's train of thought was interrupted as the first of his two guests arrived. For once, he didn't wear an artificial smile as he went out to play the role of proper host.

AHMAD HALABY WASN'T frightened—at the moment. He hadn't been seriously frightened since the spring of 1983, when the Israelis sent a pair of Phantom jets to strafe and rocket his command post on the outskirts of Beirut. Surviving the experience had taught him that a man could live through anything if he was cautious and he kept his wits about him.

Bashir Moheden had spared him the specifics when they spoke by telephone. There had been trouble with the Cyprus operation, and another meeting was required. The telephone couldn't be trusted. They must gather and discuss a means of salvaging their network before it was too late.

Halaby often hatched his best schemes under pressure, as when he had been compelled to leave the PLO and carry on his fight without support from Arafat's well-heeled connections. With his back against the wall, Halaby had devised a string of hostage incidents that netted major ransoms for his movement, swelling coffers to the point that he could field a modest army in his war against the Zionists. Of course, there had been only minor victories so far, but with the money earned from his participation in the Bekaa project, he'd launch a new offensive, carrying his fight around the world.

The Palestinian was a cautious man by nature, and a part of that was knowing when to ask a question, what to ask and when to let it go. He hadn't grilled Moheden for the details of the Cyprus problem, knowing it would eventually be explained to him. A surreptitious call to friends in Nicosia filled in Halaby on all the major details, and he recognized the loss in monetary terms, but still he wasn't worried. Cyprus was another world, and violence in the streets of Nicosia didn't phase him. He had buried far too many comrades for the deaths of Sarkis and Makarios to break his heart. As for Razmara, well, the Shiite—while ostensibly a coreligionist—had also been a zealot and a pompous ass.

The violence might not touch him, but Halaby took no chances. For the present journey, he'd brought a second vehicle, more bodyguards and weapons. Just in case. His host's villa was secure, in theory, but so had been Razmara's compound. While their enemies remained at large and anonymous, Halaby's common sense demanded that he cover all contingencies, leave nothing in the hands of fate.

He was alert, as always, to the first sight of Moheden's seaside villa—tile and stucco baking in the midday heat, with sweeping marble steps and pillars that evoked fond memories of Greece. The drug lord had installed the blessed air-conditioning and sauna bath, repaired the swimming pool and modernized the ancient plumbing. He had also fortified the grounds against attack, but one could never be *too* careful.

Standing on the marble steps, Bashir Moheden made a somber figure. There was no trace of the old familiar smile as he came down to greet Halaby.

"I appreciate your prompt response, Ahmad."

The Palestinian dismissed his partner's gratitude and nodded toward the villa. "Bakhtiar?"

"Not yet."

Halaby raised an eyebrow and frowned. Over eighteen months of meetings, the Iranians were always first on hand. It had become tradition, a running joke among the

others, but Hussein Razmara's death had evidently
changed the rules. Halaby wondered whether Bakhtiar
would come at all. Would the incidents in Nicosia doom
them to a fratricidal war among themselves?

The Palestinian didn't like the prospect of a struggle
with the Shiites. Bakhtiar and company were single-
minded, even mindless, in their dedication to the Islamic
revolution. The former Iranian leader's eight-year conflict with Iraq had been a case in point, with Muslims
spilling the blood of other Muslims while Israel sat by on
the sidelines, laughing. Such mentalities were unpredictable and, therefore, doubly dangerous.

"He knows about Razmara?"

If Moheden was surprised that Halaby knew what had
happened, it didn't register. "I would imagine so," he answered.

"Will he come?"

"I think so. Yes."

"And otherwise?"

The Lebanese stared off across the manicured lawn and
shrugged.

"Then," he suggested, "we will have to find another
way."

MIR REZA BAKHTIAR SAID nothing during the drive to
meet his business partners. His companions in the limousine knew better than to interrupt his thoughts with idle
chatter. They were busy studying the landscape, watching
out for enemies in front, and making certain they hadn't
been followed out of Tripoli.

One car had fallen in behind them on the last leg of their
journey, and Bakhtiar had insisted that his driver slow to
a crawl and force the other car to pass. His men were
armed with automatic weapons, ready at the gun ports

when the small sedan edged past them in the other lane, the driver glaring daggers. Bakhtiar permitted him the minor victory, and they didn't return to cruising speed until the other car had faded out of sight.

It was the first time in two years that Bakhtiar had made this trip alone. His gunmen didn't count, as they could never share his plans and secret thoughts. Razmara had been different, almost an equal in his dedication to the cause, and Bakhtiar had grown accustomed to his company on trips to visit Moheden. It would have been inaccurate to say that they were friends, and yet . . .

The hint of weakness startled Bakhtiar and made him scowl. The gunners noted his expression and avoided contact with his eyes, aware that Bakhtiar was dangerous at such a time. He'd been known to order executions on impulse, when he wore that look, and it would be a foolish man who risked his anger with a careless glance.

Bashir Moheden had been cryptic on the telephone, refusing to discuss the incidents on Cyprus, but he must have known that Bakhtiar would try to reach his first lieutenant for an update. Several calls had been required before the truth emerged, and Bakhtiar had seen his premonitions realized. The bloodshed in New York had simply been a taste of things to come. Their enemies were drawing closer, claiming further lives along the way.

In Bakhtiar's opinion, it was all a consequence of trusting the Americans. No infidel was ultimately faithful, but Americans were the worst of all. They stabbed each other in the back without a second thought, betrayed their wives and business partners, all the while proclaiming Christ their model of behavior. It had been a gamble, casting middlemen aside to deal with the Americans directly, and despite his acquiescence in the plan—his own attempt to

plant the seeds of revolution in America—it now struck
Bakhtiar that they had been mistaken.

Worse, it crossed his mind that they had been betrayed.

By whom? He meant to answer that himself, and settle
up the score for all his comrades who had fallen. It seemed
unlikely that Moheden or Halaby were responsible, since
they had also suffered losses in the brief, one-sided war,
but anything was possible. While enemies were unidenti-
fied, their motives were a matter of surmise. It would remain for Bakhtiar to learn their names and understand
their reasoning before he ground his adversaries into desert
dust.

The sentries at the villa recognized his car and waved
him through, securing the heavy wrought iron gates behind him. In the limousine, his bodyguards remained alert,
their weapons cocked and ready to respond in the event of
treachery. There might not be enough of them to battle
clear, but each man was a dedicated revolutionary guard
and would force the enemy to pay a fearsome toll before
he gave up his life to God.

His driver parked behind two vehicles surrounded by a
troop of Palestinians, their weapons on conspicuous display. Moheden's sentries were spread out along the driveway, others stationed on the roof and at the corners of the
house, pretending not to watch the new arrivals. They were
casual in the extreme, but there was still a hint of tension
in the air, and Bakhtiar imagined that a timely finger snap
could set the killing wheels in motion.

Bashir Moheden descended the steps to greet his guest,
a simple bow accommodating Bakhtiar's distaste at shaking hands. He made no mention of the obvious, that
Bakhtiar was late by normal standards.

"I'm pleased that you have come," the Lebanese said.
"I trust your trip was uneventful?"

"Perfectly."

He followed his host inside, along familiar corridors, until they reached the conference room. The Shiite took his normal seat, directly opposite Moheden, with the suggestion of a greeting to Ahmad Halaby. Vacant chairs around the room emphasized the message that their numbers had been cut by half since they last met.

Bashir Moheden scrutinized his two surviving partners, scanned the empty seats and cleared his throat.

"Approximately this time, yesterday," he told them, "I received an urgent call from Sarkis."

Sparing no detail, he told them everything: the strange American, his thirty-million-dollar proposition and the hints of personal involvement in Silvestri's murder, the explosive violence that had left their Nicosia operation in a shambles. He felt their eyes upon him as he spoke, but neither of them interrupted.

"And Belasko?" Bakhtiar inquired when Moheden had finished. "What has now become of the American?"

"Inquiries have been made. No trace of him was found at his hotel. An airline reservation has been purchased in his name, from Nicosia to New York, by way of Rome and London, on the day after tomorrow. I suspect he will not fly, but I have people covering the airport just in case."

"You have a photograph of this American?" Halaby asked.

"Unfortunately no." He felt their disapproval and diverted it to others who couldn't protest. "I'm afraid Makarios was lax in his security precautions. Sarkis may have ordered photographs, but they haven't been found."

"Will the police persist in their investigation?"

"For a time, but I anticipate no inconvenience. Evidence will surface, indicating that the triggermen were members of the Turkish People's Liberation Army. Terrorism will be blamed for these attacks on honest, law-abiding residents of Nicosia."

Bakhtiar was frowning through his beard. "And in the meantime? What becomes of our production schedule?"

"Names and faces will be changed," Moheden answered. "Otherwise, the operation will proceed as planned. Makarios wasn't the only businessman in Nicosia. Sarkis and Razmara will be missed, of course, but they can be replaced."

"The revolution must have vengeance for this unprovoked attack."

"Of course. But first we must identify our enemies. It makes no sense to strike off blindly, chasing shadows."

"The American," Halaby offered. "Sarkis didn't trust him, and his disappearance reeks of guilty knowledge. If we find him, he should be interrogated closely."

"*When* we find him," Moheden amended, "I will question him myself. I would suggest, however, that we keep an open mind about his offer while we strive to learn the truth. Silvestri was prepared to pay us eighteen million dollars over two years. If this Belasko is sincere about a thirty-million-dollar figure, he deserves a hearing."

Bakhtiar looked skeptical, a favorite expression worn on nearly all occasions. "I have no faith in coincidence," he said. "This man appears from nowhere, claiming—or implying—that he killed Silvestri in New York. If true, that means he also killed Kassim and Bazargan, but it appears that they have been forgotten."

"I assure you—"

The Shiite forged ahead. "Next we hear that he has thirty million dollars, just for us. Has anybody seen the money? Did Belasko name his sponsors so that we could verify their holdings?"

"He intended to discuss these matters with Makarios last night."

"And so we have the final act. Makarios is dead, with Sarkis and my countryman Razmara. Many of their soldiers have been massacred as well. We find no trace of the American in Nicosia, which suggests that either he's very fortunate, or else he's responsible for our misfortunes."

"You assume his guilt," Moheden said. It didn't come out sounding like a question.

"I suspect that he has much to answer for. Until his sponsors have been named and scrutinized, I can't trust this man on faith."

"There is another possibility," Moheden suggested.

"Which is?"

"Suppose that this American and his supporters *were* responsible for killing Silvestri. Dealers in narcotics kill each other every day. It is a fact of life in the United States. Kassim and Bazargan were caught up in the cross fire, simple casualties of war."

"Go on," Bakhtiar said with obvious reluctance.

"After dealing with the competition in New York, Belasko is dispatched to strike a bargain at the source. Unfortunately members of Silvestri's syndicate—his Family— are hungry for revenge. They know Silvestri's contacts and surmise that Sarkis or Makarios are in collusion with the enemy. Belasko is attempting to conduct his business when the hunters track him down."

"And still he manages to slip away unharmed?" The Iranian didn't sound convinced. "Why kill Razmara? What was he to these imaginary hunters from New York?"

Moheden answered with a question of his own. "Who are the New York Mafia? Sicilians, once removed. For them, revenge isn't a matter of degree. If they believed Makarios and Sarkis were involved in murdering Silvestri, they would certainly respond in kind. Razmara was a known associate, and therefore suspect. His connection with the others was enough to cost his life. As for Belasko... who can say where he's gone, or whether he's still alive?''

"I don't share your faith in strangers."

Biting off the impulse to respond in anger, Moheden replied, ''I merely think that we should wait and see before we launch misguided expeditions for revenge. Our first priority should be establishment of distribution outlets in America, as we agreed from the beginning. Once we know our friends and enemies for certain, we can deal with both accordingly."

"Agreed," Halaby said, preempting Bakhtiar's reply. "A wise man separates his friends and enemies before he kills."

"How long do you propose we wait?" Bakhtiar asked.

"Not long. A few days at the most. In any case, we can't move against Belasko or his people if we don't know who and where they are."

"I'm prepared to wait four days," the Shiite said at last. "If your investigation has produced no evidence by then, I may be forced to make inquiries of my own."

"By all means," Moheden replied. "We seek the truth, not a cover-up."

"Four days," Bakhtiar repeated.

"Four days."

And as Moheden forced a smiled, he wondered whether it would be enough.

CHAPTER FOURTEEN

"You've got the homer?" Jack Grimaldi asked.

"Right here."

"Okay. I wish the damned thing had a range of better than a hundred miles."

Mack Bolan grinned. "What's wrong? Afraid to work in close these days?"

"Oh, that's hilarious." Grimaldi made a sour face. "You should've been a stand-up comic, guy. In fact, I think there's still a chance that you could make it. Let me turn this crate around, and we can work on getting you a spot. I know this little club in Tel Aviv—"

"I'm not anticipating a career move," Bolan told him.

"No, I didn't think you were."

The two-man flight had taken off from Haifa, courtesy of the Israeli military, with a flight plan filed for Lemesos, on Cyprus. Halfway there, Grimaldi took the Cessna down below the normal radar level, veering east to cross the coast of Lebanon between Beirut and Al-Batrun. So far, except for certain startled farmers, no one seemed to be aware of the intrusion. There was only silence on their radio, but Bolan and Grimaldi kept their eyes peeled for a fighter escort, just in case.

The warrior shifted in his seat, weighed down with parachutes and gear essential for survival on the ground in Lebanon. There wasn't room for him to sit up front beside Grimaldi, but he kept in contact with the feisty pilot via mike and headphones.

"Ten," Grimaldi said without enthusiasm, marking off the minutes left until they reached the drop zone.

"Roger."

"Seems to me a couple loads of paraquat could do this job just fine," Grimaldi muttered. "Zap the poppies, put the ranchers out of business. End of story."

"Right. Except you'd have a military incident, for starters, and we'd have to use the scattergun approach—spray everything, including food crops—since we wouldn't get a second chance. Much misery, my friend, and bad press up to the eyeballs."

"Screw the press, okay? You think there won't be one hellacious military incident if someone bags you on the ground? That won't look good for Uncle Sammy."

"It's been taken care of," Bolan told him. "Plausible deniability. The cover story marks me as a free-lance mercenary. If they break that down . . . well, everybody knows that I'm a wild card."

"Damn. That stinks."

"It works," The Executioner replied. "Besides, I hadn't planned on getting caught."

"Like Syria?"

The comment took his mind back to another desert mission in the Middle East, when Bolan had been called upon to infiltrate a cult of assassins based in Syria. On that occasion, Bolan's cover had been blown, and he came close to losing everything before an air strike, with Grimaldi at the point, had saved his life. The memories of Syria were crystal clear that morning as they winged across the desert, but he refused to let them prey upon his mind.

Some thirty-seven hours had elapsed since Bolan walked away from the Razmara compound. He'd been in touch with Jack Grimaldi on the morning after to arrange for transportation, kissing off the airline tickets he'd pur-

chased under the Belasko alias. If anyone was watching for
him at the Nicosia airport, Bolan wished them luck. His
outbound flight had taken off from a secluded, private
airstrip south of town, arranged through Brognola's connections with Mossad, the crack Israeli secret service.

It hadn't been difficult to win cooperation from the
brass in Israel. Bolan's mission was a no-loss situation for
the leadership in Tel Aviv. If he succeeded, and the Bekaa
Valley pipeline was destroyed, it was a telling blow against
embattled Israel's enemies. If he should fail, the government was free to disavow connections with a foreigner who
acted on his own initiative.

"That's five," Grimaldi said. "You want to play it one
more time?"

"No point."

He knew the details of the plan by heart, and talking
through them was a waste of time. His drop zone was an
isolated region on the western outskirts of the Bekaa Valley. Justice's connections in the CIA had made arrangements for a welcoming committee, members of the
Christian underground that waged unceasing war against
Islamic terrorists and the narcotics traders. After touching base, it would be Bolan's job to win the rebels over,
turn them into allies for the short duration of his mission.
If it all worked out, if Bolan managed to survive, Grimaldi would be there to see him safely home.

He spent a moment double-checking his equipment,
starting with the main chute and reserve, the latter
strapped across his chest. His rifle was an AK-47, manufactured by the Soviets and confiscated from a PLO commando in the Gaza Strip. His side arm was the same
untraceable Beretta he'd used in Nicosia, with its silencer
secured in a pocket of his desert camouflage fatigues. Besides the parachutes, he wore a rig of military webbing,

pouches filled with extra magazines for both his guns, a
fighting knife and Russian RGD-5 antipersonnel grenades
secured to his harness. Nothing carried on his person
would connect him with America or Israel if his luck ran
out.

"One minute."

"Right."

He pulled off the headset and rose on steady legs to
reach the jump plane's exit on the starboard side. The
sliding door gave no resistance, and he braced himself with
both hands in the doorway, leaning out to scan the desert
and the rolling hills below.

The warrior took a last glance at Grimaldi. The pilot's
lips were moving, but his voice was lost to Bolan in the roar
of the wind. Thumbs-up for "Go," and Bolan tumbled
forward into space, the sunbaked desert rushing up to meet
him at a hundred miles per hour.

There was an instant after Bolan pulled the rip cord
when he wondered if his parachute would function. Then
the canopy snapped open, swift deceleration tightening the
harness straps against his armpits and his groin. He felt
himself begin to drift, his shadow tracking northward on
the desert floor. The warrior hauled against the risers,
compensating for the wind that tried to carry him off
course. It wouldn't be a pinpoint landing, but he didn't
need precision this time out. The ballpark would be close
enough.

On impact Bolan folded at the knees and let momentum take him down. A stiff breeze caught his chute and
tried to drag him, but he came up fighting, hauling on the
shroud lines, reeling in the catch. When the warrior had
pooled the silky material around him like a giant blos-
som, he hit the quick-release snaps on his harness, using

the reserve chute and some handy stones to weight the whole thing down.

A careful scan in each direction showed him nothing that would indicate pursuit—no rising dust clouds, racing vehicles or human silhouettes on the horizon. There was still a chance he might have been observed, perhaps from miles away, but any hunters on his track were safely out of range.

He unpacked the aluminum entrenching tool, assembled it and dug a grave for his surplus gear. When he was finished with the pit, he dumped the parachutes, along with helmet, gloves and goggles, then covered the lot with fresh-turned earth. A layer of lighter sand disguised the excavation site. As a final precaution Bolan used a clump of brush, uprooted from a nearby rise, to whisk his tracks away. He dropped the folding shovel down an open burrow, kicked loose sand on top of it and worked the AK-47 off its shoulder sling.

A brief examination of the weapon told him it would function on command. It had sustained no damage from the jump, and he ignored the layer of dust that had collected on the weapon's stock and barrel during touchdown. The Kalashnikov was built to function under harsh conditions, and its years of faithful service—from Siberia to Southeast Asia—had confirmed a reputation as the most reliable of modern rifles. Bolan had a live round in the firing chamber and the safety set as he struck off eastbound in the direction of the nearest hills.

The Executioner knew the dangers posed by human adversaries well enough, and he spent the first full hour of his journey running down the snares prepared for him by Mother Nature. Heat and thirst would be the killers, and his two canteens would have to last until he found a spring or water hole. There were no predators of any size, but he'd have to watch for cobras, certain other vipers, even desert scorpions. The sun would help him there, as desert dwellers normally sought refuge from the midday heat, emerging to pursue their prey by night.

And if his luck held out, he'd have made connections with his local contact well before the sun went down.

He had a name—Chamoun—and little else to go on in regard to his intended contact. There had been no photographs on file, and the description in Chamoun's brief dossier might cover half the men in Lebanon. Appearances aside, his contact was the leader of a Christian "army" that had spent the better part of six years skirmishing with Shiite revolutionaries and narcotics dealers. In the Bekaa Valley, Bolan was advised, the missionaries carried guns and weren't afraid to use them in defense of their particular beliefs.

What sort of men made such a bleak and inhospitable terrain their home? What made them fight and die for sand and thorny scrub brush when they could have built a new life elsewhere?

Bolan knew the answer going in. It was commitment, plain and simple—dedication to a cause, a place, whatever—that compelled a man to stand his ground instead of turning tail. It didn't matter in the long run whether they were fighting for a luscious garden or the far side of the moon, as long as it was home.

America had learned that lesson from the Vietcong, and Russian troops had discovered the same in Afghanistan. The history of mankind was replete with similar examples, from the stoic Apache tribes to modern Israel. Home was where a warrior drew the line, to live in peace or die in the attempt.

Bolan had been climbing over rugged ground for ninety minutes when a sudden pang of apprehension made him hesitate. The Executioner had no opinion on the controversy over ESP and psychics, but a lifetime on the firing line had taught him to respect his jungle instincts. They had saved his life on more than one occasion, and the old, familiar feeling—hackles rising as his skin began to crawl—told Bolan he was being watched.

Before he tried to find the watcher, the warrior spent a precious moment seeking cover. On his right, a narrow gully had been carved by flash flood waters in some long-forgotten rainstorm. Years ago, perhaps, but it would serve him now if he was forced to ground by hostile fire.

Pretending he had merely stopped to wipe his sweaty brow, the Executioner began a sweep of the surrounding landscape, easing off the safety on his automatic rifle. Rocky earth reflected heat and made him squint, a traveler in search of landmarks. Still, the weapons that he carried would betray him to an enemy on sight.

He nearly missed the movement, subtle as it was, but on the cautious double take he spied a gunman, lying prone between two boulders fifty yards up the slope. Another sheltered in the shadow of an outcrop on the right, his weapon trained on Bolan's silhouette. Between them, rising from the spot where he had hidden up to now, a third man showed himself deliberately, blocking Bolan's path.

The Executioner took stock of his position, keen ears picking up the sound of boot heels scuffling on stone behind him. Thirty yards? One man, if he was any judge of sound, but he couldn't afford to turn and thereby lose the three in front of him.

These might have been his contacts, but he didn't think so. There was something in their attitude that set his teeth on edge, alerting him to mortal danger. Even so, there was a recognition signal, and he felt obliged to try it.

"Arms alone are not enough to keep the peace," he said, and waited for the other half of the remark by John F. Kennedy. His standing adversary seemed confused to hear himself addressed in English, and he glanced beyond the spot where Bolan stood, eyes seeking out the gunner who was closing up on the Executioner's flank.

It was enough. His finger tightened on the AK-47's trigger, stitching four quick rounds across the nearest gunner's chest. Before the others could recover from their shock, he lunged for cover in the shallow creek bed, burrowing between two boulders for protection.

Automatic fire converged upon his hiding place from three directions, pinning Bolan down. He dared not raise his head to duel with either of the snipers on the slope above him, or the man below would pick him off with ease. Whichever way he chose to move, advancing or retreating, he was blocked by hostile guns.

He twisted over on his side, unclipped a Russian antipersonnel grenade and pulled the safety ring. An uphill pitch wouldn't be easy, but he had the forward gunners spotted in his mind, their distance and positions filed away. The rocky outcrop sheltering his chosen target posed a problem, but he needed cover more than surgical precision. Something that would help him shave the odds a little in his favor.

Bolan made the pitch, and he was counting down the doomsday numbers as he braced himself, the AK-47 pointed back down the slope along the twisting gully. As the fragmentation grenade went off, he sat up in the trench, his shoulders hunched against potential impact from above, the weapon tracking toward a target he had never seen.

He caught the flanker in the open, dazed and gaping at him from a range of thirty yards. Above them on the hillside, one of Bolan's adversaries had been blinded by a storm of dust and flying shrapnel, his companion momentarily bewildered by the blast. They hesitated long enough for Bolan to release a short precision burst that dropped the backup gunner in his tracks, and by the time they opened fire again their mark had disappeared.

Two were down, but the grenade had scored no casualties. The path was cleared for a retreat, but after thirty yards or so, the gully petered out, soil scoured down to bedrock by erosion. Falling back would cost him time and precious cover, while it seemed impossible for him to forge ahead.

The rocks and sand were warm beneath him, baking through his camouflage fatigues, reminding Bolan of his tenuous position on the slope. From where they sat, his enemies could well afford to wait him out, preserving contact, firing scattered rounds as necessary, while they waited for the sun to do its work.

Bolan braced himself to try another rush. He still had three grenades, and that might be enough to pin them down, perhaps to wound his adversaries if he threw them fast enough. Two pitches, with the one held back for use as he erupted from the ditch. Once he was clear, with the Kalashnikov in hand, they would be more or less on equal footing.

Bolan wondered who the gunners were, and quickly pushed the thought away. It made no difference now if they were terrorists or bandits, simple thieves or lookouts for a caravan of opium in transit. He'd have to kill them both, or he was finished here and now.

He palmed two grenades and was ready to release the safety pins, when heavy automatic fire erupted on the hillside. In the place of two guns, Bolan now heard six or seven hammering in unison, their bullets spattering on stone and whining into space. A heartbeat passed before he realized that he wasn't the target; there were no incoming rounds.

Confused, he clipped the two grenades back on his harness, lifting the Kalashnikov and clutching it against his chest as the explosive outburst died away. In place of gunfire now, his ringing ears heard footsteps, scuffling over sand and stone, approaching his position over open ground.

There was no time to think the action through. He was surrounded, from the sound of things, and it made little difference if they killed him now or thirty seconds later. If he chose the time himself, at least he might take one or two of his opponents with him.

Pushing off with knees and elbows, Bolan rocked back on his haunches, leveling the AK-47 at a line of dusty, grizzled warriors. Five of them had weapons leveled from the hip, prepared to cut him down on order, but the nearest of them had his automatic rifle slung across one shoulder, big hands hanging empty at his sides.

The gunner was as good as dead. And he was smiling.

"Arms alone are not enough to keep the peace," he said, repeating Bolan's recognition signal.

Almost giddy with relief, the Executioner replied, "It must be kept by men."

"I wonder," his contact said, glancing back toward crumpled bodies on the slope. "It seems that arms have done the job today. But, please, decide if you must kill me or accept my hospitality. My name is Joseph Chamoun."

CHAPTER FIFTEEN

"You took your time," Bolan said affably.

Chamoun's smile dazzled, white teeth flashing in the sturdy olive face. "I had to satisfy my curiosity," he said. "My men and I are asked to risk our lives on your behalf. I wanted to be certain it wasn't a foolish gamble."

"And?"

The broad smile softened just a bit. "You are a warrior. I believe you would have killed them all yourself... but why take chances?"

"Right."

Emerging from the ditch, Mack Bolan waited for the rebel leader to extend his hand, then shook it firmly. Dusting off his camouflage fatigues, he quickly took stock of his allies, realizing that they looked no different from the bandits who had tried to kill him moments earlier. They wore no uniforms and carried a variety of weapons, ranging from familiar Chinese knockoffs of the AK-47 to Beretta submachine guns made in Italy. A couple of them had grenades clipped to their belts, and all wore bandoliers of ammunition looped across their chests. Their eyes called up distinctive memories of other lost-cause rebels he had worked with in the past. They held the same peculiar mix of fatalism, optimism and a dash of reckless disregard. There didn't seem to be a harried, hunted face among them.

"Should we bury these?"

As Bolan spoke, the rebels were already fanning out, relieving scattered corpses of their arms and ammunition, rifling through pockets in a search for smaller items.

"We don't have time," Chamoun replied, "and it would be a waste of time in any case. The desert deals with rubbish in its own efficient ways."

The dark man cocked a finger toward the sky, and Bolan followed its direction, picking out the microscopic flecks of vultures riding on the thermals overhead. The scavengers were patient, waiting for surviving humans to evacuate the scene before they circled lower, homing on their prey.

When they were finished picking over bodies, the platoon set out, a pointman leading, Bolan walking close to Chamoun and four other rebels bringing up the rear. They marched due east through rolling hills, and while the natives seemed at ease, completely casual, their eyes were constantly in motion, overlooking nothing. Bolan let himself relax a little, falling into step beside his contact.

Joseph Chamoun wasn't a large man—maybe five foot eight and slender in comparison to Bolan's own six foot three, two hundred pounds—but he exuded confidence and strength. Beside him his companions seemed diminished somehow, though some were larger men. His leadership was absolute, and clearly based on hard-won trust.

Another ninety minutes passed before they reached the outskirts of the Bekaa Valley proper. Bolan smelled the change before he saw it, picking up the various aromas of humanity and cultivated earth, in contrast to the arid hills and desert they were leaving. Somewhere up ahead were cooking fires and livestock, families and fields. His enemies were waiting for him there—and possibly some friends.

The hills provided cover as they passed outlying farms and villages. In one such, even from a distance, Bolan picked out murals in the likeness of the late Ayatollah Khomeini, and the ayatollah's strident voice was broadcast over amplifiers in the village square. Around the blaring speakers, men and women went about their business, seemingly immune to the harangue.

"Does that go on around the clock?"

"They turn him off at sundown," Chamoun replied, "and start him up again at dawn. Even in death the great man guides them through their day—each day—with words of wisdom."

Bolan shuddered at the thought of listening to twelve- or fourteen-hour sermons every day. It was a daunting prospect, but experience had taught him human beings can adapt to almost any situation over time.

"Are these believers?"

"Some." Chamoun was studying the village with a stern tactician's eye. "The leaders of the Islamic revolution bribe the elders they can't convert on faith alone, recruit the younger peasants or intimidate them, and the rest fall into line. These people are accustomed to obeying orders—from the government, the Syrians, the warlords, hashish traders. It's in their blood. Their faith in God gives them strength to persevere."

The warrior glanced at Chamoun, surprised. "You recognize their dedication, then?"

The Christian rebel smiled. "Of course. I make no war against these people over their religion. That's for zealots in Beirut. We fight Iran's people here because they are invaders. They would subjugate our people and make Lebanon a foster child of Teheran. In the pursuit of power, they align themselves with evil men who deal in poison, and their souls are lost."

They put the village and its noisy marketplace behind them, trekking on another six or seven miles before the scouts veered off along a narrow, dusty track that climbed through rising hills. A pair of sentries recognized Chamoun and showed themselves, but Bolan had a feeling there were others, carefully concealed along the way.

The camp was simple—tents and shanties situated in a glen that featured running water and a shady grove. Among the trees, about half a dozen children hesitated in the middle of a game resembling tag, prepared to bolt and hide if there was any hint of danger from the new arrivals. Women tended cooking fires around the center of the compound, and the men kept weapons close at hand.

"My people," Bolan's contact said by way of introduction. "Some would call us rebels. I prefer to think that we are patriots, defending our homeland against traitors and outsiders. Is that so wrong?"

"I might not be the one to ask. I haven't marched in step with my elected government for quite a while."

Chamoun examined Bolan's face. "You understand, I think, what we are fighting for. The Shiites have a home here. I would not deny them that. But we don't need the Iranians to warp our minds, the dealers in narcotics to corrupt our young. I will not rest while enemies remain on Bekaa soil."

"Let's see what we can do about that, shall we?"

They were moving past the cook fires toward a tent that seemed to be Chamoun's command post, when a woman darted out in front of them and blocked their progress. She was young and lovely, with the dark complexion of her race and eyes that sparkled when she smiled.

"Is this the stranger?"

Chamoun ignored her question and addressed himself to Bolan. "Please forgive my sister's rash impertinence," he said. "Despite her age, she hasn't learned her place."

A spark of anger flashed behind the woman's eyes. "I know my place as well as anyone," she snapped. "I should be fighting at your side against our enemies. Now tell me," she addressed herself to Bolan, "have you come to help us?"

"If I can."

"One man?" Her tone was skeptical. "I hope you are a mighty warrior."

"Come with me." Chamoun brushed past his sister. "And, by all means, don't take Mara seriously."

Bolan wouldn't let himself glance back, but he could feel her eyes on him, following his every movement as he crossed the camp and disappeared inside her brother's tent. Would she be friend or foe? And did it matter in the long run? He had work to do, and enemies enough to occupy his time outside the rebel camp. And, yet, there had been something in her eyes...

Deliberately he pushed the image out of mind and concentrated on the task at hand. Distractions could be fatal in the hellgrounds, and he didn't plan on giving up his edge, however slim it might turn out to be.

If only he hadn't been captivated by those eyes.

"So, THAT IS the American."

Startled by the voice at her elbow, Mara Chamoun turned to face the speaker, nearly wincing as she recognized Amir Rashad. His smile repulsed her, and she cringed as his eyes flicked down to her breasts and back again, making her feel unclean.

"It is," she answered simply.

"He will join us?"

"That is up to Joseph."

"Of course."

Rashad was staring at her brother's tent, and despite the respite from his hungry eyes, Mara remained uncomfortable in his presence. "I have work to do," she said, and turned away from him.

Of the single men in camp, Amir Rashad stood out as one who made her skin crawl. Mara loathed the way he stared at her and sometimes even licked his lips. So far he hadn't tried to touch her, but the day would come, and when it happened, Mara thought that she might have to kill him. If her brother didn't do it first.

She concentrated on the stranger, this American who had been sent to them from more than halfway around the world. He was a warrior—she'd seen it in his face—and would have known that much without the trappings of his uniform and weapons. This one had her brother's look of dedication to a cause that may be hopeless but was never given up as lost. She wasn't certain he could help them, but she knew that he would try.

Why was she interested in the American? There had been other visitors in camp from time to time, but they were always small men from Beirut, or Europeans with their pasty faces blistered by the sun. This man was different, hardened by the life that he had led. A killer? That was given, but he wouldn't kill from spite or any other petty motive. Like her brother, the American would choose his enemies with care.

And what of allies?

Mara watched the children playing, shadows ducking in and out among the trees, oblivious to plans of violent death that her brother and the American were hatching a few short yards away. In their turn the boys would eventually become soldiers in the cause, and some or all of them would give their lives in combat with the enemy. She didn't find the prospect daunting or depressing. Such was life, and it would never change until their foes had been defeated.

Mara had grown up on war, indoctrinated by her father and her uncles in the grim necessity of fighting for the land. She hadn't been considered a potential warrior, as her sex had marked her for the more prosaic tasks of cooking, cleaning and bearing children. Thus far she'd managed to escape the latter, though she wasn't strictly virginal. Her young man had been killed in combat with the Druze militia, and the intervening months had scarcely dimmed his memory. Still, Mara was mature enough to put the past behind her, concentrating instead on the future, grim as it might be.

Would the American be helpful to their cause? What moved him to enlist with strangers in a war so far from home?

No matter. He must have his reasons. They would be made clear in time. Just now his talents mattered more than motives, and his contribution to the cause would be measured in deeds.

Her flesh was creeping, and she turned in time to catch Amir Rashad before he turned away, pretending to be occupied with other things. For just an instant, she considered speaking to her brother, having him persuade Rashad to mind his eyes, but Joseph had more important things to deal with than a lecher in the ranks. Rashad wasn't so great a threat that Mara couldn't deal with him herself.

And, meanwhile, there was the American. He might not be among them long, and she'd like to know more of him while she had the chance. It was an opportunity that might not come again, a chance to look outside her narrow orbit and behold the world at large.

Her mind made up, she waited for the stranger to complete his business with her brother. After they were finished with their talk, Mara thought, there would be time to catch him on his own.

AMIR RASHAD HAD LEARNED to cope with the disdain in Mara's eyes. She didn't take him seriously as a man, but that would change once he had proved himself, when he had wealth and power of his own. Experience had taught Rashad that women followed money as a hunting dog pursues its prey. They found the lure irresistible, and it would be the same with Mara, when his time came.

She'd have to realize that her brother was chasing shadows, living in a dreamworld. He'd never change the Bekaa Valley with his posturing and skirmishes against an overwhelming enemy. In time he'd be ground to dust and scattered to the winds. It would require imagination and tenacity to weather out the coming storm.

Rashad had both, and he was hedging by cultivating allies in the hostile camp. The errands had been trivial at first. A whisper now and then, with payment made in cash. If Chamoun prepared to launch a raid against the growers, Rashad would pass the word, allowing preparations to be made. It bothered him in the beginning to realize that people with the same beliefs were being killed because of information he supplied, but life was hard, and all survival had a price attached. If there were also risks, at least Rashad saw an immediate reward for his activities, instead of waiting months and years for the elusive victory foretold by Joseph Chamoun.

Rashad wasn't a traitor in his own, small understanding of the term. A traitor violated trust, broke faith with cherished friends, but such was not the case with him. He had no friends of any consequence within the camp, no single person who would mourn his passing if he died. There were acquaintances who tolerated him, and some who flaunted their contempt in public. None of them were interested in Rashad, except as one more body for the ranks, another pawn to be used up—and ultimately sacrificed—in Chamoun's unending war.

He might have left the camp to make his way alone, except for Mara. From the moment of their first encounter, he was smitten with her beauty, fiercely jealous of her peasant lover. In the evenings when they walked along, Rashad had followed them and watched them from a distance, brooding as their love was consummated underneath the desert sky. In desperation he'd seen a chance to end it, save her from herself, and he had spoken to his contacts, briefing them about the next raid. The peasant's death had been a stroke of luck, accepted by Rashad as God's blessing on his love for Mara.

She'd change her mind about him one day soon, when she discovered that her brother's dreams were merely so much smoke. Rashad wouldn't inform her of his own role in the unit's defeat—forgiveness might have been too much to ask—but affluence and power would conspire to make her want him, drive the peasant and his boyish good looks from her mind.

The stranger posed a problem, but Rashad wasn't discouraged. He would know Chamoun's intentions when the time came, and it would be relatively simple to inform the men who trusted him, relied upon his information. The American would be Chamoun's last chance, a bid to crush his enemies with foreign help, and once the threat was neutralized, Amir Rashad would be in a position to demand more money, more respect.

He'd been watching Mara on the far side of the compound, and she caught him at it, frowning disapproval. It made no difference. Women changed their minds from day to day and hour to hour. She'd change her mind about Rashad when he had laid the proper groundwork, gone through all the necessary moves. She simply wouldn't have a choice.

Content with his position in the scheme of things, his choice of sides in the engagement yet to come, Rashad moved closer to the tent where Joseph Chamoun was huddled with the tall American. He wouldn't eavesdrop on their conversation; that would be too hazardous. But when Chamoun emerged, there'd be ample opportunity to ask some pointed questions, learn enough to let his contacts know that he was shooting for the big time.

Soon.

He could feel it in his bones.

"YOUR PLAN IS DANGEROUS," Chamoun declared. "These people aren't fools."

"Agreed. But at the moment they're in trouble. Shaken and disorganized. They need to find another outlet for their poison in a hurry. That's where I come in."

The rebel leader clearly had his doubts. "From what you tell me of your recent clash in Nicosia, they could hardly trust you."

"My guess is they don't know what to think right now. It's fifty-fifty whether they believe I set them up in Cyprus or they've got another player in the game. They're hungry for a new connection, and they haven't got much time to put it all together. That's my edge."

"I'm accustomed to a more direct approach," Chamoun replied.

"That's fine, assuming that you have the troops to make it stick. Unfortunately, when I look around outside, you seem to be a little short on numbers."

"We are strong enough."

The Executioner had touched a tender nerve, and he retreated diplomatically. "No doubt, but if these people have a weak point, I believe it's greed. Talk money like you mean it, and they let their guard down just enough make them vulnerable."

"Then we strike?"

"You got it. Once they let us have an opening, I'll need your strength to follow through and nail them down."

"They may not welcome you. There's a chance that you will fail."

"In that case," Bolan said, "you can go on with the direct approach and have a ball. Right now I'm asking for your help to back my play. It won't take long."

"How long?"

"Two days," he said, offhand. "No more than three."

"Such confidence."

"I have a feeling for these men. They're in business—some of them, at least—to make the largest profit they can gather in the shortest time. They're earning zilch without the Cyprus pipeline, but they still have overhead. If I can reach the men on top, I think they'll play."

"Beware of Bakhtiar," Chamoun advised. "He doesn't share Moheden's lust for money."

"No," the Executioner conceded, "but he still wants something all the same. He's looking for a contact in the States, someone to circulate his product while he gives America a taste of holy war at home."

"Will he believe you're that man?"

"He might. If nothing else, the prospect ought to put me close enough to take him down." He hesitated. "What's your reading on the Palestinian?"

"Halaby? Oh, he hates the Jews all right, but he's also interested in—how would the Americans describe it?—looking out for number one?"

"That fits."

"Halaby broke with Arafat because the PLO command wouldn't adopt his schemes for more elaborate attacks on Israel. Always he'd have some plan for an invasion, with himself in charge, and Arafat rebuffed him. It isn't enough for him that everyone should hate the Jews. The world must also recognize Halaby."

"That's a bonus. I can stroke his ego if I have to. Offer him a little something extra on the side. His troops might come in handy if he got the notion Bakhtiar was starting to monopolize the spotlight."

"It's possible."

"Until I have a foothold," Bolan said, "I'd like to take the pressure off. Can do?"

"My men won't obstruct you, but you realize that there are other groups involved. Our war against the growers is a struggle shared with others. Some will listen if I ask them to postpone attacks. The rest may not."

"I'll take the chance. If you can call your markers in, it ought to give me breathing room. I don't expect a miracle."

"You may require one."

"Thanks. I like your confidence."

Chamoun allowed himself another dazzling smile. "Believe me when I say I wish you all success. A victory in your cause is a victory in mine as well. I won't profit if you fail, but I have learned that wishful thinking is a vice."

"A little hope won't kill you."

"No. I think we can afford a little hope."

But it would take a damned sight more, the soldier realized, to carry off his mission in the Bekaa hellgrounds.

Hope was fine for newlyweds and kids on Christmas Eve, but it had never saved a combat soldier on the firing line. Worse yet, unrealistic hope could be a killer.

Bolan would be going into battle with his eyes wide open, hoping for the best and counting on the worst when he made contact with his enemies. They'd be curious, for openers, and he should count on some hostility besides. How much would greed help tip the scales? Enough for him to pull it off? Or maybe just enough to get him killed?

Whatever, if it started to unravel, he'd have to try another angle of attack. Chamoun's way. The direct approach.

CHAPTER SIXTEEN

The next day was devoted to Bolan's orientation, with a guided tour of the Bekaa Valley starting shortly after dawn. The Executioner had finished breakfast—something that reminded him of curried rice—when Chamoun appeared before him in the uniform of a Syrian army officer. Bolan noted that half a dozen other rebels were dressed in similar fashion, and Chamoun carried an extra uniform, draped across one arm.

"It may not be a perfect fit," he said, handing over the khaki garments, "but I believe this should suffice."

"Are we enlisting?"

"Not quite. But to pass unnoticed in the Bekaa, you must put on a familiar guise. The people are accustomed to the sight of Syrian patrols. Our native enemies cooperate with the invaders and accept their presence in the valley as a gift from God. We've managed to acquire some vehicles and samples of their clothing, which are sometimes useful."

"I imagine so."

He didn't have to ask about the cost of acquisition. There were no holes in his uniform, but Bolan recognized the clothing as another weapon in Chamoun's unending war. If lives hadn't been forfeited to gain that edge, he'd be very much surprised.

The uniform fit passably, a little snug beneath the arms. Bolan wore his own boots, noting that the rebels were eclectic in their choice of footwear. With a standard-issue bandolier across his chest, he slung the AK-47 he'd carried into Lebanon and joined the others to begin their trek.

The vehicles were foreign copies of the standard military jeep, one sprouting a machine gun in the rear, the other one unarmed. It took a second glance, but Bolan saw the points where bullet holes and shrapnel scars had been filled in with putty, sanded smooth and painted over. There had been a price tag on the vehicles as well.

"You guys don't miss a trick."

"We can't afford to," Chamoun replied.

He chose the unarmed jeep and slid behind the steering wheel, directing Bolan to the shotgun seat. Two bogus Syrians climbed in behind them, four more peeling off to fill the second vehicle. On impulse Bolan glanced back toward the camp and saw the woman, Mara, watching through the haze of morning cook fires. Was her expression one of curiosity? Suspicion? Bolan let it go as engines growled to life, and they were off.

Chamoun drove cautiously along the narrow track, his escort rolling through a trail of dust until they reached the highway.

Forsaking comfort in the jolting vehicle, Mack Bolan concentrated on the countryside. They rolled through cultivated fields and orchards, passing isolated huts and tiny villages where people studied them with lifeless eyes. The village streets were ripe with cast-off garbage, rotting in the gutters and in mounds between the unkempt homes.

As they passed several settlements, they could hear a deep-timbred voice blaring words of wisdom from scratchy speakers. Chamoun translated some of the ubiquitous graffiti as they drove along, an endless litany of hatred for America and infidels in general, aimed at stirring up the Shiite population to a fever pitch.

"How did the Shiites get involved with the narcotics trade?" Bolan asked.

"Historically the Bekaa bandits have survived by selling hashish in Beirut and in surrounding states. Today they sell hashish and heroin around the world. New times, new markets. When Khomeini sent his 'missionaries' to the valley, they discovered that a revolutionary cadre could support itself by dealing drugs as well. The Iranian government thus saved money to invest in war with the Iraqis."

"How does dealing drugs square up with Shiite doctrine?"

"Much the same as murder, terrorism and the rest of the program. As you know, everything done in the name of the Islamic revolution is sanctified by God. Narcotics are a weapon aimed against the West. Iran has no long-range bombers, guided missiles or the like. Instead it has a hypodermic needle pointed at the heart of Europe and America."

Chamoun's assessment of the situation jibed with the reports from Stony Man, and Bolan knew it wouldn't be the first time that narcotics had become a covert weapon. Britain had used opium against the Chinese empire in the nineteenth century, and China had reversed the flow in recent times. Drugs also played a part in the subversive foreign policy of Castro's Cuba and the Nicaraguan Sandinistas. On the flip side, anti-Communist guerrillas in the Golden Triangle and in Colombia had also fattened their coffers by exporting poison to America. Whichever way you sliced it, the narcotics trade was death on the consumer, and for Bolan's money, any players in the game were marked, regardless of their leanings to the left or right.

As they proceeded north, the settlements grew larger, and the highway broadened to approximate two normal lanes. The traffic thickened, most of it pedestrian, all flowing in the same direction. Bolan understood, with some misgivings, that they were about to reach a major town.

As if in answer to his thoughts, Chamoun announced, "We're approaching Baalbek. Three, four miles to go. With any luck we may see something of our common enemies. If nothing else, you can examine their abode."

"Is there a problem with the regular patrols?"

Chamoun didn't appear concerned. "To all appearances," he said, "we *are* a regular patrol. If we meet others in the countryside there might be trouble, but there are too many Syrians in Baalbek for the troops to know each other well. A bluff, some reference to urgent business if we are detained. It shouldn't be a problem."

"I admire your confidence," he said.

"Of course."

The population center of the Bekaa Valley, Baalbek posed no challenge to Beirut in terms of size. He knew, from running down the bare necessities at the Farm, that there were something like a hundred thousand people in the city, and it seemed that all of them were on the streets this morning. Foot traffic overflowed the sidewalks, slowing progress to a crawl, but local drivers took the crush in stride, maneuvering around pedestrians who blocked the way. Bolan noted other khaki uniforms around them, and while the soldiers on patrol occasionally raised a hand in greeting, none made any move to halt Chamoun's contingent.

The rebel leader was pleased. "As I predicted, we're merely faces in the crowd. Invisible."

The Executioner reflected that "invisible" wasn't synonymous with "bulletproof," but kept the observation to himself. They seemed to have no destination as they rolled through crowded streets, but Bolan counted on Chamoun's built-in guidance system, memorizing landmarks on his own as a precaution.

Suddenly they turned a corner, and he knew precisely where he was.

"Hosseinieh," his guide announced. "Headquarters for the Shiite revolutionary guard."

They circled once around the drab, graffiti-decorated building he'd seen in slides and photographs at Stony Man. Inside that gray, foreboding structure beat the heart of the Iranian expeditionary force in Lebanon. Mir Reza Bakhtiar would occupy an upstairs suite of rooms, protected by the men and guns around him, while he served his master's pleasure. There were riflemen outside the entrance, seemingly alert, and any access from the courtyard was concealed behind an eight-foot wall, surmounted by a roll of concertina wire.

"Impenetrable, yes?"

The Executioner responded with a question of his own. "How many men inside?"

"The number varies. Thirty-five to forty on the average. Ten times that when Bakhtiar demands their presence for the monthly gatherings."

"Fixed dates on those?"

"No steady pattern. Bakhtiar sends word a day or two ahead of time, and everyone arrives on schedule."

"How long since they last got together?"

"Three weeks, perhaps a little more." Chamoun was following his drift. "My scouts advise me when the call goes out, but an assault on Hosseinieh is hopeless."

Bolan let it go and concentrated on the changing scenery as they evacuated downtown Baalbek, winding north and east through narrow, twisting streets. Beyond the sprawl of shops and civic buildings lay the residential district, homes diminishing in size as they retreated from the city's heart. Unlike the urban centers of America, where poverty and rampant crime afflicted inner-city areas, the Baalbek slums were scattered on the city's outskirts, crowded out of sight and out of mind.

Chamoun directed Bolan's gaze to an encampment on the hillside, overlooking Baalbek from the east. It looked familiar, even though his previous examination had been made through aerial photographs.

"The Sheikh Abdullah barracks," said Chamoun. "Ahmad Halaby and his Palestinians are quartered there, although the camp is dominated by the Shiite revolutionary guard. Both groups use the facilities to train their new recruits, along with visitors from Northern Ireland, Italy and West Germany."

"A regular finishing school. Can we get any closer?"

Chamoun shook his head. "The Syrians don't patrol this area. Our presence would arouse suspicion, possibly an armed reaction from the camp. There are an estimated hundred terrorists in residence at any given time."

"Can't say I like the odds."

"Nor I."

Chamoun confirmed the reading of his wristwatch with a brief examination of the sun's position overhead. It would be some time after noon, and Bolan's stomach grumbled to remind him of the hours that had flown since his meager breakfast.

"It's time we started back," Chamoun said. "There's a place where we can stop along the way and have our midday meal."

This time they skirted Baalbek, pushing south and managing to miss the bulk of traffic as they stuck to smaller roads. When they had traveled ten or twelve miles from the city, Chamoun swung off the highway and parked in a grove of trees where running water babbled somewhere just beyond the hedgerows. At a signal from their chief, the soldiers in the second jeep broke out a canvas sack of bread and cheese, salted meat and several skins of wine.

"A simple meal," Chamoun declared, as food was passed around, "but filling. It will see us through the afternoon. We're expected back in camp by dusk."

The bread was fresh, the cheese well aged, the meat and wine delicious. Bolan was about to thank his host, when he was silenced by the sound of vehicles approaching. In an instant, even as he dropped the quarter loaf and reached back for his rifle, three more vehicles filled the clearing, jammed with six or seven Syrians apiece.

"Say nothing," the rebel leader hissed, lips already molded in a smile of greeting. On the sidelines, Chamoun's commandos seemed relaxed, but each was armed and ready, poised to strike upon command.

The Executioner released his AK-47's safety, unobtrusively transferred the weapon to his lap and held his breath.

CHAMOUN RECOVERED SWIFTLY from his momentary shock. He'd been speaking English to the man who called himself Belasko, and shifted smoothly into Arabic for conversation with the Syrians. To all appearances, he was a junior officer in charge of a routine patrol. With any luck he'd be able to maintain the fiction and escape without a bloody confrontation.

They disposed of the preliminaries, with Chamoun saluting the commander of the new arrivals, silently deploring the coincidence through which he found himself outranked. His counterpart and nominal superior was shorter and heavy-set, and he retained his seat, as if by stepping down he might surrender his seniority.

"I don't recognize your face," the stranger said. "I thought I knew all junior officers in this command."

Chamoun thought fast, recovering the serve. "A recent transfer, Captain. I'm new to Baalbek."

"And your orders?"

He'd have to bluff it out. "We're assigned to search for rebels in the central district."

"Ah, then I assume your orders came from General Fawzi?"

"Certainly." The name meant nothing to Chamoun.

"How strange."

The rebel leader felt his bowels begin to tighten. "Sir?"

"There is no General Fawzi in Baalbek. *Imposters!*"

The commander of the Syrian patrol was clawing for his pistol when Chamoun whipped up his submachine gun and squeezed off a burst at point-blank range. He had no time to measure its effect, as hell broke loose along the line, with automatic weapons blazing in a lethal crossfire. Chamoun heard the machine gun on his backup vehicle cut loose, and then the general clamor drowned out the report of any single weapon.

Scrambling for safety, he slid in behind the jeep and found Belasko there ahead of him, his AK-47 spitting short, precision bursts. Chamoun knelt in the dust beside him, popping up to spray the enemy from cover. One quick glance revealed three bodies, sprawled between the hostile lines, their faces hidden or obliterated. Only three, in such a blast of concentrated fire? It was a miracle.

The storm raged back and forth, a game of numbers too intense to last. Chamoun knew they were finished if he couldn't shave the odds. His men would die—and the American—before they had a chance to face their major enemies.

Chamoun edged past Belasko, reaching up inside the jeep where he'd packed a satchel of grenades. A bullet shattered on the metal near his face, and slivers gouged his cheek, blood mingling with his perspiration as he found the duffel bag and hauled it clear. He yanked the zipper open, palmed a hand grenade and freed the safety pin. A simple pitch, no windup.

The hostile spray of bullets faltered, then started up again with less conviction. Bolan fished inside the duffel, found a hand grenade and pitched it farther down the line. Another blast before Chamoun could make his second pitch, and now the enemy machines were burning, soldiers scattering to put some distance between themselves and leaping flames.

Chamoun abandoned his secure position, firing from the hip as he advanced. He caught three Syrians on open ground and dropped two of them before his magazine ran out. Then he was left alone, unarmed in no-man's-land.

He saw the bullet coming, or imagined it, his body twisting to avoid the impact that would surely kill him at such close range. Instead the hot round drilled his shoulder, spinning him around and dumping him unceremoniously in the dust. It would require a moment for the pain to register, and he didn't have many moments left.

The Syrian looked eager, hungry, as he raised his AK-47 for another shot. The killing shot. Chamoun refused to close his eyes, and so he saw the private's tunic ripple, spouting crimson, as a spray of bullets knocked him backward off his feet.

More firing, distant, as Chamoun began to lose his grip on consciousness. His eyes were clear enough to recognize Bolan as he bent over him, and suddenly the rebel leader understood. Before the darkness took him, he summoned the strength to smile.

INCREDIBLY ONE JEEP WAS functional once they had changed a flattened tire. Eight men had started the patrol, and four of them—including Joseph Chamoun—were still alive as they began the journey home. Four men were left behind, together with the riddled second jeep, to keep the opposition guessing for a while.

Dusk overtook them on the road, and Bolan kept an eye out for the enemy. A soldier in the back had been assigned the task of keeping the pressure on Chamoun's untidy shoulder wound. The slug had gone completely through, and they had managed to control the major bleeding, but he still had need of medical attention. Would there be a doctor in the camp? If not, Bolan might have to cauterize and stitch the wound himself.

It didn't come to that. The sentries recognized their situation from a distance, and the medic was on standby when the battered vehicle pulled into camp. Chamoun was lifted clear and placed on a stretcher, then hustled toward a tent that seemed to serve as the infirmary. His sister, Mara, jogged beside the stretcher, holding tightly to her brother's hand.

The Executioner scrounged a cup of coffee and a bowl of some sort of stew. A second helping filled his belly, and the caffeine helped to clear his head. The other compound dwellers left him to himself, and Bolan took advantage of the time alone to sort his thoughts.

He didn't think Chamoun would die, but convalescence might deprive the rebels of their leader for several days. It was his second night in Lebanon, and Bolan had no time to spare in waiting for his contact to recuperate. If necessary, he'd have to try the next phase on his own and keep in touch with Chamoun as best he could.

The compound had three showers, but he opted for a visit to the bathing pool instead, and had it to himself as darkness fell. The water, warm from soaking up the sun all day, relaxed his aching muscles, helping melt the tension from his body as he floated on his back, eyes open to the starry sky. Away from city lights and camp fires, Bolan almost felt that he could count the pinpricks overhead, if only he had time.

A flicker in the corner of his eye put the warrior on alert. Three strokes and he was on the shelf with solid footing, water lapping at his chest. A solitary figure stood upon the bank, not far from where his clothes and weapon lay. He recognized the woman as she spoke.

"You saved my brother's life."

"That makes us even."

She moved closer to the waterline, moonlight falling on her face. "You have come far," she said, "to kill our enemies."

"Not only yours."

"I understand. But they are still too many."

"Someone has to try."

"We try. My brother tries each day. You see what has become of him."

"He'll be all right."

"This time, because of you. Next time, perhaps..."

"Don't sell him short."

She was unbuttoning her shirt, the moonlight casting shadows on her body as the garment fell away. Beneath it she wore nothing but her silken skin.

The soldier felt himself responding as she kicked her shoes away and stepped out of her slacks. A worm of doubt was wriggling around the back of Bolan's mind, compelling him to ask the question.

"Mara..."

"Silence."

She was in the water now and gliding toward him like some elemental spirit, dark hair spilling around her shoulders. As she slipped her arms around his neck, her body molding close against his own, Bolan's doubts and questions seemed irrelevant.

"For Joseph," she said as her lips grazed Bolan's. Fingers laced behind his neck, she raised her legs and locked them tight around his waist. "For me."

CHAPTER SEVENTEEN

"I understand. Keep trying." Slowly, carefully, Bashir
Moheden cradled the receiver, swallowing an urge to slam
it down with crushing force. He drew his hand away and
wiped his palm along the fabric of his slacks, as if it might
have been contaminated.

Once again the news from Nicosia had been disap-
pointing. Contacts on the street and on the metropolitan
police force had no word of the American who called
himself Belasko. He'd dropped from sight, one hotel room
abandoned and no others occupied. The airport had been
watched around the clock, but he hadn't attempted to de-
part from Cyprus. If he didn't show by four o'clock that
day, his scheduled flight would leave without him.

For the hundredth time Moheden wondered if the man
was even still alive. There was a possibility that he'd been
abducted by the men who murdered Sarkis and Makarios,
before they moved against Hussein Razmara's compound. If the killers were American, intent on getting even
for Silvestri's murder in New York, they might have trailed
Belasko from the States, observing him until his contact
with Makarios confirmed their dark suspicions of betrayal. Moheden knew the Mafia mentality, and once they
started leaping to conclusions, right or wrong, they gave no
quarter to their enemies.

Belasko, dead, would solve one problem, while creat-
ing yet another. If the man had been eliminated, then it
stood to reason he hadn't been part of the assault on Sar-

kis and Makarios. And, by extension, it might still be safe to strike a bargain with his sponsors in America. The downside of the matter was that Mike Belasko hadn't named his sponsors, and he wouldn't do so from his grave, wherever that might be. Unless the buyers sent another representative—and there was every chance that they wouldn't, considering the first one's fate—the Lebanese had no way of touching base with them to close the deal. And at the same time, there was every chance that one or more of New York's "Families" had turned against him, blaming him and his associates for the Silvestri strike.

Moheden cursed. The plan had been so simple in the beginning. Eliminating middlemen and moving heroin to the United States in greater quantities by cutting prices back, he should have made a fortune overnight. Instead a portion of his hard-won empire lay in smoking ruins, he'd lost connections in the States and he was looking at the possibility of violence yet to come.

His greatest fear was the prospect of a global shooting war. The Mafia didn't forgive unless there was a profit in forgiveness, and it was within the realm of possibility that Anthony Silvestri's syndicate would try to kill Moheden and his partners, even at their homes in Lebanon. It seemed farfetched, but he'd heard of other cases, where a witness or defector from the Mafia was trailed for years, to South America or Africa—wherever—and the vengeance of the tribe exacted when the subject least expected it—a bomb or sniper's bullet, poisoned food, a knife thrust on a crowded sidewalk. It was said that no place on the earth was safe once the Mafia decided you must die.

Moheden knew that there were limitations to the Syndicate's ability, but he'd also seen their work firsthand, and he'd purchased long-range contracts on his own. New York was half a world away, but Sicily was just around the corner. Blood ties held the Mafia together, and the Syndicate had earned its reputation from another kind of blood: the kind it spilled.

It was approaching lunchtime, and Moheden was surprised to find his appetite intact. With perfect logic, he decided there was nothing to be gained by going on a hunger strike. His strength and clarity of mind would be affected and, besides, the typical anxiety reaction would spell triumph for his enemies. If they could break his spirit, force him into hiding from himself, they would have won.

He was about to ring for lunch when footsteps sounded in the corridor outside his study. At the butler's knock, he struck a pose of studied relaxation.

"Yes?"

"A thousand pardons, sir. There is a stranger at the gate. A foreigner. He tells the guards you are expecting him."

Moheden frowned. "I'm expecting no one, least of all—" He hesitated. "What sort of foreigner?"

"American, I think, sir."

"And his name?" Moheden knew the answer in advance. His pulse was hammering.

"Belasko, sir. Shall I instruct the guards to deal with him?"

Moheden raised a hand, took care to keep it casual. "Not yet," he answered. "Have him searched for microphones and weapons. Send him in to me when they're finished."

"Yes, sir."

Was he making a mistake? And then again, how could the stranger harm him in the sanctuary of his own palatial home? If Bashir Moheden wasn't safe here, then he'd never be safe anywhere.

The lunch could wait, he thought, and when he dined, he just might have a guest. He drained his glass of wine, refilled it, then waited for his first glimpse of the man who was his mortal enemy, or else the key to untold wealth.

CHAMOUN HAD DISAPPROVED of Bolan's plan, but he didn't refuse to help. A dark sedan and several tailored suits were whipped up in an afternoon, no questions asked, and Bolan finalized his plans in one last meeting with the rebel leader, Mara sitting in as her brother's lieutenant while he convalesced. It was agreed that there would be no fresh attacks against Moheden's operation in the next few days, until the Executioner could organize his play and get in touch. Chamoun had been unhappy with the waiting game, disgusted with himself for having stopped a bullet, but he would perform on cue. If Bolan made no contact after three days' time, all bets were off.

When they adjourned the meeting, Bolan took a long, slow walk with Mara, through the trees surrounding the encampment. She was frightened for him, and the feeling troubled her. When Bolan took her in his arms, she wept at first and then found strength to match his passion with her own. That night, beneath the stars, they pointedly avoided speaking of the future.

Driving west from the encampment in the Bekaa foothills to Moheden's villa on the coast, Bolan carried the Beretta, his "Belasko" paperwork and fragile hopes of waltzing straight into his enemy's preserve. A thousand things could still go wrong, but the alternative—assaulting either of the Baalbek strongholds with a team of riflemen—was tantamount to suicide. If Bolan had to go that route, he'd prefer to try it on his own, a desperation measure undertaken with the very faintest hope of coming out alive.

The Lebanese might attempt to minimize his risks by killing Bolan on arrival, but it was a chance the Executioner would have to take. He was committed to the game, and there would be no turning back. If nothing else, he might get close enough to lock his hands around the dealer's throat before they cut him down.

He found the villa without difficulty, rolling up outside the wrought iron gates as if he owned the place. Three riflemen were stationed at the entrance, one of them with a strong command of English. Bolan gave his cover name and asked to see the master of the house, relaxing at the wheel of his sedan while one of them got on a walkie-talkie to the villa. Several moments passed before the English-speaking hardguy stuck his face in Bolan's open window, scowling.

"You will step outside of the car," he said.

"Sure thing."

The search had been inevitable, and he made no move to stop the hand that plucked his side arm from its shoulder rig. When he had undergone a standard frisk and turned his pockets out, he backed away and watched them search the car. It wasn't the most thorough search in his experience, but it would do.

The English-speaking sentry rode with Bolan to the house, one hand on his submachine gun, and the other clutching the Executioner's pistol. At the villa he delivered Bolan's piece to other riflemen and drove the car back to his post. Whatever might go down inside the house, there would be no quick getaway with screeching tires.

The air-conditioning took Bolan by surprise, immediately raising goose bumps on his sweaty skin. Surrounded by four guards, he marched through rooms and corridors until they reached their destination. One more frisk for anything the gatemen might have overlooked, and he was ushered in to meet his adversary.

Bashir Moheden stood beside the tall French doors, his features lost in shadow. Bolan felt the eyes examining him, inch by inch, and knew that he could make or break it here, right now.

"You're not an easy man to see," Bolan said by way of introduction.

"No. Have you been trying long?"

"I met one of your boys in Nicosia, but he had an accident."

"I'm interested in hearing more about that, if you have the time."

"I've got all day." Bolan drifted toward the open liquor cabinet and poured himself a drink without an invitation. "You don't mind?"

"By all means, help yourself."

Moheden took a seat behind his massive desk, and Bolan chose an easy chair directly opposite. "There isn't much to tell," he said. "I made your boy, Makarios, an offer on some merchandise. We were about to hash the details out when someone started busting caps. Makarios went out one exit, I went out the other. Next time I heard anything about him, he was dead, with lots of company."

"You didn't recognize the gunmen who attacked you?"

"Nah. They all had panty hose or something on their heads, you know? Like smash-and-grab guys. I was too damned busy looking out for number one to stop and check their visas."

"And you never saw Makarios again?"

"I saw his picture in the papers," Bolan answered, nonchalant. "I'm not so hot at reading Greek, but what the hell, dead's dead in any language."

"You are fortunate to have survived," Moheden told him.

"We make our own luck, don't you think?"

"Perhaps. Is that why you bring weapons when you come to visit me at home?"

"I haven't stayed alive this long by taking stupid chances," Bolan said. "For all I know, the action with Makarios was something in the family. You might have run it down yourself."

"And yet you came."

"I figured, either way, it's no skin off my nose, you follow? If you're looking at a war with someone on the outside, maybe we can help each other. If you're cleaning house, that's cool. Just tip me off next time so I can take a rain check on the party."

"For the record," Moheden informed him, "I didn't assassinate Makarios or any of the others. At the moment I have no idea who might have been responsible."

"That's rough. It makes for problems with your business, eh?"

"A temporary setback." With a frown, the dealer shifted gears. "I'm told that you know something of another recent incident in New York City. Anthony Silvestri?"

"Good news travels fast, I see. The guy was losing it. He had delusions of adequacy, biting off more than he could chew. Somebody knocked his dick in the dirt, and that's all there is to it."

Moheden's voice took on a frosty edge. "A pair of my associates were meeting with him at the time."

"Unfortunate. Sometimes you have to take your shot when it's available, know what I mean? You want to make an omelet, first you have to break the eggs."

''Silvestri's Family may disagree with your assessment of the situation.''

''The Grisanti crowd? Forget 'em. Don Patrice is looking at a string of federal indictments that'll keep him paying lawyer's fees until doomsday. He's a dinosaur, about to go extinct, and his lieutenants haven't got a working brain between them.''

''Someone planned the raids in Nicosia.''

''And you think Grisanti's got that kind of pull?'' The soldier switched from cocky self-assurance to a thoughtful frown. ''I guess it's something I could check on, if you like.''

The dealer shifted gears. ''What sort of offer did you make Makarios?''

''A two-year, thirty-million-dollar package, with an option to increase the volume after that, if everybody's satisfied.''

''You represent another Family in the United States?''

''You're warm. My people aren't hung up on all the old-world bullshit. They're concerned with profit margins and reliable suppliers. That's where you come in.''

''Perhaps.''

''You don't need thirty million?'' Bolan made as if to rise. ''Hey, look, I'm sorry that I took your time, okay?''

The Lebanese flinched, a sudden flash of panic in his eyes. ''Please, wait! You surely understand the need for caution in a venture of this magnitude, especially when there has been so much unpleasantness already.''

Bolan sat down again and smiled. ''Okay. I guess you'll want to check my bona fides? I've got a couple numbers I can give you, in New York and Washington, to get things rolling.''

The Executioner jotted down the numbers on a business card and passed it over. Dialing either one would route Moheden's call through cutouts, back to Stony Man, where Kurtzman's staff had been on the alert since his departure from the States. The dealer scanned the numbers, smiling as he raised his eyes to Bolan's face.

"Forgive my skepticism, if you will, but telephones are vulnerable instruments. Assuming that the message wasn't intercepted, it would tell me nothing. Anyone may answer, and I have no way of judging their veracity."

"You've got a point."

"If you could offer me some names..."

"My sponsors like their privacy. I'm sure they'll want to meet you when you close the deal, but first they need a reading, get me? Any time they think of buying into something major, they send me—or someone like me—to check the action. Make sure everything's on track and running smooth. They've heard good things about your operation, but they don't like flying blind."

"I feel the same myself."

"That's understandable. My people figure it's a sin to waste a big man's time, so here's the deal. Five hundred thousand for a guided tour of your operation, nonrefundable, whichever way it goes. If everything checks out and my folks like the action, I'm empowered to negotiate the two-year deal I mentioned. Even if we don't do business, you still make a fancy piece of change."

"Your offer is... unique."

"It's standard for the men I represent."

"I can't imagine carrying such sums around the countryside."

"Damn right you can't. I socked it in a safe-deposit box in Nicosia." Bolan palmed a useless railway locker key and held it up for Moheden's inspection. "When we rap the tour up, you get the key. From that point on, whatever happens, happens. No hard feelings."

He could feel the line begin to jerk, Moheden nibbling at the bait. But he was not prepared to swallow yet.

"I must consult my business partners."

"Sure, why not? That's just the flat half million, though. You want to split it up, that's your decision."

"I'm confident that we can reach an understanding."

"Glad to hear it. Shall I let you have some privacy to make those calls?"

The dealer rose and moved around the desk to shake his hand. "My servants will provide whatever you'd like. Some food, perhaps?"

"No, thanks, I'm fine."

"A moment, then."

"Sure thing."

Outside the study, Bolan trailed his escort to a recreation room of sorts, complete with wet bar, big-screen television and a VCR with racks of videocassettes. He settled for a beer and nursed it, standing at the window, studying the sun-bleached sky.

One fish hooked, apparently, and if his reading of Moheden was correct, the Lebanese would sell his partners on the "guided tour," one way or another.

He was halfway home. The easy half. From here on out the stakes would be increased, as well as the odds against him. Any slip, however small, would spell disaster.

But at least he was inside, where he could do some major damage in a pinch. They might still pierce his cover, take him down before he wrecked their poison pipeline, but the bastards wouldn't get a freebie. No damned way at all.

The Executioner had penetrated their defenses at the top, and he was hanging in until he blew their house down—or until they killed him.

AMIR RASHAD WAS restless. He had information that would doubtless fascinate his outside contacts, but he couldn't leave the rebel compound. Joseph Chamoun had ordered all his troops to stay in camp until they heard from the American, and if Rashad slipped out, his absence would be noted. Explanations would mean nothing to Chamoun, who saw through liars as another man saw through a pane of glass.

Rashad had witnessed three courts-martial in the compound. Two of the defendants had been charged with sexual assault on Shiite women, and they had confessed their crimes, believing the identity of their selected victims granted them immunity from punishment. Chamoun had executed both of them himself, a single bullet through each forehead as they knelt before him in the dust.

Rashad had been unmoved by those proceedings, but the third trial sparked a greater interest. One of the commandos was accused of spying for the Syrians, relaying information to the enemy that led to cancellation of a major raid. This time the prisoner claimed innocence, but he was contradicted by the testimony of a spy within the Syrian militia. On conviction he was handed over to the troops for execution, carried to the grove where different soldiers took their turns with knives. Rashad had joined the butchery, and no one noticed that his hands were trembling as he claimed his pound of flesh from the informer.

He didn't intend to die that way, but neither did he plan on wasting the remainder of his life in service to Chamoun's lost cause. Rashad had sniffed the wind and recognized the losing side. It might take months, or even years, before Chamoun was beaten and his soldiers scattered to the winds, but the survivors would have nothing they could call their own. The Bekaa Valley was an unforgiving place.

It nurtured winners—or at least survivors—and the rest were gobbled up alive.

Amir Rashad had chosen to survive, to win, and with the information in his hands, he could demand a higher price from his employers. They would recognize his value, not as an informer in the ranks, but as a man with leadership potential. When Chamoun was broken, they would certainly reward Rashad with a position of respect.

A runner found Rashad and told him his presence was required in the commander's tent. Acknowledging the summons, his immediate reaction was a surge of panic. Had they found him out? Was this the moment he had dreaded for the better part of two long years?

But he remembered how the traitor had been handled at his trial. An escort had dragged him across the compound, clouting him with fists when he resisted. There had been no courtly summons, certainly no chance for the accused to slip away. Rashad considered flight, abandoning his few belongings and escaping with the money that he always carried on his person. But it seemed absurd. He was accused of nothing yet, and if he bolted from a simple order to present himself before Chamoun, the act of flight would be as good as a confession to something.

At the leader's tent, he was received with courtesy by sentries who apparently suspected nothing. As he stepped inside, Rashad was instantly relieved to find himself alone with Chamoun and his sister. Smiling through the sudden rush, he even managed not to gape at Mara's breasts.

"I have a job for you to do in Baalbek," Chamoun said.

Rashad suppressed the urge to leap for joy. "As you command," he answered, carefully observing military courtesy.

"You will deliver this." An envelope, flap sealed with colored wax, was placed into his steady hands. "This information may not be entrusted to the radio or telephone.''

He memorized an address, the description of his contact and repeated them on order.

"If you are arrested," Chamoun informed him, "we will make the normal efforts to secure your release. However, you must not allow this message to be captured by the enemy. If there is trouble, it must be destroyed at once.''

"I understand, sir."

"Good. You leave at dusk.''

He was elated as he left the tent, the enveloped tucked safely in an inside pocket of his tunic. It occurred to him, in passing, that the mission might be a test to see if he might break the seal or pass the envelope to hostile hands. No matter now. There would be ample time en route to Baalbek for Rashad to plan his disposition of the letter. More importantly he would be free to reach his contacts in the city and report his news of the American.

Perhaps before it was too late.

"OF COURSE, I understand. I'll assume responsibility for any difficulties that arise. The risk is mine. That's right.''

Halaby had been easy, with his nose for profit, but predictable objections had been raised by Bakhtiar. It cost Moheden thirty minutes to ease the Shiite's mind, assuring him that every effort would be made to verify Belasko's story and absolve him in the murder of Hussein Razmara. If the facts bore out Belasko's version of events, it would be possible to overlook the deaths of Bakhtiar's two soldiers in New York.

It would take time to check the story out, however, and Moheden was concerned with handling first things first—a cool half-million dollars, for example. The peculiar offer had entirely slipped his mind when he was talking to his partners on the telephone, and it would be discourteous to ring them back, annoying them with minor details.

Never mind, he thought. With thirty million split three ways over the next two years, it wouldn't matter if the others learned about his finder's fee. He must be careful, though, to guarantee that neither learned about it prematurely.

Bashir Moheden had saved the day, and his associates would recognize that fact in time. From setbacks and potential chaos, he'd brought them to the threshold of a brand-new deal, with profits nearly double their intended take. He was, in fact, a hero.

Smiling as he joined Belasko in the recreation room, the Lebanese wondered if he could manipulate this man and his sponsors to produce an even greater profit for himself. It would require finesse, but that had always been his speciality.

"So, what's the word?" Bolan asked, his tone deliberately offhand.

"Good news," Moheden answered. "As your friends in the United States might say, we're in business."

CHAPTER EIGHTEEN

Bashir Moheden's private jet took off from Beirut airport shortly after five o'clock and made the short hop to an airstrip outside Baalbek in a little under twenty minutes. They were greeted by a twelve-man escort. Bolan and his host relaxed in the comfort of a flashy limousine while gunners took positions fore and aft in black sedans.

Moheden had returned his pistol, with apologies, and Bolan took advantage of the washroom on the plane to check its load, confirming that the piece hadn't been tampered with. A shoot-out didn't figure in his short-range plans, but the warrior recognized the value of preparing for emergencies. It was comforting to know that he could take Moheden down at any time, if he had to.

They drove through Baalbek, past the Sheikh Abdullah barracks, Moheden keeping up a steady stream of small talk as they left the town behind. The driver chose an unfamiliar highway, following the east rim of the valley, and they didn't pass the turnout where Chamoun's commandos and the Syrians had clashed two days before. They met patrols along the way, but Bolan had no way of knowing if their frequency had been increased as a result of the engagement.

"There are many growers in the Bekaa," his companion said, "but my associates and I control the largest crop. The Syrians aren't concerned with private enterprise, and they've been well paid to look the other way in any case."

"Sounds like the States. I guess payola makes the world go 'round."

Moheden smiled. "Of course, we do have minor opposition in the form of hostile paramilitary groups, but they are small and generally disorganized. I cultivate informers in their ranks, and they'll be eradicated soon."

"That's your department," Bolan said. "My sponsors don't care how you handle any of the native action, just as long as the deliveries come through on time."

"Of course. I've been doing business in the Bekaa now for many years. Our export schedule has been altered only once, by the eruption of a civil war."

"Things happen, right? But when you're pulling fifteen mill a year, it would be nice if you could get a preview on that kind of thing. Make some arrangements in advance, you follow?"

If Moheden was annoyed, it didn't show. "My contacts with the government and opposition parties have improved with time," he said. "I feel safe to say our operation is immune to critical surprises."

"Glad to hear it." Bolan scanned the cultivated fields that rippled past outside his window. "Could you fill me in on where we're going?"

"Not much farther," the Lebanese replied.

As if upon command, the scout car turned into a narrow side road, and the limo followed suit, their tail car bringing up the rear. A group of sentries armed with automatic weapons waved them past, and Bolan noted that fifty yards or so beyond the highway the rows of grain gave way to fields of poppies, standing waist-high to an average man, their yellow blossoms open to the sun. It was impossible for him to estimate the total acreage, but opium would be extracted from the poppies in sufficient quantity to keep the poison flowing. And he was prepared to bet his life that there would be other fields, as large or larger, scattered up and down the valley.

"Mass production," Moheden was saying. "Opium is harvested from late December and early March, after the poppies lose their flowers. A series of small cuts are made around the pod that remains on the stem, and the sap—raw opium—is left to seep out overnight. It's collected in the morning and transported to refineries where it's transformed into morphine and, eventually, into heroin."

"You handle all of that yourself?"

"Of course. By covering the different levels of production and supply, we minimize and eliminate contention at the grass-roots level. We're thus immune to pressure from the independent operators who supply our various competitors. Our overhead is constant and predictable, within established limits. We can fairly guarantee our price per season, and protect our foreign customers from so-called 'hidden costs.'"

"That's good to know." He made a point of hesitating, putting on a mask of reticence. "I hate to pry, okay? But with this kind of money riding on the line..."

The dealer wore a tolerant expression. "Please, feel free to ask me anything."

"All right, here goes. I heard—that is, my people heard—that there were certain strings attached to your arrangement with Silvestri."

"Strings?"

"Outside the trade, you follow? Something like, he was supposed to help your people run down hits in the United States. That sound familiar?"

"Ah. May I be frank?"

"I'm listening."

"One of my close associates—the owner of this field, as luck would have it—is a member of the Shiite revolutionary guard from Teheran. His goals are different from my own in some respects. The concept of jihad, for instance—''

"Come again?"

"Jihad, Islamic holy war against the world of infidels. As you must know, despite the outward indications of a recent thaw, some tensions still remain between Iran and the United States."

"Go on."

"The revolutionary guard is charged with tracking down defectors—runaways, what have you—and exacting punishment for any crimes they have perpetrated in Iran."

"You mean, like thinking for themselves?"

Moheden smiled and spread his hands. "My interest in the field of politics is limited to issues that affect my income. In the interest of continuing supply, I have agreed to work with the Iranians in certain minor ways. Silvestri, I believe, was acting on a similar instruction from his sponsors."

"I was afraid of that." He let Moheden sweat a moment, staring out the window with a pinched expression on his face. "My people like to call themselves a bunch of patriots, you know? I mean, *I* understand your point of view, and God knows that my backers have done business with some yo-yos—no offense—but if we're talking terrorism, here . . . I just don't know."

The dealer looked as if he were about to bust a gut. He wriggled forward in his seat and placed a confidential hand on Bolan's arm.

"There need be no participation by your sponsors in the act itself—some travel documents, a weapon now and then, strategic shelter for a fugitive on rare occasions. Members of the revolutionary guard are trained to kill themselves on capture rather than submit to forcible interrogation by their enemies. If care is taken in providing certain raw materials, your risk is minimized."

"I follow that. And frankly, I don't give a shit who ices who, as long as they leave me and mine alone. Just be aware I still may have a problem selling this at home."

Reluctantly Moheden said, "We may be able to accommodate your sponsors with a minor price reduction."

"Oh? How minor?"

"Well—"

"Hold on a sec'. Let's table that for now and keep it just between the two of us, all right? If I can close this deal for thirty mill, as planned, your discount margin might be handy for a two-way split. Assuming you don't mind a little extra profit on the side."

Bashir Moheden's smile was hungry now. "My instinct tells me our relationship is destined to make history."

"You got that right," the Executioner said.

AMIR RASHAD LEFT CAMP at dusk, by motorcycle. He carried money in a belt around his waist, a pistol tucked inside his tunic and a dagger in his boot. The envelope from Joseph Chamoun was hidden in a secret pocket where it wouldn't be revealed without a thorough search . . . unless he gave it up by choice.

The trip to Baalbeck covered close to ninety miles, one way, and he'd have to travel slowly, watching out for bandits and the Syrian patrols. Where possible, he'd proceed by moonlight, switching off his headlight to reduce the risk of being spotted by his enemies. He couldn't mask the little engine's waspish sound, but he'd stop from time to time and be prepared to swerve off-road at any hint of danger.

If he didn't sleep along the way, if he wasn't detained or ambushed, midnight ought to see him safe inside the city limits. He wouldn't approach his contact on arrival, as the handoff had been scheduled for next morning, but Rashad was certain he could find some other way to pass the time. There was a cabaret he knew of where the women were accommodating and the wine was satisfactory. He might check out the action, spend a little of his hard-earned cash and find himself a place to spend the night with company.

He thought about the tall American, Belasko, and it crossed Rashad's mind that he might be too late. If damage had been done, the culprit recognized, his information would be worthless. Even worse, he might be punished for his failure to relay the news in time.

A sudden flash of panic almost made him twist the throttle open, but he calmed himself with hollow reassurances. It would take time for the American to do his work. The first phase of Belasko's penetration was a scouting mission, if Rashad could trust his sources. Only when the targets had been singled out, identified and marked, would more aggressive action be initiated. One man couldn't crush the network on his own. Belasko was relying on assistance from Chamoun.

Rashad hoped he'd be allowed to watch the American die, as he'd watched Belasko making love to Mara in the bathing pool. The spectacle had tantalized him and enraged him all at once. He marveled at the woman's choice of lovers, always leaning toward the class of peasants and adventurers. She had no eyes for someone who would love her every day throughout his life, surrendering his pride and honor in an effort to secure her future.

Still, it made no difference. When the time was right, Rashad would make her understand precisely what she'd been missing. He would wipe the smug, contemptuous expression from her face and teach her what it truly meant to be a woman.

Soon.

When he had dealt with the American and earned his just reward.

THE MILITARY AIRSTRIP outside Kefar Blum, in Israel, was on permanent alert for enemy attacks. While no location in the country was truly secure, this installation was among the worst, positioned as it was on Israel's northernmost frontier, inside the pincer formed by southern Lebanon and the southeastern flank of Syria. At one time or another, the position had been hit with rockets and artillery, attacked by terrorists and regulars who slipped across the borders after nightfall. Twice it had been overrun, but paratroopers had reclaimed the outpost at a fearful price.

Grimaldi was acquainted with the local history, and when he left his quarters he was armed against the possibility of terrorist attack by night. The sentries recognized him, and he wasn't challenged as he moved toward the perimeter and stood, eyes narrowed in the darkness, staring off across the border into Lebanon.

The homer's maximum effective range was something like a hundred miles on paper, but it varied slightly, day by day, like any other disembodied signal beaming through the open air. Grimaldi had been forced to move from Haifa to the base at Kefar Blum when it became apparent that his man was out of range. They had him now, most times, although the signal flickered, fading now and then. But it was close enough.

Grimaldi had been watching, in his fashion, as Mack Bolan made his guided tour of the Bekaa Valley with Chamoun. The westward drive to visit Bashir Moheden had been recorded, spanning several hours, and the short hop back to Baalbek told them Bolan had been traveling by air on his return. Another run down-country—visiting the poppy fields, perhaps—and then right back to town, where he had registered no action for the past two hours.

Plotting Bolan's progress on a chart had certain built-in limitations. They could follow him along a major highway, for example, but Grimaldi had no way of knowing when he was alone or traveling in company with those he meant to kill. In urban areas, the homer lost all semblance of precision, pinning down a sector of the city, possibly a neighborhood, if they were lucky, but it would require an overflight, perhaps an agent on the ground, to single out his actual location.

Worse, the damned thing couldn't even tell Grimaldi if the man he most admired was alive.

He'd been fine, of course, until the trip to meet Moheden in his lair. They didn't have to speculate about the visit to the dealer's villa. Agents of Mossad had monitored the Lebanese's operation for a period of years, but he didn't sell drugs in Israel, and there were more pressing problems for the crack Israeli secret service than disruption of organized crime in Lebanon. The gathered information had been passed to the DEA, and on from there to Stony Man Farm, but Bashir Moheden had posed no threat to Israel prior to his alliance with Ahmad Halaby and the Shiite revolutionary guard.

The way Grimaldi pieced it all together, Bolan had secured his contact in the Bekaa, then moved on from there to make his pitch with Moheden. The dealer's gut reaction might go either way, but Bolan had been flown to Baalbek, and Grimaldi took that as a sign that he was still alive and well. Moheden didn't need to fly a corpse around the country, or conduct it on a driving tour of his opium plantations. If the Executioner had run into any problems, it would be within the past few hours, after his return to Baalbek.

Was his cover solid? How long would it take before Moheden or his contacts in New York got wise? It made Grimaldi furious to realize that Bolan could be fingered, tortured, killed, and he'd never even know about it if the homer's beacon kept on sounding loud and clear. Of course, if Bolan's enemies discovered the device...

Grimaldi cursed the darkness, almost wishing there would be a raid, some outlet for his simmering aggression and anxiety. It didn't matter who or why; he simply needed to lash out, allow himself the luxury of action in the midst of all this waiting.

The pilot had been raised a Catholic, but he hadn't been to church—much less confession—for years. He knew some dusty prayers, but none of them were quite appropriate for the occasion, and he let it slide. The Executioner had been in rugged spots before, and he was still alive.

So far.

Grimaldi had a helicopter gunship and a Phantom standing by, each armed and ready for a swift response in different situations. If it came to lifting Bolan out, the chopper could run north as far as Baalbek, westward to the outskirts of Beirut. If Bolan was confirmed as KIA, Grimaldi had a list of targets for retaliation—starting with Moheden's desert villa—and he was prepared to take the whole damned air force on if necessary.

Whichever way it played, he'd be there for Bolan at the finish.

One way or another, Jack Grimaldi still had dues to pay.

THE HOTEL ROOM WASN'T luxurious, but it was comfortable. Bolan had a view of downtown Baalbek, mostly dark and shuttered after nightfall, and he didn't mind the extra bit of privacy, the chance to spend some time away from Bashir Moheden.

The dealer had his own apartment in the city, where he stayed infrequently, and he'd rented Bolan one of the best rooms in town. They were supposed to meet bright and early for breakfast, followed by a visit to Moheden's drug refinery that would complete the guided tour. If Bolan couldn't force a meeting with the other partners, he was ready to eliminate Moheden and proceed from there as best he could.

Communicating with Chamoun would be the problem. Once he secured a fix on the refinery, he'd be needing men to launch a swift, precisely timed attack. There were too many targets now, too many enemies for him to try it on his own.

But if he couldn't make contact with the rebels, Bolan knew that he'd have no choice. He hadn't come this far to let a breakdown in communications trash the mission. Nicosia had been practice, a rehearsal for the main event in Lebanon, and if it came to flying solo, he'd do his best with what he had.

All afternoon and evening the warrior had been plagued by nagging apprehension, vague misgivings that he couldn't name. He wrote it off to combat jitters, a condition that afflicts the seasoned veteran along with green recruits. No matter that a soldier might have faced the enemy a dozen or a hundred times before. On each occasion that he took the firing line, there was a fleeting moment when he questioned his ability, the wisdom of his orders, enemy positions or the state of his equipment and support. The Executioner, on hold in Baalbek, questioned all these and more.

He trusted his ability to do a job in combat, but mature self-confidence didn't make Bolan bulletproof. The most professional of soldiers died eventually—from an oversight, some marginal miscalculation, or the fact that they were simply out of time. If Bolan's number came around this time, security meant nothing.

His mission, as a concept, was a sound one. He'd known the odds at the beginning, and refusal of the task had never been an option. Bolan's sense of duty forced him to accept, and made him grateful for the opportunity to strike another blow against the savages. If this should be the last time out, at least he had a chance to make it count for something.

His enemies were numerous, and the warrior didn't have a solid fix on all of their positions yet. It scarcely mattered, since a single man could never take them all in the allotted time, but he'd still feel better when he knew precisely where they were. Each member of the pack eliminated would be one more predator removed from circulation, extra frosting on the cake.

Equipment-wise, the warrior recognized his limitations. He couldn't conduct a war with the Beretta and its two spare magazines, but he could make a start and hope to pick up other arms along the way. As for support, he had Chamoun, the rebel troops, and Jack Grimaldi waiting to assist him when he gave the word. Assuming, always, that he had a chance to get the message through.

A simple case of combat jitters, right. He smiled and cranked the window open, listening to Baalbek's night sounds as he killed the lights and lay down on the double bed. His thoughts flashed back to Mara, but he pushed her image out of frame and concentrated on tomorrow and his scheduled tour of the powder factory. With that location fixed, he'd be in position to inflict substantial damage on the Bekaa pipeline. Cripple it, perhaps, or even bring it down.

But first it would be necessary to establish contact with Chamoun, coordinate the strike before his cover started smoldering around the edges. Once it flamed, there would be no time left, no other chance to save the play.

Tomorrow? Possibly before the day was out?

He focused on the dark abyss of sleep and hoped he wouldn't dream.

CHAPTER NINETEEN

Amir Rashad awoke with the sensation that a furry animal had crawled inside his mouth to die. His breath was rancid, his throat was parched from too much alcohol the night before. He glanced around the tiny bedroom, fearful of awakening the pain that lurked behind his eyes, and found that the woman had departed.

Pale morning stabbed through rips and moth holes in the ancient curtains, forcing him to squint against the light. It would be early yet, but he had no spare time to waste. His contact would have been alerted to expect the envelope first thing.

The more important task came back to him, its urgency sufficient to disperse his mental haze. This morning he'd graduate from errand boy and spy to the position of a valued player on his master's team. There would be no more menial assignments, no more hiding in the shadows. Once he proved his worth, by turning over the American, he'd be clearly marked for better things.

Unless he hung about the room all day and missed his contact.

Groaning with the pain it cost him, he threw back the rumpled, musty sheets and dragged himself into an upright posture. Walls and furniture revolved around him for a moment, finally stabilizing. It required a major effort of will for him to stand, but once erect, he thought he might survive.

There were showers down the hall. Rashad propelled himself along the corridor on wooden legs and stood beneath the tepid spray while life crept back into his body. Other tenants of the cheap hotel were starting to arrive when he departed, bundling his threadbare towels and dropping them inside a hamper by the door.

There was no question of consuming breakfast. He couldn't have kept it down, and it was pointless to waste money on a meal that would inevitably wind up in the gutter. Suffering didn't destroy his business sense or blind him to his main objectives for the day.

A cautious man, Rashad decided to cover all the bases and run the errand for Chamoun first thing. It wouldn't take much time, and if his expectations for the second lap weren't entirely realized, his cover with the rebels would be safe. Accordingly he took no steps to read the message, making certain that its seal of wax was still intact.

His rebel contact was the owner of a humble pawnshop, several blocks away from the hotel where he'd passed the night. The shop was open early, its proprietor expecting him, and he approached the place like any other customer. He waited while the seal was broken and the message read. The old man glanced up when he was finished.

"You have read this?"

"No." His voice was steady as he spoke the solemn truth.

"There is no answer."

"Very well."

He left the shop and spent a quarter hour wandering around the streets with no apparent destination, pausing frequently to window-shop and check the faces of pedestrians around him. If he was being followed, the tail was clever—he couldn't spot him.

When Rashad was satisfied, he walked back to the hotel, retrieved his motorbike and set off northbound through the crush of morning traffic. In the shadow of Hosseinieh, the Shiite stronghold, he turned off into a maze of narrow side streets, dodging dogs and ragged children as they crossed his path. The streets hadn't been swept in living memory, and mounds of garbage lined the gutters. On his left a block of houses had been scoured by fire. More children scampered through the ruins, hands and faces black with soot.

His target was a seedy warehouse on the outskirts of the residential district. Pulling up outside, Rashad turned off his engine and dismounted, wheeling the bike ahead of him as he approached the doors. He pushed the buzzer, waited and was just about to try again, when footsteps sounded on the concrete floor inside. A bolt was thrown and the door eased open. A baleful eye examined him as if for symptoms of disease.

"I have an urgent message for Selim."

"Your number?"

"Seventeen."

"Come in."

He pushed the bike inside and propped it on the kickstand, safe from thieves and urchins on the street. The watchman took his knife and pistol, waited while he turned his empty pockets out, then led him down an empty corridor that terminated with the entrance to the warehouse proper. Swinging doors gave access to the cavernous interior. A glassed-in office stood in the corner to his left.

Rashad was patient while his escort entered, muttered something to his contact and emerged to wave him through. The watchman held his weapons in one hand, thick fingers wrapped around the lethal steel.

"You pick these up before you leave," he said, and then the door snicked shut behind him, leaving them alone.

Selim didn't stand up. He put no stock in courtesy and dealt with his informers brusquely, wasting no more time than he found absolutely necessary.

"Yes?"

Rashad breathed deeply, marshaling his thoughts. It was important that Selim should be impressed, or his report might go no further, and he'd be cheated of his just reward.

"I have a message for the man in charge."

"Go on, I'm listening."

"I must deliver it myself."

Selim expelled a weary sigh. "You have no business with the masters," he replied. "If they saw everyone who brings them urgent messages, there would be time for nothing else."

"You don't understand. There's a stranger, an American—"

Selim was on his feet before Rashad could finish, gripping his lapel with one hand, flourishing a slim blade in the other, pressing it against his captive's throat.

"The name!" he demanded.

Rashad's life didn't flash before his eyes, but he saw Death, up close and personal. If he didn't speak swiftly, truthfully, there would be no reward. No riches. Nothing.

Sucking in a ragged breath, he held it long enough to feel the blade bite deeper, nearly drawing blood.

"Belasko."

AFTER BREAKFAST Bashir Moheden drove Bolan to the powder factory that was disguised as an evacuated tenement in Baalbek's dreary slum. There were no sentries on the street, but Bolan made a rapid scan, detecting snipers in a couple of the upstairs windows, opposite. The children of the streets were wise enough to quit their games and run for home when they recognized the dealer's limousine.

Inside, two Arabs sporting automatic rifles, pistols strapped around their waists, snapped to attention as Moheden entered. One of them was also carrying a walkie-talkie on his belt, and Bolan knew the lookouts in surrounding tenements had radioed word of their arrival.

An elevator took them up three floors, and they were greeted by another pair of gunmen on arrival. One peeled off and led them down a murky corridor, through double doors that opened on the lab itself. Before they entered, both men were handed surgical masks. They took a moment to fit the gauze rectangles over nose and mouth. Inside, they were delivered to a swarthy overseer who did everything but bow and scrape before his master.

The overseer, guards and chemists all wore masks against the risk of breathing caustic fumes or residue from the narcotics in production. With their lab coats and their swimming goggles, the technicians all resembled extras from a 1950s science fiction movie, bent on whipping up a monster in their lab. In fact the poison they produced had been responsible for putting countless monsters on the street. But these men never gave a second thought to consequences.

Moheden's eyes betrayed a hint of pride as he led Bolan down the line, delivering a minilecture on the technique of refining heroin from opium. "The raw material is first converted into morphine," he explained, "a relatively simple process, which reduces the original bulk by ninety percent. In the final stage, morphine is boiled with acetic anhydride—a chemical closely related to the acetic acid found in common vinegar—and the resultant product is diacetylmorphine. Heroin.''

They moved along the sturdy tables, past retorts, beakers and Bunsen burners hissing flame. The chemists never glanced up from their work, and Bolan wondered whether they were industrious or frightened of the man who paid their salaries.

"Our product is ninety-nine percent pure," the Lebanese went on. "It isn't, in your charming vernacular, 'stepped on.' A bargain at four thousand dollars per kilo, I'm sure you'll agree."

"And the volume?"

"I estimate three thousand kilos per annum from this plant alone. A second lab wouldn't be difficult or costly to establish, if your business should require a larger quantity."

"That's something we can talk about in time. Six thousand kilos over two years, at a cost of four grand each, makes twenty-four million, give or take."

"You mentioned thirty."

"So I did. Let's say I sell the package to my sponsors at a kilo-price of five grand each. That's half the going rate in Hong Kong, and they shouldn't bitch. If you can satisfy your partners with the four-grand tag, that leaves us three mill each to play with, when we're finished."

"Ah. The wonders of mathematics."

"Have we got a deal?"

Before Moheden could reply, someone rapped sharply on the door. The foreman waddled over to admit a sentry from the corridor, with two men on his heels. One of the tagalongs struck Bolan as familiar, but he couldn't place the eyes, and all the rest was hidden by a square of gauze. The new arrivals were glaring at Bolan, and he felt a worm of apprehension squirming in his gut.

These guys were trouble.

The foreman beckoned Moheden, glancing over at a gunner on the sidelines nearest Bolan. The dealer wore a puzzled look as he excused himself and crossed the floor. The gunner, meanwhile, seemed to know precisely what was coming, and he moved to stand behind the Executioner, almost within arm's reach.

It clicked for Bolan as Moheden huddled with the new arrivals. He's seen the shorter of the men just recently, when he was staying in the camp of Joseph Chamoun. A traitor! And his presence in the powder factory—the burning glance from Bashir Moheden—could only mean that Bolan's cover had been blown.

He moved before the opposition had a chance, reaching inside his jacket and snaring the Beretta as he spun to face the nearest gunner. Bolan shot him in the face, a single round that turned his nose into a gaping wound. He caught the folding-stock Kalashnikov before it dropped from lifeless fingers, pivoting to bring the second laboratory gunner under fire.

His target was responding, but it was too little and too late. The second round from Bolan's pistol drilled the shooter's throat and knocked him off his feet, already dead before his body hit the floor. Still spinning, Bolan found the AK-47's trigger, held it down and watched all hell break loose.

His first rounds swept along the table, exploding glassware, raising clouds of million-dollar dust. One lab technician stopped a bullet and went down, thrashing in the sudden snowstorm. Others scattered in search of cover that didn't exist.

The floor boss had a pistol in his hand as Bolan spun to face him, but the other members of his tiny group were leaping wide to save themselves. He had a glimpse of

Bashir Moheden's retreating back before the dealer reached the outer corridor and disappeared. Then the warrior's attention was consumed by details of the task at hand.

He nailed the foreman with a straggling burst that stitched across his chest from right to left and slammed him over in his tracks. The new arrivals, strange and familiar face alike, were breaking for the doors, to follow Moheden, when Bolan cut them down and left them writhing on the floor. He had a moment's grace before the guards arrived, and it was time enough to spot a fire escape outside the nearest window.

Bolan moved on instinct and tried to raise the window, but it had been nailed or painted shut. He swung the folding-stock Kalashnikov against the flyspecked pane and battered out the glass, stepping through as cursing figures filled the narrow door behind him.

The Executioner let them have a parting burst, which kicked up another storm of powder. Then he was out, but it could still go either way, and all the odds lay with the house. He was outnumbered, easily outgunned.

And he was running for his life.

MOHEDEN WAITED in the corridor outside the lab, prepared to flee again if necessary. He wasn't a hero and had never posed as one. If necessary, he could kill, but decades had elapsed since he'd been called upon to fight with weapons like a common soldier.

With a measure of relief, he heard the sounds of battle fading, muffled as the sentries took their hunt outside. The fire escape! He turned and barked an order to the gunmen standing at his side. They bobbed their heads and retreated toward the elevator at a run to call up reinforcements on the street below.

The dealer pushed the door back and stepped inside the lab, his nose wrinkling at the smell of cordite and the stench of human waste. After one step across the threshold, he nearly lost his footing in a slick of blood spread out before him, seeping from two prostrate forms. His spy, Selim, and the informer from the rebel camp—what was his name?—had fallen almost side by side. Moheden edged around their bodies, found the operation supervisor lying crumpled in his path and paused to take stock of the carnage.

At least five men dead, with the equipment shot to hell and merchandise destroyed. They might save some of it if they were quick enough, but the American had cost him roughly thirty thousand wholesale dollars in about ten seconds.

Moheden had been blind. The bastard was an agent of some kind, perhaps assigned to gather information on their network, and he had invited him inside, conducting what amounted to a guided tour of future targets. They would have to move the laboratory now, or what was left of it, before the police arrived. Long years of bribery would slow them down, but they were still a factor to be reckoned with, and the Americans might prod them into swifter action.

But, the fields . . .

A laboratory could be moved in hours—even moments, if the bulk of its equipment had been trashed like this one—but a thousand-acre farm wasn't exactly portable. He thought about the prospect of a sweep along the Bekaa, ripe fields withering before a wall of flame, and cringed inside. It took a moment for him to regain composure, realizing that the threat he visualized, while awesome, had no basis in reality.

Assuming the Americans had struck some kind of bargain with the Beirut government—a prospect that was
difficult to swallow—the crucial problem would be practical enforcement. Lebanese police and military officers
had carried no authority within the Bekaa Valley for a decade, yielding tacitly to occupation by the Syrians and local
strongmen as their troubles had multiplied around Beirut.
Whatever deal the White House or its newly christened
"drug czar" might attempt to make with Lebanese officials, Washington had no significant influence with the
Syrians, much less the Shiite warlords of the Bekaa.

Around him, various survivors of the shoot-out were
attempting to bring order out of chaos, turning off the
Bunsen burners, picking shards of glass from drifts of
snowy powder, sweeping up around the tables. Snapping
orders right and left, Moheden chose another foreman on
the spot, dismissed the startled chemist's thanks, demanding that the lab be broken down and moved within
the hour. Sooner, if they had it in them.

Turning from the mess, the dealer left them to it. He had
other, even more unpleasant duties to perform. He'd be
forced to tell his partners now that he had been deceived.
His judgment on the tall American had been mistaken. All
of them were presently at risk because Moheden had been
thinking with his purse instead of with his brain.

He wouldn't phrase it quite that way, of course. It was
important to preserve at least a thin facade of injured innocence, defuse the anger of his comrades—and especially Bakhtiar—before it reached a lethal flashpoint. If he
had to fight his friends as well as the American . . .

Moheden pushed the thought away. They would believe
him, stand behind him in the hour of crisis. Bakhtiar, for
all of his fanaticism, couldn't be mistaken for a fool. His

own best interests lay in solidarity, a strong united front
against the enemy.

It sounded good.

If only Moheden could manage to convince himself.

IT WAS A TWISTED REPLAY of the action in New York, with
Bolan as the hunted. He felt the rusty fire escape shiver as
he pounded down the steps, heard the gritty sound of bolts
attempting to work free of ancient masonry. His pursuers
used a burst of automatic fire to clear the windowframe
before they scrambled through.

He spun to face them, squeezing off with the Kalashnikov before he had a solid target. Sparks flew off the steps
and spindly railing, brick dust spurting from the wall on
impact. One of Bolan's adversaries took two rounds below the belt, the momentum of his fall dragging him across
the railing.

Number two was angling for a shot around his dying
partner, but he never found it. Bolan held down the AK-
47's trigger and used his last half-dozen rounds to drop the
gunner on his backside, stepping clear before the dead
meat reached the landing. He discarded the Kalashnikov
and leaped across the rail, with fifteen feet between him
and the ground.

The alley ran from east to west beside the building Bolan had evacuated, one end opening upon the street where
Moheden had parked his limousine, the other granting
access to a cluttered street in back. The front was covered,
and just to emphasize the point, a rooftop sniper started
pegging shots at Bolan, gravel flying as the first few rounds
went wild.

The warrior sprinted along the alley, the Beretta in his
hand, and picked up speed when he heard voices raised
behind him. Bullets whined off the alley walls, and he

hunched his shoulders, waiting for the impact that would knock him sprawling in a final flash of white-hot pain.

Stacks of wooden crates and cardboard boxes filled his path, brimming with the refuse of the streets. He sidestepped, ducked behind the nearest pile and dropped into a fighting crouch. Before he had a chance to catch his breath, two riflemen appeared from nowhere, blocking off the near end of the alley, closing fast. They hadn't spotted him.

He braced the automatic in a firm, two-handed grip and stroked the trigger twice. His first round struck the gunner on the left and drilled a hole beneath his jawline, clipping vertebrae before it blew a fist-sized exit wound behind one ear. The second guard was still recovering from his surprise when Bolan put a bullet through his heart at thirty feet. The gunner folded like a rag doll, going down in the filth without a whimper.

The Executioner left the cover of his makeshift sanctuary, moving fast and low, his weapon spitting rounds in rapid fire as soon as he made target acquisition. Three men armed with submachine guns spread out in a ragged skirmish line. The warrior tracked his fire from right to left, his first rounds punching through the chest of number one and blowing him away.

It was a tie with number two, the gunner ripping off a hasty burst as Bolan shot him in the face, the explosive impact toppling him backward. His partner, all alone now, nearly made the tag, but he was firing high, his bullets slicing empty air a foot or two above his prostrate target. Bolan made it three for three, a relatively simple shot at twenty yards, and he was on his feet, a man in motion, by the time the gunner fell.

He half expected further opposition on the street, but Moheden hadn't laid on the same security in back. It was an oversight, and it would cost the dealer, as Bolan holstered his Beretta, dodging spotty traffic in his rush across the street. In a few more moments he'd be absorbed by the teeming crowds.

When he'd covered several blocks, the Executioner began to take stock of his situation. He'd pulled it off, survival-wise, but he was stranded in a hostile city where his enemies had free run of the streets. His features and his clothing marked him as a foreigner, a moving target, and he couldn't count on finding friends among the native populace. Unless he could obtain a rudimentary disguise and some form of transportation, he was lost.

The Executioner had walked away with one hand, but his adversaries weren't ready to concede the game. All things considered, Bolan wasn't happy with the cards he had been dealt. The more he studied them, the more he wondered if they might not be a dead man's hand.

CHAPTER TWENTY

It took an hour and a half for Bashir Moheden to gather all the scattered bits of information necessary for his plan. By that time he had heard the worst of it—Belasko had escaped, against all odds—and he had issued promises to his unhappy partners that the situation would be rectified. Of course, if they were willing to provide material assistance, he would be most grateful.

Half the ninety minutes were consumed by Moheden's attempt to name the dead informant. In the end, he never learned the man's identity, but that was secondary to uncovering his rebel contacts. When the name of Joseph Chamoun came up, the dealer knew that he had solved a least a portion of the mystery.

For years the Bekaa Valley's Christian population had been locked in conflict with their Muslim neighbors, echoing the tremors of religious warfare from Beirut. Around the Bekaa, though, the Christians weren't satisfied with sniping Druze and Shiite targets. Rather, they had taken it upon themselves to strike at organized narcotics dealers, doing everything within their power to disrupt the flow of drugs that were the region's single largest-selling export item.

Granted, all their efforts to the present time had been relatively minor—an ambush, here and there; small shipments hijacked; runners executed and relieved of cash. It was annoying, but the rival dealers did no less to one another in the normal course of business, and reprisals had been more or less successful in containing Christian rebels to the valley's southern quarter. One day, if they grew too troublesome, a concentrated push would wipe them out entirely.

Now Moheden wondered if the moment for that push had come.

The troops of Joseph Chamoun had been his most persistent enemies among the scattered Christian forces. They had clashed with members of the Shitte revolutionary guard on more than one occasion, and while there had been no stunning victories for either side, Chamoun's commandos had revealed themselves as tough, determined fighters. They were dangerous, in short, because they wouldn't quit.

Moheden—through his spy, Selim—had cultivated turncoats in as many of the Christian "armies" as he could. It was a stroke of luck to place a man inside Chamoun's contingent, and the traitor's fingering of Belasko had been nothing short of providential. What might the American have done if he had been admitted to a meeting of the cartel leaders? Would any of them have survived?

The dealer had no way of knowing if Chamoun had forged official ties with the Americans, or whether he had simply hired a mercenary to advance his cause. The action in New York was clearly separate from any localized offensive by the Christian troops, and that implied at least a tenuous connection with the West. It didn't matter if Belasko or Chamoun had made the overture. Together they were doubly dangerous, and it would be Moheden's task to crush them into the dust.

It took the second half of ninety minutes to collect and arm a raiding party from the Sheikh Abdullah barracks. Half of the men were Palestinians donated by Halaby, while the rest were members of the Shiite revolutionary guard. Each group had leaders of its own, but after some discussion, they agreed to take their orders from an officer selected by Moheden for the job.

A background check of Joseph Chamoun had helped to give those orders their direction. Realizing that a raid might somehow miss Chamoun, Moheden had decided on a backup plan. It was, with all due modesty, a master stroke. If executed properly, with all dispatch, he was convinced that it would bring the rebel leader to his knees.

If not, at least it would provide the troops with exercise, a bit of sport. They had been getting stale of late, in the dealer's opinion, training constantly for raids and revolutions that were first postponed, then canceled. How long had it been since any of Halaby's men had sortied against the Israelis? How long since any of the revolutionary guard had trashed a U.S. embassy or taken hostages?

This would be a dress rehearsal, practice with a living enemy who could and would return their fire. They should be grateful for the opportunity to test themselves, assuming they survived.

One final task. Arranging for the helicopters hadn't been supremely difficult, but it required some time, the crossing of strategic palms with gold. Four ships would be available upon demand, with pilots borrowed from the military. In a region like the Bekaa, where the lines of jurisdiction and authority were blurred, the deal wasn't unusual.

Bashir Moheden would be waiting for the raiders when they came back with the head of Chamoun, or with their prisoner. In either case he'd have struck a telling blow against his enemies, while winning back a measure of respect from his associates. If luck was on his side, he might transform abject humiliation into triumph.

THE PROBLEM of Bolan's clothing had been relatively simple to resolve. As he roamed the streets, alert to any indication of a tail, he passed a thrift shop and ducked in to buy himself a suitable disguise. Avoiding the extravagance of all-out Arab garb, he settled for the military surplus apparel so popular in Lebanon, the drab material a striking contrast to the navy outfit he'd worn on entering the shop. The owner was startled when his customer insisted on discarding what was obviously an expensive suit, but as a businessman he made no protest.

Transportation was a bit more difficult, but Bolan had to make the effort. He couldn't remain in Baalbek any longer, and the hike to reach Chamoun's encampment, nearly ninety miles away, might take a week. With wheels he could complete the journey in an afternoon, and so he started searching for a vehicle to fit his needs.

He chose a taxi after weighing all the pros and cons of just taking a vehicle from the curb. In Lebanon—and more particularly in the Bekaa Valley—poverty restricted ownership of cars to members of the merchant class, the civil service and the military. Auto theft was rare, and the alert for stolen vehicles would bring a swift police response. Instead of bagging wheels from any one of several downtown parking lots, therefore, the Executioner decided on a more direct approach.

He flagged down the taxi a mile from where he'd escaped Moheden's trap. The driver didn't seem surprised to hear himself being addressed in merely functional Arabic, and he followed Bolan's vague directions to the southern quarter of the city. There, when Bolan showed him the Beretta on a quiet side street and commanded him to climb inside the trunk, he made no argument.

Avoiding major thoroughfares, he cleared the city limits in another quarter hour, running south along the highway where Chamoun and company had met the Syrians. How long ago? A lifetime. Twenty miles from town he stopped and freed his hostage, allowing cash to take the place of an apology. The cabbie might encounter a patrol five minutes up the road and send them after him, but Bolan had to take that chance. At least this way he had a shot at leveling the odds.

He drove with the Beretta on the seat beside him, one eye on the rearview mirror. Bolan's mind was racing toward his destination, sorting out the facts that he would lay before Chamoun. The powder factory would be dismantled and removed before a raid could be initiated, but he had obtained the address of Moheden's home away from home in Baalbek, and there still might be a chance to catch the dealer on the scene. If not, the soldier had a backup plan in mind.

But first he had to reach Chamoun's encampment, find out whether the rebel leader was fit to travel, much less fight. They wouldn't have a better chance to move against their common enemy, but every moment counted now, with Moheden and company undoubtedly preparing their defenses for the coming storm.

He checked the taxi's gas gauge, saw that he had fuel enough to make a one-way trip and put more weight on the accelerator. Grumbling, the taxi picked up speed and carried Bolan south.

THE SILENCE DIDN'T WORRY Joseph Chamoun. He had agreed with the American that premature communications could betray them and alert their enemies before they were prepared to strike. The absence of a message simply meant that he was close to Moheden, absorbing secret details of the enemy's defenses.

Of course the silence might mean he was dead.

Chamoun dismissed the thought. He hadn't known Belasko long, but he believed himself to be a decent judge of men. By any name, the tall American was a survivor. Granted, he took risks that other men might well consider foolish, but his every move was calculated, mapped out in advance for maximum effect. If anyone could pierce the heart of the cartel...

The sound of helicopters startled him. Some distance yet—a thousand yards, perhaps—but they were audible above the normal racket of the camp, and drawing closer by the moment. Rolling from his cot, he grimaced at a stab of protest from his shoulder wound, retrieved a submachine gun from the folding table as he thrust the tent flaps back and stepped outside.

The others were alert. Men abandoned their routine jobs in search of weapons, women scooped up stray children and hurried to their tents. Chamoun couldn't make out his sister anywhere. Too late he realized the helicopters were equipped with special mufflers to allow them the advantage of surprise. His thousand yards might only be two hundred or less, and as they broke the cover of the trees, he cursed himself for being such a fool.

Three airships grazed the treetops as they closed in for the kill. He heard the crackle of machine-gun fire and watched the spurts of dust begin to march across the compound. One tent rippled, flapping in the breeze, and then another. Bullets swept the camp like the initial scattering of raindrops that precede a cloudburst. Here, however, when the rain from heaven fell on human flesh, it left its mark.

A number of the men were firing back, peppering the whirlybirds with automatic fire, but they had nothing in the way of cover, and their time was short. The pilots kept their ships in motion, while below them human targets ran in circles, dropping where the bullets found them, rolling over in the blood and dust. One sprawled across a cooking fire, past feeling as his khaki shirt and pants burst into flame.

Chamoun whipped up his submachine gun, taking time to aim before he squeezed the trigger. Did he imagine the hit, or had his bullets cracked the windscreen of the nearest helicopter? There! Firing again he saw them strike, the pilot hauling backward on his joy stick as he tried for greater altitude.

The rebel leader ran out of ammunition as he tracked the rising target, fumbled for another magazine and cursed as he remembered he'd left the bandolier inside his tent. Retreating, he was barely through the flaps when an explosion rocked the camp, immediately followed by another, then the world fell in around him.

Something struck him smartly on the skull, and he went down, the tent collapsing on him like a shroud. Chamoun experienced a sense of drowning as he wormed his way along the ground, one hand still wrapped around his empty submachine gun, groping with the other for an exit.

He was running out of time. Suppressing panic, he retrieved a clasp knife from his pocket, opened it and started hacking at the tent material. It snagged his blade at first, then yielded, and he cut a slit approximately three feet long. Emerging from the gap, blood streaming from a scalp wound, he resembled something in the nature of a freakish newborn entering a hostile world. With weapons clenched in both hands and a savage grimace on his blood-streaked face, he made a perfect war child.

They had set the helicopters down nearby, their weapons silent now as gunmen fanned out through the camp. One passed Chamoun without observing him, and it was all the edge he needed, scrambling to his feet and swinging his SMG against the gunner's *keffiyeh*. The raider staggered and slumped to his knees. Chamoun was on him, slashing with his knife. The blade slid home beneath his adversary's ear and ripped across the jugular, releasing gouts of crimson. The rebel leader retrieved the dying soldier's rifle, left him to his final heartbeats and broke for the cover of the trees.

A pair of gunners on his left had spotted him. They shouted and opened fire. He returned a withering blast with the captured rifle. One of his assailants caught a rising burst and staggered, fell. The other went to ground, apparently unharmed, and then Chamoun was in the trees, the sound of shots and shouting voices all around him.

He had torn the stitches on his shoulder wound, the fresh blood soaking through his tunic. Never mind. There would be time enough to bind it if he managed to escape the hunting party on his heels. Had he been recognized? What had become of Mara? How many of his people would survive the raid?

He wondered fleetingly if something evil had befallen the American. It didn't follow automatically. There were a hundred ways in which the opposition might have found his camp. They had, perhaps, remained in one place for too long a time.

Gunfire chattered behind him. He was tempted to return, confront the enemy and try to save his people, but he knew the gesture would be wasted. There was nothing he could do to stop them, and he wouldn't improve their lot by dying needlessly. Instead he would survive and find a way to inflict the appropriate revenge on the men who had decreed this massacre.

He prayed that Mara might escape, his people find a sanctuary from the storm. Above all else, he prayed for strength to find his enemies and strike them down.

MARA HAD BEEN WORKING in the mess tent, helping to prepare the midday meal when first she heard the helicopters. Stepping outside she was in time to see them break the tree line to the north and come in with machine guns blazing from their open loading bays. A bullet snapped past on her left, another closer on her right, and instinct took control, propelling her across the compound in a sprint.

Around her, men were cursing, firing, falling. Mara saw a boy of six or seven cut down in his tracks, unmoving as the bullets danced around him. She was searching for her brother, but he might be anywhere. If he was still inside his tent—

A grenade went off, immediately followed by another, dust and gravel raining down on Mara as she ran. Disoriented, she suspected she was running in a circle, but the gunfire and explosions had her trapped. She felt the blast of rotor blades and knew the helicopters were coming in for a landing. She tried to veer away, but there was one on either side of her, another squatting just across the compound.

One chance left, she ran in the direction of her brother's tent and the grove of trees beyond. Where *was* his tent? She saw it now, collapsed and rippling in the artificial gale produced by rotorwash.

Forgetting danger, Mara ran to find her brother, stopping short beside the shambles of his tent. A dead man lay nearby—an enemy, his throat slashed open—and she turned away from him, intent on rescuing the living.

Where to start? She grabbed at the stiff material of the tent, discovering that it was torn in places. Bullets, she decided, or the jagged shrapnel from explosions. There were shapeless lumps beneath the shroud, all deathly still as Mara crawled around them. Furniture, perhaps, upended when the tent collapsed. There was no sound, no movement, to betray the presence of a living man.

Had her brother been elsewhere when the explosion struck his quarters? Was he safe? She glanced around the compound, saw more enemies than friends, and knew that it was time to save herself. She scrambled to her feet and struck off to the west, where trees and undergrowth would cover her retreat—if she could get that far. Sporadic gunfire cracked around her, weak resistance falling in the face of the assault, but Mara concentrated on her destination, jumbled thoughts competing for attention in her mind.

The gunman came from nowhere, tackled her and brought her down. The jarring impact emptied Mara's lungs, but she fought back with all the strength she had, claws raking at her adversary's face and drawing blood. He cursed and tried to pin her hands. Mara kicked him in the groin.

She scrambled to her feet, prepared to run, but other men surrounded her, eyes wary, fingering their weapons. Mara waited for the bullet that would end her life, and when it didn't come, she understood that these men meant to capture her alive. It gave her an advantage if the enemy was under orders not to kill her, and she seized the moment, breaking full tilt for a weak point in the line.

A Palestinian stepped out to intercept her, and she saw the butt of his Kalashnikov as it swept through a narrow arc, directly toward her face. She raised an arm to shield herself, to absorb the crushing impact, but the blow threw Mara off her stride. She lost her footing, stumbled and fell. They were on her in an instant, pinning down her arms and legs.

Immobilized, she felt a rough hand work its way along her neck in search of the carotid artery. She tried to bite the probing fingers, but her head was pinned, a gunman standing on her hair. The searching hand made contact, pressed and Mara saw dark motes begin to dance before her eyes. Another moment and her world went black. She didn't feel the gunmen lift her body.

THE DRIVE TOOK LONGER than Bolan had anticipated, with patrols twice forcing him off the road. Each time he saw them coming from a distance, pulling into turnouts, and hoped they would pass him by without a second glance. If he was stopped and questioned, it was over. He didn't speak fluent Arabic—couldn't even attempt any of the regional dialects—and his Beretta wouldn't get him far against a rifle squad with automatic weapons.

Luck was with him. The patrols were intent on other missions. Bolan watched them pass and counted down the moments after, each time giving them a decent lead before he put the stolen cab in motion. It was creeping on two o'clock before he reached the narrow side road leading to the rebel compound. He slowed as he made the turn, leaning out the driver's window so the sentries could identify him.

Bolan had been ready for a challenge, but there seemed to be no guards on duty. Startled by the lapse, then worried, he pushed on, avoiding swift acceleration in case there might be spotters he had overlooked. It would be bitter irony if he was shot down by an ally this close to his goal.

Within a hundred yards of camp, he met two stragglers, both armed with submachine guns. They were braced to fire when recognition saved him, and the men came forward, speaking to him excitedly and gesturing in the direction of the compound. Bolan couldn't understand much of what they said, but one of them was bleeding through his shirt from what appeared to be a superficial wound, and both were caked with battle dust. He gunned the taxi forward, and within another moment he was on the outskirts of the rebel camp.

Before him, in the aftermath of combat, was chaos. Tents lay scattered, flattened by the firestorm. Retrieval teams were lifting bodies from the field and laying them along the sidelines. Bolan counted eighteen silent shapes so far, with others on the way, but he was more concerned with an examination of the living. He was searching for familiar faces, hoping for survivors.

Joseph Chamoun approached him, looking weary and beaten. Blood had stained his shirt and plastered it against his wounded shoulder, and the rebel leader's face was streaked with rusty abstract patterns. Bolan didn't need to ask what happened, so he chose another question.

"When?"

"Perhaps an hour," Chamoun replied. "They came in helicopters, from the north. The ships were military, but the men were Palestinians and revolutionary guards."

He made the link immediately, scowling at the memory of frightened eyes above a scrap of gauze.

"One of your men turned up while I was with Moheden," Bolan said. "He fingered me. I didn't get a clear look at his face, but he was average height, slim build, with longish hair slicked back. I recognized him from the camp, but we were never introduced."

Chamoun was staring at him, boring holes in Bolan with his eyes. "Rashad," he snarled. "I sent him into town myself. He had a message to deliver."

"More than one, I'd say."

"The filthy Judas has betrayed us all."

"He paid the tab."

"You killed him?"

Bolan nodded.

"I regret that I couldn't have done the job myself, and slowly."

"We've got other things to think about right now. How many people did you lose?"

"Two dozen, at a minimum. More likely three."

Chamoun was holding something back, and Bolan didn't have the time to dance. "There's something else," he said. "What is it?"

"Mara. She isn't among the dead, and all the others have returned from hiding." Chamoun's expression had become a mask of pain. "The enemy has taken her away."

CHAPTER TWENTY-ONE

Moheden had been waiting for a quarter of an hour when he heard the helicopters. He stood on the veranda of a spacious ranch-style house, with poppy fields surrounding him on every side. The yellow flowers blazed as if the fields were burning, and he watched the helicopters skimming low above the crop, maintaining speed as they approached.

The ranch, as with the rest of it, had been Moheden's brainstorm. Bakhtiar had favored dropping off their hostage at Hosseinieh, the Shiite stronghold, while Halaby had preferred interrogation at the Sheikh Abdullah barracks. It had taken precious time for them to be convinced the helicopters shouldn't be observed delivering their human cargo inside Baalbek. Thus far, members of the military and police force had agreed to play along on the dealer's assurance that they wouldn't be involved directly in the conflict. The appearance of three army helicopters landing at a point controlled by terrorists and revolutionaries would incite discussion and, perhaps, investigation.

Thus, the ranch was perfect. They had privacy, security and all the time Moheden needed to prepare for the elimination of his enemies. Chamoun, his sources said, would stop at nothing to preserve his sister's life. A "private" meeting would be scheduled, and Chamoun would keep the date because he had no choice. His final act as leader of the Christian rebels would be suicide.

Communication with the hit team had been minimized to shave the risks of being overheard and spotted by legitimate authorities. Moheden knew that they had found the girl, whose photograph they'd studied prior to takeoff, and that damage had been suffered to at least one helicopter. He would have to pay for the repairs, as well as something extra for the officers who risked their jobs by renting him the airships. But it would be worth the cost.

The helicopters hovered briefly, whipping up a storm of dust, then settled to the earth like giant prehistoric insects. One of them was scarred around the nose and flank by bullet marks, and a spider web design was etched on its windshield. Shiite riflemen ran out to meet the new arrivals, ducking low beneath the rotor blades, off-loading bodies first, before the others disembarked. He counted five dead—three Palestinians, two revolutionary guards—before the girl was dumped unceremoniously through the loading bay of number one.

Her hands were tied behind her, and the short drop sent her sprawling. She resisted briefly as a pair of gunmen lifted her and marched her toward the house. She didn't meet Moheden's eyes, and probably wouldn't have recognized him anyway. He watched her go, then turned and waited for the leader of the strike team to report.

The man was tired and dusty, but his military bearing was intact. "We lost five men," he reported, "plus three more wounded. And the damage to one helicopter, which you see."

"How many of the enemy were killed?"

"No less than twenty-five. Perhaps twice that."

The estimate was almost certainly inflated, but Moheden didn't care. Substantial casualties had been inflicted on a force with limited reserves, and the specific numbers didn't interest him.

"Chamoun?"

The soldier braced himself as if expecting to be beaten. "He was seen, but managed to escape."

"No matter." It amused the Lebanese to observe the fighting man's reaction. "While we have the woman, he cannot go far."

"Yes, sir."

"You are dismissed."

Was it the truth? he wondered, as he turned back toward the house. Their late informant in the rebel camp had filed reports of Joseph Chamoun's devotion to his sister, but there was a chance the man had been mistaken. If Chamoun decided that his cause was more important than the girl, Moheden would be back where he had started.

No. Not quite.

His enemies were damaged, reeling from the unexpected blow, and their attempt to infiltrate his operation had been foiled. It troubled him that sweeps of Baalbek hadn't turned up the American, but there was time enough for that. Belasko had retarded the dealer's production schedule, but the heroin refinery would be operating at a new location in another day or two. All things considered, it could easily have been much worse.

It *would* be worse for Chamoun and his American accomplice. They would suffer for their interference in the schemes of more intelligent, sophisticated men. Moheden meant to see them suffer, wanted to relish every moment of their pain before he granted them the sweet relief of death.

But first there was the girl.

THEIR FIRST PRIORITY had been evacuation of the camp. It seemed unlikely that the raiders would return, but while the slightest possibility remained, Chamoun couldn't afford to take the chance. Aside from any risk of secondary strikes, there was a danger that the Syrian patrols might be informed about the battle by civilians in the area and come to check things out.

Reluctantly Chamoun gave orders for the bodies to be loaded on a truck held for burial when camp had been established at a new location. Fortunately he already had another site in mind, selected with an eye toward the necessity of swift evacuation, and by dusk they had the makings of another camp, some twenty miles away.

Survivors labored on past dark, erecting tents and cooking up a frugal meal. In the desert heat, the recent dead were going ripe before they finished supper, wafting an aroma of corruption over the encampment. Bolan took a shovel and assisted in the preparation of a common grave. His mind was off and running while he worked, unraveling the mystery of Mara's disappearance.

Certain facts were plain enough. She hadn't been selected randomly, the single prisoner abducted while her captors gunned down other women in their tracks. A solitary hostage stood for little in the scheme of things, unless the prisoner's identity supplied the hostage takers with a special edge.

He thought about the traitor who had lived and worked beside Chamoun, perhaps for years, and wondered what the man had told their enemies. Presumably he had discussed the close relationship between Chamoun and Mara, somehow kicking in a photograph or two to help the raiders choose their target. Mara would have been abducted as a weapon to be used against her brother if he managed to survive the first assault. Moheden would be counting on the rebel leader to submit, agree to anything, on the condition of his sister's liberation.

Bolan wondered if the girl was still alive. Had she been wounded in the raid? Would she be executed or allowed to die upon arrival at her destination? Moheden might anticipate resistance from Chamoun, demands to see or speak with Mara prior to making any deals, but it was difficult to guess the dealer's mood. He might be so enraged by recent setbacks that he'd take his anger out on Mara, using her to punish Chamoun. Conversely if Moheden wanted further information, Mara might be subject to interrogation by techniques producing disability or death.

If she was still alive, her time was limited. A day or two at most—perhaps no more than hours. Bolan felt the urgency, but he was still confronted with the problems of location and retrieval. Would the raiders take her back to Baalbek? And if so, would she be caged in the Sheikh Abdullah barracks or among the Shiites at Hosseinieh? Was there some other unknown holding pen Moheden might prefer?

He'd have to put himself inside his adversary's mind, examine the contingencies from the Lebanese's perspective. Were there drawbacks to confining Mara at a given site? Would risks outweigh advantages if she was caged at one place rather than another? Was it safe to let her live at all?

The answer came to Bolan in a sudden flash of insight. Could he manage to convince Chamoun in time? Were they too late already? Only one approach could prove him right or wrong, and if he was mistaken, they would be committed to a full assault—their last assault—before his error was discovered.

Still, he *knew*. And if Chamoun wouldn't accept his logic, Bolan would be forced to test the theory on his own.

FOR JOSEPH CHAMOUN, the night seemed dark and hopeless. In a few short hours he'd seen his life turned upside down—his people driven like a herd of sheep before the enemy, his sister carried off by men who would inevitably kill her...if she wasn't dead already.

Twenty-seven persons had been killed in the attack, another fifteen wounded as they ran for cover in the trees. Their medic, stunned by a grenade blast, had been carried from the field to safety, working overtime to help the others after he recovered from the shock. New stitches in his shoulder and a fresh batch in his scalp had made Chamoun presentable, but he cared nothing for the pain. Instead he burned with grief and anger.

It would be difficult, he knew. Twenty-three of his commandos were among the dead and wounded, a reduction in his fighting force of more than twenty-five percent. With sixty-two armed men remaining, he could never hope to mount a killing thrust against the enemy at either of the Baalbek strongholds, where his force would be outnumbered from the start.

Whatever happened, he wouldn't allow himself to rest until he learned his sister's fate, her whereabouts. If it was possible to set her free, Chamoun would take all steps within his power, even if it meant surrendering himself, his life, in an exchange.

Could that have been their plan from the beginning? If it was, then Bakhtiar and Moheden couldn't afford to let his sister go, whatever they might promise in negotiations. She was bait and nothing more. When Mara had served her purpose, she would become expendable, a piece of excess baggage to be cast aside and soon forgotten.

Staring at the cook fires, listening to shovels rasp on sandy soil, he thought about Amir Rashad, regretting that the man had died so easily. Chamoun's idea of justice would have brought the traitor back to camp alive, for special handling by the men he had betrayed. He might have yielded crucial information while he lived, and even if he managed to resist, he would have been rewarded for his treachery.

Too late.

The American had been right to kill him while he had the chance. At least Chamoun knew how the enemy had singled out his sister—how they would have had him, too, if he hadn't escaped. Rashad had doted on his inexpensive camera, recording aspects of their daily life around the camp on film—"for history," as he'd explained it. Group shots, panoramas, candid photos of action around the camp—all perfectly innocuous until they were delivered into hostile hands, laid out to form the blueprint for a sneak attack.

On learning of Rashad's betrayal, Joseph Chamoun had gone directly to the dead man's tent, hauled back the crumpled canvas and rummaged among his things. The metal strongbox had been dented by a bullet, but its contents were secure. The photos lay before Chamoun, arranged in stacks, and they included several dozen that Rashad hadn't seen fit to show around the camp.

Snapshots of Mara. At the bathing pool.

The photos clearly spanned a period of months. In some her hair was shoulder-length, whereas it had been cut a few weeks earlier into a shorter, almost boyish style. He could tell nothing from her clothing, as she wore none in the photographs Rashad had saved.

He stacked the photos back inside the box and made a mental note to burn them all before he went to bed that night. It was ridiculous to think that he could sleep, but he would still go through the motions. There was nothing else to do.

He heard someone coming, then recognized the tall American from his silhouette.

"Chamoun?"

"Come in."

Bolan took a seat across the folding table, pushed the box of photographs aside and leaned in closer. "Can you have your people ready in the next half hour?"

"Ready?"

"There may still be time."

"For what?"

Bolan's eyes were burning coals. "I think I know where Mara is."

SHE HAD AWAKENED in the helicopter, with her wrists bound tightly behind her back. A dead man lay beside her on the metal floor, and combat boots were pressed against her spine. She closed her eyes at once, but one of her captors had seen her stirring, and he started prodding her with his feet, making lewd remarks until the officer in charge demanded silence.

In a rush the fractured memories came flooding back. Mara saw a child cut down by flying bullets, and the tattered shroud that was her brother's tent. Was he alive? How many of the others had been killed or wounded? Why had she been spared by the attackers?

Even as the thought took shape, it came to her that the fates hadn't been kind in leaving her alive. She was a prisoner, completely helpless, and it troubled her that she'd been selected by her enemies from all the others in the camp. Was she the only hostage? And if so, how had the raiders picked her out? What was their purpose in abducting her?

The first faint stirrings of imagination painted nightmare portraits in her mind, and Mara shut them out immediately. She'd need her wits about her when she faced her enemies, and manufactured terrors only made her weaker at the outset. She'd cling tenaciously to life while hope remained, and when it faded, she'd find a way to spare herself the worst of it.

The rotors had changed their pitch, and Mara felt the ship descending. On touchdown she lay still and watched the dead man carried off ahead of her. A moment later, rough hands pulled her upright, dragged her toward the open loading bay and shoved her through. She tried to catch herself—and failing that, to roll aside—but with her hands bound, there was little she could do. The ground rushed up to meet her, bruising knees and cheek on impact, but she bit her lip and made no sound.

She wouldn't let the bastards see her cry.

A pair of gunmen hauled her to her feet, one brushing at her clothes as an excuse to touch her breast, and Mara tried to kick him in the shins. He sidestepped, grinning, and the soldiers gripped her arms, a warning twist sufficient to remind her of the pain they could inflict. She walked between them through the dusty rotorwash, in the direction of a long, low ranch house thirty yards away. She glimpsed an older, well-dressed man on the veranda, speaking with the officer who had protected her in flight, but Mara didn't recognize his face. A man of influence, perhaps, but who?

It made no difference at the moment. Everything would be revealed to her in time, and she was in no special hurry to confront her enemy. Delays could work in Mara's favor now, allowing time for...what?

Inside the house she was delivered to a pair of revolutionary guards, stern-faced and clad in customary black. They led her to a room devoid of windows, freed her hands and locked the single door behind them as they left. The furniture consisted of a cot, a straight-backed chair and a ceramic chamber pot. She grimaced at the latter, wondering if she should fill it quickly, even hurl its contents at her jailers, or deny herself in protest. In the end she split the difference, waiting for the need to grow more pressing.

She examined her surroundings, found no exit other than the door and sat down on the cot to take stock of herself. Aside from minor scrapes and bruises, she was fit enough. She wasn't strong enough to overpower several men at once, but she was sleek and swift. If they sent one man with a meal, or removed her from her cell for any reason, she might have a chance to seize his weapon or to strike him with the chair or chamber pot. Do *something.*

Whatever else might happen, Mara was determined to resist her own humiliaton and destruction. There had been no opportunity to put up serious resistance at the compound. Now, though it might be too late, she felt obliged to try.

And if they killed her for it, she would have the satisfaction of resisting with her dying breath. For now, it was the only concrete hope she had.

MIR REZA BAKHTIAR HAD changed his mind. Initially he had decided to remain in Baalbek, safe inside his fortress, and allow Moheden to interrogate the prisoner alone. On further thought, however, he decided that the Lebanese had been given ample opportunity to prove himself, without result. Thus far, Moheden's men on Cyprus had been killed while dealing with a spy—an error that rebounded in the death of Bakhtiar's close friend, Hussein Razmara—and Moheden had repeated the mistake in Baalbek. Blinded by his greed, he had invited the American to tour their facilities, with a result that echoed Nicosia's violence. Now he tried to save the day by burning out a rebel camp and capturing a female prisoner. At best the plan seemed ill-considered. At the worst it smacked of rank incompetence.

Emerging from the courtyard of Hosseinieh, the Shiite leader traveled in his armored limousine, with two staff cars in front and two behind. He had perhaps two dozen soldiers at the farm, but they would do him no good on the journey, and if rebels were involved in their misfortune, reinforcements might be helpful.

To this point Bakhtiar had kept the news of their embarrassment from Teheran. The government didn't smile on failure, and had a record of impulsive actions—cancellation of a salvageable program, execution of the persons deemed responsible—that didn't fit his reputation for infallibility. The prophet was a genius; Bakhtiar wouldn't dispute that fact. But as a holy man, he was accustomed to dispensing theory and interpreting Koranic scripture. There were times, as evidenced by conduct of the war against Iraq, when practical decisions went astray and wound up in disaster.

Of course, Teheran had been informed about Razmara's death. There had been no way to disguise the fact, and so it was reported as an act by renegades and infidels, coincidental with Razmara's duties for the drug cartel. Before top officials were informed of the ''mistake,'' the problem would be solved, their enemies wrapped up and tucked away in graves.

It was a promise Bakhtiar had made himself, and he would keep it if it killed him.

Leaving Baalbek in the waning light of dusk, the convoy hastened south along the valley's second-widest road. They passed one Syrian patrol and then another, but his vehicles were recognized and spared the ritual of stop-and-search reserved for peasants, members of the merchant class and other human flotsam. The Syrians did business with Iran for imports, and inside the Bekaa Valley they had recognized political reality. A word from Bakhtiar—or from Teheran—and Shiites would have risen in a howling mob against the soldiers who had dared molest their spiritual leaders.

It was comforting, he thought, to have both God *and* the large battalions on his side.

Moheden had been wise, for once, in carrying his hostage to the farm. Her people—if they looked for her at all—would doubtless start in Baalbek, chasing leads among the Palestinians and revolutionary guards. While they were grinding out their fruitless plans for an assault upon Hosseinieh or the Sheikh Abdullah barracks, all their precious secrets would be spilling from the woman's lips. She would destroy them in her effort to escape the pain, and when she found the sweet release of death, her passing would be symptomatic of the infidels' destruction.

Sometimes life was sweet, despite the fact that Bakhtiar's religion largely barred him from the realm of earthly pleasures. When an enemy betrayed himself and his comrades, and the noose closed tightly around them all, he knew that God smiled upon the holy revolution. Someday, when jihad had set the world on fire instead of simply burning out the Middle East, there would be cause for genuine rejoicing. On that day the Shiite thought that he might take a woman for himself, or even sip a glass of wine.

But first they had mistakes to rectify and enemies to kill. He wouldn't rest while the assassins of Hussein Razmara were at large and plotting his destruction. The American must be discovered, captured and eliminated. Slowly. Painfully. And in such a manner that his mind would vomit up its darkest secrets prior to death.

On impulse Bakhtiar decided they should tape the girl's interrogation. Film wasn't appropriate, since she would have to be undressed, but he would have the cameras ready when they captured the American, Belasko. His confession would be very useful as a piece of propaganda in the endless running battle with America. The White House would be forced to finally admit its sabotage against the people's revolution. And if this Belasko turned out not to be an agent of his government, the film and tape could still be doctored to support a charge of CIA complicity.

Outside the ranch house, revolutionary guards snapped to attention as Bakhtiar's limousine pulled up and stopped. Moheden, taken by surprise, was slower off the mark and met him in the foyer.

The dealer forced a smile and lied. "I'm glad that you have come."

"I will assist you with the prisoner," Bakhtiar said, admitting no debate. "Some questions may occur to me that should be answered."

"As you wish."

"Of course. We shall begin at once."

CHAPTER TWENTY-TWO

It had to be the farm. Examining the other possibilities in detail, Bolan had discovered fatal flaws in each. For starters, both Hosseinieh and the Sheikh Abudullah barracks were too public, too accessible to the authorities. Despite security precautions they were also vulnerable to attack by snipers, rockets, even drive-by gunners on the street. An incident of any kind would bring police, who might feel duty-bound to check the premises and log complaints of hostages confined therein. It might amount to nothing in the long run, but a public link between Teheran's "holy men" and the narcotics trade would clearly damage their prestige.

The farm, by contrast, offered privacy, defensible perimeters and distance from the deputized authorities. A fair pitched battle could be waged without alerting anyone outside, and the casualties made to disappear without a trace. If Syrian patrols caught wind of the disturbance, they would be more apt to shrug it off, allowing Bakhtiar to deal with it himself.

Logistically the farm put Bolan closer to his enemies, located as it was midway between the current rebel camp and Baalbek. Closer meant less wasted time in transit, and a better chance of bringing Mara out alive—provided they could pull it off.

In hasty conversation with Chamoun, he tried to second-guess their enemies and gauge the strength of the opposition. On his whirlwind tour of the farm, he had

observed at least a dozen guards, but they were bound to
beef up that contingent now that war had been declared in
earnest. Leaving a dozen men to guard the camp, he would
have fifty to assault the dragon's lair. Against how many?
If Moheden called out reinforcements from the Baalbek
strongholds, Bolan's team could find themselves outnumbered by a ratio of eight or ten to one.

It seemed unlikely that the enemy would strip his urban
fortresses of personnel, and Bolan cut the gloomy estimate in half. Two hundred sentries on the farm would still
provide Moheden with a healthy edge, unless the strike
force could achieve surprise. But how?

He thought about Grimaldi and the feasibility of calling up a one-man air strike, but he instantly dismissed the
notion. He'd have to broadcast in the clear, on Joseph
Chamoun's equipment, and the call might easily be intercepted by their enemies. Assuming it wasn't, Grimaldi
would need time to reach his target, and a flying strike
against the farm might finish Mara. All in all, the risks
seemed greater than the possible rewards.

That left an infantry assault, bedeviled by the all-
important question of surprise. Moheden's sentries on the
farm wouldn't be taken in by humble peasants congregat-
ing on the highway, and a group of fifty men would instantly excite suspicion. Once inside the poppy fields, the
raiders might be able to conceal themselves, but getting
there was half the battle. All approaches would be
guarded, and a force of any size would be contested instantly, unless . . .

He leaned across the table toward Chamoun, his elbows rumpling a large map of the Bekaa Valley they had
spread between them. Glancing up from his consideration
of an unpaved access, Chamoun appeared to recognize the
spark in Bolan's eyes.

"You have the answer?" There was something close to desperation in his voice.

"I might," the Executioner replied. "But first we have to get ourselves arrested."

BASHIR MOHEDEN HAD BEEN caught off guard by Bakhtiar's arrival at the farm. They had agreed beforehand that the girl would be the Lebanese's personal responsibility, his final chance to make things right with the cartel. By dropping in to take a hand in her interrogation, Bakhtiar was signaling a lack of confidence in Moheden, demeaning him before Ahmad Halaby and the other members of their team who might be quick enough to catch the nuance.

Furious at Bakhtiar for what he saw as rank betrayal, Moheden succeeded in disguising his reaction. He was civil, even cheerful with his cold, distrustful partner, reassuring Bakhtiar that every possible security precaution had been taken. With their enemies still reeling from the raid that afternoon, it was unthinkable that Joseph Chamoun could track his sister down, deploy his small remaining force and stage a counterstrike so soon. As for Belasko, he might still be hiding out in Baalbek, cut off from his allies. If he managed to escape the city, journey southward, he would find the rebels decimated, their small community in shambles.

Bakhtiar wasn't impressed by his assurances. The holy man had brought another twenty gunmen with him, and his first act on arrival was to radio for more. Nearly one hundred guns would be on duty, and Moheden hoped that they wouldn't be needed.

If the enemy made any move at all—other than a plea for peace, the Lebanese thought that it would come in Baalbek. He'd brought his hostage to the farm specifically to put a buffer between himself and the most likely combat zone. A major shift in troops could easily alert the enemy, but Bakhtiar refused to see the folly of his actions. As the owner of the farm and principal supplier of the drug cartel, he was within his rights to fortify the place at any time, for any reason. Moheden could only watch and hope the shift didn't betray his scheme before he had the necessary information in his hands.

He had intended to approach the girl with sympathy at first, relying on her simple peasant background to ensure a measure of stupidity. Commiserating with her plight, he would have offered favors, sanctuary from the brutes who had abused her during transit, swift release if she would answer certain minor questions. Only as a last resort would he fall back on violence—not because of any private squeamishness, but rather based upon the fact that victims under torture might say anything. A man or woman, driven past the threshold of endurance, would confess to crimes committed years before their birth, fictitious incidents dreamed up by their interrogators—anything at all. How many "witches" had been hanged or burned upon their own detailed confessions of consorting with the devil? In more recent times, how many Soviets, Chinese and Cubans, Eastern Europeans and Vietnamese had publicly confessed their "crimes against the state" before they shuffled off to prison camps or firing squads?

Coercion had its uses in a system where conformity was sought at any price. Beyond a certain point, however, it began to earn diminishing returns. A military leader who relied on torture for his battlefield Intelligence might find himself deploying troops against a nonexistent enemy. Police who leaned on the third degree in building cases frequently sent blameless men to jail, while leaving hardened criminals at large. A cautious man, Moheden didn't wish to risk his life, his fortune, on the garbled pleadings of a tortured soul.

With Bakhtiar at hand, however, he'd have no choice. Physical abuse was second nature to the Shiite zealots, and with Bakhtiar in charge of the interrogation, there would be no room for subtlety.

It was a pity, the Lebanese thought. He'd seen the woman in selected photographs, so different from the dusty, battered victim who had been unloaded from the helicopter, and in other circumstances, free of interference, Moheden might have approached her *as* a woman. He wasn't devoid of charm, and in her current situation, much could be accomplished with a friendly smile, a well-placed compliment. She might have tried to bargain with her body, and he might have let her, but that wouldn't be an option now that Bakhtiar was on the scene.

Instead of teaching her to serve him, picking up her vital information in the process, now Moheden would be forced to tear the girl apart. And based upon his past experience with torture victims, it might all be wasted effort. They would stand no better than a fifty-fifty chance of learning anything worthwhile from Mara once the operation had begun.

A pity.

Still, if he could strike some happy medium with Bakhtiar, secure agreement to the use of low-key torture in the early phases, they might have a chance. He badly wanted to destroy his enemies, not merely rout them as he had that afternoon. Destruction meant elimination of the threat, together with a lesson for the other peasants who considered launching armed resistance on their own. Eradication meant smooth sailing, safety, higher profits all around.

Determined not to fail, he motioned for Ahmad Halaby to accompany him, and both men fell in step with Bakhtiar, en route to the interrogation room.

WHEN MARA'S TIME arrived, two Palestinians were sent to fetch her from her cell. Her spirits slumped, but she had promises to keep, and she had worked to fill the chamber pot against this moment. Now as they advanced upon her, Mara seized the pot and flung its contents squarely into one man's face, delivering a solid crack across his skull as hands flew up to wipe his stinging eyes.

Her adversary staggered, fell, and when the chamber pot didn't explode on impact, Mara swung on his companion, missing as he came in low, beneath her guard. His shoulder struck her in the solar plexus, momentarily short-circuiting commands between her brain and lungs. Momentum drove her backward, pinned against the nearest wall, and Mara felt like she was drowning. Suddenly, incredibly, she had forgotten how to breathe.

And still she fought. Her strength was fading, but she slammed the chamber pot across her captor's shoulders, lost her grip and heard it shatter on the floor. The Palestinian backed off a foot or so and lunged again, the impact turning Mara's legs to rubber. She was certain that he hardly felt the blows she rained upon his back, and when he stepped away from her, she crumpled to the floor.

She saw the first man struggle to his feet, hair plastered to his scalp with urine, one hand pressed against the swelling there. His face was twisted into a mask of rage, and he would surely have attacked her if his comrade hadn't intervened. A whispered word restrained the Palestinian and finished Mara's hopes. Instinctively she knew the man wouldn't have spared her, under any threat of punishment, unless he was convinced that she faced something worse.

She was propelled along a corridor, through several twists and turns, until they stopped outside another door. No knock this time; her escorts merely threw the door back, hauled her across the threshold and closed the door again behind them.

Mara glanced around another room devoid of windows, where the furniture was even less hospitable than in her cell. A single heavy chair was planted in the middle of the room, and at a second glance she saw its legs were bolted to the floor. The leather straps affixed to both arms and the forward legs left Mara in no doubt about its function. In one corner, jammed against the wall, a smallish folding table held a bright array of pliers, cutters, probes and blades. The centerpiece appeared to be a compact hand-crank generator.

Mara let them pull her toward the middle of the room. She offered weak resistance when the urine-smelling guard began to fumble with the buttons of her shirt, but then his partner fired a solid fist against her kidney and she folded, sinking to her knees. They hauled her upright, stripped her bare without preliminaries and conveyed her to the chair. Its polished wood was cool against her back and buttocks as they strapped her in.

She was completely helpless now, deprived of all mobility beyond a wriggle here and there. She couldn't even tip the chair and try to knock herself unconscious in the fall. Instead she sat before her captors, trying to return their gaze defiantly, aware that she was failing. The one with urine in his hair stepped closer, his rough hands prowling over her.

The door clicked open, and the probing hands were gone. She saw her guards, both standing at attention, opposite three new arrivals. Two of them, Ahmad Halaby and the bearded Shiite Bakhtiar, she recognized from photographs. The other, tall and clean-shaven, had been out on the veranda when she first arrived.

Her escorts were apparently Halaby's men. The swarthy Palestinian stepped forward, almost rubbing noses with the urine-scented guard, and fired off several rapid questions Mara couldn't follow. When her captor answered in a weak affirmative, Halaby's open palm lashed out and rocked the soldier's head, its livid imprint branded on his cheek. A left and then another right followed, the guard accepting it without a whimper, his companion carefully avoiding any visible reaction. Finished with the dressing-down, Halaby ordered both of them away and waited for the door to close before he started scouring his palm with a clean handkerchief.

The three inquisitors surrounded Mara in a semicircle, studying her face and body inch by inch. Halaby's eyes were small and piggish, lustful, like the eyes of his disgraced subordinate. Mir Reza Bakhtiar examined her with clinical detachment, nothing in his gaze suggesting that he was alive below the waist. The tall, clean-shaven man fell somewhere in between the two. She saw appreciation of her body in his eyes, but knew that he would hurt her all the same.

"Ahmad?" The tall man's voice was soft, yet firm.

Halaby fetched the hand-crank generator, brought it back and set the box in front of Mara, on the floor between her feet. She saw that both the generator's cables had been fitted with ugly alligator clamps.

"My name is Bashir Moheden," the tall man said. Her sneer produced no visible reaction. "I'm forced to ask you certain questions. If your answers satisfy, there need be no...unpleasantness. Refusal on your part will lead to pain beyond imagining, and I will learn your secrets all the same. Be wise. Cooperate."

"I have no fear of you," she lied.

"So brave," Moheden said. "So foolish."

Kneeling on the floor between her open knees, he scooped up the generator cables and spent a moment flexing the clips in his hands, their jaws clicking on empty air.

"Once more," he said. "I ask you courteously. No?" The shrug betrayed complete indifference. "Then we must begin at the beginning."

IT TOOK THE BETTER PART of forty minutes for the lookouts to report a Syrian patrol approaching on the Bekaa's secondary north-south highway. With a pair of motorcycle scouts and four other vehicles—a half-ton truck among them—Bolan thought it sounded perfect for his needs. If only they could pull it off without a hitch.

He parked his stolen taxi in the middle of the highway, pulled some wires on the distributor and settled down to wait. Before he heard approaching engines, Bolan loosened the Beretta in its shoulder rigging and left his army surplus jacket open for a quicker draw.

This time would be cold blood, at least for starters, but he told himself that Syria was playing an aggressor's role in Lebanon, while simultaneously training terrorists at home and sponsoring their raids around the world. The Bekaa occupation was an act of war, disguised as "military aid." Above all else, these troops, in death, might help him rescue Mara and defeat his enemies.

It was a chance the Executioner couldn't afford to miss.

He heard the motorcycles now, outriders gliding into view a moment later. Following behind were two jeeps, an open personnel carrier and the slat-sided half-ton, with perhaps a dozen riflemen in back. That made it close to thirty uniforms, but it would have to do.

He hunched beneath the taxi's open hood, one hand on the Beretta, seeming not to notice as the motorcycles pulled up close on either side. Inside the taxi, Joseph Chamoun—his "passenger"—sat stiffly, with an Uzi submachine gun in his lap.

One of the motorcycle scouts called out to him, and Bolan glanced up from the taxi's engine, putting on the face of one who is surprised to find himself with unexpected company. He shrugged in answer to the question, already measuring the angles, waiting for the other vehicles to stop behind his cab.

The second, closer scout was speaking now, but Bolan scarcely heard him, and he offered no response. The jeeps, the APC and truck were all in place now, lined up neatly ten or fifteen feet between them, with his taxi leading the parade. It was as nearly perfect as a set would ever be.

He drew the Beretta, fired one round at point-blank range and saw the starboard scout go down before he spun to face the other. Both of them were wearing flap-style holsters, and the pointman never had a chance to reach his gun before a quick round drilled through his upper lip. He toppled backward, pinned beneath the bike, as firing broke out all along the line.

Chamoun's commandos had concealed themselves along the road on either side, and at the sound of Bolan's first two shots they opened up with everything they had. Chamoun had twisted in his seat, the Uzi spitting through an empty frame where glass had been removed to offer him a better field of fire. He caught the driver of the nearer jeep and knocked him from the saddle with a 3-round burst, his weapon tracking on to nail the shotgun rider where he sat.

In motion, Boland heard the half-ton's driver fighting with his gear shift, grating hard to find reverse, when a rifle bullet cracked his windshield, drilling him between the eyes. His human cargo was pumping rounds in all directions, scarcely taking time to aim, and some of them began to scatter as they realized the truck had stalled. The driver of the second jeep was wounded, but his men were fighting back. He had the four-wheel-drive in motion, whipping out around the lead car, breaking for the open road.

Two rounds from the Beretta snapped the driver's head back, and he lost it as he passed the taxi, veering to the right, tires spinning hopelessly until the jeep gave up its bid at climbing the embankment. Snipers had already killed the shotgun rider, and they dropped one of the gunners in the rear before he scrambled free. His partner, quicker to retreat, was on his feet and sprinting in a futile search for cover, when another round from Bolan's pistol dropped him in his tracks.

The personnel carrier was putting up a respectable fight, its machine gun lacing the night with tracer rounds, but its open top left crew members exposed to gunmen on the overhanging bluffs. Bolan saw one of Chamoun's rebels fall, then another, but their collected fire was scoring, hot rounds rattling around inside the APC until they burrowed into flesh.

He took a chance and dodged across the pavement, ducking rifle fire from both sides as he ran, and leaped up onto the fender of the moving APC. The driver saw him coming, turned to grapple with a weapon on the seat beside him, but there simply wasn't time. The man was cursing helplessly as Bolan reached inside the cockpit, his Beretta spitting twice at skin-touch range.

He sprang away and let the snipers finish it, a burst from the machine gun chewing pavement at his heels before a well-placed round retired the gunner. Thirty yards down-range, survivors from the half-ton truck were keeping up sporadic fire against their enemies, but only four or five were still in any shape to fight. As Bolan watched, their ranks were whittled down to zero, and a pall of silence fell across the battlefield. Chamoun's remaining troops emerged from cover, scurrying around the scene and mopping up with careful head shots where the fallen soldiers still showed signs of life.

A quarter hour of concerted effort cleared the highway. The bodies were stacked inside the half-ton and the APC, and the vehicles maneuvered to a side road out of view. Unloading was a grisly task, but grim determination saw them through, as they began to sort the bodies out by size and strip them of their clothes.

The uniforms were mostly torn and bloodstained now, but it was dark, and they would serve their purpose under cursory examination, if the worst of them were kept inside the truck and APC until the final moment. At a glance, the military vehicles appeared no worse than usual, the bullet scars and dings familiar sights around the Bekaa Valley. Joseph Chamoun had briefed his soldiers on the need for clean, precision fire, and so the vehicles were fully functional, despite their superficial wounds. No tires were flattened, and the engines all responded smartly, grumbling together in the darkness.

Dressing in the largest uniform that he could find, a bloodstain tucked beneath one arm, Mack Bolan shouldered a Kalashnikov and slipped a bandolier of extra magazines across his chest. The shirt was small, but comfort was irrelevant. They had their edge, if they could only use it to its best advantage.

Chamoun had stubbornly ignored the Executioner's advice, insisting on a frontline place among the members of the raiding party. Settling in the lead jeep's shotgun seat, while Bolan took the wheel, he kept the Uzi primed and ready on his lap. Behind them, signals flashed along the line, the other gunmen settled in their places, ready to begin.

"We go?" Chamoun asked.

"We go," the Executioner replied.

He only hoped that they weren't too late.

CHAPTER TWENTY-THREE

Ahmad Halaby had excused himself from the interrogation after half an hour. He wasn't a squeamish man by any means, but it appeared to him that Moheden was getting nowhere with his prisoner. Halaby thought that Bakhtiar would soon take over, and he didn't care to witness what would follow.

He had used the guards as an excuse, reminding Bakhtiar of his responsibility for keeping the perimeter secure. It didn't matter if the Shiite bastard thought him weak, unmanly. It wasn't Halaby who avoided touching women in a normal way, extracting pleasure only from their pain and suffering. He would be glad to challenge Bakhtiar at any time, one man against another, with their contest to the death.

Of course, he knew it would never come to that. While Bakhtiar wasn't a coward, he had lately grown obsessed with "dignity," a need to place himself above the level of his troops. He had become a combination holy man and bureaucrat, too proud to soil his hands with common labor or the simple chores of killing. Thus, it struck Halaby as peculiar that the man would seem so eager to interrogate a prisoner—this prisoner—himself.

The Palestinian dismissed his train of thought, the other images it brought to mind, and concentrated on his mission. His concern for the perimeter defense hadn't been a total fabrication after all. Moheden was convinced that they were safe, the Christian rebels wounded and confused. But supposition didn't satisfy Halaby. Granted, it was probable their adversaries would go looking for the girl in Baalbek, if they still had men enough to hunt for her at all. However, probability and certainty were very different things. Halaby had seen men lose everything by betting with the odds, and he wasn't about to make the same mistake.

The ranch was vast, and he didn't have time to tour the perimeter and check every outpost. Instead he took the walkie-talkie offered by his first lieutenant and touched base with his teams. They responded smartly on the north and west. Halaby was beginning on the south, when he was interrupted by a burst of static from the radio.

A sentry on the east-west access road identified himself and blurted out, "Emergency! A Syrian patrol has just turned off the highway, moving toward the house. Advise!"

Halaby frowned and answered crisply, "Take no action. Let them pass. They will be dealt with on arrival."

He would have to summon Bakhtiar, an interruption the Shiite was unlikely to appreciate. But as the master of the house, it was his place to deal with uninvited visitors, and most especially those in uniform. Halaby wondered what the Syrians could want, decided it was probably another, larger bribe, and retreated through the house.

A muffled scream was audible outside the interrogation room. Halaby waited for the sound to die away before he entered. He kept his face deliberately impassive as Moheden spun the crank again, his captive lurching at her bonds. The scream cut like a razor blade across the Palestinian's nerves.

"What is it?"

Bakhtiar seemed out of breath, as if he'd been interrupted in the middle of a distance run. His face was flushed, unusual color present in his cheeks.

Halaby swallowed his disgust and said, "The lookouts have reported a patrol, just off the highway, moving toward the house. They should be here at any moment."

"Syrians?" Moheden asked, distracted from his work.

Halaby nodded. "I've allowed them to proceed."

The Shiite seemed about to question the decision, then thought better of it. "I will speak to them myself," he said, and led the way outside.

Behind them, the Lebanese expelled a weary sigh and stood. "We shall resume when you return," he said.

"*I* shall take over," Bakhtiar informed him coolly. "You are wasting too much time."

With that he swept along the corridor, Halaby on his heels. The door to the interrogation chamber snicked shut behind them. They were almost to the parlor when a burst of automatic fire erupted in the courtyard, and Halaby saw his world go up in smoke.

THE COLUMN HAD MADE decent time. Behind the half-ton, half a dozen mismatched vehicles were loaded with the gunners who had come up short of uniforms, assigned to park a full mile back and wait until a summons or the sound of combat called them in to join the party. If the plan worked smoothly, Bakhtiar's defenders would be sucked away from their perimeter positions to defend the house, and so the second wave would slip in, nearly unopposed.

If everything proceeded on its proper schedule.

Bolan recognized the access road and turned off the highway, holding to a steady thirty-five and trusting that the other vehicles would match his pace. Two sentries were ahead, their flashlights stabbing through the darkness, but he didn't even brake. If they were sidetracked here, so far from the selected target, they might never make it to the house. He would ignore the sentries, trusting the authority of their uniforms until such time as someone opened fire.

There were more sentries now, and they made no attempt to hide themselves, their weapons on display as Bolan and his convoy rumbled past. He saw confusion on their faces, but it didn't translate to concern. They weren't frightened, and he sensed that they had seen patrols come down this road before. Considering the vast plantation's staple crop, it would have been peculiar if the troops weren't familiar visitors, collecting periodic payoffs as the price of their official blindness.

The road looked different in the dark, a tunnel brightened only by their headlights, but he recognized the house immediately. They could see the blaze of floodlights from a distance, like a beacon guiding them home. Bolan let the motorcycle set the pace and pulled his AK-47 closer, propping it between the jeep's front seats.

Around the final bend and they were entering the courtyard, with guards on every side. "Your call," he told Chamoun. "If Mara's in the house, it could go either way."

"I love my sister," the rebel leader replied. "Her life is precious to me, but her dignity means more. I will not bargain with her soul. When we are close enough, we strike."

The motorcycles rumbled past the wide front porch, and Bolan followed, switching off the jeep's ignition as they coasted to a stop. A couple of the closer guards were squinting at Chamoun's commandos, noticing the bloodstains on a number of their uniforms and recoiling in surprise. Before they had a chance to analyze the evidence, Chamoun had raised his Uzi, rattling off a burst that dropped two gunners in their tracks.

It hit the fan behind them, and on every side. The motorcycle scouts peeled off in opposite directions, firing pistols at the darting silhouettes of sentries on the run. One of them tried to climb the porch but lost it on the stairs and toppled over, rolling clear before the heavy bike could pin him down. He had, perhaps, five seconds to reflect on his predicament before a burst of automatic fire came in on target, blowing him away.

His comrade, on the other bike, had doubled back to make a run across the open courtyard, scattering a group of sentries, dropping two with pistol fire before a spray of bullets knocked him from his seat. The bike ran on without him for another thirty yards, fuel spraying from its punctured tank, and disappeared into the nearest poppy field.

So much for signals to the backup force. If they were listening, the night wind ought to tell them that the battle had been joined. How many guards on the perimeter would leave their posts and race to help their fellows at the house? He hoped the members of the secondary team would watch themselves. Their numbers—and their timing—could make all the difference in the world.

Just now, however, Bolan's mind was focused on the more immediate concern of personal survival. Bullets filled the air around him, gouging divots in the courtyard, striking sparks on impact with the jeep. He had to move or die, but cover was a rare commodity. The farmhouse, given all its dangers, still appeared to be his only hope of sanctuary.

Braced for anything, the Executioner erupted from his crouch, the AK-47 blazing in his grip, and sprinted for the house.

AT FIRST the distant, muffled sound of automatic weapons didn't register with Mara. Deafened by her own shrill screams, the fierce, internal hammer of her pulse, it took a moment for her senses to absorb the message. Something must be happening outside, but what?

She could recall an interruption of the torture. Was it moments earlier or days? The Palestinian, Halaby, had been watching her at first, then he had disappeared—some kind of trick, perhaps—and when she next stopped screaming, he was back again. What was the message he had passed to Bakhtiar?

She shook her head and tried to focus on the floor in front of her, the generator with its trailing wires. Moheden had removed the alligator clips when the others left, but Mara felt them just the same. She wondered if her flesh was torn or merely burned where they had been attached.

The message. Something barely understood, a fleeting respite from the pain. Halaby whispering in Arabic, about . . .

A Syrian patrol.

She was mistaken, obviously. Bakhtiar was friendly with the Syrians. He paid them for protection. They would have no cause to fire upon his men, unless . . .

Her mind refused to function properly. She raised her head a fraction, caught Moheden staring at the open door and tried her bonds again. The perspiration helped a little, but the straps were cinched too tight for her to free herself. In her condition, weakened, racked with pain, she would have offered him no challenge anyway.

Assuming that the Syrians had turned on Bakhtiar for reasons that she couldn't comprehend, what would it mean to her? Her family had no friends among the occupation troops. If they discovered her, identified her, it would be a toss-up whether she was executed on the spot or carried off to jail. Whichever, it was still a brighter prospect than continuation of Moheden's questioning, and Mara found herself silently rooting for the attackers, wishing them well.

The Lebanese knelt before her, soft hands resting on her knees. It disappointed Mara that she couldn't find the strength or energy to spit at him. Unlike her flesh, still glistening with sweat, the inside of her mouth felt dry as dust.

Moheden's voice seemed small and faraway. "I have been negligent," he said. "I underestimated Joseph and the American, but there may still be time to make amends."

The man was raving. How were hostile Syrians connected to her brother and Belasko? It amused her to believe his mind had been unhinged by pressure in the past few days, and yet ...

He fumbled with the strap around one ankle, and Mara found that she could move her foot. The other next, and she suppressed an urge to kick the man, knowing she would still be helpless with her arms securely bound.

He rose and stood beside her chair, unfastening the strap around one wrist and then the other. Mara flexed her fingers, willing circulation to return and marshaling her strength for one last effort. It would be her only chance. If she could pull it off—

Moheden grabbed a handful of her hair and lifted her from the chair as if she had been weightless. Twisting in his grasp, immune to pain with all that she had suffered, Mara tried to claw his face, but he was quicker, striking with his free hand and bloodying her nose. The second punch struck home with stunning force, and Mara crumpled to her knees as he released her, whimpering in her frustration. When she raised her eyes to look at him again, there was a pistol in his hand.

The dealer found her clothing in the corner and dropped the slacks and tattered shirt in front of her on the floor. "Get dressed," he snapped. "I give you thirty seconds."

"And if I refuse?"

He shrugged. "The choice is yours. We are about to leave this house together. If you choose to travel naked, I shall not object. It may be days before I have the time to find you other clothing."

Days? The glimmer of a hope made up her mind. Still kneeling, Mara slipped her shirt on, leaving it open in the front where all the buttons had been torn away. The slacks presented greater difficulty as she had to stand, but after nearly falling once, she got it right. They fit her snugly, and she grimaced as the seams chafed wounded flesh.

"You first," Moheden ordered, waggling his pistol toward the door. "Be quick about it!"

Mara did as she was told, her spirits lifting as the sounds of automatic fire drew closer. Now, unless she was mistaken, she heard firing from inside the house as well.

She had a chance. No more, no less. Moheden wanted her alive, and she would take advantage of that fact, until she found a weapon and the opportunity to use it.

Hope would linger while she lived, and Mara's fondest hope was for a chance to kill this man. It was the single-minded goal that gave her strength to carry on.

CHAMOUN'S FIRST Uzi blast had sent two gunmen sprawling, and he followed with a move that dropped him into a crouch beside the jeep. He saw that the American was unloading on the other side, his rifle hammering at someone on their flank, and the commandos seated just behind him were in motion, scurrying for shelter as they laid down cover fire.

The newest stitches in his shoulder hadn't separated yet, and Chamoun ignored the stabbing pain that emanated from his wound. There was no time to think of personal discomfort when his sister's life was riding on the line, his men outnumbered and surrounded by their enemies. If he could only catch a glimpse of Bakhtiar, just long enough to put a bullet through the Shiite's brain, Chamoun could face his death with feelings of accomplishment.

A near miss struck the jeep's rear bumper, inches from his face, and shards of metal stung his cheek. Chamoun wormed backward, searching for the sniper, but he had too many enemies to choose from. They were everywhere, their numbers multiplying by the moment, reinforcements racing from the fields and somewhere out of sight, behind the house.

Too many.

He'd been a fool to play along with Belasko, but what choice did he have? A lesser man might have abandoned Mara—and his conscience—but the American must have known that duty would compel Chamoun to make the effort. He'd seen his people slaughtered earlier that afternoon, and when the opportunity for payback was presented, he couldn't resist.

If nothing else, he thought, they could inflict a telling blow on their enemy before they died.

He found a moving target, stroked the Uzi's trigger, and a member of the Shiite revolutionary guard pitched forward on his face. Another broke from cover, firing as he came, and Chamoun squeezed off another burst, the rag doll figure dancing with the impact of his well-aimed slugs.

That made it four, and if his men could do as well across the board, they just might have a fighting chance.

He saw the hand grenade in flight, and barked a warning as he rolled beneath the jeep. A choking cloud of dust erupted with the blast, and jagged shrapnel clattered off the body of the vehicle above him. Gasoline cascaded from a ruptured jerrican and splashed around him, spattering his face and scalp. Chamoun crawled backward, praying that another ricochet wouldn't strike sparks before he had a chance to scramble clear.

Ironically it was a member of his own command who nearly killed him. Staggered by a chest wound, one of the support troops from the second jeep released a dying burst as he collapsed between the vehicles, his muzzle blast igniting potent fumes. Chamoun was lunging for the open air as flames licked past his face, his eyebrows singed away, and he could feel his own hair burning, hear it crackling as he wriggled through the dust.

It was the dust that saved him, handfuls mashed against his scalp and forehead, smothering the flames before they could do more than superficial damage. He was twenty feet away before the jeep went up, a fireball rolling skyward, oily smoke obscuring the battlefield. A secondary blast pushed baking heat waves through the air, but Chamoun had found his sanctuary in the shadow of the APC.

Above him one of his commandos braved incoming rounds to man the light machine gun, playing automatic fire across the door and facing windows of the ranch house. Craning for a glance in that direction, Chamoun imagined that he saw Belasko, there and gone, around the northwest corner of the building.

A mistake? Hallucination? It didn't matter. He wished the tall man well, wherever he might be, and concentrated

on the task at hand. They each had a job to do, and if they
never met again, it would be God's own will. Until he felt
the hand of Death upon his shoulder, Joseph Chamoun
would keep on fighting, carrying the battle to his enemies.

And, at the moment, his priority was gaining entry to
the house.

To find his sister and the men whom he had risked so
much to kill.

MACK BOLAN'S RUSH had been diverted by a storm of
gunfire from windows facing on the courtyard, driving him
to ground beside a flatbed truck that had been parked beside the house. It offered decent cover, and he dropped two
sentries when they tried to root him out, the hot rounds
from his AK-47 reaching out to slap them down.

He saw the frag grenade go off, the forward jeep erupt
in leaping flames, and he was grateful for the glimpse of
Joseph Chamoun retreating, more or less intact. Away to
Bolan's right, fresh smoke was rising from the poppy field,
flame visible among the stalks, and he was puzzled for a
moment, wondering about its source, before his memory
kicked in.

The motorcycle with its punctured fuel tank. Clearly it
had capsized in the field, a spark or simple engine heat igniting gasoline that spurted from the several bullet holes.
It might not be enough to torch the crop, and then again...

He put the question out of mind and concentrated on
the more immediate concern of entering the house. His
only hope of finding Mara, of eliminating Bashir Moheden and company, lay inside those walls. Unfortunately
the defenders seemed to know their job, and Bolan
couldn't count on them to make a critical mistake.

Whatever he achieved, from here on in, the Executioner would have to do on his own. The backup force would be en route by now, but he couldn't depend on them to save the day. If Moheden had panicked at the sound of gunfire—if he was even *here*—then Mara might be dead already. There was no more time to waste.

The rooftop sniper nearly bagged him as he wriggled out from underneath the truck. A burst from Bolan's AK-47 caught the gunner as he lined up for a second shot, his tunic rippling with the impact as he toppled out of sight. Unless the rifleman was sporting body armor underneath his clothes, the odds had just been shaved another fraction in favor of the challengers.

The warrior ditched an almost-empty magazine and snapped a fresh one into the Kalashnikov. His guided tour of the establishment, though brief, had planted something of a blueprint in his mind. In the rear there was a service entrance for food deliveries to the kitchen, and a pair of sliding plate glass doors located on the south, adjacent to a carport. Bolan couldn't reach the latter, but with any luck it would be covered by the gunners from the half-ton. His job, meanwhile, included entry to the house, discovery of Mara's whereabouts and the destruction of his ranking enemies.

Initial doubts aside, he knew that he would find Moheden—and perhaps his partners—in the house. The volume and ferocity of the defense told Bolan there were influential visitors on hand, but he would only learn their names and number by direct approach, and that meant slipping past the guards.

All Bolan had to do was cover thirty yards of open ground to reach the corner, ten or fifteen more to gain the service entrance. There, assuming he hadn't been dropped along the way, he would be left to make his way inside the house, past heaven knew how many guards and find the room where they were holding Mara captive.

Simple.

And there was no time like the present to begin.

He spent a moment staring at the poppy field, where flames were leaping briskly in the night, and then came up firing, driving toward his goal.

CHAPTER TWENTY-FOUR

From the moment that the shooting started, Bashir Moheden had struggled with a rising sense of panic, knowing that he must control himself if he was to survive. His hostage had provided him with a solution, but it still might blow up in his face. The enemy was all around him, and the dealer recognized his peril. He could die here if he wasn't quick enough and tough enough to save himself.

He thought about the enemy and knew, regardless of Halaby's warning from the sentries, that they weren't Syrians. It made no sense for a patrol to barge in after nightfall, and the guards on duty wouldn't open fire on uniforms without an order from the top. That meant the "Syrians" were the aggressors, and it narrowed down the field of players to a single choice.

Somehow, against all odds, Chamoun had found out where his sister was confined. There might be any one of several explanations, from a lucky guess to a report from traitors in the ranks and yet—

Belasko!

He had slipped away from them in Baalbek and had managed to avoid the sweep that followed. Nothing would prevent him, theoretically, from pushing south and joining forces with Chamoun. He would have been too late to watch the airborne raid or interfere with it, but there had been survivors, and Belasko was a fighting man. He could have whipped them into shape, secured the necessary uniforms—reports of missing Syrian patrols wouldn't be logged until the morning—and prepared the strike himself.

How had he known where Moheden would take the girl? Again, an educated guess would serve, and the American had nothing much to lose. If he was wrong about the farm, he would have found a token force on duty, wiped them out and gone about his business of destroying Bakhtiar's investment. Strong resistance meant that VIPs were on the scene, and the American could pull out all the stops in his assault.

Moheden was counting on the woman as his ticket out, but there were still unanswered questions in his mind. Would the American be interested in saving her? Was he merely using Joseph Chamoun as a convenient source of cannon fodder? What precisely did the bastard want?

No time for futile speculation.

Moheden steered his hostage through one corridor and down another, taking care that they didn't get close to the battle lines. If he could reach his car and get a fair head start while members of the rebel strike force were distracted, there was still a chance. The rest of it could wait, from answering those nagging questions to the quest for retribution. After he was safe at home, there would be ample time to feast upon the sweet meal of revenge.

Survival and escape were Bashir Moheden's priorities, and he would use the woman to protect himself. When she had served her purpose, he would kill her and dispose of her remains. Perhaps, he thought, it would be interesting to package her up and mail her to her brother. One piece at a time.

But first things first. They moved past silent bedrooms set aside for members of the staff, across a smallish parlor, toward the sliding plate glass doors. The draperies were closed, and the dealer kept Mara covered with his pistol as he edged them open and checked out the carport. The reports of automatic fire were louder here, but he saw no one in position to obstruct them.

A sudden movement near his limo caught his eye, on the driver's side. One man, from all appearances, attempted to conceal himself behind the car.

"This way," Moheden ordered, sliding back the lefthand door and shoving Mara through. She offered no resistance, but he kept the pistol jammed between her shoulders, just in case.

They crept along the wall, with Mara leading, to approach the prowler on his blind side. They were fifteen feet away before Moheden recognized the man and called his name.

"Halaby!"

Startled, the guerrilla leader spun to face them, leveling an automatic of his own. He registered relief at the sight of Moheden, his weapon lowered toward the floor. "I thought that someone should protect the cars," he said.

The dealer let him hide behind the lie. "And where is Bakhtiar?" he asked.

"We separated." There was obvious reluctance in Halaby's voice as he continued. "Should I try to find him?"

"No," Moheden answered. "He has made his choice. We're leaving. Now."

THE FIRST RUSH carried Bolan to the northeast corner of the house where he paused, braced for opposition. But the sentries were needed elsewhere, and he had the rear veranda to himself. The service door was locked, and the warrior took a chance with the Beretta, gambling on a silenced round. The latch disintegrated, and he stepped across the threshold into semidarkness.

He was in the kitchen, facing toward a pair of swing doors with light behind them. The sounds of combat were muffled, but clearly audible. A shadow moved in front of Bolan, taking human form and separating from the bulk of the refrigerator. There was no time for speculating on the fine points, whether he'd stumbled on a slacker or been intercepted by a guard on duty.

The Beretta chugged a single note, and Bolan watched the opposition fade away. He scanned the room, alert to any sounds of a response beyond the swing doors. When there was none, he let the pistol lead him through a dining room, where a partially eaten meal had been hastily abandoned.

He had no clear fix on his targets, but he moved out along a corridor that split the house in two from north to south. The war was close at hand now, rattling the walls, and Bolan had a choice to make. He could pursue his own objectives, or he could assist Chamoun and the commandos with their stalemate. The warrior tossed the mental coin, and "heads" came up with Mara's face. The troops would have to get along without him for a while.

At once, as if in response to his decision, a door flew open just in front of Bolan, spilling riflemen into the corridor. He counted three before he started squeezing off the pistol, spitting 9 mm rounds, his opposition reeling in the face of concentrated fire. One of them lasted long enough to raise his submachine gun, and held down the trigger as he died. Bolan ducked below the hail of bullets, flattening against one wall while plaster rained around him.

For an instant he imagined that the sounds of battle faltered, gunmen in the nearby rooms acknowledging the presence of a foe inside their stronghold. Reinforcements would be detailed to investigate—if any could be found—

and Bolan would be tied up fighting for a stretch of corridor that seemed, in essence, indefensible.

He chose to move instead, but it wasn't that simple. As he rose, a sudden blur of motion farther down the corridor alerted Bolan to the presence of another gunner. A pistol shot rang out, the bullet sizzling past the Executioner's head. Recoiling, he glimpsed the gunman for an instant, as he ducked around another turn and disappeared. They hadn't met, but he remembered photographs from Stony Man, and Bolan would have recognized the face in any lineup.

Bakhtiar.

He scrambled to his feet and set off in pursuit along the corridor.

MIR REZA BAKHTIAR HAD been disgruntled when Halaby called him out of the interrogation room. Moheden had been pampering the woman, toying with her and getting nowhere. Bakhtiar was on the verge of stepping in before the Palestinian returned from his excursion to "review the troops," with the announcement that a Syrian patrol was on the way.

The news had come as a surprise to Bakhtiar for several reasons. First and foremost was the fact that he'd grown accustomed to delivering his bribes in Baalbek to a ranking officer, and months had passed since anyone in uniform had set foot upon his rural property. A second problem was the timing. No patrol had ever called at night, and the coincidence of an appearance on *this* night, specifically, defied all logic. Finally, if a legitimate patrol was stopping in—to hit him up for cash, or any other reason—the troops would normally have waited on the highway, clearing their approach by radio before they started through the fields.

Accordingly he was prepared for trouble when the shooting started, scowling at Halaby's bald expression of surprise. He slipped a hand inside his caftan, palmed the automatic that he wore holstered around his waist and moved in the direction of the battle. Hanging back, Halaby laid a hand upon his arm to slow him down.

"What is it?"

"We shouldn't expose ourselves to danger," Halaby said. "The responsibilities of leadership—"

"Include the act of leadership itself. Come, don't tell me you are frightened."

"Nonsense!" Anger brought a trace of color back into Halaby's cheeks. "My first concern is the protection of our mutual investment. Dead commanders have no value to their troops."

Disgusted, Bakhtiar threw off the Palestinian's restraining hand. "Command, then, if you think that you can find a place to hide."

He turned away without another word, convinced Halaby wouldn't have the nerve to shoot him in the back, and moved in the direction of the battle. With a bitter curse, Halaby broke and ran, confirming Bakhtiar's assessment of the man, and Palestinians in general.

He had halved the distance when a loud explosion rocked the house, immediately followed by another. Somewhere close at hand, the shouts and curses of defending troops were changing into cries of panic.

Bakhtiar was torn between an urge to join his men and the compelling instinct for survival. Could he face Halaby if he turned and ran as the Palestinian had done? Would it be courage or insane bravado to proceed? He hesitated for a moment longer, felt the first small cracks in his determination start to widen, growing into fissures, letting fear seep through. It was a strange emotion for a man of Bakhtiar's conviction, and it hit him hard.

The girl!

He fixed upon her as a symbol of his plight and as a means to personal salvation. If—as he was certain—the attackers were associates of Joseph Chamoun, they would be fighting under orders to retrieve the girl at any cost. If Bakhtiar could spirit her away in time, before the raiders found her on their own...

He turned and ran, content to know that he wasn't retreating from the fight, so much as taking steps to seize the victory. If he could pull if off, he would deserve a hero's laurels.

The door to the interrogation room was standing open. Bakhtiar rushed through and found himself alone. The chair was empty, buckles dangling, the generator squatting in a snarl of cables on the floor. The atmosphere was redolent with pain and perspiration.

It would have taken several moments for Moheden to decide, more precious time for him to free the girl and—yes, her clothes were gone—to get her dressed. Where would they go? Not toward the fighting, that was certain. Through the back? It wouldn't suit the dealer to escape on foot across the fields.

That left the vehicles, and Bakhtiar was moving as the conscious thought took shape. Moheden wouldn't hesitate to leave without him, manufacturing some lame excuse if Bakhtiar survived, but he wasn't about to get the chance. The girl would slow him down, perhaps resist along the way, and more time would be wasted on a choice of vehicles, while the Lebanese steeled himself to run the gauntlet past his enemies.

A chance, and it was all he needed. Bakhtiar raced back along the way that he had come, veered left in the direction of the carport, shutting out the sounds of battle that were closer, more insistent now.

He was within a dozen yards, when gunfire suddenly erupted on his heels. He spun to find three members of his revolutionary guard collapsing in a heap, a khaki-clad intruder rising from a combat crouch, a silenced pistol in his hand.

Instinctively the Shiite sighted on his enemy and fired, forgetting not to jerk the trigger, cursing as his shot went wild. Before the stranger could respond, he flung himself around the corner, pounding toward the carport, feeling Death's foul wind upon his neck.

CHAMOUN HAD LED THE RUSH across the wide veranda with a volley of grenades and automatic fire. Men fell on either side of him, but the defenders had begun to crack, retreating from their posts in groups of two and three. The gradual retreat became a rout when one of Chamoun's commandos gunned the APC across the porch and rammed its armored nose directly through the wide front doors, machine guns laying down a screen of cover fire. The carrier's retreat left the rebel leader and those around him with a means of access to the house.

Inside he found the first line of defenders dead or dying, bodies crumpled on the floor where they had fallen in the final hail of fire. The curtains were in flames, and two of his commandos ripped them down while Chamoun pushed on, the other members of his spearhead fanning out to check adjoining rooms.

The steady beat of automatic fire continued outside, and Chamoun knew it could still go either way. He closed his mind to the uneven odds—improved, however slightly, by their access to the house—and concentrated on the search for Mara.

Where to start? She might be anywhere, alive or dead. He focused on the sound of her voice, imagining she was calling him, and chose a corridor that opened off the smoke-filled living room. It was a *dying* room today, and there would be more death before he finished with his enemies.

A number of the enemy had passed this way, and Chamoun had moved past half a dozen doors before a scuffling sound attracted his attention. He signaled for a member of the team to cover him, before he smashed the door in with a driving kick and followed through, his wounded shoulder sending shock waves through him as he hit the floor.

He caught one gunner trying to conceal himself inside a wardrobe, while another crouched behind the bed. Chamoun squeezed off a short burst from his Uzi, and the standing target crumpled, dying silently before he hit the floor. The other came up firing with an automatic rifle, stitching abstract patterns on the wall, and the rebel leader responded with a second well-placed burst before his backup had a chance to intervene.

The spray of rounds was dead on target, lifting the man off his feet and slamming him against the nearest wall. He left a smudge of crimson as he sank into a seated posture, head slumped forward with his chin supported on his chest. From where he lay, Chamoun could see the dead man's eyes locked open, staring at the answer to his final question.

On his feet, Chamoun retreated from the bedroom, feeding the Uzi a fresh magazine as he continued down the corridor. Ahead of him another door stood open, spilling stark fluorescent light across the hall. The rebel leader didn't slow his pace, compelled to step across that threshold and confirm what he already felt inside.

It was a torture room. That much was evident on sight, and Chamoun was sickened by the pent-up smell of desperation. Glancing at the generator on the floor, he stepped around it, stretching out one hand to touch the chair. Its seat still damp, still warm.

His mind unleashed a cry of anguish, but he kept it locked behind his teeth. Instead of screaming, he turned to his first lieutenant, nearly whispering in his attempt to keep control.

"They aren't far ahead of us."

Removing Mara from the torture room would mean that she was still alive, whatever damage she had suffered in captivity. Moheden and the others wouldn't waste their time or energy transporting a corpse. If Chamoun could place himself inside the dealer's mind, there yet might be a chance to cut him off.

A given: Mara was alive.

She still had value to the opposition as a hostage, but they couldn't use her here if they were overrun. They must escape, but how? What was it that his mind had overlooked? A minor thing, of no importance at the moment of assault, essential now.

The carport!

Lunging from the torture room, he raced along the corridor, turned right, then caught himself and doubled back. He was retreating now, and his initial view of Bakhtiar's command post must be looked at in reverse. A mirror image of his first glimpse, as their motorcade approached the house.

Were they too late? Was *he* too late?

Deliberately he closed his mind to failure, concentrating on directions. And the havoc he would wreak among his enemies, if he wasn't in time.

As Bakhtiar emerged through the connecting door, Moheden shouted, "Go! Now!"

Ahmad Halaby didn't hesitate. He had the limousine in motion instantly, tires squealing for a moment on the gravel of the courtyard. In the back seat, Moheden twisted to observe the Shiite standing dumbstruck in the middle of the carport.

Suddenly the car was taking hits, and he gave thanks for the expensive armor plate, the triple thickness of the windows. Who was firing at them? It made little difference now. The dealer didn't plan to stop for anyone or anything, until he reached the Baalbek airstrip where his private plane sat waiting. He would let himself relax a bit when they were safely in the air.

He could see the poppy fields burning, one more signal of disaster. Given the recent dry weather, half the crop might be ravaged. But he had other things on his mind at the moment.

Like survival.

One of Bakhtiar's commandos blundered out in front of them before they reached the access road. Halaby never even touched the brakes. The rag doll figure flew up and across their hood, a panicked face pressed tight against the windshield for an instant, sliding clear when the Palestinian gave the steering wheel a twist. The leaping flames reached out to stroke them on his right, but the vehicle was on the road now, leaving the smoke and death behind.

If Bakhtiar survived, there would be problems. Moheden could swear that he hadn't seen the older man, but that would count for little. He was running, with his tail between his legs, and while the move made perfect sense, it would inevitably strike the Shiite as evidence of cowardice. Bakhtiar would doubtless try to sever their connection, and the dealer thought it might be best that the man's crop was burning. That way the competition would be minimized while Moheden went looking for another partner to complete the picture.

Still, it would be better if someone did the world a favor and eliminated Bakhtiar. Without him, all his damning accusations silenced, there would be no trouble from the revolutionary guard when Moheden began to shop for other partners in the Bekaa Valley. He might even deal with the Shiite's successor, if the man seemed reasonable, someone who could put his holy war on hold to make a profit.

There was ample time for such considerations later, after he was safe and sound. Moheden swiveled in his seat to check their backtrack, as Halaby reached the highway and swung north toward Baalbek. The horizon was on fire, a ruddy glow of flames appearing to run on for miles, but the Lebanese saw nothing that would indicate pursuit. No doubt their enemies—and friends—were too concerned with killing one another to give chase.

Moheden concentrated on the task at hand. Escape was paramount, and once he made himself—and his hostage—secure, he could start to think in terms of realignment, reconstruction. If the flames behind him ate up most of Bakhtiar's crop, that simply meant the addicts in New York would have to pay a higher price for their relief in months to come. A few more stereos and television sets to steal, and as the price increased, so too would profit margins.

It was simple economics, but the dealer had to be alive before he could cash in.

The woman stirred beside him, and he jammed the automatic tight against her ribs. She grimaced, but said nothing.

"We're going on a journey," he informed her. "You will be my guest. A taste of luxury, perhaps, before..."

He left it there, unfinished, taking pleasure from the certain knowledge in her eyes. Her death had been foretold, but he would let her cling to the illusion that some hope remained. That way, while they were waiting for her brother or Belasko to make contact, she might wish to please him, swing the odds a bit in favor of herself.

And in the long run, it would hardly matter what she wanted. He owned her absolutely. He could dress her up in silk and jewels, or strip her naked for his pleasure. He could kill her, if she bored him or didn't perform upon command.

But not just yet.

She might be useful in another way before Moheden was finished with his enemies.

CHAPTER TWENTY-FIVE

On impulse, Bolan took the corner in a slide, collecting mat burns on his elbows and jolting into impact with a wall. Downrange his prey snapped off another shot and vanished through a doorway, leaving the warrior short of targets for his AK-47. Scrambling to his feet, he followed, slowing his approach.

It was an outside door, according to the close-up sounds that emanated from the other side, and Bolan knew that they had reached the south end of the house, where vehicles were stashed inside a covered carport.

Dammit! He was breaking out!

Discarding caution, Bolan made it to the door in six long strides. He skipped a beat, lunged through, and was in time to see Moheden's limo veering off in the direction of the access road, absorbing hits and gathering momentum on the way. A glow of leaping flames from somewhere on his right reminded Bolan of the burning poppy fields.

A scuffling on his left pitched the warrior forward in a desperation dive, the bullet that was meant to kill him smacking into plaster somewhere overhead. He caught a glimpse of Bakhtiar before the Shiite ducked behind another car, and in a flash the Executioner knew that he hadn't missed out entirely.

Bakhtiar was his, if he could make it stick. But who was splitting in the limo?

The inevitable answer settled on his shoulders like a weight, designed to press him through the floor. He'd been so damned close, and now—

His enemy was on the move, a darting shadow, weaving in between the cars. A glimpse of feet by firelight gave him all the target he could hope for, and he fired a burst beneath the undercarriage of a dark sedan. He was rewarded by a yelp of pain and the heavy impact of a body.

Shifting, Bolan circled to his left, attempting to outflank his opposition. Bakhtiar was also on the move, but he was slithering along the ground, groaning.

The Executioner felt nothing that would pass for sympathy.

He crouched behind the car, imagining the open space between them when he showed himself, aware that Bakhtiar would have a slight advantage then, despite his wounds. It would be easier to let his AK-47 do the work, fire blind around the jeep and hose his target, but that might damage one or both of the remaining cars.

And Bolan saw that he would need them.

Enough. His mind made up, he lunged from cover, going low and easing off the trigger for a fraction of a heartbeat, long enough to mark his target for the kill. Ten feet away, Mir Reza Bakhtiar was on his knees, one pale hand clenched around the outside mirror of the jeep, desperately trying to haul himself erect on broken ankles. It was costing him, and when he started squeezing off in rapid fire, the rounds he threw at Bolan came in three feet off the mark.

A short, precision burst was all it took. The Shiite holy man was dead before he knew it, spastic fingers clinging to the jeep a moment longer, giving up their grip when gravity took hold.

Bolan stepped across his fallen enemy and glanced inside the dark four-door sedan. The keys were there, and the warrior felt a surge of hope.

He had a chance.

Without another thought or moment's hesitation, Bolan cracked the driver's door and slid behind the wheel. A moment later the vehicle roared to life and shot forward, the warrior hunched behind the wheel to make himself the smallest target possible. A glance had told him that the chase car didn't have the limo's armor plating, but it was a safer bet than trying out the open jeep, which was his only other choice.

Unfortunately there had been no way of tipping off Chamoun's commandos to his plan. They saw the limousine escape, and then, just when they had returned to dueling with their scattered enemies, another vehicle erupted from the carport, racing off in hot pursuit. All things considered, there was only one response that made good sense.

Incoming fire began to strike the car from every side, exploding glass and driving Bolan under cover of the dashboard, forcing him to steer blind. Praying that he wouldn't miss the road, he kept his head down, crumbled safety glass rolling down his collar. Bullets hammered at the bodywork, but Bolan's luck was holding out.

Until the left front tire exploded.

The warrior felt the car begin to swerve and fought the wheel to keep the vehicle more or less on track. He risked a glance above the dash, in time to see a plume of smoke escape from somewhere underneath the hood.

He cursed silently. He was finished, and his prey was running free, with Mara. There was nothing he could do to stop Moheden.

A bullet splintered on the nearest window post and stung his face with bits of shrapnel. Cover was essential now, before the gunners found their mark. He aimed directly for the nearest row of poppies, bearing down on the accelerator. Flames were licking out, where only smoke had showed before, and he had moments left before the liberated vehicle became a rolling funeral pyre.

His charger reached the cultivated ground and lumbered on, its bare rim plowing brand-new furrows on the left. He felt the back tires losing traction and wondered whether he would make it far enough to gain some cover. But he had no other options. When he was twenty yards inside the field, the hood blew skyward, and he knew that it was time to try his luck on foot.

He left the car in motion, diving clear, and came up in a combat crouch. It wouldn't do for him to hike back the way that he had come. Chamoun's men would be quick to recognize his uniform, but in the darkness and the excitement, they might not be quick enough. Accordingly he set a course that led him toward the access road. From there, a short hike back would bring him to the courtyard battleground.

An explosion marked the end of the sedan, and flaming gasoline rained down on the upturned faces of the poppies. Soon another portion of the field was burning, one fire sweeping outward from its point of origin to join the other, merging in a single sheet of flame. The Executioner had time to reach safe footing on the road, but he could feel the heat behind him in the last few yards.

Emerging onto one-lane dirt and gravel, the Executioner started back in the direction of the house. It was in sight when Joseph Chamoun's reserves erupted from the poppy field ahead and to his right. They came in firing, easily distinguishing their own in uniform and the defenders who were taken absolutely by surprise.

It would be over quickly now, a victory despite the odds. And yet the unfamiliar bitter taste of failure stayed with Bolan. Mara and the dealer had eluded him, one still a prisoner, the other running for his wretched life. There might not be another chance to save the girl or to collect Moheden's debt of blood. Unless...

Hopeful, Bolan trudged back toward the house.

CHAMOUN HAD REACHED the carport moments after Bolan sped away, and he had nearly fired on the retreating vehicle before he glimpsed the crumpled form in front of him and recognized Mir Reza Bakhtiar. It struck him, then, but there was no way to communicate with his commandos in the courtyard, and he watched, crestfallen, as they shot the American's car to pieces.

Was the man alive? Despite his bitterness at losing Mara one more time, Chamoun was still concerned about Belasko. They had come this far—this close to saving her—because of the American, and if she still had any hope at all, Chamoun suspected that Belasko's strength, his cunning, would provide the key. It would be grievous irony indeed if one of the rebel leader's own soldiers crushed that fragile hope.

He was cautiously emerging from the carport when an explosion in the poppy field sent fiery streamers skyward. The sedan was finished, and a mushroom cloud of flame was rising in its place when Chamoun's expected reinforcements burst from cover on the eastern flank. A group of revolutionary guards were pinned between the new arrivals and a group of khaki gunners huddled near the APC, cut off from any hope of cover or survival. Even so, they died like men, and Chamoun admired their courage at the last.

More mopping up remained, inside the house and at the barracks building out in back, but for the most part it was over. Through surprise and perseverance, they had overcome a larger force, destroyed a major portion of the dealer's crop, and Bakhtiar was lying dead, not thirty feet away. It was a triumph to be celebrated, but the rebel leader couldn't find it in his heart to cheer. The cost had been too high.

A realistic man, Chamoun was ready to accept the fact that Mara might be lost forever. He would cling to hope, of course, but action was required to set her free, and so far he had failed at every turn. What did it matter if he killed a hundred soldiers? Or a thousand? While Moheden lived, with Mara in his clutches, victory would taste like ashes on his tongue.

A body count would take some time—and there was scattered killing to be finished yet—but from the evidence before his eyes, he estimated friendly losses in the rough vicinity of twenty-five percent. Of those who had set out that night to strike a blow against the common enemy, no less than one in four were dead or gravely wounded. Coupled with his losses of the afternoon, that meant Chamoun's commando force—his people—had been nearly cut by half. They couldn't chase Moheden back to Baalbek now, much less across the country to his coastal hideaway. It would be suicide.

Alone perhaps—or with Belasko if he lived—Chamoun might have a chance. He could pursue the dealer on his own, exact a toll of vengeance in his sister's name. Moheden might be momentarily triumphant, but he wouldn't live to gloat. From this day forward, he would have a shadow. Death would follow him until he paid the final price.

His reinforcements had moved on around the house and toward the barracks. Chamoun heard scattered gunfire as they finished mopping up, but his attention was commanded by a solitary figure on the access road. Emerging from the smoke, a tall man with a rifle in his hands was moving closer, making no attempt to hide himself.

At fifty yards the rebel leader recognized Belasko. From appearances, he hadn't suffered any lasting injury.

Chamoun experienced a surge of hope and rushed forward to confront the grim American. One glance into Belasko's eyes and he could read the man's thoughts.

"We go together," Chamoun informed him.

"Fine. But first I need a radio."

IT WAS A DESPERATE PLAN, but Bolan had exhausted all his other options. Tracking Moheden along the highway was a waste of time, and they didn't have men enough to storm Hosseinieh or crack the Sheikh Abdullah barracks if their rabbit went to ground at either stronghold. They would have to bank on stealth, and hope the dealer had been spooked enough to quit the area completely. With his private plane and pilot waiting on the Baalbek airstrip, he could easily be home by dawn, inside his fortress villa on the coast.

It was a gamble, but it was the only hope they had. Chamoun had promised help with transportation, but the Executioner had one more detail to arrange, and he would have to do it on his own.

Grimaldi.

It would be a waste of precious time and fuel to have Jack pick them up. Instead the soldier hatched a backup plan. Grimaldi wouldn't like it and would grouse and grumble to himself, but he'd be there when they needed him. With bells on.

The rest of it amounted to a waiting game, with Chamoun on edge but bearing up, pretending that he wasn't worried sick about his sister. Bolan learned that he had seen the torture room, but they said nothing else about the subject. Mara had been breathing when she left the farm, or else Moheden would have run without her. There hadn't been time to formulate more subtle plans around a corpse.

So be it.

Mara was—had been—alive, and they would act on the presumption that Moheden needed her to stay that way, however briefly. He would wait to see the outcome of the battle on the farm, then he would bluster, threaten, barter—anything at all to save himself. Above all else, the dealer would attempt to dupe his enemies and throw them off guard. He might suggest a meeting, for delivery of the woman, where his troops would lie in wait and bring the curtain down.

That is, he would if he had time.

But time was running out for Bashir Moheden as well as for his hostage. Either way it played, with Mara safe or dead, Bolan meant to take the dealer down. There would be no white flags or cease-fires for Moheden.

Their business at the farm was finished in another fifteen minutes. Bakhtiar retained no noncombatants on his staff, and members of the Shiite revolutionary guard were willing martyrs, fighting to the death against their enemies. A number of the Palestinians had attempted to surrender, but by that time there had been no mercy left in Chamoun's commandos. Bolan calculated that a few had likely slipped away to take their chances in the burning poppy fields, but it would make no difference now.

His mission lay in front of him, unfinished. The Executioner would have liked to leave Chamoun behind, but he couldn't deny a brother's right to see it through. And on the side, Chamoun might still be useful for his knowledge of the countryside, its people and their languages.

It would be two of them against the dragon in his lair, and Bolan understood the odds. If taking down the farm had been a risk, assaulting Moheden's retreat looked more like suicide.

The Executioner preferred to view it as a challenge. And he had a feeling it might be the challenge of his life.

GRIMALDI TOOK THE CALL at half-past midnight, read between the lines of Bolan's guarded speech and signaled an immediate affirmative. He kept his reservations and his questions to himself, aware that Bolan would be running short on time, perhaps in danger of attack by hostile forces homing on the beacon through triangulation.

Still, the gutsy pilot had misgivings as he made the final takeoff preparations, and he ran them over in his mind as he was suiting up.

For openers, it bothered him that he wouldn't be picking Bolan up. It meant the Executioner was pressed for time, his quarry moving fast, and coded references to "dropping by the dealer's place" told Jack that they were chasing after Moheden. There had been briefings on the smuggler's hideout—photos, with a sketchy rundown on defenses—but Grimaldi figured there was no way on God's earth that their informants could have covered everything.

So he was looking at a crapshoot.

Bolan had obtained some other means of transportation to the coast, and he was going in as usual, against the odds, perhaps alone. Grimaldi would be there to help him crack the box, but there were further complications. Bolan's passing reference to a "friend inside" told Jack that he'd have to watch his step. Somewhere within the villa there was someone Bolan wanted to protect. Grimaldi had no way of knowing who that someone was, or if the "someone" might be plural. When the hit came down, he'd be forced to choose his targets carefully, with almost surgical precision—which, in turn, meant his effectiveness would be severely limited from the beginning.

It had to be the chopper, then. He would have opted for the Phantom on a simple hit-and-run maneuver, and Grimaldi could have guaranteed a wipe with rockets, bombs and napalm, but the "friends inside" would fry along with hostile personnel.

And at the same time, there was Bolan's safety to consider. Knowing the man the way he did, Grimaldi knew the guy wouldn't be satisfied to find himself a vantage point and drop Moheden's sentries from a distance. If the big guy had a "friend inside," that meant that he'd be inside, too.

Grimaldi cursed and muttered to himself, but he finished running down his preflight checklist in approximately half the normal length of time. A number of Israelis stood around the sidelines, watching, no doubt wondering what the American was up to. As he made his final takeoff preparations, Jack examined them, returned their stares and marveled at the kind of men who spend their lives forever on the edge.

Like Bolan.

And it would be Grimaldi's job to guarantee that the soldier didn't lose his edge when it was needed most. He didn't have to understand the details of the plan, or give it his endorsement. All he had to do was follow through and be on time.

So they were dropping in to see the dealer. The unwelcome wagon, loaded down with goodies no one in his right mind would be anxious to receive. A one-time-only special, just for Bashir Moheden.

It would be Bolan's show, Grimaldi flying backup, but if something happened...

Scowling into lift-off, knuckles white around the joystick, Jack Grimaldi took his chopper out to find a long-lost friend and slay a dragon.

CHAPTER TWENTY-SIX

The pilot was a friend of a friend, bound to Joseph Chamoun by politics and religion. His aircraft was a twenty-year-old single-engine job of European manufacture, from a firm that Bolan didn't recognize by name. Spot welding marked the fuselage in places, but the engine sounded healthy. It would only have to serve them for a short while, and Bolan hoped that it would hold.

He climbed aboard, with all of his misgivings, and buckled into a jump seat behind Chamoun, who rode in the copilot's place.

"There was another plane," Chamoun informed him, shouting to be heard above the engine noise. "A pilot and three passengers. Two men, one woman. They flew west."

So, they were on the scent at any rate. West meant the villa, and it ruled out an eleventh-hour change of plans, with Mara stashed somewhere in Baalbek. That meant sixty minutes, give or take, to touchdown on the coast. A vehicle was waiting for them—or it would be—and with a fair wind at their backs, they should be closing in on Moheden before the first full light of dawn betrayed them.

They had taken time to change en route to Baalbek, swapping bloody uniforms for dark civilian clothes. It was the best that they could do in an emergency, and Bolan would be forced to get along without the blacksuit, camouflage cosmetics and the other penetration gear that had supplied him with an edge on other raids.

At least, he thought, their weapons would suffice. Both men were packing AK-47s, with enough spare magazines between them for a full-scale war. Beneath a lightweight jacket, the warrior wore the Beretta's shoulder harness, while Chamoun's chosen side arm was the venerable Browning Hi-Power, manufacutured by Fabrique Nationale. Both men carried fighting knives, and each had taken on the added weight of half a dozen frag grenades, retrieved from Bakhtiar's own private armory.

If they went down, it wouldn't be from lack of hardware. Bolan was concerned about Chamoun, his stamina and state of mind, but there was no denying him a piece of the attack on Moheden's estate. Whichever way it went, the guy had paid his dues. He had a vested interest in the raid, and one more gun could only help.

Brognola's briefing back at Stony Man hadn't included numbers for Moheden's household staff. A dozen sentries had been visible on Bolan's visit, but the force would have certainly been increased, with all that the dealer had suffered in the past few hours. Guessing numbers from a distance was a futile game, and Bolan didn't waste his time. He had enough to occupy his mind with the mechanics of the raid.

It would be rocky going in, but they would have to manage. Coming out was something else entirely, and he didn't bother trying to predict the game. Survival went down one step at a time, and they were in the starting gate.

MOHEDEN STOOD outside his villa, waiting for the sun to rise. He had always found the pre-dawn hours peaceful and serene, but now the darkness filled him with foreboding, every shadow hiding unknown enemies. He longed for daylight, when the sun would burn his fears away.

His apprehension was irrational, the Lebanese realized. His enemies—if any still survived—were miles away, confined within the Bekaa Valley and environs. They would be hard-pressed to reach him here, unless . . .

An image of Belasko sprang to mind, implacable and
unforgiving. Moheden wouldn't be satisfied until he saw
his adversary dead, but in the meantime, he believed that
he'd taken every possible precaution to protect himself.
The normal complement of fifteen sentries had been doubled, using up the last of his reserves, and he'd placed
Ahmad Halaby in command of the detachment, seeking to
calm the Palestinian's nerves with busywork.

The dealer lighted a thin cigar and blew a cloud of
smoke in the direction of the sea. He wished that he was on
a ship, going anywhere at all, but he couldn't escape his
problems with a cruise. They would be waiting for him
when he came ashore, unless he dealt with them directly
and eliminated his opponents in the ruthless style that had
become his trademark. Weakness would jeopardize his
empire by encouraging attacks from other quarters. Any
peasant with a rifle and a dream would feel himself
equipped to challenge his superiors and threaten the security of the established syndicate.

How much of that was left after tonight? Moheden
didn't think that he would hear from Bakhtiar again, and
he was already considering the best means of approaching
a successor. The alternative was finding a completely new
supplier. Not impossible, by any means, but it would take
more time, and that meant money out of pocket while his
customers went begging and, perhaps, found new suppliers of their own.

It would be easier, for all concerned, to make his peace
with the Iranians and thus maintain the status quo. Moheden thought that he could pull it off, as long as he was
first to speak with Bakhtiar's successor and describe the
grim events that had transpired. A little sympathy, a little
charm, the promise of revenge. The Shiites were like
spiteful children in their view of the Americans. Belasko's

name—and better yet, his head—would go a long way toward absolving Moheden of any guilt in the affair.

Appearances were everything, the dealer knew, and he had taught himself to be a master of disguise.

He thought about the woman, locked away inside the villa, and considered visiting her cell. He might feel better with some exercise, and she could offer him relief from his frustration.

Soon, perhaps, when he had finished his cigar and satisfied himself that they were safe. He'd take another tour of the grounds before he spared the time for pleasure. It would irritate Halaby, having someone double-check his preparations, but the situation clearly called for extraordinary measures, and they couldn't stand on protocol.

How long until the dawn? he wondered.

Not soon enough.

DARK WATER SLID away beneath the helicopter as Grimaldi broke his northern course and headed east toward land. His flight plan was a repetition, more or less, of the approach that he'd used for dropping Bolan on the outskirts of the Bekaa Valley. This time, though, he wouldn't have to make his way across hostile territory. He was homing on a coastal target, flying low to beat the radar, hoping for complete surprise.

Grimaldi liked to think he was prepared for anything. The gunship came complete with lethal hardware, though it lacked the Phantom's power punch of bombs and napalm. What he *did* have was a 20 mm Gatling mounted in the nose, prepared to greet his enemies with a blistering six thousand rounds per minute. Backing up the gun, twin rocket pods provided him with an explosive edge, though he would have to use them cautiously. The automatic pistol on his belt and Uzi submachine gun mounted by his seat

were standard flight equipment, but he didn't plan on getting close enough to use them this time out.

Flying on instinct, Grimaldi replayed the last conversation with Bolan in his mind. The mission wasn't slated as
a pickup operation, but Grimaldi planned to leave his options open, just in case. The big guy's "friend" might need
a lift, and you could never tell when the Executioner might
find himself cut off from the established exits. Anything
could happen once the play went down, and while a pickup
hadn't been requested, neither had it been specifically
ruled out.

For now, Grimaldi would be satisfied to play by ear and
improvise as necessary. It was a familiar story in the Bolan wars.

The rushing darkness called up memories of other missions, other times when they had faced the enemy together, coming out on top with nothing more than guts and
nerve. Each time, Grimaldi wondered if the run might be
his last with Bolan, but they had always pulled it off. So
far.

In childhood he'd once been taught that God mistook
such pessimistic thoughts for prayers and sometimes
granted the unwitting supplicant his "wish." Grimaldi
didn't buy it, any more than he believed in lucky rabbits'
feet or four-leaf clovers. But he didn't like to gamble,
either. From experience he knew that apprehension and
distractions jeopardized a fighting man's performance in
the field—or in the air. The raid against Moheden's fortress would require his concentration to the max, and he
wasn't prepared to jeopardize the mission on a whim.

Another twenty minutes. He was almost close enough to
taste it now, and trusted Bolan to be in position when the
time came. Darkness was an ally when it came to launching an assault, but it could also hide your human allies,
turn them into moving targets in the crunch. Grimaldi's

orders were precise, in terms of timing, and he couldn't wait for dawn to light the killing ground.

If Bolan was delayed somehow, Grimaldi wouldn't get the word before he started his approach. He wasn't captivated by the notion of a one-man show, but he could play it that way, too, if necessary. There was no provision for a scrub at this point in the game.

Ten minutes and Grimaldi concentrated on his instruments, deliberately blanking out the thoughts of death. Whatever happened in the crunch would happen. He'd done his best to be prepared, and there was nothing more that he could do. Case closed.

Ahead of Jack Grimaldi, dawn lay crouched and waiting on the far horizon, hanging back to let the deadly games begin before it came onstage.

AHMAD HALABY HAD no taste for waging a defensive war. Since his enlistment with the PLO in younger days, his specialty had always been the hit-and-run assault—a bold, aggressive strategy that never failed to take his targets by surprise. It went against the grain for him to sit inside a fortress, waiting for the ax to fall.

They had already tried it once, with Bakhtiar, and the result had been unqualified disaster. How many men had been lost on the farm? How many lives thrown away so that Moheden could toy with the woman? And now they were preparing for a reenactment of the travesty, with fewer troops to man the ramparts.

Granted, there was something in Moheden's argument about their distance from the enemy, the losses that their adversaries had undoubtedly sustained. It wouldn't qualify as any kind of victory, but if it slowed down the opposition and sapped his will to fight, it might achieve the same affect. Halaby hoped Moheden was correct about the

villa being safe. He had already seen enough danger for
one night.

Of late, the Palestinian had come to wonder if his nerve
was failing. In the old days, prior to—and immediately
after—his defection from the PLO, Halaby had been
known for his aggressive fighting spirit. He had led the way
on raids that passed from action into legend overnight.
While Black September hired the Japanese Red Army to
assault Lod Airport, members of Halaby's faction struck
against the very heart of Tel Aviv, attacking Zionist officials in their offices and homes without a second thought
to risk. Halaby sometimes led the raids, and he was always close at hand, providing backup and support in case
of complications.

Lately, though, he worried that responsibility had
changed him, weakened him. He lacked a certain energy
these days, and for the better part of two years he had done
his fighting from an office, letting others do the dirty work
on his behalf. A leader had responsibilities, of course, but
there were times when he began to wonder whether duty
had, in fact, become a fair excuse for staying safe behind
the lines.

If someone else had voiced those doubts, Halaby would
have been compelled to kill his critic, as a show of strength.
In private, now, he found that he couldn't escape the nagging questions that beset him. His actions earlier that evening, when he broke and ran from Bakhtiar, provided
something in the way of final confirmation for his own
worst-case scenario.

The tiger had become a timid house cat, wary of the
hunt. With any luck, the guilty secret might have died with
Bakhtiar, but other tests would come in time, and he
couldn't be certain of his own reactions in another crisis.

Still, Moheden trusted him to oversee the guard around
his villa. It was something in the nature of a ceremonial

position, but considering the dealer's panic when they fled the Bekaa poppy farm, Halaby felt a little better. Frightened as he had been, Moheden had been worse. He pegged Halaby as a man of strength and resolution, capable of managing the palace guard. It was a start, and if Halaby kept his wits about him, it might be the start of winning back his self-respect.

The job was not difficult. He made the rounds, initially, to satisfy himself that all approaches via land and water had been covered. If the enemy did come, Halaby's soldiers would be ready. They wouldn't be taken by surprise this time.

It was a promise to himself, and one that he couldn't afford to break. Halaby recognized that Moheden would need a strong right arm now that the Shiite holy man had been removed. If he could prove himself tonight and in the days to come, the post would certainly be his. From such a vantage point, Halaby could do great things for his cause . . . and for himself.

He felt a bit more confident as he began to make another tour of the line. In fact he almost wished the enemy *would* show himself. Ahmad Halaby's hour of redemption was at hand.

THEY DROVE along the coastal road with the lights off until they came within a mile of the target. Moonlight would betray them if they ventured any closer in the jeep. Bolan parked the vehicle in a stand of trees, well off the road, where it wouldn't be spotted by Syrian patrols. A narrow track wound down the cliff face to the sea, and Bolan led the way, with Chamoun close on his heels.

The beach was narrow and rocky, but it ran for miles in each direction. Moving south, they hugged the bluffs and kept alert for watchers on the ground or on the ledges overhead. A single slip would spell doom, and Bolan didn't intend to throw his final chance away on careless errors.

The plan had been agreed on in advance, while they were airborne, and they didn't need to talk about it now. During Bolan's earlier visit to Moheden's villa, he had noted how the cliffs were scarred with narrow, twisting paths— no more than goat trails for the most part—granting access to the beach from higher up. In Bolan's mind, it stood to reason that the dealer's troops would watch the highway first, and then the sea approaches. He hoped they would forget about the beach as anything except a landing zone, and thereby open up a breech in their defenses.

It was still a gamble, but it seemed to be their only chance. A more direct approach along the highway would be suicide, with gunners waiting for them at the gates. Chamoun had promised that his wound wouldn't delay them or prevent him from scrambling up the trail, and so far he had kept his word.

In fifteen minutes they were poised beneath the cliff where Bashir Moheden's estate lay basking in the moonlight. Bolan found the trail that he'd picked out earlier, its general location filed away for future reference. He waited for Chamoun to scan the cliff face, frowning at the narrow track. Another moment and the rebel leader nodded, signaling that he was ready to begin.

The Executioner took the lead. With twenty feet to go before they reached the top, he hesitated, turning back, and risked a whisper to Chamoun. "From here it's all or nothing. I expect some backup, but it might not help. There are no guarantees."

"I ask for none," Chamoun replied. "The only guarantee in life is that inaction leads to failure. Let's go."

The Executioner released his silenced side arm from its shoulder harness, easing off the safety as he started climbing. Here the trail was almost vertical, and Bolan used his free hand for support, testing each step in advance to prevent a noisy rock slide. Chamoun, behind him, gave no indication that his wounded shoulder was protesting under the strain.

He reached the top, peered over and found a sentry less than thirty feet away. The young man was intent on studying the sea, prepared to shout a warning at the first sign of amphibious assault. If he had any company, they weren't visible from Bolan's vantage point.

It would be now or never. If they didn't forge ahead, and quickly, they were finished.

Bolan sighted down the slide of his Beretta, stroked the trigger once and watched the young man crumple in a silent heap. He waited, half expecting a response, and counted off ten seconds in the ringing silence. Finally satisfied, he scrambled up and over, settling in a combat crouch as Chamoun joined him.

CHAPTER TWENTY-SEVEN

"Is everything secure?"

"Of course." Halaby's smile was forced, unnatural. "I've toured the perimeter twice already, and will examine everyone again in a half hour."

"All right."

Moheden wasn't satisfied, but there was nothing else for them to do. He had to let himself unwind, forget the screaming panic he had felt short hours earlier when he was fleeing for his life. The coastal villa was a different world, impossibly removed from the Bekaa Valley in a nation where peasants frequently lived and died without traveling more than ten miles from their ancestral homes.

His enemy had twice suffered major losses today—no, it was yesterday by now—and if Chamoun was rash enough to follow him outside the Bekaa, it would be a simple matter for authorities to mop up his survivors. All he had to do was hold them off, like any homeowner entitled to defend his property.

Or he could simply kill them all himself.

The dealer frowned. He was anticipating trouble where he knew none should arise. The rebels might know where he lived, but reaching him was something else entirely. Mounting a successful raid against the villa he had fortified with extreme care would be the last act of a madman. Surely Joseph Chamoun, if he still lived, was wise enough to know he'd been beaten.

Thinking of Chamoun reminded him of Mara. Truthfully the woman had been in his thoughts since he dispatched the troops to fetch her from the rebel camp. He had participated in her torture with a mixture of reluctance and excitement he couldn't explain. Her beauty, even in the midst of suffering, enthralled him.

And he wanted her. Right now.

There was no reason to deny himself. The woman was his property, in essence, to be dealt with as he liked. She must remain alive for now, against the possibility of trading her for peace and quiet, but she wasn't sacrosanct. She could be his. She *was* his.

Moheden dismissed Halaby, leaving him to supervise the outside troops. His mind was occupied with Mara and the pleasure she could give him while she lived.

There was no question, ultimately, of releasing Mara. She'd seen too much to live, but it was necessary to postpone her execution while his other enemies were still at large. When Moheden had isolated them, determined their names and numbers, he would kill them all. But in the meantime he would use her for the purpose God had intended female flesh to serve.

Inside the house, he poured himself a glass of wine and drank it down, as if for courage, without taking the time to savor the bouquet. Another, and he felt vitality returning, spreading through him with the ebb and flow of liquid fire. He pictured Mara, naked in the straight-backed chair, and felt himself respond.

At first the warning shouts refused to register. Someone—a member of the guard?—had raised his voice, but Moheden couldn't make out the words, which were immediately smothered by a burst of fire from automatic weapons. Flinching as the shout became a scream, the Lebanese tugged the automatic pistol from his waistband, nearly dropping it before he flicked the safety off.

A raid against the villa was impossible, but it was happening. The enemy had played into his hands, and it was time to make the bastards pay. Beginning with the woman.

THE SENTRIES HAD BEEN placed strategically, one gunner every hundred feet or so, but in the darkness they were sometimes out of contact with one another. After taking down the lookout on the cliff, Mack Bolan found a corner of the property where trees and shadows helped conceal a solitary gunman from his fellows. Bolan studied his position from the branches of a twisted cedar just outside the wall, deciding that they wouldn't find a better place to make their surreptitious entry.

First the takedown. It would have to be accomplished silently, before the mark could open fire or shout a warning. Bolan wrapped his legs around the limb that held his weight, his silenced automatic steady in a double-handed grip. The range was something over forty feet, but there was nothing in the way, and if the man stood still a moment...

The warrior stroked the trigger twice and watched the sentry topple forward on his face. Another moment, waiting to be certain that the others hadn't heard, and then he scrambled down to join Chamoun. The rebel's wound hadn't restricted his activities so far, but Bolan knew it must be hurting him. Beneath the outer wall, he made a cradle of his hands and hoisted Chamoun up first, then passed the weapons over prior to scrambling across.

They stood beside a dead man in the darkness, studying the house and grounds. A few more seconds and their quest would take them into no-man's-land, where cover was provided only by a piece of sculpture here, a bit of manicured shrubbery there. A rush across the open ground was perilous, but it would be their only chance.

Chamoun was reading Bolan's mind. He shrugged resignedly and pointed toward the house. A cautious flash of teeth, a quick thumbs-up and he was ready. Bolan wondered what was going on inside that mind—concern for Mara, fury at her captors—but he had run out of time. Their course lay straight across the lawn, beside the swimming pool. And, he decided, it was time to raise or fold.

The move had possibilities, but Lady Luck was dozing when they broke from cover. Up ahead on Bolan's left, a gunner was emerging from the shrubbery, startled eyes locked squarely on Chamoun and Bolan as they made their break. He shouted to his comrades on the wall, and he was grappling with his submachine gun when Chamoun unleashed a burst that cut him down. The guard managed one short scream before he fell, and triggered off a burst in the direction of the stars.

At once, selected sentries broke formation, answering the call to action. Others held their posts, prepared to handle any danger from outside the walls, but ten or fifteen men would be enough to do the job on sitting targets.

He took the precious time to check his watch, afraid to trust his ears when they were ringing with the sounds of shouts and automatic fire. He might not hear the helicopter coming, but he knew that Jack would be on time, no questions asked. Their task, meanwhile, must be to penetrate the house.

He fired a burst along their backtrack, toppling one of Moheden's soldiers. Without another moment's hesitation, Bolan swung in the direction of the sliding doors that were his target, firing as he ran. Bullets from his AK-47 raked the plate glass windows, bringing down both panes like sheets of falling ice.

Still firing, Bolan plunged across the threshold and inside.

GRIMALDI CAME IN low over the estate at treetop level, rotors whipping at the cool night air. The floodlights had blazed on when he was still two hundred yards offshore, a signal to the pilot that the hit was going down on schedule, and he let the beacons guide him in.

He skimmed past startled sentries on the wall and drew some scattered fire as he completed one quick circuit of the property. No sign of Bolan, but he noted gunners racing for the house, and when he flicked the small receiver on, a blast of feedback from the homer told him his friend was somewhere just below.

That made it easier for now. He could assume that Bolan's "friend inside" was somewhere in the house, and anybody moving on the grounds was playing in a free-fire zone. He took the chopper down and made a quick run past the swimming pool, a short burst from the 20 mm Gatling wreaking havoc with a squad of riflemen who made the grave mistake of stopping in the open.

Two of the survivors headed for the wall, their weapons lost along the way, and Grimaldi pursued them far enough to meet another team of gunners moving toward the house. He hit them with the chopper's floodlight and the Gatling simultaneously. Grimaldi left them where they fell and circled back in the direction of the villa.

He spotted several vehicles lined up along one side, and froze them in his sights. The starboard rocket pod belched twice, three times, and the expensive cars were swallowed in a rolling tidal wave of flame. The shock wave jarred his chopper, and Grimaldi lifted off to give himself some breathing room. He wasn't quick enough to miss the human torch that staggered from the wreckage, trailing sparks from arms that beat in vain against the hungry flames.

So much for quick and clean.

He circled back around the house, reversing his direction, and surprised another group of riflemen advancing on the source of the explosions. Two or three of them were quick enough to open fire before he pressed the Gatling's trigger, blowing them apart. One round cracked the windscreen to his left, a quick reminder that the birdman wasn't bulletproof.

He took the helicopter up and spied a rooftop gunner on the way. The guy was pegging shots in his direction, firing wide—so far. Grimaldi let him have a quick two-second burst and watched the target dive for cover as his sixty rounds tore up the roof. The guy had gone to ground behind an air-conditioning compressor, and Grimaldi didn't feel like playing cat and mouse. Instead he closed the gap between them with a rocket, and the hulk of the compressor went to pieces, spewing shrapnel for a radius of twenty yards.

No point in looking for the gunner after that. His mother wouldn't know him on the undertaker's slab, and there were other targets begging for attention on the ground. Grimaldi couldn't do a thing for Bolan in the house, but he could thin the ranks outside, and he would concentrate on that.

It felt like shooting tethered ducks, but he rejected the analogy. The targets were predatory animals, responsible for countless murders, untold suffering through export of their poison to the States and Europe. Judgment day had been a long time coming, but it was upon them now.

Grimaldi swept across the floodlighted grounds in search of targets, carrying the cleansing fire.

AS SOON AS THEY HAD crossed the threshold, Joseph Chamoun turned back to scatter their pursuers with a burst of automatic fire. He saw one runner stumble, sprawling on the grass, and two more peel away in opposite direc-

344   ASSAULT

tions, seeking cover. One of them slid home behind a piece
of statuary, but the other had no luck at all. Chamoun
could almost feel the gunman's desperation as he fired
another burst and brought his target down.

A bullet smacked the wall beside the rebel leader, and he
spun to find the American dueling with a pair of gunners
crouching on a marble staircase. Chamoun fired off a
burst that pinned them down, while Bolan unclipped a frag
grenade and pitched it overhand, a toss that dropped the
lethal egg three steps above his targets, letting gravity take
over.

The explosion loosed a rain of plaster from the ceiling,
shrapnel gouging into walls and shattering a fortune in
expensive glasswork. Neither of the gunmen was in fighting shape as Bolan rushed the stairs, Chamoun falling in
behind him and hesitating as he recognized the chopping
noises of a helicopter engine. Close upon that sound, another: gunfire, fast and furious, much like the droning of
a giant wasp.

"The cavalry," Bolan informed him. "He's on our
side."

Chamoun drew some relief from that, until he took the
measure of their task. Moheden's house was huge, gar-
gantuan. It might take hours to locate Mara in the maze of
rooms and corridors. Instinctively he knew they were running out of time.

"Which way?" he blurted, praying that Belasko would
somehow be right the first time.

Then, before the tall American could answer, other
gunmen found them, bursting through a massive pair of
double doors that granted access to a formal dining room.
Chamoun reacted swiftly, flattening himself behind a
padded couch as bullets sliced the air above his head. He
heard the American's weapon answering the challenge, and

he wriggled backward, looking for an opening from which to join the fight.

In fact the battle came to him. Six inches from his face, the hand grenade bounced once and spun around before it stopped. With no time left for conscious thought, Chamoun kicked backward, rolling, scuttling away on hands and knees. Beyond a certain range, the bulk of shrapnel would go upward, but if he was trapped inside the point-blank killing zone—

The shock wave lifted Chamoun completely off all fours and flattened him against the nearest wall. He couldn't muster fear, and so he settled for surprise as darkness carried him away.

BASHIR MOHEDEN WAS approaching Mara's room when an explosion on the roof sent tremors through the house. He panicked and rushed forward, bursting through the door. She recoiled from what she read in his face. He felt an urge to kill the woman where she sat, her back against the wall, but she might still be useful if he could negotiate with the attackers.

Somehow he would have to make his way outside. The vehicles were there, and if they were disabled, he might still escape on foot. It was not hopeless yet.

"Get up."

She hesitated, and Moheden crossed the room to drag her out of the room. Mara twisted in his grasp and landed one swift kick against his shin before he pressed the automatic to her skull.

"Enough!" he snapped. "My patience is exhausted. Life or death—the choice is in your hands."

She glared at him with hatred in her eyes, but ceased her struggles. Prodding her ahead of him, the dealer reached the corridor and pointed Mara toward the left, in the direction of the secondary stairs. He recognized the sounds of combat and knew his enemies had breached the house, but there was no escape from any of the upper floors without a leap that might have left him incapacitated. He would have to brave the killing ground and try to make his way by stealth.

They reached the stairs a moment later, Mara hesitating until she was prodded with the pistol at her back. She started down reluctantly, Moheden close behind her. So far it seemed as if his enemies were concentrated on the far side of the house, toward the veranda, and the dealer hoped to slip away before they gained a greater foothold.

"Hurry!"

Mara staggered as he shoved her and nearly lost her footing, cursing as she caught herself. She bolted, but Moheden was on her in an instant, fingers tangled in her hair to drag her back. She spun and aimed a kick in the direction of his groin, but he avoided her and whipped an open palm across her face. The scream that pierced his brain seemed equally comprised of fear and rage.

Moheden stepped in close before she could retreat and cracked the automatic hard across her skull. She crumpled at his feet, and he bent down to grasp the cuffs that pinned her wrists behind her back. Employing them as handles, he began to drag her prostrate form across the polished floor.

THE FRAG GRENADE DROVE Bolan under cover, but it caught a couple of his adversaries by surprise. The warrior came up firing in the aftermath of the explosion, finishing both men before they had a chance to fall, and catching one more as he tried to duck behind an easy chair. The AK-47 nailed his target broadside, dropping him before he reached his meager sanctuary. Only one more adversary was on the field—the man responsible for lobbing the grenade. He broke from cover now, a submachine gun stuttering before he found a target, and the Executioner was waiting for him, lining up the shot and squeezing off from thirty feet away. The 3-round burst was dead on target, stitching crimson blooms across the gunner's chest and blowing him away. Bolan had barely glimpsed his face, but it had been enough. Ahmad Halaby would be leading no more raids across the border.

Bolan doubled back and found Chamoun where he lay. His shoulder wound had opened, and his nose was bleeding, but there seemed to be no other further damage. The warrior shook the prostrate form and gently slapped his cheeks, rewarded with a groan before the dark eyes fluttered open, swimming in and out of focus.

"Can you hear me?" Bolan asked.

"I . . . yes."

"We're short on time," he said. "I'll have to leave you here." He found the rebel's weapon, placed it in his hands and waited for the grip to tighten. "You'll be needing this."

"Where are you going?"

"Upstairs, first."

"I'm coming with you."

Halfway to his feet, Chamoun collapsed, one hand thrown out to catch himself, a dazed expression on his face.

"No time," the soldier said again, rising. "Take care."

And he was on the stairs, stepping over one dead gunner when he heard a woman scream behind him, somewhere to his left. Retreating, Bolan risked a glance around the nearest corner, peering down a hallway that appeared to pass by other stairs. He saw two figures struggling and recognized them, as Bashir Moheden reached out and brought his pistol down on Mara's skull.

The woman dropped to the floor, and Moheden was dragging her in the direction of a nearby exit when the warrior made his move. A shot was risky with the figures hunched together, so he took a chance and showed himself.

"That's far enough," he said.

Moheden froze, immediately dropping to a crouch and pulling Mara upright, propping her before him as a human shield. "Stop there," he called, "or I'll kill the woman."

"I don't think so," Bolan countered. "She's your ticket. Cash it in and you've got nowhere left to go."

"It seems that I have no alternative."

Moheden's tone was fatalistic. Bolan hesitated, waiting to discover which way this one would decide to play his final scene.

"A question," the dealer said.

"Fair enough."

"Who are you?"

"Someone who resents you pushing poison in the streets."

"Who sent you? Interpol? The CIA?"

"What difference does it make?"

Moheden shrugged. "No difference. It's enough that I have beaten you."

"I think you've got that backward," Bolan told him, edging closer. "You're a little short of men, from where I stand."

"No matter." There was cunning in the dealer's voice. "You want the woman. I'll never let you have her."

Bolan tried to keep his tone indifferent. "Suit yourself. If that's the way you want to play it."

"I don't seem to have much choice."

Moheden straightened slightly, offering a portion of himself to Bolan as he raised the automatic, aiming it at Mara's skull. It was a tricky shot, but there would be no second chance. Bolan snapped the AK-47 to his shoulder, stroking off a burst, deliberately firing high.

Several rounds were off the mark completely, slicing empty air instead of boring into Mara's flesh. The first was all it took, however. It ripped through Moheden's shoulder, flinging him away from Mara, with his own shot angled somewhere overhead. Released from her restraint, the woman toppled sideways, clearing Bolan's field of fire before the dealer could recover from his stunning wound.

Moheden tried to rise, and Bolan let him make it to his knees before he said, ''That's all.'' From twenty feet, he held the AK-47's trigger down. In the sudden, ringing silence that followed, something ike a wistful sigh escaped Moheden's lips. Then he was still.

The Executioner whirled at a shuffling sound behind him, the Beretta in his fist. Joseph Chamoun limped past Bolan, knelt by his sister's side and took her in his arms. Another moment passed before she stirred, eyes coming into focus on her brother's face.

Outside, the chopping sound of rotor blades was closer, reaching Bolan through a door that had been blasted from its frame. Grimaldi was outside, and he was waiting.

''Time to go,'' he told the pair. ''We've got a flight to catch.''

Take
4 explosive books
plus a
mystery bonus
FREE

DON PENDLETON's
MACK BOLAN.

More SuperBolan bestseller action! Longer than the monthly series, SuperBolans feature Mack in more intricate, action-packed plots— more of a good thing

			Quantity
STONY MAN DOCTRINE follows the action of paramilitary strike squads, Phoenix Force and Able Team.	$3.95		
RESURRECTION DAY renews a long-standing war against the Mafia.	$3.95		
DIRTY WAR follows the group on a secret mission into Cambodia.	$3.95		
███████████████	$3.95		

Total Amount
Plus 75¢ Postage   .75
Payment enclosed

$400.00

Please send a check or money order payable to Gold Eagle Books.

In the U.S.A.	In Canada	SMB-2A
Gold Eagle Books	Gold Eagle Books	
901 Fuhrmann Blvd.	P.O. Box 609	
Box 1325	Fort Erie, Ontario	
Buffalo, NY 14269-1325	L2A 5X3	

Please Print
Name: _____
Address: _____
City: _____
State/Prov: _____
Zip/Postal Code: _____